The
Arrangement

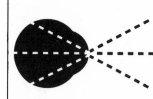
This Large Print Book carries the
Seal of Approval of N.A.V.H.

The Arrangement

Joan Wolf

Thorndike Press • Thorndike, Maine

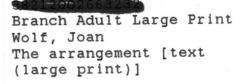
Copyright © 1997 by Joan Wolf

Published in 1998 by arrangement with
Warner Books, Inc.

Thorndike Large Print ® Basic Series.

The tree indicium is a trademark of Thorndike Press.

The text of this Large Print edition is unabridged.
Other aspects of the book may vary from the original edition.

Set in 16 pt. Plantin by Juanita Macdonald.

Printed in the United States on permanent paper.

Library of Congress Cataloging in Publication Data

Wolf, Joan.
    The arrangement / Joan Wolf.
        p. (large print) cm.
    ISBN 0-7862-1359-0 (lg. print : hc : alk. paper)
    1. Large type books.   I. Title.
[PS3573.O486A89   1998]
813´.54—dc21   97-47257

For Aaron Priest, agent extraordinaire, with gratitude and appreciation.

CHAPTER 1

Some people may say that I am rash and headstrong, but at least I have enough intelligence not to get myself stranded in the middle of a blizzard. This is a comment I have made (rather frequently) to the Earl of Savile, but he seems never to pay it any mind.

"How was I to know that the benighted inn had burned down?" is his invariable reply. "And if you throw that up at me one more time, Gail, I swear I shall do something you will very much regret."

I am getting ahead of my story, however. It begins on a late afternoon in February, in the middle of the aforementioned blizzard. Nicky, my eight-year-old son, and I were staggering from the house down to the stable to take care of the horses, when, through the thickening dark, we saw a coach turn in through the gate of my small establishment. As we stood gaping, it came to a halt some dozen or so feet from where we were standing.

"Good heavens," I said to Nicky. "What in the world is that?"

"It's a coach, Mama," Nicky said with an amazement that equaled my own.

To have a coach come tooling into one's yard under such circumstances was extraordinary indeed, but even more extraordinary was the voice of the coachman. "Is this the Saunders house?" he shouted down to me, in an accent that was purely Eton and Oxford.

I had a wood muffler draped like a mask around my face, and I pushed it away from my mouth as I went closer to the vehicle. "Yes, it is," I screamed back into the wind. "Are you lost?"

In answer, the coachman swung down from the box. Even though he was covered from neck to ankles in a many-caped greatcoat, he managed to move with athletic grace. "Not anymore," he said. "I had planned to put up at the Red Lion, but it isn't there."

I had automatically reached up to hold the rein of the left leader when the coachman jumped down, and now he came to relieve me of that task. The first thing I noticed about him was that he was very tall.

"The Red Lion burned down two months ago," Nicky offered, his voice floating up from under the wool hat I had jammed over his forehead and ears.

8

"So I discovered — rather too late for my comfort, I'm afraid!" the coachman replied.

At this moment the coach door opened and another man stepped out. "Have we landed straight, my lord?" he asked.

"It seems so," the coachman answered in his flawlessly aristocratic voice. "Come to Rusty's head and we'll get these horses under cover, John."

I felt as if I had landed in the middle of one of Mrs. Radcliffe's more imaginative novels.

At least one thing was clear, however. The carriage horses could not be left standing in the wind.

"Follow me," I said, and once more raising my muffler to cover my face, I led the way across the stable yard to my rather ramshackle carriage house. As I grasped the door to open it, the wind gusted, almost ripping it out of my hand.

The coachman's gloved hand grabbed the door above mine, and with a brief, "Let me," he opened it without allowing it to slam against the building. Then the men led the horses and the snow-encrusted coach inside.

Once the horses were standing quietly, the coachman, whom the other man had addressed as "my lord," turned to me and said, with a gleam of white teeth in the gloom,

"You must be finding all this rather odd, Mrs. Saunders."

" 'Rather odd,' is an understatement," I said frankly. "How do you know my name? Were you looking for me, sir?"

"Yes," said my unexpected visitor in a deep and extremely pleasant voice, "I was. Allow me to introduce myself, ma'am. I am the Earl of Savile, and I must hasten to assure you that when I set out this morning I had no intention of placing any demands upon your hospitality. As I indicated earlier, I had expected to find accommodations at the Red Lion."

The Earl of Savile! The shock of hearing that name almost caused me to miss the rest of his polite little speech.

What can Savile want with me?

I was grateful for the dark in the carriage house. It hid the look of terror that I was certain had flashed across my face.

Nicky asked, "If you really are an earl, then why were you the one driving the coach?"

"Poor Grove was in danger of getting frostbite, so I took a turn," came the disarming answer. Once more the earl looked at me. "Dare I hope that you have stabling for my animals, Mrs. Saunders?"

My body was rigid with fear. I drew a long,

unsteady breath and pressed two thickly gloved fingers against my forehead. "Let me think for a minute," I said, trying to force my brain to function.

"Two of our stalls are empty, Mama," Nicky said helpfully.

I came to the unwelcome conclusion that I would have to offer Savile shelter. Much as I wanted to do so, I could not throw him back out into the storm.

"I suppose I can open up two more stalls if I put my ponies at the end of the aisle behind a rope," I said to the earl curtly. "If you will unharness these poor beasts, I will endeavor to create some room for them."

The Earl of Savile appeared not to notice my inhospitable manner. "You are very good," he said. He had stripped off his gloves and was blowing on his hands.

I left him to his job as Nicky and I once more fought our way out into the blizzard.

Settling the horses proved to be little trouble. My groom, Tim Haines, had mucked out all the stalls before he had gone home a few hours earlier, so Nicky and I had only a little picking out to do. I moved the ponies, put fresh straw in the four empty stalls, and when the men came in leading the tired carriage horses, I had a place to put

11

them. My horses lifted their heads from the hay I had just given them to watch the arrival of the newcomers, then went back to the main business of their lives. The two ponies I had put together in a straw-bedded area at the end of the aisle were exploring their new home with a succession of enthusiastic snorts.

"God knows what mischief they will get into," I said to Nicky as Fancy poked her nose inquisitively over the rope that I hoped would keep her from roaming the aisle. "Are you certain there is no tack around for them to chew on?"

"I didn't see any, Mama, and I looked."

"Very well, then let us return to the house." I looked up at the man who was standing next to me and asked shortly, "Have you eaten?"

He began to rebutton his greatcoat. "Not since breakfast, Mrs. Saunders."

"You must be hungry, then," I said.

"I rather fear that I am," he replied apologetically.

I pulled my muffler up over my face, shoved Nicky's hat back down over his ears, and said to the men, "Come along, then." We ducked out once more into the snow.

Mrs. MacIntosh must have been looking out the window for us, because she opened the door before I had a chance even to lay a finger on the latch.

"Get you on in here, lassie, before you turn into a block of ice," she said. "Master Nicky, take off that coat and hat and leave them right here at the door."

The four of us stamped our feet to knock away the snow before we entered the dark, shabby front hall of my rented house. Mrs. MacIntosh regarded with curiosity the two men who accompanied me and said, "Did you lose your way in the snaw, gentlemen?"

Savile removed his hat and looked down at the small Scotswoman, who did not stand as high as the top button on his coat. "I beg your pardon for this invasion, ma'am," he said, "but I was planning to put up at the Red Lion and discovered — too late, alas — that it no longer exists."

"My lord, this is my housekeeper, Mrs. MacIntosh," I said woodenly. "Mrs. MacIntosh, the Earl of Savile and his coachman, Mr. Grove, will be staying with us for the night."

Mrs. MacIntosh's pale blue eyes bulged when I said the earl's name.

Savile said with disarming courtesy, "How do you do, Mrs. MacIntosh. I wonder if I might remove my greatcoat?"

"Of courrrse you must remove your coat,

my lord!" Mrs. MacIntosh replied immediately, rolling her *r*'s in the true Scottish fashion. "You and Mr. Grove must be starrrving from driving through that dreadful snaw."

"You have hit the nail straight on the head, ma'am," the earl replied. "*Starving* is the appropriate word, isn't it, John?"

"That it is, my lord," Grove replied fervently.

"Well, dinna ye fret," my housekeeper graciously assured my unwanted guests. "There is plenty of supper for everyone."

I said, "I'll show his lordship and Mr. Grove to the two bedrooms at the end of the passage, Mrs. MacIntosh."

The housekeeper gave me an appalled look. "You canna put his lordship in sich a room, lassie!"

Her Scottish accent always grew more pronounced when she was upset.

"Please don't worry about me, ma'am," Savile said charmingly. "I shall be grateful for any space you might be able to spare."

I did have two decent bedrooms, which I used for clients, but as I was in the middle of painting them, they were not fit to be occupied.

"The rooms at the end of the passage will do fine," I said impatiently to my housekeeper. "Please bring some hot water up for our guests now, Mrs. MacIntosh. You can put linen on the beds after dinner."

Nicky spoke up in a plaintive voice, "I'm starving too, Mrs. MacIntosh. Will dinner be ready soon?"

"It is ready now, laddie," the little Scotswoman said, her face softening as it always did when she looked at Nicky. "Go along upstairs with you now and change your clothes."

"I believe that is good advice for us all," I said briskly. "If you will follow me, gentlemen, I will show you to your rooms." As Mrs. MacIntosh went to the kitchen for hot water, I escorted the men upstairs to the bedroom floor.

I had been renting Deepcote for the past eight years, and, despite my annual requests, the landlord had not seen fit to do anything about refurbishing the house, whose interior had become irretrievably shabby about fifty years before. When my husband was alive we had decided on Deepcote more for its decent stabling and its proximity to London than for the beauty of the living quarters.

Suffice it to say that the Earl of Savile did not appear impressed with what he saw of my home. He was too polite to comment, however; he merely passed into the frigid, spartan room I had assigned him and assured me he would be downstairs in a trice.

I was sure he would be. The room contained one bed, one battered armoire, and one hard chair, certainly nothing to tempt him to linger.

I went to my own room, in which Mrs. MacIntosh, bless her, had kindled a big fire, and began to take off the warm wool dress I had worn to take care of the horses. It had some hair on it, so I did not return it to the wardrobe but laid it over a chair so I could brush it later. Then I took out one of my more decent-looking afternoon dresses. I had no intention of dressing up in evening garb for the sake of the Earl of Savile.

What can Savile want with me?

I walked to the window and pulled aside the threadbare crimson drapes. The cold air that had been trapped between the window glass and the drapes rushed out at me, and I shivered. Outside, it was now completely dark. I could hear the howling of the wind and the swish of the snow as it brushed against the leaky glass panes of my window.

I shut the drapes and went back to the fire to finish dressing. I was running a comb through my close-cut black hair when there came a knock on the door of my bedroom. I opened it to find Mrs. MacIntosh standing on the threshold.

"Lassie," she said worriedly, "his lord-ship's coachman will eat in the kitchen with MacIntosh and me, but where is Master Nicky to have his meal?"

Nicky had been eating with me in the dining room since he was three years old.

"Where he always eats, of course," I said.

"But, lassie, his lordship willna expect a child at the dinner table."

This was unarguably true. In his lordship's world, children ate in the nursery. Perhaps, occasionally, they might be allowed to join a family party, but never would an unrelated child of Nicky's age sit down at the same table as the Earl of Savile.

Mrs. MacIntosh said, "Canna Mr. Nicky eat wi' us in the kitchen?"

"No." My voice was adamant. "Nicky will eat in the dining room tonight, Mrs. MacIntosh."

While it was perfectly true that Nicky had taken his evening meal with the MacIntoshes on the very occasional evenings when I had guests, I thought it was one thing for him to eat with a couple who were almost grand-parents to him, and quite another for him to eat with some strange coachman.

I have to confess, the thought that my son's presence would effectively prevent the

17

earl from stating his business to me during dinner was another reason for my decision.

When Mrs. MacIntosh seemed inclined to try to persuade me, I cut her off. "This is Nicky's house, Mrs. MacIntosh, and if the Earl of Savile does not care for the company of an eight-year-old boy, then he may find his dinner elsewhere."

Mrs. MacIntosh looked at my face, sighed, and went away.

I slapped the comb down on my scarred dressing table and went out without bothering to consult the mirror that hung on the wall.

I went directly to the kitchen and found Mr. MacIntosh presiding over the ancient stove. The MacIntoshes had been the caretakers of Deepcote when Tommy and I had first taken it, and at that time Mrs. MacIntosh had been the cook. Then Mr. MacIntosh had an accident that left his left leg crippled. The property's owner had been ready to fire the couple, as Mr. MacIntosh was no longer able to perform the physical labor he was employed for, but I had volunteered to pay for a daily man from the village to do Mr. MacIntosh's chores.

So the couple had stayed, but Mr. MacIntosh had become severely depressed by his uselessness. It was his wife who had suggested that he assist her by taking on the cooking.

The man had proved to be a genius. The simple soup that he was serving this evening would be hearty, filling, and have such a symphony of flavors that you would dream about it as you drifted off to sleep. I almost wept with joy as I inhaled the aroma coming from the stove.

"I hope you don't mind being saddled with these extra mouths to feed, Mr. MacIntosh," I said.

"Of course not, lassie. Janet tells me that we have a lord come to dinner?"

"The Earl of Savile. He'll eat in the dining room, of course, but I'm afraid that you and Mrs. MacIntosh are going to be graced with the company of his coachman."

"That is no a trouble, lassie. The gentlemen may be accustomed to fancier fare, but there is plenty of soup and bread to fill their stomachs."

I looked at his narrow, dark, intelligent Scottish face. "They will dine like kings, and you know it," I retorted.

He smiled.

The kitchen door opened and John Grove stepped inside. "I hope I am in the right place?" he asked apologetically.

"Come in, man, come in," Mr. MacIntosh

19

said hospitably, and I left the two men to get acquainted and went on down the hall to the drawing room.

How to describe my drawing room?

Once, more years ago than I care to contemplate, the drapes had been yellow. Once the upholstery had not been threadbare and the stuffing had not poked out of it in unfortunately strategic places. It is true that the walls were freshly painted, but tonight the warm golden color I had thought so pretty seemed only to point up more sharply the travesty of the furnishings.

Most of the time I did not notice the defects of the room quite so vividly. Perhaps I was conscious of them tonight because they contrasted so strongly with the tall, slim figure of the Earl of Savile, who was standing before the blazing fire dressed in pantaloons and a long-tailed coat of fine blue cloth, with a pristine white necktie arranged around his throat. This costume was morning dress, not evening dress, of course, but he looked as out of place in my decayed room as a Thoroughbred would look in a pigsty.

I looked at my decidedly out-of-fashion afternoon gown and thought gloomily that I probably looked as drab and unattractive as my surroundings.

Nicky had preceded me and was standing

next to the earl in front of the fire, talking animatedly about his pony. He looked very neat and I was thankful to see that he had put on his church clothes.

"There you are, Mama!" he said when he spied me standing at the door. "I have been telling his lordship all about Squirt."

"That is nice, Nicky," I said. "I believe dinner is ready."

"Oh good," Nicky said happily. "Shall I go and help Mrs. MacIntosh?"

"Yes, sweetheart, if you please."

I glanced quickly at the earl and said, "If you will come with me, my lord?"

We walked out of the drawing room and progressed, side by side but not touching, to the room that lay directly next to it off the central hall of the house. As soon as we walked in the door I noticed that Mrs. MacIntosh had put out wineglasses. I never had wine with my meal.

I gestured the earl to the seat at the head of the small table and sat down. Nicky came into the dining room carrying a bottle of wine.

"Mrs. MacIntosh found some old wine of Papa's," he said brightly as he set the bottle on the table in front of Savile. He turned his beautiful little boy's face to the earl and said blithely, "Won't that be nice?"

"Very nice," the earl said in his deep and courteous voice. "I shall appreciate a glass of wine after a day spent fighting the snow."

Mrs. MacIntosh appeared carrying a tureen of soup, which she placed in front of me. As she returned to the kitchen to fetch the bread, Nicky came to stand beside me so that he could carry the bowl of soup I was filling to our guest. Then he returned for his own bowl.

Mrs. MacIntosh returned with the bread as I was filling my soup bowl. Nicky looked at me, waiting expectantly. I folded my hands, bowed my head, and said, "Thank you, Lord, for your gifts of the day and for this food which we are about to eat."

"And thank you for bringing our guests safely through the snowstorm," added my kindhearted son.

The earl's voice joined ours as we said, "Amen."

I always said a prayer of thanksgiving before meals. There had been a time when I was not certain from one day to the next if a meal was going to be on the table at all.

Prayers finished, Nicky picked up his spoon and applied himself to his soup. I picked up my spoon, but before I began to eat, I took a deep breath and made myself look across the table, directly into the face of my enemy.

Savile's dark gold, beautifully cut hair glowed in the candlelight. His eyes looked as if they were light brown. His facial bones were long and cleanly chiseled.

I had been right in my earlier assessment, I thought. He was a Thoroughbred all right.

He tasted a spoonful of the soup and his eyes flew up to meet mine.

I couldn't stop myself from smiling. "Not bad, is it?"

"Not bad?" He took another spoonful. "It's ambrosia!"

"I know about ambrosia," Nicky said. "I learned about it from Mr. Ludgate. It is the food of the gods."

"Very good," the earl said approvingly. Nicky beamed.

I didn't know whether to be pleased that Savile was being kind to Nicky or annoyed that my son's presence had failed to annoy him.

"Who is your cook?" Savile asked me.

I told him a little about the MacIntoshes.

"I have a garden in the summer and Mr. MacIntosh saves all the vegetables to use in his winter cooking," Nicky said.

"How splendid," the earl replied with a friendly smile. "There are not many boys

23

responsible enough to help their mama with the gardening."

"Nicky doesn't help me," I said coolly. "I don't garden; I haven't the time. He does the garden all by himself."

The earl had finished his soup. He poured himself a glass of wine.

"Would you like some more soup, sir?" Nicky asked. He added proudly, "All of the vegetables in it are from my garden."

I said, "I feel that I must explain to you, my lord, that the soup *is* the dinner. There is plenty more of it, however."

"In that case, I will have another bowl," the earl said.

Nicky jumped up from his seat and went to do the honors.

CHAPTER 2

As dinner consisted of only two courses, the soup and a pudding for dessert, we were not at the table for very long. When the meal was over, I sent Nicky upstairs to do his studying and invited the earl to join me in the drawing room for a glass of the sherry I kept for Mr. Ludgate when he came to visit.

I even took a glass of sherry myself. Unfortunately, there was no way to avoid hearing what had brought Savile to see me, and I thought that I was likely going to need all the fortification I could get.

The two least dilapidated of my grayish drawing-room chairs were placed on opposite sides of the fireplace and I invited Savile to take one. I sat in the other, drank half of my sherry, and placed the glass on an old walnut table within my reach.

For ten long seconds we regarded each other in silence across the tattered rug.

Then, "You're not what I expected," he said abruptly.

I lifted my chin. "I cannot imagine what your lordship means."

"Can you not?" He took a sip of his drink and watched me over the rim of the glass. That was when I realized that his eyes weren't an ordinary light brown at all, but amber-gold, like the sherry.

I looked away from him, into the leaping flames of the fire. "No, I can't," I said. My muscles were tensed against the blow I feared was coming. I struggled to keep my face expressionless.

He lowered his wineglass. "I have come here to Surrey directly from Devane Hall, Mrs. Saunders," he said. "I am afraid that I bring you the news that Lord Devane is dead."

It was not what I had expected to hear. I kept my face carefully guarded and very still, and after a moment I asked, "Why should you think I would care about that?"

"I think you might care very much when you learn that your son is named in Lord Devane's will," Savile returned. I could see out of the corner of my eye that he was leaning back in his chair, watching me.

I shut my eyes.

Finally, "How is Nicky named?" I asked desperately.

"I don't know precisely what is written in George's will," the earl answered. "All I know for certain is that my cousin left him some money."

I stared despairingly into the fire. "Tell me about it."

I could feel Savile looking at my averted face. "It happened less than a week ago. George overturned his phaeton and was caught under one of the wheels. It crushed his chest."

He paused, as if expecting some response from me.

"How sad," I said, my eyes still fixed upon the fire.

"Indeed it was," Savile replied. "My cousin was not yet dead, however, when they carried him into the house."

Too bad, I thought grimly.

"We put him into his bed and sent for the doctor," Savile went on. "Lady Devane fainted when we carried George in, so it was left to me to stay with him as we waited for the doctor to arrive."

The earl picked up his glass and took another sip of sherry. "I had thought he was unconscious, but when we were alone his eyes opened and fixed themselves upon me with such an expression of pained urgency. . . ."

Oh damn, I thought. *Damn, damn, damn.*

"He said my name," Savile continued. "It was hard to understand him, because when he talked, blood and saliva bubbled from his mouth, but he kept repeating my name."

The fire I was watching snapped and crackled, and I wanted to hold up my hands to push away what I was afraid was coming next, but there was nothing I could do.

Savile continued his tale. " 'Yes, George,' I said, leaning close to him. 'I'm here. What can I do for you?' "

I saw the earl turning more toward me as he got closer to the revelation I did not want to hear.

Savile went on, " 'Find the boy,' George said, with those desperately urgent eyes still glued to my face. 'You must . . . find the boy.'

" 'What boy, George?' I asked."

I was gripping my hands together so tightly that they ached. *Here it comes,* I thought. *Oh God, here it comes.*

" 'In my will,' George said. 'He must have the money I've left him in my will.'

"I took my cousin's hand in mine and his grip was astonishingly strong. I said, 'How shall I find this boy, George?' "

Savile stopped. When finally I could stand it no longer and turned my head to look at him, he continued quietly, "He told me to 'find Gail.' "

Our eyes held. I didn't say anything.

"He begged me, Mrs. Saunders," Savile

said. " 'Promise me, Raoul,' he said. 'Promise me that you will find the boy.' "

I tore my eyes away from his. I forced myself to breathe deeply and slowly and tried to keep my face expressionless.

"I promised him, of course," Savile said, "and less than five minutes later, he was dead."

His voice ceased, and for what seemed a long time the only sound in the room was the ticking of the clock on the mantel.

I had hated George Melville for many years and had often wished him dead, and now it seemed that even in dying he had managed to cause me trouble.

Savile said soberly, "He was thirty-one — a year younger than I am."

I tried to organize my thoughts. It could have been worse, I thought. George had not told Savile everything.

"How did you find me?" I finally asked.

"Through your aunt, Miss Longworth."

I nodded. It was the answer I had expected. I had always remained in communication with Aunt Margaret.

"So now you know why I have sought you out, Mrs. Saunders," the earl said. "Clearly, your son, Nicholas, is the boy my cousin was referring to. I am the executor of Devane's will and it is to be read at Savile Castle, my

29

home in Kent. I have come to escort you there so that you may be present when the will is made public."

My mind was in a whirl as I considered the implications of this bequest. "Why isn't the will being read at Devane Hall?" I asked, playing for time.

"Under the circumstances, I thought you might prefer not to return to Hatfield," Savile said quietly. "I understood from your aunt that you have not returned home since your marriage."

The village of Hatfield had never been home to me. It was just the place where Deborah and I had been forced to live after our parents had died. I cared not the snap of my fingers what they thought about me in Hatfield.

This, however, was not something I was about to discuss with the Earl of Savile.

I had made up my mind about what I should do, and I said in an extremely calm voice, "As there is absolutely no reason for Lord Devane to have made any financial provisions for my son, I see little point in my being present for the reading of this will."

"Don't be a fool," Savile said forcefully. He leaned forward in his chair, as if he would persuade me by sheer masculine force. "My cousin told me that he had left a sum of money to your son, Mrs. Saunders, and from what I can judge of your situation, you need it."

His eyes flicked insultingly around my shabby drawing room.

I clenched my hands and said fiercely, "My house may not be elegant, but I can assure you that Nicky does not lack for any of the important things in life! *My lord,*" I added with deliberate disdain.

His golden eyes were inscrutable. "I believe I know more about your financial situation than you realize, Mrs. Saunders," he said. "When I was still in Hatfield I had a talk with your late husband's mother, and she informed me that you had inherited nothing from him. Nor, according to the same source, have you ever possessed any money of your own."

I lifted my chin. Lady Saunders had hated it when Tommy married me. He was her youngest son, and her favorite, and she had wanted him to marry a lady who had money. To her mind, I had qualified under neither of those categories.

I thought, *I will not let the thought of Lady Saunders discussing me with the Earl of Savile upset me!*

I set my jaw, turned my face to the fire, and said coldly, "I have no need of inherited money, my lord. I have been earning a living for myself and my son ever since my husband died."

Silence.

"I see," he finally replied. "And may I ask what you do to earn your living, Mrs. Saunders?"

His voice was quiet, but there was a note in it that set off an alarm in my head. It was a moment before I understood what it was that he thought I did to earn my living.

White-hot fury flamed through me. I gripped the arms of my chair to keep myself from jumping up and hitting him. I glared at him instead, and said succinctly, "I teach riding, my lord. My clients are the children of the newly rich — men who have made a great deal of money in banking or in manufacture and who want their children to have the same advantages as the sons and daughters of the upper class. Most of these children have grown up in the city and have had no opportunity to learn to ride. They come here and I teach them."

He could not disguise his surprise, nor could I prevent the color burning my cheeks. My fingers opened and closed on the chair arms. I absolutely *longed* to hit him.

At last he said slowly, "So *that* is why your stable is so full."

"Yes." I was still livid with him for what I suspected he had been thinking. "Besides my own horses, I have three horses I teach on, as well as the two ponies whose stalls I commandeered to accommodate *your* carriage horses, my lord!"

He looked me up and down. "You do this all by yourself?"

I thought his look was insulting. Nor did his frankly incredulous tone do anything to soothe my temper. It is true that I am small boned and consequently tend to look rather delicate, but in fact I am as hardy as a mountain pony.

"Yes," I said through my teeth. "I do it all by myself."

The fire had begun to lag, and I picked up the poker and went to stir it up, wishing I could use the iron staff on the earl instead of the logs.

Savile said, "Was this originally your husband's business?"

I glanced at him over my shoulder. The light from the leaping flames made his dark gold hair look very bright. "We undertook it together," I said. "Then, when Tommy died, I continued it on my own."

"That must have been difficult."

I shrugged and gave another savage poke to the fire.

"Difficult" did not begin to describe the horror of that first year after Tommy's death. Had it not been for the MacIntoshes, and for Mr. and Mrs. Ludgate, our local vicar and his wife, I don't think I would have made it.

I put the poker down reluctantly and turned to face Savile. I said, pronouncing each word as carefully as if I were communicating with someone who did not know the language well, "I do not desire Lord Devane's money, nor do I desire to travel to Savile Castle with you, my lord. You may consider that your promise to Lord Devane has been fulfilled. You have found Nicholas. You may now go away from here with an easy mind."

Savile listened to me with polite attentiveness. When I had finished he said smoothly, "Let me remind you, Mrs. Saunders, that I have no idea of what my cousin wrote in his will. All he told me was that he had left money to a boy whom I must suppose to be your son, Nicholas. Whether or not he further identified this boy remains to be seen."

It took a moment for the meaning of his words to sink in.

Then they did.

Oh my God! I thought in horror. *What if*

George has claimed in his will that Nicky is his son?

Suddenly my legs felt too weak to hold me up, and I made my way back to my chair. I sat as straight as I could and once more tried to breathe slowly and deliberately.

It would be just like George to say after he was dead what he was afraid to say while he was alive, I thought bitterly.

"Does George's wife know anything about Nicky?" I asked Savile abruptly.

"I have said nothing to Lady Devane about my cousin's last words to me," he replied. "She is grieving for her husband and I did not wish to add to her distress."

"Well, if George has mentioned Nicky in his will, there is no way you can prevent her from being distressed, my lord," I said tartly. "Particularly since I must suppose that the money George so generously bequeathed to my son is money that really belongs to his wife!"

An ironic look came over Savile's eyes and brows although his mouth remained grave. He said, "The money, I must suppose, will come from George's private funds, but since those funds originated from the handsome settlement Lady Devane's father bestowed upon my cousin at the time of his marriage, then what you say is undoubtedly true, Mrs. Saunders."

I rested my head against the back of my chair and closed my eyes. "God in heaven, what a spineless creature George was," I said.

Silence.

"Perhaps you have cause to think so," Savile replied at last.

I opened my eyes. "I spoke from general observation, my lord, not from personal experience!"

He nodded, but it was evident that he did not believe me.

Under the circumstances, I supposed I couldn't blame him, but this did not make me any the less furious.

I stood up. "I will sleep on what you have told me and let you know my answer in the morning."

"Very well." He had risen when I did, and now we stood facing each other, with six feet of the faded and frayed rug between us.

I said as politely as I could, "I will leave you the sherry bottle, my lord, and if you should like a book to read, please choose one from my collection." I nodded to the two glass-enclosed cabinets along the wall that held my scant but treasured library.

It was nine o'clock at night. He was probably accustomed to having his dinner at that time. On the other hand, he most likely did not rise until nine in the morning.

I got out of bed at six.

"Thank you, Mrs. Saunders," he replied with beautiful courtesy. "You are very kind."

I thought of the inhospitable bedchamber that awaited him and had to acknowledge that he was behaving very well. I don't know why this should have irritated me, but it did.

"We must hope that the snow has ended by the morning," he added. And smiled.

How to describe Raoul Melville's smile? Its radiance? Its warmth? Its profound intimacy? All I can say is that its effect on me was much stronger than the sherry I had drunk.

"Good night, my lord," I managed to croak.

"Good night, Mrs. Saunders," he replied very softly.

I left the room as quickly as I decently could.

Nicky was looking out his window when I came into his room to kiss him good night. "It's still snowing, Mama," he said, and I went to join him.

It was indeed still snowing hard. The wind was also blowing as strongly as it had all afternoon; one could hear it moaning in all the chimneys.

"Whatever am I going to do with the earl if he can't get away from here tomorrow?" I muttered distractedly as I stared out at the falling snow.

"I think he's nice," Nicky said.

"You think everyone is nice," I retorted.

"Well, Mama, usually everyone is."

I put my arm around him and hugged him.

If I tell you that my son is the sweetest, kindest child who ever lived you will no doubt think that I am prejudiced. But my opinion has been seconded by any number of people who are not related to Nicky. Mr. Ludgate, who is a very lovely man himself, adores Nicky, and has often told me that he would make a very fine clergyman.

Nicky looked up at me out of blue eyes that were as clear and lucent as the sky on a summer afternoon. "Don't you like him, Mama?"

I prevaricated. "It is just that I don't know what to do to entertain an earl."

"I promised to show him Squirt," Nicky said helpfully.

I dropped a kiss on the top of his silky, light brown hair.

"Time to get into bed," I said.

He turned to give me a hug. "Good night,

Mama. See you with the sunshine!"

It was our nightly ritual. "See you with the sunshine, sweetheart," I returned.

I waited until Nicky was in bed before I went down the passage to check that Mrs. MacIntosh had made up a fire in the earl's room.

She had, and the bed was made up as well. The same was true for Grove's room next door.

Nothing would ever make those bedrooms attractive, but at least they were no longer frigid, and the chimneys were not smoking too badly.

I did not climb right into my bed but sat for a long time in front of my bedroom fire, wrapped in a blanket and trying to decide what would be the best thing for me to do about this will.

Nicky must not know anything about George.

That was my chief consideration. My mind scurried first this way and then that, trying to fathom what course of action would best achieve that end. It was almost ten-thirty when I finally made up my mind.

I would go to Savile Castle with the earl, but I would leave Nicky here at Deepcote with the MacIntoshes.

My reasoning went something like this: If I refused to accompany the earl, and Nicky was named as George's son in his will, then the lawyers would be required to see that George's wishes were carried out. They would seek us out and Nicky would learn what George had claimed.

On the other hand, if I was present at the reading of the will, I could deny George's claims and refuse the inheritance.

Really, I thought, *if I refuse to acknowledge George as the father of my child, who will be in a position to gainsay me?*

I had no choice, really. I had to go.

I blew out my candle and got into the bed that I had once shared with Tommy.

It was not my husband's face that floated before my closed eyes, however, as I snuggled my head into my pillow and prepared to go to sleep.

My last conscious thought was, *How did he come to be given a French name like Raoul?*

CHAPTER 3

It was still snowing steadily when I awoke the following morning. I lit my fire and dressed quickly in front of its welcome heat. Mr. MacIntosh had the stove going in the kitchen, and I ate a big bowl of oatmeal at the old oak table before I went down to the stable to feed the horses.

The sky was just beginning to turn from black to leaden gray as I stepped out my front door. The snow was falling almost as heavily as it had the day before. Some of the drifts in the stable yard looked to be as high as my waist.

Damn, I thought as I fought my way through the high-piled snow down to the stable. What was I going to do to entertain Savile if I was saddled with him for the entire day?

I had to dig out around the stable door before I could open it, and when I finally entered, all the horses nickered eagerly. I set down the lantern I had been carrying and went to light the charcoal brazier, which would give off enough heat for me to do my chores with a fair degree of comfort.

Then I climbed the ladder to the hayloft and began to drop hay down into the stalls.

The nickering got louder as I went up the line of five stalls on the right side of the aisle, the horses on the left side growing impatient as they heard their comrades beginning to munch.

By the time I had finished the last of the horses, the two ponies in the temporary pen at the end of the aisle were whinnying fretfully.

"I'm coming, I'm coming." I threw more hay down the ladder, climbed down, and took it into their makeshift stall.

Quiet miraculously descended on the stable. The only noises were the crunching sounds the horses made as they ate and, from outside, the faint howling of the wind.

I smiled. I loved morning in the stable. It was so peaceful.

The stable door banged as someone opened it, and I turned to see Grove coming in the door. He closed it quickly against the blowing snow.

"Lord, Mrs. Saunders," he said. "I would have seen to the horses for you! There wasn't no call for you to be out here before the sun is even up!"

"I feed my horses every morning at this

hour, Grove," I said calmly. "It was no trouble to drop some hay to your animals as well as mine."

"Well, I thank ye, Mrs. Saunders." He gave me a smile. Grove's hair was grizzled but the slight space between his two front teeth made him look oddly boyish. "Dare I hope ye might have some extra grain for my boys, too?"

"Of course I do," I replied. "First, however, I was going to see to the water buckets."

"Have they iced over?"

"Probably," I said with resignation.

He went into the stall that contained the earl's good-looking right leader. "How are you this morning, Rusty my boy?" he asked in the soft voice of a true horse lover. He patted the chestnut's arched neck, then bent to check the water bucket.

"He's drunk two-thirds of it," he reported with satisfaction. "The rest is frozen, though."

He came out of the stall. "If you'll show me where the pump is, Mrs. Saunders, I'll refill all of the buckets."

I accepted his offer with gratitude. The one thing above all else I hated about the winter was having to cope with frozen water buckets. Once you got your gloves wet, your hands froze unmercifully.

While Grove took care of the water, I measured out appropriate amounts of grain into each horse's manger. There was a bit of a ruckus as Polly tried to eat Fancy's grain as well as her own, but I soon got the ponies sorted out.

By now the brazier had warmed the barn to a more pleasant temperature.

I sat down on the bench next to the brazier and undid the buttons on Tommy's old coat.

The door opened and Grove came in with the last bucket of water.

"Aren't your hands freezing, Grove?" I asked sympathetically. "Come and hold them in front of the brazier."

"Thank ye, Mrs. Saunders," he replied. "They are a mite chilled at that."

I leaned my shoulders against the wall and watched as Savile's coachman stripped off his gloves and held his bare, reddened fingers out to the glowing charcoal.

I said, "Was that the earl's coach you arrived in yesterday, Grove?"

"It was not," he replied emphatically. "You don't think his lordship would own such an old-fashioned rig as that?"

I shrugged and said noncommittally, "One never knows."

It had been quite a few years since the

old-time coach had been replaced by the lower-slung, more comfortable chaise. Chaises were not driven by coachmen, either, but by postillions, who directed the horses by riding them.

Grove obviously felt it was incumbent upon him to explain to me how the fashionable Earl of Savile had come to be riding in so dated a carriage. "We started out in his lordship's chaise, but we had not gone above two miles from Devane Hall when a linchpin broke," he said. "We knew the snow was coming, ye see, and his lordship decided to take Lord Devane's old coach rather than wait to have his own vehicle repaired."

I took off my wool hat and ran my fingers through my short hair, fluffing it up. "I take it, then, that you are not employed as his lordship's coachman?"

Grove lifted his chin with pride. "I'm his groom, my lady, as I was his father's groom before him. Taught his lordship to ride his first pony, I did."

I could find nothing satisfactory to reply to this momentous information, and silence fell.

I broke it at last by saying gloomily, "The snow doesn't show any signs of letting up, does it?"

"Afraid not, Mrs. Saunders. From the

looks of it, we're going to be laid up here for another day at least."

With difficulty I refrained from groaning. I sighed instead and stood up. "Ordinarily I have a lad come from the village to muck out the stalls in the morning, but I strongly doubt we will see him today. That leaves us to do the job, Grove. If you will take care of your horses, I will take care of mine."

"Not a bit of it!" he said emphatically. "I will see to all the horses, Mrs. Saunders. You get yourself back into the house and have your breakfast."

"I've already had my breakfast," I said.

Once more the stable door opened, and this time it was my son who came in. "Good morning, Mama," he said. "Good morning, Mr. Grove."

"Good morning, sweetheart," I replied cheerfully. "Did you sleep well?"

"Yes."

Nicky always slept well, and once more I swore to myself that I was going to make very certain that nothing would happen to change that.

"I don't think Tim is going to get to Deepcote this morning," Nicky continued. "You and I had better do the stalls ourselves, Mama."

"I was just saying the same thing to

Grove," I said. "There is only room to put two horses in the aisle at once, so why don't you and I work on our horses, and Grove can do his lordship's."

"All right," Nicky said cheerfully. "I'll get the pitchforks and the wheelbarrows, Mama."

Grove protested once more that he would do all the stalls, but again I refused.

There was no way on this earth that I was going to be beholden to the Earl of Savile.

By the time the horses had been fed and watered and the stalls had been cleaned and bedded with fresh straw, it was almost nine o'clock. We returned to the house and were removing our outerwear in the front hall when his lordship came down the stairs. He was impeccably dressed in a morning coat and pantaloons, with a fresh shirt and a new snowy-white neckcloth tied around his throat. His dark gold hair was brushed and tidy. His Hessian boots gleamed. He looked at us in surprise.

"The horses have been seen to, my lord," Grove said cheerfully. "Mrs. Saunders feeds almost the same grain we do at home, I'm glad to say, so we shouldna have problems with their digestions."

I picked a piece of straw off my coat and

said woodenly, "If you will go into the dining room, my lord, I will ask Mr. MacIntosh to cook you some breakfast."

"Have you been down to the stable already, Mrs. Saunders?" Savile asked in amazement.

"Yes," I said.

Nicky elaborated on my reply. "We got all the horses mucked out, sir. Mama says that if the wind lets up later we can put them out in the paddock for a half an hour or so, just so they don't go mad from confinement."

The earl's golden eyes were on me. "Don't you have a man to see to your horses, Mrs. Saunders?"

"Someone usually comes from the village to help, but he couldn't make it in this snow," I said shortly. "It's nothing new for Nicky and me to do stalls, my lord, I assure you of that. Now if you'll excuse me, I must go and change my shoes."

Mrs. MacIntosh came into the hall. "I have a fire going in the dining room, lassie," she said to me. "MacIntosh will have breakfast for you and his lordship in a trice."

"I have already had breakfast, Mrs. MacIntosh," I said.

"A bowl of oatmeal three hours ago is not a full breakfast, lassie," Mrs. MacIntosh said firmly. "Now go wash your hands and come

48

and eat a proper meal as you always do."

"What about me, Mrs. MacIntosh?" Nicky asked. "I only had a bowl of oatmeal too."

"The three of us will eat in the dining room," I said quickly.

Mrs. MacIntosh beamed at Nicky. "Would ye no rather eat in the nice warm kitchen, Master Nicky? Ebony has been missing you."

Ebony was our cat. She hated the cold and usually spent the entire winter in the kitchen, where she was warm but bored.

"Poor Eb," said Nicky. "Of course I'll come and pet her, Mrs. MacIntosh."

As I could hardly order Nicky to eat in the dining room, that left me with the earl.

I gave Mrs. MacIntosh a sour look and trudged upstairs to wash my hands and brush my dress.

The earl was enjoying a plate of cooked eggs and bannock bread when I came into the dining room and took my place opposite him at the table. I was wearing an old blue kerseymere dress for warmth, not for style, and once more I was uncomfortably conscious of how shabby I must appear beside my elegant guest.

The eggs that Savile was eating were from the chickens in Mrs. MacIntosh's henhouse, and they were unaccompanied by bacon or grilled kidneys. I was quite certain that the earl was accustomed to eating meat for breakfast, but meat was not served very often in the Saunders household. I couldn't afford it.

I poured myself some coffee and offered a fresh cup to Savile. Then I said, "I have decided that I will accompany you to Savile Castle after all, my lord."

He put down his coffee cup. "A wise decision, Mrs. Saunders. You owe it to Nicholas to take advantage of any bequest George may have made to him."

I didn't reply. It occurred to me suddenly that the prudent course right now was to keep my mouth closed about my intention to refuse any money from George. If Savile knew my intention, he would doubtless spend the entire journey to Kent trying to get me to change my mind.

At that moment, Mrs. MacIntosh came through the door bearing more eggs, bread, and fresh coffee. I filled my plate, refilled my cup, and tucked in to my food.

Silence reigned as I ate my second breakfast. When finally I was finished, I looked up and found Savile regarding me with that infuriating amusement in his eyes.

"I was hungry," I said defensively.

"You have every reason to be hungry if you have been out at that stable since six-thirty in the morning," he returned. "There was no need for you to do that, you know. Grove would have seen to the horses."

"I have no intention of asking your groom to see to my horses," I said evenly. "I will see to them myself, as I always do."

His brows drew together, but he did not reply.

I took a deep breath, then trotted out the little speech I had prepared on my way down to the dining room. "I fear I have little to offer you in the way of entertainment, my lord. Perhaps you were able to find a book that interested you?"

As I finished speaking, his face underwent a remarkable change, the golden eyes narrowing, the well-cut mouth setting into a hard, straight line. To my astonishment, I realized that he was angry.

"What kind of a cursed dandy do you think me?" he said in a clipped, hard-edged voice. "If there is work to be done, I am perfectly capable of doing my share. I certainly have no intention of sitting around reading a book while you break your back mucking out horses!"

Well, well, well. He was insulted. Suddenly I felt much better.

"The horses are finished until lunchtime, my lord," I said sweetly, "and that is three hours away."

"What do *you* plan to do this morning, Mrs. Saunders?" he countered.

I gave him my most angelic smile. "I am painting one of the bedrooms that I use for my clients."

He actually looked shocked.

"Painting?" he said. "Surely you don't mean you are painting the *walls?*"

"I assure you, I am not painting murals, my lord," I replied even more sweetly. "I finished the molding and the window trim yesterday and am all ready to begin the walls this morning."

"Good God," he said.

"Just so," I returned.

He looked slowly around the dining room. As in the rest of the house, the old walnut furniture was scarred and shabby. The walls, however, were painted the same pale gold that I had used in the drawing room.

"Did you paint this room as well?" he asked.

"This room was last winter's project," I replied.

He leaned back in his chair and regarded me across the table. "You haven't yet got around to the two bedrooms at the end of the passage, I notice," he said dryly.

"No one ever uses them," I replied. "My time is precious, my lord. Once my clients start to arrive in the spring, I can hardly turn the house upside down with painting. I have to get my work done during the winter, when no one is here."

He nodded. Then he said in a perfectly amiable voice, "Well, if you can spare me a paintbrush, I will be happy to assist you, ma'am."

I stared at him across the table, not quite sure I had heard him correctly.

"I am perfectly able to wield a paintbrush, Mrs. Saunders." His voice had taken on that clipped tone once more. He obviously felt it was an insult to his manhood that I didn't think him capable of painting a wall.

I felt a shiver of unholy glee at the thought of the Earl of Savile painting my house. I raised my brows and gave him a look that was deliberately provoking. "Really, your lordship, I don't think it would be at all commensurate with your rank for you to be undertaking such common labor."

I had intended him to be annoyed by my remark, but he surprised me with a smile. "No, they would certainly drum me out of the House of Lords should anyone hear about it," he said. "I must rely on your discretion, ma'am."

He probably was accustomed to moving mountains with that smile, I thought crossly. Well, it was not going to move me.

I rose from my chair. "If you are serious about this, my lord, then I suggest you change out of those elegant garments. I will also try to find you a smock."

"A smock," he repeated in deepening amusement as he stood up. He shook his head. "My reputation is in your hands, Mrs. Saunders. If it should ever become known in the London clubs that I actually wore a smock . . . !"

I was standing behind my chair and now I lifted my hands and rested them upon its laddered back. "Would you be drummed out of White's as well, my lord?" I asked lightly.

He gave me a pained look. "I must inform you, ma'am, that I am not a member of White's. White's is a Tory club. All the Melvilles are Whigs. I belong to Brooks's."

I said gravely, "I beg your pardon for even suggesting that your lordship might be a Tory."

At this moment the door from the kitchen opened and Nicky came into the dining room. "I've finished my breakfast," he announced. "Is there anything else I can do for you, Mama?"

"No, thank you, sweetheart. Do you have something to work on for Mr. Ludgate?"

"Yes, I do, Mama."

"Well, why don't you do your schoolwork. If you need my help I will be in the guest room. The earl and I are going to paint."

Nicky's blue eyes grew huge. He looked at the tall aristocrat standing at the foot of the table. "Are you really going to help Mama paint, sir?" he asked in awe.

"I can see that if I don't do a decent job with this painting, I shall never live it down," Savile said. "Why are we standing here dawdling, Mrs. Saunders? There's work to be done!"

I had been working on the bedroom next to Nicky's for about a week, so all of the furniture was pushed into the middle of the room and swathed in covers. The floor was also covered so that I didn't splatter it with paint, and a ladder was propped against one of the walls.

I had begun my painting project five years ago, when I finally realized that if I kept waiting for my landlord to paint the house, I would wait forever. This particular bedroom was the first room I had done, and this winter I had decided to do it again.

I had swathed myself in a smock and was

briskly stirring my bucket of blue paint when the door opened and the Earl of Savile came into the room.

He had removed his coat and his shoes and his neckcloth and had rolled up the sleeves of his shirt. As he crossed the room toward me on silent feet, I thought fleetingly that he moved with the fluid strength and grace of a lion. I stood with the paint stirrer in my hand and looked up at him as he came to a halt beside me.

He was a full head taller than I, and without his coat I could see how slim he was through the waist and hips. The skin exposed by his open shirt collar was faintly golden, and the crisp hairs on his bare forearms were the same color as the hair on his head.

I felt almost overpowered by the sheer masculine force of him and had to exert all my willpower not to betray myself by stepping back. My fingers tightened around the paint stirrer.

Savile slowly looked around the room, taking in the fresh white paint on the moldings, the two windows, and the mantelpiece. Finally his eyes settled on my face. "I'll take the ladder and start painting the upper part of the walls," he said. "Why don't you begin to outline the window frames, Mrs. Saunders."

I replied in a voice that was supposed to sound repressive but unfortunately just sounded breathless, "I rather thought *you* were working for *me*, my lord."

His eyes crinkled faintly in amusement. "I beg your pardon, ma'am. What would you like me to do?"

"Oh, go ahead and paint the upper walls," I said irritably, and was relieved to hear that my voice sounded normal once more. "You have a longer reach than I have."

"Such was my reasoning," he returned with that faint amusement I found so disconcerting.

I set my lips and handed him the smock I had brought for him. As soon as he slid one arm into it, it became obvious that it was not going to fit across his shoulders.

"I shall be fine without it," he said, stripping the smock off and handing it back to me. "Now, if I can just pour a little of this splendid paint into another bucket, I shall be ready to start."

I went to fetch the second bucket, he poured the paint, and we began work.

Fifteen minutes or so went by in silence. I was carefully outlining the first window in blue, and thinking about how I was going to break the news to Nicky that I would be leaving him for a few days, when I was struck by another uncomfortable thought.

I turned to look up at the earl on the ladder. "My lord," I said, addressing his broad back, "it has just occurred to me that you could not have had an opportunity to inform your wife that you would be bringing me to Savile Castle. What if she . . . I mean, suppose she —"

I broke off, scowling, unable to find a tactful way to say that perhaps Lady Savile would not find Mrs. Abigail Saunders a respectable enough person to be welcomed into her home.

The earl did not stop painting as he answered, "Since I am not married, Mrs. Saunders, there is no reason to concern yourself with my wife's supposed sensibilities. I can assure you that my housekeeper is perfectly prepared to welcome any guests I might suddenly introduce."

"I see," I said. But as I turned back to my window I was conscious of feeling surprised that a man who bore such an ancient title and lineage was not yet married.

The morning went by in relative silence as we worked carefully to smooth the fresh blue paint over the cream color that I had originally painted the room five years before. While I painted, I cudgeled my brain for some way to explain to Nicky that, once the weather cleared, I would be going away with the Earl of Savile.

At the end of two hours I still had not found an answer. I had finished outlining the two windows, however, and had begun to paint carefully along the molding at the edge of the floor. When I looked up to inspect Savile's work, I had to confess that he had gotten much farther than I ever would have in the same amount of time. He had, in fact, managed to finish the top third of two of the walls and was a quarter of the way across the third wall.

The quiet concentration of our work had been broken only twice — both times by Nicky, who had come in from his bedroom next door with some questions about his schoolwork. One of the questions I had known the answer to, the other I had not.

"Persepolis was the capital of Persia," Savile had informed us from the heights of his ladder.

"But what was Susa then?" Nicky had asked. "It says in my reading that the king lived in Susa."

"Susa was the capital until Darius built Persepolis," Savile said. "The Persian kings spent part of the year in both places, but the ceremonial capital was Persepolis."

"Oh," Nicky said happily, "thank you, my lord." And he had returned next door to write down his newly acquired information.

At eleven-thirty Mrs. MacIntosh came to the door to announce the time. I straightened up from my kneeling posture and stretched my cramped back and legs.

Savile looked down at us from his ladder. "Do we have to stop already? I was hoping to get all of these walls finished this morning."

"Noon is lunchtime in the stable," I explained, looking up at him. He did not look as tidy as he had two hours ago. A lock of hair was hanging over his forehead, and his shirt was pulling loose from the waistband of his pantaloons.

"When is lunchtime in the dining room?" he asked.

"One-thirty, my lord," Mrs. MacIntosh said.

"Very well," he said. "I'll continue working here for a while longer, Mrs. MacIntosh. Mrs. Saunders can go and see to the horses."

While I did not at all enjoy being dictated to in my own home, I had to admit that I would be extremely happy to have the top part of all the walls finished. I didn't mind doing the trim, but I found the process of covering vast spaces of wall with a small, four-inch brush extremely tedious. It was tiring as well.

I said, "Very well, my lord. I will have Mrs. MacIntosh call you an hour before lunch so you may change your clothes."

"Mmm," he said. He brushed his forearm across his forehead, trying to push back his hair. Then he dipped his brush into the paint bucket once more and lifted it to the wall. "Do that, Mrs. Saunders."

I scowled at him, but he had his back to me and didn't see.

CHAPTER 4

The snow was letting up as I walked down to the stable with Nicky and Grove.

"If the snow stops soon, the roads might be passable by tomorrow, ma'am," Grove said.

I certainly hoped they would be. Having made the decision to go with Savile to hear the reading of George Melville's will, I wanted nothing more now than to get it over and done with.

"The Brighton Mail goes through Highgate," I said. "Once the snow stops, I'll ride into the village and ask Walker, the blacksmith, to let us know as soon as he has seen it go by. If the mail can make it through, then his lordship's chestnuts should be able to get through as well."

"That is so, Mrs. Saunders," Grove replied with obvious pride in the quality of his master's horses.

Nicky gave a little bounce and said, "We shall miss you and Lord Savile, Mr. Grove. It has been fun having guests in the middle of winter."

"Thank 'ee, Master Nicky," Grove said gruffly. "You're a good lad."

Once more I worried about how to explain to Nicky that I would accompany the earl while he would remain at home.

I put my mare and Nicky's pony out together in the side paddock and Polly and Fancy together in the back paddock. While I carried piles of hay to the horses in the paddocks, Grove and Nicky picked out the stalls, gave hay to the horses in the stable, chopped through the thin layer of ice in the water buckets, then filled them to their tops.

I then returned to the house and went upstairs to wash my hands. Before going down to the dining room, I decided to take a quick look to see how far the earl had progressed on the guest-room walls.

To my amazement, he was still up on the ladder.

"Good heavens, my lord!" I said. "Did Mrs. MacIntosh forget to call you?"

He didn't even spare me a glance; all his concentration was on the even strokes of his brush. I had to admit that he was working as easily and efficiently as any tradesman.

He said, "I told Mrs. MacIntosh I would get something in the kitchen later. I want to finish this last wall before I eat."

"I can't believe how much you have done

63

in just one day!" I confessed.

He lowered his paintbrush, turned to look down at me, and smiled ruefully. "My sister could tell you that once I begin something, I'm a bear until I finish it."

He had a long streak of blue paint along the line of one chiseled cheekbone and a daub on his chin. I laughed. "Wait until you see your face, my lord. It is very artistically decorated."

He chuckled. It was a deep, warm, utterly delightful sound.

The part of the wall behind me that Savile had painted was well above my head, so I leaned against it, folded my arms, and gazed up at him. "I have to admit that you have surprised me, my lord," I said. "I never dreamed you would be so accomplished."

He lifted his brush. "Thought I was useless, did you?" he said as he began once more to apply the blue paint.

His shoulder and back muscles moved smoothly under the thin cotton of his shirt as his arm went up and down, spreading paint evenly on the wall. He certainly did not have the physique of a "cursed dandy."

I said, "Well . . . let us say, rather, that I did not picture you as a painter."

The brush continued its up-and-down motion, and I noticed that he had an impressive set of muscles in his upper arm as well.

I realized what I was thinking and blushed.

Good heavens, Gail! I scolded myself. *Stop staring at the man. You see bigger muscles than that every time the blacksmith shoes your horses.*

Savile said, "It is not that difficult to apply paint to a flat surface, ma'am."

I cleared my throat and fixed my eyes on an expanse of wet blue wall. "Not difficult, no. But it is a tiring sort of thing to do. Not at all the sort of activity that one would choose if one had other options open to one."

"It is not precisely enjoyable, I will agree," he said. He lowered his brush and turned his body a little so that he could look around the room. "But I must say that it is rather satisfying to see how well the room is looking. This is a very pretty color you have chosen."

He had a rather disconcerting way of saying things that did not at all coincide with my image of a great earl. After a moment I admitted candidly, "I have often felt that way myself."

He looked up. "You didn't repaint the ceiling."

"Painting ceilings is horrid," I said firmly. "I did it five years ago, when I first painted this room, and I have no intention of ever doing it again."

He nodded, then said, "Go and have lunch, Mrs. Saunders, and don't worry yourself about me."

I took him at his word, and went.

I didn't see the earl again until a bit later in the afternoon. I was sitting at my desk in the corner of the drawing room, going over bills, when he came in. He made scarcely a sound, but such was the forcefulness of his presence that he had advanced but a few steps before I felt him there behind me.

I turned to look at him.

"Don't disturb yourself, Mrs. Saunders," he said. "I found an interesting book last night and am just going to sit here in front of this nice fire and read for a while."

He was wearing a black cutaway coat, and the blue paint no longer adorned his face. I nodded at him a little distractedly, my mind on the sum I had just toted up.

Surely the hay bill can't have been that high! I thought in dismay as I turned back to my desk.

The winter was always the hardest time for me financially. My income stopped in the autumn, along with my clients, leaving me with approximately a third of the year to get through on my savings alone.

I added up the bills for hay and straw and grain once more and got the same depressing answer.

I thought bitterly that I would have to dip in to the money I had been putting aside for Nicky to go to Oxford.

I must cut costs, I thought.

But where?

There's Maria, I thought for probably the two-hundredth time since Tommy had died. *I don't need a horse of that quality, I know I don't. I could sell her for a nice sum and buy myself something else at a quarter of the price I realize.*

But I knew I wouldn't sell Maria. She had been Tommy's wedding present to me, a beautiful bay Thoroughbred with nearly perfect conformation.

"She reminds me of you, Gail," my husband had said when first he had taken me to see her. "She looks so delicate, with that exquisite head and neck, and those elegant long legs, but her heart is full of courage." He had given me his endearing, mischievous grin. "Not to mention the fact that she has such a fiery temper that I got her at a steal from Rogers's, who didn't know what to do with her!"

I knew she would have magnificent babies,

and every year I had hoped to find enough money to pay the stud fee to breed her to a Thoroughbred stallion.

Every year I had failed to do so.

Maria was twelve now — growing old to have a first foal.

I chewed on the end of my pen and stared at the sums listed before me.

If I used George's money to pay for Nicky's education, I would have those savings available to put toward operating costs.

The idea popped into my mind before I could block it out.

No. My lips moved to form the word, although I did not speak it aloud. I did not want to take anything from George. I would not take anything from George.

I would manage.

I always had.

Savile's voice came from behind me. "I was talking to Nicky in the kitchen a while ago, Mrs. Saunders, and I received the distinct impression that he does not yet know that you plan to accompany me to Kent."

I turned in my chair to face him. "I haven't told him yet," I confessed. "I have been trying to invent a reason for my making such a trip, and so far I have not been able to come up with anything satisfactory."

"Telling him the truth is out of the question, I gather." The ironic note in Savile's voice was unmistakable.

"I do not want Nicky to know anything about Lord Devane." I scowled in sudden alarm. "You didn't say anything to him, did you, my lord?"

He was sitting in one of the fireside chairs, a book that looked like my well-read copy of Lady Greystone's *On Equitation* in his hands. He said, "No, I held my tongue. I do not agree with your decision, Mrs. Saunders, but I will respect it. Nicky is, after all, your son."

"Thank you," I said in an ironic tone that matched his.

He changed the subject. "Was that your mare I saw out in the paddock earlier? The bay Thoroughbred?"

I smiled. "Yes, that is Maria."

"She is beautiful."

"Thank you. I agree, she is beautiful."

His long fingers smoothed the red leather cover of the book. "She looks as if she would be fast."

"She has never raced, so I don't know how fast she is," I replied. "I got her when she was three." I heard my voice soften. "She was a wedding gift from my husband."

A little silence fell, then he said, "Have you bred her?"

I carefully placed my pen back into its holder. "No."

"Does she have any vices?"

"No," I repeated. "She is a trifle hot at hand, but that is only because she is full of courage."

His golden eyes looked puzzled. "Then why haven't you bred her, Mrs. Saunders? The foal of a mare like that would go for a very handsome price."

"I can't afford the stud fee," I said baldly.

He raised his brows. A little silence fell.

I was about to turn back to my account book when he said thoughtfully, "Do you know, I rather think I might just have discovered an acceptable reason for you to accompany me to Savile Castle."

I stared at him blankly.

"You are going to look at my stallion to see if he will be an acceptable mate for Maria," he explained.

"Do you have a stallion?" I asked in surprise.

A log fell and he got up to poke it deeper into the embers. "Not at Savile Castle," he replied, "but Nicky does not need to know that."

I turned his suggestion over in my mind and could find only one flaw in it. "If I am going to look at a horse, then Nicky will never understand why he cannot accompany me."

Once again the straight, dark gold eyebrows lifted. "What about his studies with this Mr. Ludgate?"

"Mr. Ludgate is always flexible."

The earl shrugged, his big shoulders moving easily under his superbly fitted coat. "Are you required to produce a reason for leaving him behind, Mrs. Saunders? I have no children myself, but I have a number of nieces and nephews, and I know that they would never expect to accompany my sister and brother-in-law on all of their jaunts, even when school is not in session."

I considered trying to explain to Savile that Nicky and I did not have an ordinary kind of mother-son relationship. When Tommy died, all of my communication with the world of our mutual childhood had died with him. Lady Saunders disliked me, and she disliked my son as well, so Nicky had grown up with no contact with any of the members of his father's family. My parents and my sister, Deborah, were dead; the only remaining member of my family was Aunt Margaret. As Aunt Margaret had never once, in all the years that Deborah and I had lived with her, set foot outside the confines of her house and garden, she was incapable of com-

71

ing to Deepcote to visit me. And my returning to Hatfield had simply been out of the question.

This lack of family had caused Nicky and me to bond together in a way that parents and children in ordinary families, who shared their affections with a number of other people, did not. To put it simply, Nicky was everything to me — as I was to him.

It was impossible to express all this to the Earl of Savile.

I said, "It is a good suggestion, my lord, and if you don't mind, I will make use of it."

He put down the poker, returned to his seat, and said mildly, "I do have a stallion, you know. Actually, I have several of them. They are standing at my stud near Epsom. Come spring, you are more than welcome to breed Maria to any one of them, Mrs. Saunders."

I felt the color burning my cheeks. I raised my chin. "I am not an object of charity, my lord," I said fiercely. "I do not accept what I cannot pay for."

"My dear girl," he returned in the same mild voice, "I was only suggesting a loan. You can easily repay me the stud fee when you sell Maria's foal."

My heart jumped. It was true that I didn't want charity, but an offer like this was manna from heaven. I said carefully, "I shall have to wait until the foal is a yearling if I want to realize a decent sum."

"I would be in no hurry to be repaid, I assure you."

Thankfully, there was no amusement in his voice when he said this.

"Well . . ." I drew a deep breath. "If that is indeed the case, I should be very happy to accept your offer, my lord."

"Good." He smiled at me. "I should hate for Nicky to think you had found my stallion wanting, you know."

That beguiling smile caught me at a weak moment, and I smiled back.

Something leaped in the air between us, and suddenly my heart began to hammer so hard that it felt as if it were going to break through my rib cage. The smile left his face, his expression hardened, his eyes narrowed.

Oh no! The thought was sheer panic. *No, no, no, no, no.*

I jumped up, my only thought to get away from him, away from the dangerous look I saw in his eyes, away from the dangerous feeling I had in my stomach.

I stammered, "If you will excuse me, my lord, I must find Nicky." And heedless of how rude or stupid I might appear, I fled the room.

There was no fire in my bedroom during the middle of the day, so I wrapped myself in a blanket and sat staring into the cold grate.

I had been a widow for six years now, and during that time there had been a number of men who wanted to warm what they imagined must be my cold and lonely bed. There had even been two men who wanted to lie with me so badly that they had offered to marry me.

So I understood very well what I had seen in the Earl of Savile's face.

It wasn't Savile who was worrying me, however. I was perfectly capable of handling unwelcome male ardor. What worried me was the response I had felt in myself. That was something altogether new.

Don't be a fool, Gail! I thought. *Just because the man looks like some kind of a god doesn't mean you have to play the role of a smitten Greek maiden.*

I gripped my hands together under my ancient warm wool blanket.

Just because the man painted a few walls for you doesn't mean he is entitled to jump into your bed.

I breathed deeply, drawing the cold, damp

air of the bedroom into my lungs.

Just because the man has a smile that could melt ice in the arctic doesn't mean you have to fall into his arms like a love-starved widow.

I had never felt like a love-starved widow before.

I shut my eyes and rocked the chair back and forth.

Perhaps I had imagined it all, I thought. Perhaps nothing had happened between us. Perhaps he was wondering what in the name of heaven had caused me to bolt from the room like that.

I rocked back and forth, back and forth, until gradually the rhythm soothed my jangled nerves. I let my head rest against the back of the chair and closed my eyes. I would just sit here for a few more minutes, I thought, and then . . .

"Mama!"

I opened my eyes and sat up abruptly, feeling the chill in my bones, the stiffness in my neck.

"Mama, you fell asleep!"

I blinked and looked into Nicky's blue eyes, which were but inches from mine.

"I must have," I said in surprise.

"It has stopped snowing," Nicky said, straightening away from me. "Lord Savile put his chestnuts out in the paddock an hour ago, Mama, and he is bringing them in now. He wanted to know if you wished him to put Elijah and Noah out for a while."

I unwound myself from my blanket. "What in God's name is Savile doing in the stable?" I asked. "Where is Grove?"

"Mr. Grove rode Sampson into the village to see if he could get any news of the Brighton Mail."

I had said that I would ride into the village, but then I had fallen asleep. I was furious with myself.

I struggled to my feet. "What time is it, Nicky?"

"It is after four o'clock, Mama."

I had been asleep for almost an hour! I never slept in the afternoon. Perhaps that was why my brain felt so fuzzy.

"Certainly Elijah and Noah may go out for a while," I said, "but I will do it. His lordship does not have to attend to our horses, Nicky."

"Oh, he doesn't mind," my son assured me blithely. "He's a great gun, Mama. Do you know he has two nephews who are my age and a niece who is still a baby?"

"Does he?"

"Yes. Charles and Theodore are the ones my age. They are up at Eton at present."

"Fortunate boys," I said lightly. I had

more chance of flying to the moon than I had of sending Nicky to Eton.

"I don't think they're fortunate, Mama," Nicky said. "I would hate to go to school away from home. It is much nicer studying with Mr. Ludgate."

I hugged him and said, "Go tell his lordship that I will be down to the stable in a trice."

Nicky raced from the room, and I went to fetch Tommy's old coat.

Mrs. MacIntosh caught me as I was going out the door, and by the time I reached the stable the geldings were already out in the front paddock. The day was growing dark but the wind had ceased along with the snow. Savile had left the stable door open to let in some fresh air, and the first thing I heard as I stepped inside was Nicky's delightful peel of merriment.

"Cleverest horse I ever knew," the earl said with a chuckle.

He emerged from one of his horses' stalls with a pitchfork full of manure. "Ah, here you are, Mrs. Saunders," he said cheerfully.

He was wearing his extremely expensive caped driving coat, which made him look enormous. I decided not to apologize for my absence; I most certainly did not want him to know that I had been napping while he had been doing my chores.

"Hasn't Grove returned yet?" I said a little stiffly. "It will be dark very shortly."

Savile tilted his head, as if he had heard something. Then I heard it too: the sound of a horse's hooves muffled by the snow.

"I believe he has arrived," said the Earl of Savile.

Grove brought the news that the Brighton Mail had gone through Highgate at two-thirty in the afternoon. "The storm is clearing from the west to the east, my lord," Grove reported. "The mail's driver is a friend of the local blacksmith, and he stopped long enough to tell him that while they hit some pretty heavy drifts, the horses had been able to get through without too great a struggle."

"That answers our question, then," Savile said. "We shall set out ourselves directly after breakfast."

His eyes met mine over Nicky's head, and he quirked an eyebrow in inquiry. I shook my head slightly.

"Nicholas, my lad," Savile said cheerfully, "I have persuaded your mama to come to Kent with me for a few days to take a look at a stallion I own. I have told her that I would be honored if she found him worthy to breed to her beautiful Maria."

It was growing quite dark inside the stable, but I could see the quick eagerness that lighted Nicky's face. "Do you really have a Thoroughbred stallion, sir?"

"I do."

"That is wonderful!" Nicky enthused. "Mama has wanted to breed Maria for years, but . . ." His voice died away as he remembered the reason why I had been unable to fulfill this longtime dream of mine. His eyes flew to mine.

I said calmly, "Lord Savile has offered to let me defer payment of the stud fee until after Maria's foal is sold, Nicky."

"Oh," said Nicky. He turned back to Savile with a big smile. "I say, that is kind of you, sir."

I had never had to teach Nicky manners. Courtesy came to him as naturally as breathing.

Savile ruffled Nicky's hair, a casual gesture that looked as if he had performed it many times. I remembered that he had told Nicky he had nephews.

The earl said to his groom, "Did you find Tim Haines?"

"Yes, my lord, I did. He said he would be happy to come and stay with Master Nicholas and the MacIntoshes until Mrs.

Saunders returns home."

"Good," said the earl. He turned to me. "Now you won't need to fret about who is taking care of your horses, ma'am."

The nerve of the man!

I believe my mouth might have been open as I stared at him. I finally managed to say, with biting sarcasm, "Thank you so much for attending to *my* business, my lord."

"You're welcome," he replied with imperturbable good humor.

"But, Mama," Nicky said in a small, puzzled voice, "aren't I coming with you?"

My heart ached. I had not informed the earl that I had never before spent even one night away from Nicky. It was only my horror at what would happen if Nicky found out about George that gave me the strength to say, "I will only be gone for a few days, sweetheart, and you ought not to miss your lessons with Mr. Ludgate."

"I'm afraid that I am the ogre who has insisted that you remain behind with your schoolwork, Nicky," Savile said. "If either of my nephews ever learned that I had entertained a boy of their age during the school term, I should never hear the end of it. They are constantly trying to find reasons to come to Savile Castle, you see, and so far I have been very good about holding firm. I most certainly do not wish to give them any kind of a lever to use against me."

I saw Nicky duck his head quickly, a little gesture that wrung my heart even more.

"You can come and see my stallion in the spring, when your mother brings Maria to be bred," Savile said kindly.

Nicky straightened up a little in the gloom. "That would be nice." His voice was still very small.

I swallowed hard around the lump in my throat, then said, "Have you finished mucking out your horses, my lord?"

"Yes, Mrs. Saunders. I might add that I have mucked out yours as well."

"Then I shall throw them down some hay."

I marched stiff-backed to the ladder to the hayloft, put a foot on the first rung, and stopped as I realized that I could scarcely climb the ladder in a skirt with Savile and Grove standing there below me.

I turned around, a scowl on my face.

Savile was grinning.

I clenched my fists.

Grove stepped forward. "Let me drop the hay, Mrs. Saunders," he said. "You and the lad and his lordship go on back to the house and get ready for your dinner."

In fuming silence I trudged back through

the snow, with Savile on one side of me and Nicky on the other.

I was growing very tired of being ordered about by the Earl of Savile.

CHAPTER 5

For dinner Mr. MacIntosh served potted chicken stuffed with herbs, and I realized that Mrs. MacIntosh had sacrificed one of her hens to the necessity of feeding a man the size of the Earl of Savile. There was a fragrant potato casserole to go along with the chicken and a large loaf of delicious crusty bread. I gave a big helping of chicken to Savile, a smaller one to Nicky, and served myself just the potato casserole.

Nicky was very quiet as he ate his chicken. I kept shooting worried glances in his direction as I made halfhearted conversation with the earl.

"Do you know, Nicky, I suspect that your mama is worried about leaving you here with the MacIntoshes," Savile surprised me by saying suddenly. "I have tried to reassure her that an eight-year-old boy can survive for a few days without his mother, but I do not think she is convinced."

The earl's tone was humorous and colored with just the sort of odious "we males together" condescension that a young boy was guaranteed to find flattering.

Sure enough, Nicky lifted his chin and, for the first time since we had sat down, looked at me directly. "I shall be perfectly fine, Mama," he said. "I'm not a baby anymore, you know."

"Those were my exact words," Savile said in the same odious tone he had just used.

Nicky basked in the light of the earl's approval. He sat up taller in his seat.

"You will have plenty to keep you busy," I said. "I'll want you to keep an eye on Tim to make certain he does what he's supposed to do with the horses. And you have your schoolwork for Mr. Ludgate as well."

"Yes, Mama," Nicky said with commendably superior male patience.

I forced myself to smile at him as I said, "I suppose you *are* growing up."

He looked so small and slight as he sat between Savile and me at the large dining-room table. My heart shivered with love and fear as I met his innocent blue gaze across the dinner plates.

"Yes," he returned with surprised pleasure. "I rather believe that I am."

I left Savile with the dregs of the sherry bottle and went upstairs to pack. The will was scheduled to be read on the nineteenth, which was the day after next. I reckoned that I would arrive at Savile Castle on the afternoon of the eighteenth, hear the will read sometime on the nineteenth, and depart on the morning of the twentieth. This meant that I would be eating two dinners at the castle, and, unfortunately, I owned only one decent evening dress. This was the gown I had purchased in December to wear to the annual Christmas party the squire always hosted for the neighborhood.

I removed the gown from my closet and laid it out on my bed. It was made of celestial-blue silk, the exact same color as Nicky's eyes, and it had a fashionably deep, square-cut neckline, short, puffed sleeves, and a scalloped flounce along the hem. The dressmaker in the village had copied it from a picture I had picked out in the *Ladies Magazine*. It was the first new evening dress I had purchased since Tommy's death, and I loved it.

The blue silk would not be an embarrassment at the table of an earl. The same could not be said for my two other evening dresses, however. I took out the better of them, a yellow muslin done in the plain empire style that had been popular during the war, and laid it on the bed next to the blue.

In addition to its being a dress for a very

young girl, the yellow looked tired and dowdy and out of fashion. I decided it would be better to wear the same gown twice than to make an appearance in the pathetic yellow. I picked up the blue, held it up against myself, and looked in the mirror that hung over the old walnut dressing table next to the window.

Except for the short feathery hair that had once been a long ripple of ebony, and an expression of gravity in the dark blue eyes, the girl who looked back at me did not appear very different from the "witch's brat" who had married Lady Saunders's youngest son nine years ago.

"Witch's brat" was the name that had been bestowed upon Deborah and me by some of the more unkind denizens of Hatfield. It had not been earned by any activities of our own, but was due to Aunt Margaret, who was famous throughout our part of Sussex for her many herbal concoctions.

Let me hasten to assure you that Aunt Margaret was *not* a witch. She never cast spells or foretold the future or any of the other silly activities one associates with the witches in *Macbeth*. Aunt Margaret was an herbal healer, which is a different thing altogether.

About some things, however, I have to

admit that Aunt Margaret was very peculiar. For example, she was incapable of leaving her house and garden. I do not mean that she didn't wish to leave; I mean that she *could not* leave. It made her physically ill to attempt to do so.

As we grew up, this infirmity proved to be a serious problem for Deborah and me. All of the other Hatfield girls had mamas to chaperon them, but Deborah and I had nobody. Deborah, who was by nature a serious and dignified person, managed to rise above this social handicap, but I freely confess that I was something of a hoyden.

In my more honest moments, I also have to confess that Lady Saunders had reason to object to Tommy's and my marriage. There was nothing she could do about it, however, as Tommy was twenty-one and I had the approval of Aunt Margaret.

I stood in front of my mirror now, contemplating the twenty-seven-year-old woman who was reflected in the rather tarnished glass. A short lock of black hair had fallen across my brow and I tossed my head to flick it away.

I love this dress, I thought, as I turned this way and that, holding the gown up against me. The blue of the dress picked up the blue of my eyes, which were so dark that they often looked black.

I was profoundly grateful that I had decided that this was the year I absolutely had to have a new dress. The thought of appearing at Savile Castle in the old yellow was appalling.

Not that I wanted to impress the Earl of Savile, I assured myself hastily. Rather, it was a matter of pride. I did not wish George's relations to know how poor I really was.

I was carrying my portmanteau toward the stairs early the following morning when Savile called to me from behind, in the passageway. I stopped, and he came to take the bag from my hand. I opened my mouth to protest, then closed it again. If the man wanted to carry my portmanteau, let him.

Tim Haines was down at the stable doing the morning chores, so Nicky and Savile and I sat in the dining room and had breakfast. Nicky was remarkably cheerful, and I tried not to let either him or the earl see how dreadfully apprehensive I was about leaving him.

It wasn't until we went out into the cold morning air, and the coach steps were let down for me, that I saw a flicker of uncertainty on my son's face.

"I shall be home on the twentieth," I said to him, and reached out to give him a brisk, reassuring hug. In return, his arms came up to hold me tightly. I kissed the top of his head, closing my eyes as I felt the silky texture of his hair under my lips. Then I forced myself to relax my grip on him and step away.

"Take care of him, Mrs. MacIntosh," I said lightly.

"You need na fear for Master Nicky, lass," my faithful housekeeper said firmly. "He is as dear to me as if he were my verra ain bairn."

I think that the only thing that enabled me to get into the coach was that I knew she was speaking the truth.

I scarcely registered the fact that the Earl of Savile had entered the coach after me and was sitting on the cushioned seat at a distance of barely a foot.

We pulled out of my stable yard and onto the road that would take us to the village of Highgate and thence onto the highway to Kent.

I didn't say anything, I just stared blindly at the empty seat opposite mine, trying desperately not to cry.

At last Savile spoke. "He really will be all right, you know." His voice was surprisingly gentle. "Most boys of eight are packed off to school, separated from their mothers for many months at a time."

I knew this was so.

I said in a constricted voice, "It is just that since my husband's death, Nicky and I have been rather on our own. It has made us very close."

"I can understand that." His voice was, if possible, even gentler. "But you cannot smother him, Mrs. Saunders. He must learn to stand on his own."

A jolt of healthy anger shot through me. "I have always been of the opinion that it is extremely easy for those who have no children to give advice to those who do," I snapped.

"Doubtless you are right," came the serene reply. "I did have a son once, but both he and his mother died two days after he was born. I can only assure you that I have two nephews and a niece whom I am often called upon to entertain, and so my knowledge of children is not totally theoretical."

Well, of course I felt utterly dreadful. The poor man — to lose a wife and a child like that!

"I am so sorry, my lord," I said with genuine contrition. "I did not mean to stir up an old wound."

"It happened eight years ago," he returned. "I can assure you that though the scar is still there, it no longer aches."

I had lost Tommy six years ago. "I know exactly what you mean," I said.

We sat in sympathetic silence for perhaps ten minutes.

Then I began to be aware that we were shut up together in the coach and that his thigh was not a foot away from mine. I felt a flush of heat course through me.

What is the matter with you, Gail? I asked myself in agitation. *You never feel like this!*

I cleared my throat and asked, "Who is likely to be at the reading of this will, my lord?"

He leaned his shoulders against the rather worn blue velvet squabs, slid down a little on his spine, closing infinitesimally the space between us, and folded his arms across his chest. "Harriet will be there, of course, draped in her new blacks. She was not pleased that I refused to have the will read at Devane Hall and instead forced her to make the trip to Savile Castle."

There was a dry note in the earl's voice when he spoke of Lady Devane that one could not miss. I said nothing, however. Harriet Melville, Lady Devane, could be the most angelic person in the world and I would still have hated her.

Savile continued, "Harriet will, of course, be accompanied by her father. She is always accompanied by her father. His name is Albert Cole, and he made his money working poor wretches to death in the cotton mills of Manchester."

Savile did not even attempt to disguise his dislike of George's father-in-law. "It was Cole money that bought Harriet her position as George's wife, of course. My uncle's pockets were all-to-let; poor George had no choice about whom he could wed. It was marry money or flee the country."

He spoke in a soft, even tone, clearly conscious that he was treading on very precarious ground.

I could feel how my whole body had stiffened. "If George had resisted, I am convinced that another way out of the family financial difficulties could have been found," I said coldly.

"I really do not think there was another way," Savile said. "My uncle should never have put poor George in such a position to begin with, of course. But a gambler is a gambler, and by the time Uncle Jack had finished, the entire estate was mortgaged to the hilt."

I did not want to hear this story. I did not

want to hear anything that might cast George in a sympathetic light.

I said, "Will anyone else be there besides the grieving widow and her father?"

Savile agreeably followed this change of topic. "My cousin, Roger Melville, will be present. Roger is the new Lord Devane."

I thought that it would not be easy for Lady Devane to be in the company of her husband's successor.

All those daughters and no son, I thought piously, thinking of George and Harriet's family. For all the money that Mr. Cole had paid for Devane Hall, he would not be able to retain it after all. His daughter had not provided George with a male heir.

"My elder sister will undoubtedly be present as well," Savile went on. "Not be-cause she expects anything from the will, but because she is incurably nosy." His voice sounded half amused, half exasperated.

"What is your sister's name?" I asked.

"Regina."

"I meant, by what title should I address her?"

"Oh. She is married to a commoner, so her name is still Lady Regina. I doubt that her husband will come with her. He is Gervase Austen — you know, the fellow who discovered that new comet everyone was talking about last year. Gervase is far more interested in the stars than he is in people."

I had heard of neither Mr. Austen nor his comet. I smiled faintly to indicate my interest and wisely said nothing.

"My cousin John Melville will be there as well," the earl went on. "John lives at Savile and is kind enough to act as my steward. I really don't know how I should go on without him."

"And who is the attorney who has charge of the will?" I inquired.

"Old Middleman of Middleman and Ambrose. He resides in London, of course, and that was another reason to have the will read at Savile Castle. We are much more convenient to London than is Devane Hall."

I said carefully, "Do any or all of these people know that George has left money to Nicky?"

We were so close that I could actually feel him stiffen. "No," he said in a clipped voice. "I have not confided that delightful news to anyone but you."

I had insulted him.

"I wasn't sure," I said. "If what George told you is true, then they will all know it soon enough."

"I am the executor of George's will, not the town crier."

He was *really* insulted.

"I beg your pardon, my lord," I said softly. I truly had not meant to offend him.

He gave me a swift, eagle's glare and said nothing.

I turned my head to look out the window. The sun had turned the snowy landscape into a sparkling scene of crystal splendor. The world was eerily quiet; even the horses' hooves were muffled as they fell on the packed snow of the roadway.

I drew in my breath with an audible catch.

"It is beautiful indeed," Savile said quietly. Evidently he had gotten over his ill humor.

I said with a forced laugh, "And when it melts we shall be knee deep in mud!"

Silence descended on the coach.

"How long before we arrive?" I asked at last in a muffled voice.

"It depends upon the road," came the reply. "From what we have experienced thus far, I should say another five hours."

Five hours! I could not possibly remain cooped up with him there in that coach for five more hours, I thought.

"I get sick if I ride too long inside a coach," I said with inspired invention. "Do you think it would be possible for me to ride up on the box with Grove for a while?"

I could feel him looking at my profile,

which I tried to keep expressionless.

"It will be cold up on the box," he said.

The cold on the box was infinitely preferable to the heat I was beginning to feel inside the coach.

"I am dressed warmly," I said firmly, "and I would rather be cold than sick."

"Very well." He opened the window, leaned out, and shouted to Grove to stop the horses. We alighted in the middle of the road, which was the only area not covered in snowdrifts. I could see the tracks of the Brighton Mail that Grove was following.

Before I could protest, Savile put his hands on my waist and swung me up next to Grove on the high box. I felt the touch of his hands all the way through my wool dress and my pelisse.

Grove looked at me as if I were insane. "It's too cold for you up here, Mrs. Saunders," he said.

I trotted out my lie about feeling sick.

Grove's mouth set in a disapproving line, but he unwrapped the plaid wool blanket from around his legs and handed it to me.

"No, no, no!" I protested in distress. "I do not mean to rob you of your blanket, Grove. I shall be fine, I promise you."

From his position on the ground beside us, Savile recommended, "Tuck the blanket around yourself, Mrs. Saunders. I can promise you that as long as you're beside him, Grove won't use it himself, so someone might as well get the benefit of its warmth."

I looked at the set of Grove's jaw and knew that Savile was speaking the truth. I felt terrible. "Thank you, Grove," I said in a small voice.

"Ye're welcome, Mrs. Saunders."

The earl disappeared, and Grove picked up the reins after he heard the coach door slam closed. He clucked to the chestnuts and we moved off again at a slow trot.

I hunched up, wrapped the blanket around myself, and tried to convince myself that I wasn't freezing. I could have ridden in that temperature, because when you ride you are exercising. Driving is sedentary, however, and after an hour I was shivering badly. I was just about to ask Grove to stop so I could get back into the coach when the earl once again called for Grove to halt the horses.

"Time to switch places, John," Savile said as he came to stand beside the box. "I'll drive while you get in out of the wind for a bit."

"It ain't windy, your lordship," Grove protested.

"It is when you're sitting on an open box behind trotting horses," the earl returned. "Come on, man. Get down."

Grove wrapped the reins and slowly got to his feet. He moved stiffly, and I realized that the cold had gotten into his joints.

I felt even more guilty about stealing his blanket.

Grove jumped to the ground, staggered, and was supported by his lordship's gloved hand.

Savile looked at me. "You too, Mrs. Saunders," he said. "Your stomach must be feeling better by now."

"Yes, it is," I said through chattering teeth.

The earl reached up, and without any hesitation I put my hands on his shoulders and let him lift me to the ground. He held the coach door for me and I got in, followed by Grove. Savile shut the door and after a minute we felt the coach rock a little on its springs as the earl climbed up onto the box. Then we were once more moving forward.

"Oh dear," I said. "I still have the blanket!"

"Keep it, Mrs. Saunders," Grove recommended.

I felt a flash of irritation. *If the two of them are so determined for me to keep this benighted blanket, then I will!* I thought. I tucked it around my waist and leaned back, grateful for the soft squabs and the lack of wind. I closed my eyes and pretended to go to sleep.

The slow trot of the horses was extremely soporific and I was almost asleep for real when the carriage stopped again and the men once more changed places. I lifted my heavy eyelids and regarded them sleepily. Then the carriage moved off and once again my eyes closed.

Someone rearranged the blanket around me. I mumbled a word of thanks and drifted off into oblivion.

I opened my eyes to feel a strong male arm holding me snugly against a big warm body. I realized that the wool under my cheek was that of a man's coat.

I struggled hazily up from the depths of unconsciousness.

"Tommy?" I said.

"I'm afraid not, Mrs. Saunders," said the Earl of Savile.

I jerked away from him and sat bolt upright, horrified that I had been sleeping on his shoulder.

He appeared not to notice my reaction. "You woke up just in time," he said. "Savile Castle is just ahead."

CHAPTER 6

I gazed through the coach window and saw what looked like a magical castle right out of the Arthurian legend rising before me out of the snow.

"Good heavens, it really *is* a castle," I said.

"Yes," agreed its owner, "it is."

I stared at the distant, high gray stone walls, cornered with four perfectly symmetrical towers, and wondered if I would find noble knights and damsels in distress within. Surely they had to be in residence somewhere!

Savile said, "You can't see much of it now, because it's frozen and covered by the snow, but there is a moat. Well, actually it's a small lake. The castle is built on an island."

I turned from the window and gave him an incredulous look. "This amazing edifice actually has a *moat?*"

He grinned, something he should not have been allowed to do.

I turned back to the window, thus averting my eyes from that criminally attractive smile. "When was it built?" I asked. "During the same period as Camelot?"

He laughed. "Not as early as that. One of my ancestors built it during the reign of Richard II." His voice was pleasant and informative, but I could hear the pride he was trying to conceal.

I couldn't blame him.

"The Hundred Years War was going on and there was fear of a French invasion," he continued. "At that time the River Haver, which creates the lake, was a passable tributary of the Thames, so the king issued my ancestor a license to crenellate the manor house, which stood on the shore of the lake" — he gestured — "over there. My ancestor, the first Raoul, decided instead to pull down the manor house and build a fortified castle on the island."

I looked at the walls and towers we were approaching. They appeared less magical and more formidable the closer we got. I stared at the notched battlements and said, "Well, it is most certainly crenellated and fortified."

"Yes, we are well equipped to pour slaked lime, stones, and boiling tar or water on any enemies who might make it past our outer defenses," he assured me.

I laughed.

The coach bounced once and then rolled

forward more smoothly. I could see from my post at the window that we had passed onto a narrow roadway from which all the snow had been cleared.

"At one time, this causeway was made of timber," Savile said. "Today, of course, it is made of stone."

The coach tooled along the cleared roadway, which apparently was really a bridge, until we reached a free-standing stone tower some two hundred yards in front of the main door set into the castle wall. I looked up, rather expecting to see Elaine hanging out the window searching for her long-lost Lancelot.

"We are now on an island that is only a little larger than the tower next to us," the earl informed me. "At one time this was the first line of defense for the castle."

The coach stopped, the tower door opened, and an elderly man stepped out. Savile rolled down his window and a blast of cold air rushed into the coach.

"Welcome home, my lord!" the elderly man called. His face was beaming. "We made certain to get the causeway cleaned off for ye!"

"Good job, Sims," the earl said good-humoredly. "Tell me, has Lady Devane arrived yet?"

The smile disappeared from Sims's face. "That she has, my lord. And Mr. Cole with her."

"That's no surprise," Savile muttered under his breath. He nodded to the elderly gatekeeper, rolled up the window, and settled back against the squabs as the coach moved forward once more, a small frown between his brows.

The earl had so obviously forgotten my presence that I hesitated to question him. Instead, I watched in silence as we passed through the huge, arched stone gate, which must once have been closed by a portcullis, and entered within the castle walls.

Suddenly the Middle Ages vanished, and my amazed eyes beheld a snow-filled courtyard in the center of which stood an exquisitely beautiful Renaissance house built of rich golden-yellow stone streaked with reddish brown.

It was a totally unexpected sight and I must have made a sound indicative of my astonishment, for at last the earl's attention swung back to me.

"It does that to everyone the first time they see it," he said humorously. "I think it was the seventh Raoul who decided to tear down most of the medieval buildings and put up a modern residence for himself."

By "modern" I judged he meant either Elizabethan or Jacobean.

"Your family rather went in for tearing down and starting fresh," I said.

He laughed.

"Your family crest is the lion?" This was far from being a wild guess on my part, as stone lions topped all of the gables as well as the main entrance before which we had halted.

"Yes," said Savile, "as a matter of fact, it is."

A butler in full livery was coming out the front door. Savile opened the coach door on his side and stepped down before anyone could come to open it for him. For perhaps a minute he stood talking to the butler not far from the arched front door of the house, then the butler turned and went back into the house while Savile came to my side of the coach. A footman appeared with portable steps, and Savile assisted me to alight onto the snow-cleared drive.

"I've sent Powell to find my sister, Mrs. Saunders," the earl said genially. "She will see to it that you are made comfortable."

It annoyed me no end, but I suddenly found myself extremely nervous about staying in that great house.

"Does Lady Regina know I am coming?" I asked Savile.

"No one knows you are coming," he returned. "In fact, I rather think your presence is going to be a shock."

He sounded pleased.

That made me even more nervous.

There were no stairs leading into the house; we simply went in the immense front door and found ourselves in what at one time had obviously been Raoul the Seventh's Great Hall. I shot a glance at the stone fireplace, with its massive chimneypiece carved with lions and its ornate strapped overmantel, and thought incredulously, *Do people really live in a place like this?*

The sound of piano music drifted into the hall from a room close by. It stopped abruptly, and Savile said to me, "That was Ginny at the piano. She should be here in a moment."

I nodded tensely.

A woman came into the Great Hall from the doorway on my left.

"Raoul," she said warmly. "You're here at last. You'll be mortified to hear that everyone else made it before you. What an insult to your famous chestnuts!"

She crossed the polished wood floor to the earl, who bent and kissed her on the cheek.

"I'm late because I had to stop to pick someone up," Savile said to his sister.

"Ginny, let me make Mrs. Abigail Saunders known to you. Mrs. Saunders, this is my sister, Lady Regina Austen."

"How do you do, Lady Regina," I murmured.

"Mrs. Saunders," she said, giving me a mystified look.

"Mrs. Saunders figures in George's will," the earl said, "and I thought she should be present to hear it read."

Lady Regina's look went from mystification to astonishment. She said feebly, "Indeed."

A small silence fell, in which I regarded Lady Regina gravely. She had her brother's dark blond hair and finely sculpted face, but her eyes were brown, not gold.

"You will have Mrs. Ferrer show her to a room, won't you, Ginny?" the earl said.

Lady Regina's good manners reasserted themselves. "I will show her to a room myself," she said, and smiled at me.

The earl smiled at me also and said, "I will leave you in the capable hands of my sister, then, Mrs. Saunders." He departed in the opposite direction from which Lady Regina had come.

I wanted to beg him not to leave me, but obviously that was not feasible, so I straightened my spine and resolutely followed Lady

Regina across the floor to the beautiful staircase that, after the fireplace, was the room's outstanding feature.

Graciously, charmingly, relentlessly, Lady Regina began to quiz me. "Did you have a long drive, Mrs. Saunders?"

"Rather long," I replied quietly. "The roads were still quite filled with drifts, but we were able to follow the path of the mail."

"Ah," said Lady Regina.

We had reached the top of the stairs and I looked around at the imposing room I found myself in.

"What a magnificent room," I said, trying to turn the subject.

"This used to be the Great Chamber," Lady Regina told me. "At the time the house was built, rooms like this were used to entertain one's noble guests."

From ornate ceiling to marble floor, the room was intimidatingly magnificent. The paneled walls were decorated with a wealth of curious carvings, which later I would discover included winged horses, chimeras, and mermaids. The chimneypiece was what caught my immediate attention, however. I stared at it in unabashed awe. It was a truly remarkable piece, made of alabaster and black, white, and gray marble, and decked with strapwork, acanthus scrolls, and garlands of musical instruments and flowers.

Lady Regina saw where my eyes had lighted. "The chimneypiece has been described as one of the finest works of Renaissance sculpture in England," she told me, with the pride I had detected in her brother's voice earlier.

"It is magnificent," I said. I glanced at the room's only furniture, which were some carved oak chairs set along the wall. "Is the room in use today?"

"My parents occasionally used it as a ballroom," Lady Regina said.

She turned to her right and began to lead me through a succession of smaller, less formal rooms, all the while asking me questions.

"Where do you live, then, Mrs. Saunders?"

"In Surrey," I said, "in a town called Highgate."

I was quite certain that Highgate would mean nothing to her, and from the small frown between her brows I saw that I was right.

"I wonder, how did my brother know you were named in my cousin's will?" came the next question.

"I understand your brother is Lord Devane's executor," I replied. "One would expect him to know something about the contents of the will."

"Well, he never said anything about it to me!" This was obviously a sore point with Lady Regina.

The passageway turned to the right and we entered what was apparently one of the bedroom wings. We walked halfway down the hall, past at least six closed doors, until finally Lady Regina stopped in front of one, turned the latch, and pushed it open.

"Good," she said. "I thought this room would be ready."

I followed the earl's sister into an utterly charming room. It had a wide window with diamond-shaped glass, under which was a comfortable-looking window seat. The four-poster was covered with a faded gold tapestry spread, which matched the faded gold canopy over the bed. The floor was covered by a deeply colored rug that had come from the Orient. There was a wonderful blast of warmth coming from the coal fire in the fireplace.

There was a partially open door set in the middle of the wall to the right.

"The dressing room is through that door," Lady Regina told me. "Shall I send one of the maids to unpack for you, Mrs. Saunders?"

"No, thank you, Lady Regina. I am accustomed to doing for myself."

Lady Regina did not look at all surprised by this revelation. "Hot water will be coming momentarily. Dinner is in an hour and a half. I will send a footman to show you the way to the drawing room."

"Thank you," I said, and stood in the middle of the floor, hands clasped in front of me, waiting for her to leave. When finally the door closed behind her, I let out a long, slow breath and went to sit in the window seat, my mind awhirl.

Once, I had thought Devane Hall was the height of luxury. But Devane Hall was like a peasant's cottage compared to this place.

I did not want even to contemplate what the Earl of Savile must have thought of my ramshackle establishment.

Then I thought defiantly, *Why the devil should I care what the Earl of Savile might think?*

Another thought struck me, and I grinned. *Don't become too awestruck, Gail. Remember, you had the owner of this magnificent pile painting your extra bedroom!*

My portmanteau was delivered and I unpacked it in my dressing room, which contained a modern dressing table made of rosewood banded by yellow satinwood, a large rosewood wardrobe with brass knobs in the form of lion masks, and a brass-trimmed cheval glass. I washed my face and hands in the hot water that Mrs. Ferrer had provided and scrutinized my silk evening dress, thankful to see that it had collected a minimum of wrinkles. I hung it up in the wardrobe, put on my dressing gown, and went to sit in the window seat and look out at the snow.

Tonight I would meet George's wife for the first time. Of course, she was not his wife any longer, I corrected myself. Now she was his widow.

I knew that my hatred of Harriet Melville was irrational. It was not her fault that George had married her for her money. But strong emotions are never rational, and I did hate her.

I had been delighted when her three children turned out to be girls.

Was this petty? Yes, it was.

Was this un-Christian? Yes, it was.

Was this honest? Yes, it was.

Was I looking forward to seeing her face when George's bequest to Nicky was read out by the solicitor? Yes, I was.

I looked at the clock on the mantel and realized that I had better get dressed if I was to be ready when the footman came to fetch me.

I put on my evening dress and sat at the dressing table, thinking about what I might do with my hair. I had few options, as I kept it cut short and close to my head. In the end I just threaded a blue velvet ribbon through my feathery curls and fastened my only jewelry, my mother's small, diamond drop earrings.

When I looked at myself in the full-length mirror I thought I looked presentable.

The footman, a tall young man in the blue and gold livery of the Earl of Savile, arrived. He led me back down the bedroom passageway, through the small parlors and the ballroom, down the stairs into the Great Hall, through what appeared to be the music room, and into a splendid-looking formal drawing room done all in pale blue damask, where a group of people were gathered before the coal fire.

"Mrs. Saunders! Do come in," said Lady Regina, advancing to meet me. She took my hand in a friendly way and began to draw me forward.

The earl was standing with his shoulders against the wall next to the ornate fireplace and he gave me a nod and a pleasant, "I hope you have recovered from the rigors of our journey, Mrs. Saunders."

I looked at him. He was wearing evening dress: white shirt and neckcloth, perfectly fitted black coat, and tight-fitting black trousers. He smiled at me but his eyes looked somber.

"Yes, thank you, my lord," I replied, "I have."

"Allow me to introduce you to my cousin Lady Devane," Lady Regina said next, and I turned to look at the woman seated in a Sheraton chair at a little distance from the fire.

The first thing I noticed was that she was rather stout. The second thing I noticed was that the corners of her eyes drooped oddly, as if she were fatigued. The third thing I noticed was that she was looking at me with undisguised suspicion.

"Saunders?" she said to me. "Are you any connection to Squire Saunders from Hatfield?"

I could feel Lady Regina snap to attention next to me.

"I am his daughter-in-law," I returned with dignity. "Or rather, I was his daughter-in-law. My husband died some six years ago."

Her brows, which were thick and sandy-colored and looked like twin caterpillars, drew together. "Good God, you must be the witch's brat who married the squire's youngest son!" she blurted.

By now everyone in the room was staring at me.

Savile said coldly, "Witch's brat? What on earth are you talking about, Harriet?"

George's widow turned to look at him. "There is this extremely odd woman who lives in Hatfield, Savile. All the locals think she is some kind of a witch and go to her for everything from medicines to love potions. She used to have two nieces living with her," her strange, dark eyes swung back to me, "and evidently this is one of them."

"My aunt is an herbalist, Lady Devane," I said, and even I could hear the contempt in my voice as I spoke her name. "Only ignorant persons could possibly confuse an herbal healer with a witch."

An unattractive red flush suffused Lady Devane's face.

Before she could reply, however, a harsh-sounding male voice said, "Watch your mouth, missy. You talk that way to my daughter, you got to deal with Albert Cole."

I lifted my eyes to look at the man who was standing just to the right of Lady Devane's chair. He appeared to be somewhere in his upper sixties and his clothing proclaimed him to be of the merchant class. His old-fashioned suit was of brown broadcloth, with a full-skirted coat. He was wearing knee breeches with stockings, not the newly fashionable trousers such as were being worn by Savile. His shoes were old-fashioned as well, square-toed and adorned with buckles. Savile's waistcoat was snowy white; Mr. Cole's was embroidered with what looked to be an assortment of brightly colored tropical birds.

I stared at the waistcoat in amazement.

"Mrs. Saunders," Savile said, and I could hear the underlying amusement in his voice as he took in my fascination with Mr. Cole's waistcoat, "may I present Mr. Albert Cole, Lady Devane's father."

I dragged my eyes away from that many-hued garment and met the small, shrewd, light-colored eyes of the man whose money had bought George.

"How do you do, Mr. Cole," I said in what I hoped was an expressionless voice.

"What's this Saunders woman doing here, Savile?" Mr. Cole said, ignoring my greeting. "This is a family gathering."

"Mrs. Saunders is here because she figures in George's will," Savile said in a very soft voice.

Shocked silence filled the room.

115

Then Mr. Cole took a step toward me. His face began to grow very red. "I won't have it!" he said. "My girl has just lost her husband and I won't have one of —"

"That is quite enough, Cole," Savile said, and his tone stopped Albert Cole dead in his tracks. "Mrs. Saunders is here because it is her legal right to be here and because I invited her. If you do not care for my guests, then *you* may leave."

"Don't make a fuss, Papa," Harriet said in a strained voice.

Lady Regina took my arm and said smoothly, as if nothing uncomfortable had just happened, "Mrs. Saunders, I have not yet presented you to my cousin, Mr. John Melville."

One of the two men who stood together in front of the fire bowed to me. "Happy to make your acquaintance, ma'am," he said.

I looked steadily into a nice-looking, unremarkable face and murmured some-thing polite.

"And my other cousin, Mr. Roger Melville, who is the new Lord Devane."

Devane Hall was entailed, of course, and so Harriet's girls would not be able to inherit either the title or the property. I looked with interest at the slim, blond young man who would be George's successor.

He smiled at me. His eyes were as blue as Nicky's. "So nice to meet you, Mrs. Saunders," he said.

The butler, Powell, appeared in the doorway and announced that dinner was served.

The earl took in Lady Devane, the new Lord Devane took in Lady Regina, and Mr. John Melville took in me. Mr. Cole followed behind, his hands behind his back, his face fixed in a scowl.

I foresaw that we were going to have a pleasant dinner and steeled myself for battle.

CHAPTER 7

Large folding doors led from the drawing room directly into a large and splendid dining room. The immensely long mahogany table looked as if it could seat forty people easily. I looked from the table to the painted ceiling, which featured lions among its richly colored scenes, to the two huge crystal chandeliers, to the magnificent display of silver plate on the mahogany sideboard, and knew that my blue evening dress was not equal to the room.

Fortunately, however, the dining room was not prepared for dinner. The gleaming wood surface of the table was naked except for two matching black urns, and the dozens of carved gilt chairs in the room were lined up along the splendidly carved walls.

I took in all of this magnificence in a few quick glances as I accompanied Mr. John Melville across the short side of the dining room and through the door that was directly opposite the doorway through which we had come.

We were now in another dining room,

large by my standards but not intimidating like the one we had just passed through. The table in this room was round and supported by a central pillar ending in three great carved paws. The sideboard was made of rosewood with brass inlays, and the display of silver and china reposing upon it was remarkably restrained, considering what I had just beheld.

Fresh flowers, presumably from the earl's greenhouse, adorned the table, together with place settings of china that bore the lion of Savile against a blue and gold background.

"I am so glad that you purchased this table, Raoul," Lady Regina remarked as we all took our places. "A round breakfast table is so much cozier for the family than that old mahogany monstrosity Mama used to have in here. After all, the whole point of having a family dining room is so that one can dine informally with one's family."

"If I remember correctly, Ginny, it was *you* who purchased this table," the earl retorted. "My only part in the transaction was to pay the bill."

Lady Regina did not look at all discomposed. "Well, someone has to look after the inside of this house, Raoul," she said. "And since you have proven so recalcitrant about acquiring a second wife, of necessity the task must fall to me."

Savile's dark gold eyebrows drew together and he said a little irritably, "I am perfectly capable of seeing to my own house."

"You see to the grounds and the property admirably," Lady Regina agreed. "Allow me to mention, however, that the withdrawing room needs new draperies, the morning room needs new wallpaper, the . . ."

Savile held up his hand. "Enough."

"Ah, the ladies. They always know how to sport the blunt, don't they, m'lord?" Albert Cole said genially.

I could see the muscles tighten under Lady Regina's lovely skin. She opened her lips, then shut them together, hard.

The earl shot his sister a look of wicked amusement. When he spoke, however, he proved himself a faithful brother. "Much as I hate to admit it, Ginny is right, Cole. My interests do lie with the land rather than the house."

I said, trying to lighten the atmosphere, "It seems to me that a round table is extremely appropriate for this house. When I first saw its walls and towers rising out of the snow, I thought I must surely be coming to Camelot."

The new Lord Devane, who was seated to my left, laughed. "You are thinking of Arthur's round table, are you, Mrs. Saunders?"

"Yes, my lord, I am."

He gave me a look of approval. "I had the same feeling myself the first time I came to Savile," he said, and while the soup was being served he proceeded to regale the table with the amusing tale of his first visit to the castle.

I sat with my soup in front of me, my hands folded in my lap, waiting. On either side of me, the men dipped their spoons into their bowls and began to eat. At this point I realized that grace was not going to be said, so I picked up my spoon and took a sip of the steamy liquid in front of me.

I had just decided that it must be some kind of vegetable soup when the earl, who was seated to my right, murmured softly, "It doesn't stand up to Mr. MacIntosh's, does it?"

It didn't, of course.

"It is very good, my lord," I said politely.

He made a noise indicative of disbelief, and I smiled into my soup.

The soup was removed and a fish course was set out next: a turbot in some sort of butter and herb sauce. It was good and I was hungry. I let the conversation eddy around me while I ate.

After the fish dishes were removed, I was

amazed to see the butler set a large roast turkey in front of the earl. I stared at the huge bird in wonder. Surely I wasn't expected to eat *that* along with everything that had come before?

It seemed that I was.

The earl rose to his feet and took a large carving knife from Powell. I watched in astonishment as his long, slim hands, wielding the knife with decisive authority, slashed easily through the fowl, slicing off the succulent meat and depositing it on the plates, which a footman then brought to each of us seated around the table.

The second footman poured more wine. I had drunk only about a fourth of my first glass, but I noticed that everyone else's glass was almost empty.

The third footman took an array of covered side dishes from the sideboard and arranged them on the table. The dish in front of me contained what I thought might be oyster stuffing for the turkey. It smelled delicious and I regretted having eaten so much turbot.

Once the turkey had been served, everyone chose their side dishes. Two footmen assisted in this process; if the dish one wanted was out of reach, one simply asked a footman to bring it to one.

I had some of the oyster stuffing and a few pickled beans. I looked at the amount of turkey that the earl had heaped upon my plate and wondered how I was going to get through all that food.

How paltry Savile must have thought his dinner at Deepcote, I thought.

"How did we fare with the snowfall, John?" the earl asked as we began our main course.

Mr. John Melville, whom I remembered was Savile's steward as well as his cousin, finished chewing his meat before he answered, "Not too badly, Raoul, from what I can see. At any rate, I have had no damage reports from any of the tenants."

Savile nodded and proceeded to ask a few specific questions, demonstrating that he was indeed aware of what was happening on his land.

Mr. Cole interrupted rudely, "What time is this solicitor fellow coming tomorrow, Savile?"

There was a pause as the earl turned to look at his guest. Then, "I expect him by early afternoon," Savile said pleasantly.

"I still don't understand why Papa and I had to travel from Devane Hall all the way to Savile Castle in order to hear George's will read," Harriet said. "The weather was terrible, the journey was most unpleasant, and we had to put up overnight at a very inferior inn. One would think that you would show more concern for a newly made widow, Savile!"

I could not help but notice that the newly made widow's plate was heaped with food.

"I am sorry that you were inconvenienced, Harriet," Savile said, "but it was easier for Middleman to come to Kent than to Sussex."

"It ain't for us to consider Middleman's convenience, it's for him to consider ours," Mr. Cole said bluntly. His plate was heaped even higher than his daughter's.

"I also had to fetch Mrs. Saunders," said the earl.

Next to me, Roger Melville, the new Lord Devane, said gently, "Ah yes, the mysterious Mrs. Saunders."

I took a small bite of turkey and didn't look at anyone.

Harriet Melville's rather high-pitched complaining went on. "It's bad enough that I have to look at Roger and picture him throwing me and my beloved daughters out of my own home, but to be asked to sit down to take my dinner with the niece of our local witch! Really, Savile, I think it is too much."

"My girl's right," said Mr. Cole. "I call it

scaly behavior all 'round, that I do."

Roger Melville whispered in my ear, "It doesn't seem to have affected their appetites."

I had to bite my lip to keep from smiling.

The earl said, "I would much prefer not to hear any more about this so-called witch, Harriet. I have met Miss Longworth myself and she most certainly is not a witch."

"She is an herbal healer," I repeated. "People come from all over the area for her medicines."

"They come to her for love potions," Harriet said defiantly. She stared at me, her dark eyes glittering beneath their odd, sleepy-looking lids. "Everyone knows that. Everyone knows that that's how you got Tom Saunders to marry you. You used a love potion!"

I laughed. I couldn't help it. The idea of Tommy as the victim of a love potion was so absurd that it was hilarious.

Savile said coldly, "I think it is perfectly clear to anyone with eyes why Tom Saunders was attracted to his wife, and it has nothing to do with love potions."

"Good God," said Lord Devane in exaggerated amazement. "Surely only an ignorant servant girl could be so unenlightened as to believe in love potions, Harriet!"

Harriet's face went scarlet.

Albert Cole slammed his hands on the table, making some of the side dishes jump. "Are you callin' my girl ignorant?" he demanded, staring truculently at Lord Devane.

As Devane made a faintly amused, superficially polite reply, I stared at Harriet's fiery face. For some reason, I didn't think her embarrassment came from being likened to an ignorant serving girl.

Good heavens, I thought. *Could she possibly have asked Aunt Margaret for a love potion to use herself?*

I felt a sudden, unwanted stab of pity. It could not have been pleasant, being married to a man who was in love with another woman.

Then she shouldn't have married him, I thought.

The earl took charge of the conversation, turning it firmly in another direction. He said to his sister, who was seated across the circle from him, "Why is Gervase not here with you, Ginny?"

"He is in London for a meeting of the Royal Society," she replied. "You know how they are always dying to hear him talk abut his comet, Raoul. One would have thought they would have heard everything he had to say on the subject by now."

"What is the name of this comet?" I asked.

"Austen's Comet," she replied with a laugh. "What else?"

The warmth in her eyes was at odds with the casual humor of her voice. It was perfectly clear to me that Lady Regina was enormously proud of her husband.

"Gervase is one of the great mathematical brains of our time," the earl said to his sister. "Men of science will always want to hear him talk."

"Not *one* of the greatest, Raoul," Lady Regina returned with sparkling eyes. "*The* greatest. There can be no doubt of that."

Albert Cole wiped his mouth with a large white linen napkin and said, "Waste of time if you ask me, using mathematics to look at the sky. Mathematics should be used to make money."

"Well, if making money is to be our measure of greatness, then certainly you, Cole, must be the greatest man of our time." The amused, malicious voice belonged to Lord Devane.

I shot him a quick look and saw that the same amused malice danced in his very blue eyes.

Mr. Cole returned seriously, "You are probably right, Devane. Did you know that I started as the son of a collier?"

John Melville said gravely, "Yes, I believe you have mentioned that fact once or twice."

Across the table I saw John Melville's eyes meet the earl's. Savile coughed, picked up his napkin, and covered his mouth.

Lady Regina said firmly, "For heaven's sake, Mr. Cole, do not regale us once again with the saga of your journey from the depths of poverty to the heights of enormous wealth. We have all heard that tale more often than we care to, I can assure you of that."

Albert Cole was not insulted. "You can't bamboozle me, Lady Regina," he said. "You and that genius husband of yours would be mighty happy to have my money, I can tell you that."

Lady Regina's eyes narrowed dangerously, and she began to open her mouth.

Before she could speak, however, John Melville cut in. "Gervase would just spend it trying to make a more powerful telescope, or something like that. Money means nothing to a man like Gervase Austen, Cole."

Mr. Cole's little, light eyes shone like twin lamps in the darkened flesh that surrounded them. "Money never means nothing, Mr. Melville," he said.

All of the Melvilles sitting around the table looked politely incredulous.

I had met many men like Mr. Cole in my

time — they were the mainstays of my client list — and I thought I understood far better than the aristocratic Melvilles the frame of reference from which a man like Albert Cole operated.

Yes, he was a boor. Yes, he was rude and unpolished. But it was a fact that he had been born into bitter poverty and that he had made himself a fortune with nothing but his wits and his hard work to sustain him.

In one thing, certainly, Albert Cole was right and the Melvilles were wrong: Money can only mean nothing to those who have it.

The butler came to stand behind the earl and murmur softly, "Have you finished, my lord?"

"Yes, I think so, Powell. You may remove the cloth and set out the sweet."

To my astonishment, that is precisely what the servants did. The table was cleared and the cloth was removed to reveal another immaculately clean one beneath it. Clean glasses were set before each diner, along with dessert plates, knives, forks, and fresh napkins. A sweet wine was served for the ladies and decanters of claret and port were set before the earl.

Then Powell set an immense apple pie upon the table.

"Will you have some, Harriet?" the earl

inquired courteously of the grieving widow.

"Yes, thank you, Savile, I will," she replied.

Powell cut a piece, put it upon a plate, and gave the plate to one of the footmen, who brought it to Harriet. This procedure was then repeated for each of us at the table.

Even though the pie looked wonderful, I declined. I had eaten a much larger dinner than I was accustomed to, and my stomach felt uncomfortably full.

Throughout the rest of the dinner, the earl and John Melville talked determinedly about things that were going on around the estate. Everyone else was silent as they applied themselves to the pie.

After the pie was finished, Lady Regina rose.

"Shall we retire to the Little Drawing Room for tea, ladies?"

Harriet and I stood up obediently, and the three ladies filed out, leaving the men to their port and their conversation.

We did not return to the room where we had met before dinner, but went instead up the great stairs and into the comfortable-looking parlor that was the first room to the right of the Great Chamber. The walls of this room were covered in pale green damask and the armchairs were gilt beechwood with green velvet upholstery. A very pretty rose-wood book cabinet with brass trellises along the glass front stood against the wall between two large, green-draped windows. A settee was placed at right angles to the fire, and Harriet sat upon it. She looked at me.

Suddenly, I couldn't face the thought of spending one more minute in her company.

I said to Lady Regina, "I am so sorry, but I am truly exhausted from today's journey. Please make my excuses to the gentlemen, but I am going to say good night now and go to bed."

"Oh, don't leave us to our own company, Mrs. Saunders," Lady Regina said, and the look she gave me was heartfelt.

I was not inclined toward mercy, however. "I would be no company at all, I assure you." I looked toward the settee. "Good night, Lady Devane."

"Oh, good night," she replied petulantly.

Lady Regina sighed. "Shall I call a foot-man to escort you to your room?"

"That won't be necessary," I assured her.

"Then I will send one of the maids to help you undress."

This service I declined as well. I had managed to get into my evening dress without help; I would get out of it the same way.

The bedroom passageway was very cold,

but a blast of warmth from the fireplace wafted out to greet me as I opened my bedroom door. The bedside and fireside oil lamps had been lit, and as I undressed in a leisurely fashion I compared the comfort of the room with the way I had to scramble out of my clothes and jump into bed at home in order to stay warm.

I was just going to turn out the lamps and get into bed when there came a soft knock at the door and a maid entered.

"I have a hot brick for your bed, ma'am," she said.

I watched as she folded down my bedclothes and slipped the hot brick down to the foot of the bed.

"Thank you," I said.

She gave me a prim little smile and exited quietly.

Now, normally when one gets into bed in the wintertime, the sheets at the bottom are like ice. This was not the case at Savile Castle, however. The hot brick radiated heat all through the bottom part of the bed and I wiggled my bare toes blissfully.

I had to admit that even though I had felt like a beggar girl dining at the table of King Cophetua, I had enjoyed my dinner immensely. I had never seen such a lavish display of food.

And that was only a family dinner! I thought. What must a formal party be like at Savile Castle?

That was one thing I would never find out, I thought, wiggling my toes again comfortably. Both birth and economic situation firmly excluded me from the kind of society in which the Earl of Savile moved.

It was not that my birth wasn't perfectly respectable; it was. My father was a doctor in the city of York and my mother was the daughter of a clergyman. When my sister and I were children, my family had automatically been included in the "good society" of York and its environs. It had never occurred to either Deborah or me that we were not every bit as good as everyone else we knew.

Then my parents went on a short trip to a seaside resort and were killed in a hotel fire. Deborah was eleven and I was eight. Our world had never been the same again.

I wrapped my arms around my knees, stared into the glowing coals, and remembered how frightened the two of us had been as we rode the stagecoach from York to Hatfield on our way to live with Aunt Margaret, my father's sister and our only surviving relative. We had sat in mute silence all the way, our hands clasped together, our eyes focused unseeingly out the window.

We had never before met Aunt Margaret, and when we did, she was a definite shock. Older than my father by ten years, she had been a semirecluse for years. The addition of two lively children to her home had probably been as difficult for her as adjusting to her had been for us.

It was not that she did not care about us. When she remembered us, she cared very much. But for the part of the day that Aunt Margaret spent in her garden, Deborah and I did not exist for her. And Aunt Margaret spent virtually her entire day in her garden.

The result of this situation was that Deborah and I had brought ourselves up. In childhood we had been allowed to roam freely about the countryside, but as we grew into young womanhood, this lack of adult restraint started to become scandalous. The rector's wife, Mrs. Bridge, had spoken to Aunt Margaret about her duty to chaperon her nieces, but poor Aunt Margaret was utterly incapable of leaving Littleton Cottage. To give Mrs. Bridge her due, she tried to include us along with her own daughter in many of the activities organized by the local mamas in order to introduce young men and women to one another as prospective spouses.

I was fifteen when I first met Tommy, who

was home from Eton for the summer. I was fishing at the pond that lay to the southeast of town when he came along, whistling and carrying his fishing pole. I liked him immediately because he did not patronize me the way so many of the older boys did. It was not until the following year, however, when I had begun to develop a figure, that Tommy began to pay me the kind of attention a young man pays to a young woman.

The year after that, George made his appearance in neighborhood society. I remember very clearly the first occasion upon which I saw him. It was at a picnic given by Mrs. Bridge. George had come down from Cambridge for the summer and for some reason or another — boredom probably — he had decided to join Mrs. Bridge's expedition to some local ruins.

All the girls except me instantly fell in love with him. He was very handsome as well as being the next Lord Devane.

From the day he'd first appeared at that benighted picnic, George had given me nothing but trouble. I devoutly hoped that tomorrow, when I declined his legacy, I would be able to say goodbye forever to George Melville, Lord Devane.

CHAPTER 8

I awoke at my usual early hour the next morning, but as I was quite sure that none of the family would be stirring until much later, I decided to remain in bed. The only way I could keep myself from worrying about what might come out in George's will that afternoon was by turning my brain to what seemed the eternal problem of my life: money.

The money that I was presently making from my business was not going to be enough to see me through the next few years. Consequently, I had to either (a.) spend less or (b.) earn more. Since I had already cut my expenses to the bone, the only solution was to earn more.

I would have to raise my rates.

This was a course of action I had been resisting for several years. For one thing, my present rates were not cheap. My particular business had a very high overhead: horses to stable and feed, plus rent to be paid on a house and property large enough to accommodate both horses and clients. As I rarely had more than one client at a time, I had to charge a fairly steep sum in order to cover my costs.

During the two years that Tommy and I had run Deepcote together, we had done quite well. Clients had been more plentiful in those days, with Tommy teaching the men and the boys while I taught the girls. After Tommy died, however, business had fallen off drastically. I had largely kept my female clients, but the men and boys had stopped coming, and my income had plummeted. I was beginning to regain some of the male business — parents who had been pleased with the job I had done with their daughters had started to send me their sons — but I was afraid that if I raised my rates, I would turn away some of the new clients whom I might otherwise attract.

I had learned that while men like Albert Cole might own a vast amount of money, they wouldn't pay a penny higher than what they judged a product to be worth.

I had just come to the gloomy conclusion that I was going to have to take a chance and raise the rates anyway, when a housemaid came into the room bearing hot chocolate and a pitcher of hot water on a tray.

"Lady Regina has asked me to tell you that breakfast will be put out in the family dining room from nine until ten-thirty, ma'am," she said as she put the tray down and went to pile more coals upon the fire.

"Thank you," I said politely.

The maid lifted the tray, put it across my lap, and poured me a cup of chocolate; then she took the pitcher of hot water into the dressing room and poured its contents into the elegant porcelain basin. Next, she returned to the bedroom and asked, "Would you like me to help you get dressed, ma'am?"

"No, thank you," I said as politely as before.

After a few minutes the maid went away, and I waited for the room to warm up a little more before I got up.

My green merino wool morning dress was plain and serviceable and not nearly as appropriate to the elegance of my surroundings as last night's blue gown, but it was the best I owned and would have to suffice.

I washed my face in the basin of hot water, then sat before the elegant little dressing table to comb my hair. A little piece was sticking up at my crown where I had slept on it last night, and I dipped my comb in water and damped it down.

My stomach was in a knot, so I breathed deeply and slowly, trying to make myself relax. I shut my eyes.

Please, Dear God, please, I prayed. *Don't let there be anything in George's will about Nicky's parentage.*

I opened my eyes, put down the comb, stood up, and smoothed the skirt of my dress with slightly trembling hands. Then I straightened my spine and my shoulders and went down the stairs to the family dining room to a breakfast that I knew I would not eat.

I saw immediately that the earl was not present; Lady Regina and Lord Devane were the only people in the dining room when I went in. She gave me a friendly smile and said, "My brother and Mr. Melville are out somewhere on the estate, Mrs. Saunders, and Harriet and her father are breakfasting in her dressing room. The food is set out on the sideboard. Please, help yourself to whatever you would like."

My first thought was that I had been right about Savile being accustomed to having meat with his breakfast. The sideboard was laden with food; bacon and kidneys and even pork chops were set out along with cooked eggs and a great variety of breads and muffins. I took a muffin and went to sit next to Lady Regina. The footman who had been standing by the sideboard came to fill my cup with coffee.

"Surely that is not enough food, Mrs. Saunders!" Lady Regina exclaimed when she saw my plate.

"I am not very hungry," I said. "This will be perfectly sufficient, I assure you."

I took a bite of muffin and drank some coffee.

Lady Regina and Lord Devane were staring at me in a way that I thought was extremely rude. I put down my coffee cup and said evenly, "Is something wrong? Do I have a spot on my face?"

Lady Regina laughed gaily. "Of course not, Mrs. Saunders."

"The fact is, we are dying of curiosity about you, ma'am," Lord Devane admitted with a charming smile. "Savile has told us nothing, you see — just that you figure in George's will and must be present to hear it read."

"I too am curious about what can be in the will, my lord," I said quietly.

They exchanged looks, clearly frustrated by their inability to pry any information out of me.

I sipped my coffee and took another small bite of muffin.

"Harriet ain't happy about your being here," Devane said, testing to see what my response would be to that.

She was going to be even less happy after the will was read, I thought.

I nodded.

Their frustrated looks deepened.

I have to admit that I might have enjoyed mystifying them had I not been so sick with worry about what would happen in a few hours' time.

Lady Regina and Lord Devane were too well bred to pursue a subject that was clearly distasteful to me, so we fell back upon that most useful of English topics: the weather.

When I had finished eating, Lady Regina offered to show me the family portraits in the Long Gallery and I accepted her invitation with relief. I would have welcomed anything that would keep my mind from dwelling upon the reading of George's will.

The Long Gallery was the room just to the south of the family dining room. It was well named, I thought, as I contemplated the three large Persian rugs placed one after the other on the polished parquet floor. The high arched ceiling was painted in richly colored murals. Portraits painted in oil and framed in ornate gilt marched up and down both sides of the lovely, delicate, chestnut-brown–paneled walls.

"You see before you the history of the Melville family, their friends and their relations," Lady Regina said, with a lavish gesture toward the walls. "I will give you the abridged tour since I am sure you don't want to remain incarcerated in this room for another week."

I laughed. "The abridged tour will be quite adequate."

"We will begin, then, with the third baron, who built this castle," Lady Regina said, leading me to the first picture on the left wall. "He was called Raoul, of course. The first son is always called Raoul. It is a tribute to our ancestor, the Raoul de Melville who came over with the Conqueror."

I made a noise to indicate that I was impressed.

"He probably wasn't anything more than an impoverished mercenary," Lady Regina said candidly. "He made rather a good thing out of his trip to England, though."

The most fascinating thing I found about our trip around the gallery was not the family history that Lady Regina rattled off so glibly, but the strong likeness that prevailed among the faces of most of the previous earls and that of the present one.

I commented upon this when we reached the portrait of Raoul the Eighth.

"The Melvilles have always bred true," Lady Regina announced with undisguised pride, just as if she were talking of horses.

I stared at the face of Raoul the Eighth, who was standing before what was clearly the chimneypiece in the Great Hall here at Savile. The defined, dark gold eyebrows were exactly the same as the present Raoul's, as were the elegant cheekbones and the long, almost sensual mouth. But Raoul the Eighth's eyes were brown, like Lady Regina's. I didn't see a pair of eyes the color of the present earl's until we stopped before the portrait of an extremely lovely woman.

"My mother," said Lady Regina with a mixture of affection and pride.

One couldn't tell what color hair the woman in the portrait had, as it was powdered in the style of the last century, but her eyes were amber-gold.

"She is very beautiful," I said sincerely.

"And this is my father," Lady Regina was saying, but my eyes had fastened themselves on the portrait of another lovely young woman. I walked over and stood before it. This woman was dark haired and green eyed, with a long, elegant neck and a slim, extraordinarily graceful body.

Lady Regina saw me looking. "That is Georgiana," Lady Regina said, "my brother's wife."

I looked at that quintessentially exquisite

143

aristocrat and remembered how she had died.

"Savile told me she died in childbirth," I said softly. "How very tragic it must have been for him."

"It was, of course," Lady Regina replied. "She was only twenty, and then, he lost the baby, too. He was devastated."

I could understand. I knew what it was like to lose a spouse. But, unlike Savile, I had my boy.

Georgiana Melville looked down upon us with her cool green eyes.

"Poor girl," I said, and meant it.

Mr. Middleman, George's solicitor, arrived in time for luncheon, which was a very subdued affair. Afterward, Savile invited us all into the library, a tremendously high-ceilinged room, with a gallery running around the top of it and the bottom walls filled with chestnut wood bookcases. I recognized the portrait over the fireplace as that of the Raoul who had built the house during the reign of King James.

Chairs had been set in a semicircle around a great library desk. The earl seated me at the end of the semicircle and then sat beside me, placing himself in such a way that his big body shielded me from the view of most of the others in the room.

Mr. Middleman was a small, rotund man with a face one wouldn't remember ten minutes after one had met him. He had the room's undivided attention, however, as he put on his spectacles and unrolled the official-looking document that was George's will.

The small amount of luncheon I had eaten was lying like lead in my stomach and I hoped I would not disgrace myself by being sick.

The opening words of the will were ordinary enough. In the usual way, George assured us that he was of sound mind and that the dispositions he was about to make were done of his own free will.

George's chief possession, of course, had been Devane Hall, but since Devane Hall was entailed, it was not within George's power to dispose of it. The entail meant that it must go to George's nearest male relative, and since George and Harriet had no son, that person was his cousin Roger Melville.

This information was briefly stated in the will, and then George bequeathed a sum of his personal money to Roger in order to help him "pay off whatever debts he may have incurred so that he may begin his tenure as Lord Devane with a free mind."

"Decent of him," the new Lord Devane said.

"You can be sure that that was Middleman's idea," Savile murmured in my ear.

Next came a series of small bequests to old servants.

Then Mr. Middleman glanced at me, and I knew my time had come. I think I might have stopped breathing. All motion stopped among the spectators and the room grew intensely quiet. The little solicitor deliberately pushed his spectacles higher on his nose, then began to read slowly and clearly: " 'To Nicholas Saunders, son of Abigail and Thomas Saunders, I bequeath the sum of twenty thousand pounds, to be administered for said Nicholas until he reaches his majority by my executor, Raoul Melville, Earl of Savile.' "

A roar erupted from the throat of Albert Cole.

Harriet screamed.

My first thought was: *"Son of Abigail and Thomas Saunders." Thank God!*

"I won't stand for it! Do you hear me, Savile?" Mr. Cole roared. "That's *my* money and I won't have it given away to any of Devane's by-blows!"

"I can assure you that I have no trouble hearing you, my dear Cole," Savile returned acidly. "In fact, you are in danger of permanently damaging my eardrums. Do please moderate your voice."

My second thought was: *Twenty thousand pounds!*

"I won't see a penny of my money given to that witch's bastard!" Harriet screamed.

"Twenty thousand pounds is a huge amount of money to give away from the estate," Lord Devane said. "Is it within George's gift, Mr. Middleman?"

"Yes it is, my lord," the solicitor returned bluntly. "It is not money from the estate at all. It came from the money settled upon his lordship by Mr. Cole at the time of his marriage to her ladyship."

Albert Cole had evidently paid highly to get a baron for his daughter.

"And that's why it ain't going to his bastard!" Mr. Cole boomed.

Mr. Middleman said sharply, "Lord Devane has made no claim of parentage to this boy, Mr. Cole. In fact, he goes out of his way to name him as the son of Mr. and Mrs. Saunders."

"You can't bamboozle me!" Mr. Cole shouted. His face had become alarmingly red. "There's only one reason Devane is giving money to this brat and that's because it's *his* brat!"

"Papa is right!" Harriet screeched.

I looked at the scene before me with comfortable detachment. Both of the Coles had open mouths and puce faces. Lady Regina looked bemused and was speaking to Lord Devane, who was scowling. I glanced up at the earl's face and my eyes widened.

He was angry.

"That is quite enough."

His voice sliced through the room like a sword, creating instant quiet.

He stood up.

"Mrs. Saunders is a guest in my home and I will not have her slandered."

There was something in his voice that sent a shiver down my spine. I wasn't surprised when the Coles shut their mouths.

The earl turned to look at the lawyer, who was standing behind the desk. "If I understand you correctly, Middleman, the money that my cousin has bequeathed to Nicholas Saunders was his by law to leave as he chose."

"That is correct, my lord," the little solicitor replied.

The earl turned next to regard Albert Cole. "That money was legally settled upon my cousin at the time of his marriage to your daughter, sir. It is not your money. It has not been your money since the marriage settlements were signed."

Albert Cole twitched.

"I do not ever wish to hear you refer to Nicholas Saunders as a bastard again. Do I make myself clear?"

Albert Cole stared back at Savile. It was perfectly clear to me that he wanted to argue with the earl but was afraid. I didn't know how Savile was doing it; no one thought that he would physically harm Mr. Cole. Nevertheless, there was no doubt that Albert Cole was thoroughly intimidated.

"Yes, my lord," he mumbled grudgingly.

Since the situation had suddenly become so dramatic, I decided that now was a good time to make my own announcement.

"There is no need for anyone to fret about Lord Devane's twenty thousand pounds," I said. "I am not going to accept it."

"What!" said Lady Regina. "Are you mad, Mrs. Saunders?"

Probably, I thought glumly.

"Why on earth would you do such a thing?" Lord Devane said in amazement, peering around Savile to get a look at me.

The earl sighed and sat down.

"She's only saying that," Harriet announced. "No one would refuse twenty thousand pounds."

Albert Cole glared at me suspiciously but,

still intimidated by Savile, didn't say anything.

"I have no idea why Lord Devane should make such a provision for my son," I said firmly. "I am going to refuse it because it leads other people to make incorrect assumptions."

Here Lady Regina's brown gaze fell away from my face. Obviously it was not only the Coles who had been making those assumptions.

"I am perfectly able to take care of my own son," I finished grandly. "I refuse to accept Lord Devane's legacy."

Stunned silence descended upon the room.

It was Savile who finally broke it. "If I understand the terms of the will correctly, Middleman," he said mildly, "the legacy was not left to Mrs. Saunders."

"You are indeed correct, my lord. The legacy was specifically left to Mr. *Nicholas* Saunders."

I stared at the lawyer suspiciously. "Are you saying that I cannot refuse it?"

"That is precisely what we are saying," Savile replied.

I turned my head to glare at him. "But I don't want it!"

He bent his head a little and said in a soft

voice, for my ears only, "It will provide for Nicky's schooling, Gail."

I was so furious that I didn't even notice that "Gail."

"*I* am saving money for Nicky's schooling. I do not want to touch a penny of that money, Savile."

"If the woman don't want the money, then don't give it to her," boomed Mr. Cole.

Now that Savile's attention was on me, he had recovered his courage.

Everyone ignored him.

"You have no choice, Mrs. Saunders," the little lawyer explained to me with commendable patience. "The money is not intended for you but for your son. You do not have the right to refuse it."

"Very well. I'll take it and then I'll give it away," I said recklessly.

Mr. Cole groaned loudly.

Harriet shrieked.

Lord Devane said with amusement, "This place is fast becoming like a circus."

Mr. Middleman said, "The money is not yours to administer, Mrs. Saunders. Until Nicholas reaches the age of twenty-one, that responsibility has been given to the Earl of Savile."

I sat in silence as the rest of George's will

was read. It didn't take very long. The bulk of his personal fortune, about thirty thousand pounds, was left to Harriet and their daughters, Maria, Frances, and Jane.

When Mr. Middleman had finished, I rose, intending to retreat upstairs to my room so that I could think. Savile put a hand under my elbow, however, and said quietly, "Come along to my office, Gail. I want to talk to you."

This time I did notice the "Gail."

We walked through the Long Gallery, the family dining room, the formal dining room, the drawing room, the music room, the Great Hall, and the withdrawing room, until finally we were in the room that the earl called his office. It was far less grand than the other rooms I had thus far seen, and I had the distinct impression that this was a place where work was indeed done. The big, old oak desk was covered with papers, all neatly arranged in piles, and several ledger books reposed on what looked like an old refectory table set against a simply paneled wall.

A green velvet sofa was placed at right angles to the fireplace, and the earl guided me to sit upon it. He sat next to me.

I stared at my hands, which were clasped tensely in my lap. "I don't want that money, Savile," I said.

"Is the good opinion of other people more important to you than this chance to secure your son's future?" he said.

My head snapped up. "Do you really think I care what other people might think of me?" I said bitterly, staring defiantly into his eyes. "Think for a moment, Savile. Can you tell me how I am to explain to Nicky that a man who is a perfect stranger has left him such a huge sum of money? He might not question it now; he's only eight. But as he grows older he will question it, and I don't want that to happen."

The golden eyes looked gravely back into mine.

"Yes," he said after a minute. "I see what you mean."

Hope flickered in my heart. "Then you will allow me to refuse the inheritance?"

His eyes narrowed slightly. Suddenly, all my senses were acutely conscious of him, sitting at a respectable distance from me on the sofa, but still much too close.

He said, "What if I find a way to give the money to Nicky without him ever knowing that it came from George?"

But I would know it came from George, I thought.

"No," I said in a hard voice. "I don't want it."

He leaned toward me, compelling me with the extraordinary power of his physical nearness. "Let it go, Gail," he said softly. "Whatever wrong George may have done to you, let it go. Take the money for Nicky."

I shook my head. "You don't know," I said. "You don't understand."

"You won't be punishing George by refusing to take his money," Savile said reasonably. "You will be punishing Nicky."

I jumped to my feet and backed away from him until I fetched up against the desk on the opposite side of the fire from the sofa.

"I will never forgive that man," I said. "Never! And I will not take a penny of his money."

Slowly Savile rose to his feet. He did not move away from the sofa, however, and when he spoke his voice sounded oddly flat. "You look like a piece of delicate porcelain, but you're as adamant as rock, aren't you?"

I met his eyes challengingly. "No, I'm not delicate, my lord. I can't afford to be delicate. I've learned to survive on my own, and I am going to continue to do just that. I have no need for George's blood money; I can provide for my son myself."

"Blood money?" he said.

I could feel my nostrils quiver with tension. I had said too much already. I shook my head, turned my shoulder to him, and did not answer.

The silence between us lasted for what seemed a very long time. Then he said, "Very well. If at any time you change your mind about this, let me know. Otherwise I will hold the money in trust for Nicky until he is twenty-one."

I started to protest, then closed my lips. It would be many more years until Nicky turned twenty-one, I thought. I would deal with the problem of George's legacy then.

CHAPTER 9

The remainder of my stay at Savile Castle passed in an uneventful and civilized manner. The Coles, apparently still swayed by fear of Savile, were subdued at dinner, and once more I retired to my room early, although with a much easier mind than I'd had the night before.

The worst had not happened. George had confirmed Tommy and me as Nicky's parents, and I was free to go home to my son and pretend that I had simply been looking at a stallion.

Life would go on as usual.

And so it did.

February passed, then March and part of April. I was beginning to think that Savile had forgotten his promise to let me breed Maria to one of his stallions when I received a communication from him that he would be arriving at Deepcote in two days' time to help me take Maria to his stud near Epsom.

I had never expected to see Savile himself. If he had remembered his promise at all, I had fully expected him to send a groom.

I did not at all like the excitement that jolted through me at the thought of meeting him again.

Don't be a fool, Gail, I told myself firmly. *Savile is probably coming because he wants to keep an eye on Nicky. He is just the sort of man who will feel obligated by that absurd will of George's. He most certainly is not coming to see you.*

I did my best to put all thoughts of Savile from my mind, but this proved rather difficult, as Nicky talked about nothing else until the afternoon when the earl arrived at Deepcote.

I was working with a client in the paddock behind the stable when I heard Nicky shouting, "Mama, Mama! His lordship is here!"

The man I was longeing on Sampson turned and gave me a startled look. "Pay no attention to Nicky, Mr. Watson," I commanded. "Concentrate on what you are doing."

Samuel Watson took a deep breath and nodded.

Sampson's trot had begun to lag a little and I clicked to encourage him to step forward.

"Up — down — up — down — up — down," I counted. "That's the way, Mr. Watson," I approved as my student rose and

157

fell to the rhythm of Sampson's trot. "Try to keep your legs under you. That's very good."

I had found that teaching new riders to post to the trot on the longe line was the best way to help them find their balance and feel the motion of the horse. Consequently I was standing in the middle of the paddock, with the longe line in one hand and a long whip in the other, while Sampson went around me in a big circle. As I turned with Sampson and Sam Watson, I saw Savile come around the corner of the stable and approach the paddock.

I rotated away from him.

"Look down, Mr. Watson," I said. "Can you see your toes?"

"Yes," came the breathless reply.

"Then your legs are too far forward. Move them back."

Mr. Watson moved his legs back.

"Straighten your shoulders. Try not to hunch forward."

Mr. Watson's shoulders came back. He sat up straighter. He continued to post to the motion of Sampson's trot.

"Excellent!" I said with sincerity. "You are one of my best students, Mr. Watson."

The tense, concentrated face of my client broke into a quick smile.

The lesson was finished fifteen minutes later, and I held Sampson while Mr. Watson dismounted the way I had taught him, then the two of us walked toward the stable and the Earl of Savile, who was standing outside the paddock fence, watching us.

He was hatless, his dark gold hair bared to the spring sun. I had forgotten how tall he was.

"I am very glad to see you, my lord," I said with a smile I tried to make merely pleasant. "May I introduce Mr. Samuel Watson to you?" I looked at Mr. Watson. "Mr. Watson, this is the Earl of Savile."

I saw Sam Watson's blue-gray eyes flicker with surprise. He had not made a fortune in the city, however, by giving away his feelings. "A pleasure to meet you, m'lord," he said with dignity.

Savile let a small silence fall as he looked down at my client from the other side of the fence. Then, "Mr. Watson," he replied in a voice that was definitely frosty.

I was surprised. I had never thought that Savile would be too high in the instep to be on pleasant terms with a Cit.

I said, "Mr. Watson has taken the Edgerton estate on the other side of Highgate, and I have just begun to give him lessons. I think he is going to be one of my best students."

Mr. Watson gave me an engaging grin. "You've a kind heart, Mrs. Saunders. I appreciate it."

"I take it that Mr. Watson is not staying in the house then?" Savile said in a voice that was only marginally less frosty than before.

I looked at him thoughtfully. "No," I replied. "He drives over each afternoon for his lesson."

Nicky said, "Edgerton is a bang-up place, my lord. It even has a maze! Mama got lost in it and Mr. Watson had to find her."

"Indeed," Savile said.

I hesitated, wondering what to say next. In the last few days, after his lesson Sam had come into the house for some refreshment before driving home, but Savile sounded so forbidding that it didn't seem a good idea to try to throw the two together.

Sam saved me. "I had better be going, Mrs. Saunders," he said. "The same time tomorrow?"

Sampson pulled at the rein I was holding, as if to remind me of his presence. Absently I reached up to rub his forehead.

"I think we will have to take a few days off, Mr. Watson," I said apologetically. "I hope you don't mind."

He smiled easily. "I shall miss coming, but of course you must see to your own affairs,

Mrs. Saunders. Just send me word when you are ready to begin again."

I smiled back at him. I liked Sam Watson. Like Albert Cole, he was a self-made man, but unlike Albert, Sam had imagination. He understood that there was more to life than making money — something that I thought was probably very rare in a man who had literally worked his way out of the sewers of London.

Sam was in the process of remaking himself. He had learned to speak without his original, disfiguring accent; he had learned to drive and to dance; he had acquired a country house; now he was learning to ride.

There was a sense of adventure about him that reminded me very much of Tommy.

Now he quite calmly ducked through the paddock fence and straightened up so that he was standing next to Savile. Sam was not a tall man and he had to look quite far up to meet the earl's eyes. "Good day, my lord," he said calmly. "It was nice to meet you."

Humor softened Savile's mouth. "I am delighted to have met you also, Mr. Watson," he said, with much more courtesy than he had shown thus far.

Sam walked off toward the carriage house, where his phaeton and groom awaited him.

As soon as he was out of earshot, I turned

to Savile and said hotly, "I'll have you know that Mr. Watson is one of my best clients. He is paying me a small fortune to teach him to ride. I'm not asking you to socialize with the man, but you could at least be polite!"

"I was polite," Savile replied calmly.

I snorted.

Over the earl's shoulder I saw John Grove approaching. "We've got the curricle and two horses, plus another horse to use to pony your mare to Epsom, Mrs. Saunders. Is there room for the three of them in your stable?"

"Yes," I said. "I have an empty stall, and my ponies can spend the night in the paddock. You may put your horses in their stalls, Grove."

As we walked around the corner of the stable, a fashionable phaeton came from the direction of the carriage house and headed toward the open gates. It was pulled by a neat pair of grays and was driven with smooth competence by Sam Watson.

"He drives very well," the earl said dispassionately.

"He's a remarkable man," I said. "I was not flattering him when I said that he is an excellent student."

"You know him socially as well?"

"Yes," I said, and rubbed Sampson's forehead again. "He has been a welcome addition to our small neighborhood."

A small frown drew Savile's dark gold eyebrows together in a look I took to be one of disapproval. I said haughtily, "*You* may be too exalted in rank to inhabit the same room as a Cit, my lord, but I can assure you that I am not."

His mouth set in a grim-looking line. "I did not say that."

"Well, that is how you looked."

"What is a Cit, Mama?" Nicky asked.

"A Cit is someone who has made money in investment or banking in the City of London," I answered promptly. "Some people look down on Cits because their parents were poor and landless and because their taste is usually uneducated. A situation which is *not* their fault."

"Oh," Nicky said doubtfully, not quite certain what I meant. He looked at the earl. "Mr. Watson is a good'un, really he is, my lord. He's paying Mama a lot of money to teach him to ride. And he can hit a ball farther than anyone I've ever seen." Nicky turned back to me. "Can't he, Mama?"

"He certainly can, sweetheart," I replied.

"He sounds like a perfect paragon," the earl said smoothly.

I didn't reply to that provocative remark and instead led the way into the house.

* * *

Mrs. MacIntosh was thrilled to see Savile again and Mr. MacIntosh outdid himself with dinner. We started with a light vegetable soup, then progressed to wild ducks served with a shallot sauce. For dessert there was a trifle.

It was a very simple meal compared with the dinners served at Savile Castle, but for us it was lavish. Nicky's eyes were enormous as he regarded the three different vegetables served with the ducks.

"Mr. MacIntosh has outdone himself for you, my lord," I said. There was no point in pretending otherwise; Savile had seen what our normal fare consisted of.

He put a morsel of duck in his mouth and closed his eyes. "Magnificent," he intoned.

Nicky giggled, and even I had to smile.

"Do you know how tempted I am to lure the MacIntoshes away from you?" Savile said. "It is only my sense of honor that keeps me from making them an offer."

"It isn't your honor at all," I retorted. "It's that you know they wouldn't go."

He turned to my son. "I think I have just been insulted, Nicky."

Nicky laughed. "Mama knows you were making a joke, sir." Then he added, with just the faintest undertone of worry in his voice,

"You wouldn't take the MacIntoshes away from us."

"You're right," Savile said, his face suddenly grave. "I wouldn't."

I changed the subject. "How are you planning to get us all to Epsom tomorrow? Did I hear Grove say something about ponying Maria?"

"Yes," Savile replied. "I thought I would take you and Nicky in the curricle with me, and let Grove ride Domino and lead Maria. Domino is a nice, steady old campaigner and will be a calming influence on her."

I said, "I think I had better ride Maria myself. One has much more control over her from the saddle than from the back of another horse."

He looked at me. He took a sip of wine, then carefully replaced his glass in exactly the same spot as it had been before he picked it up.

"Do you think Maria will be unsafe on the road?" he inquired softly.

I gave him one of my best smiles. "Only if she is handled by a stranger."

We continued to look at each other.

"She will be fine with me," I said seriously, answering the worry that I saw in his eyes. "I ride her on the road all the time around here."

"Country roads are not the same as a highway," he pointed out.

"You have never seen me in the saddle, have you, my lord?" I asked.

"I have not had that pleasure."

"If you had, you wouldn't worry," I returned.

A smile glimmered in his eyes. "Such modesty," he said.

"Modesty has its place," I agreed, "but sometimes truth is more useful."

At that he laughed.

"Mama is a wonderful rider," Nicky assured the earl.

"Very well then. It looks as if it will be just you and me in the curricle, Nicky."

Nicky's face glowed. "How long will the ride be, my lord?"

"About four hours, I should think — my stud is about twenty-five miles from Deepcote. If we leave in the morning we can be there well in time for me to show you around the farm. You can meet the gentleman who is to be the father of Maria's baby" — Nicky laughed merrily at this sally — "and your mother can assure herself that Maria is going to be well cared for and happy."

Maria would have to remain at Savile's stud until she came into season so she could be bred to his stallion. I would go home without her the following day.

Nicky helped Mrs. MacIntosh clear the dishes from the main course and then the trifle was brought out and set before me. After we had finished the dessert, I sent Nicky up to his room and Savile and I moved to the drawing room. Mrs. MacIntosh had started a fire while we ate, but I was acutely conscious of how the room must look to a man who called Savile Castle home.

We took our places on either side of the fire and I picked up the poker to push an imaginary branch back into the grate. I said, without looking at him, "I am very grateful to you, my lord, for this chance to breed Maria."

I knew my voice sounded a little stiff. It was not that I wasn't grateful, it was just that it galled me that after I had made such a point of being able to support Nicky on my own, I was forced to accept Savile's generosity this way.

"There is no need to be grateful, Mrs. Saunders," he returned easily. "I know I will get my money from you in time."

His reply soothed my pride, and I felt some of the stiffness drain out of my body. I said a little too fiercely, "I will repay you the moment I sell Maria's foal."

He didn't answer, and when I looked at

him he was regarding me with a grave expression.

I said quickly, "It was very kind of you to come for us yourself, my lord. Nicky is thrilled to have a chance to ride behind your famous chestnuts."

He nodded and transferred his gaze to the fire.

A dreadful suspicion suddenly leaped into my mind. Would Savile take the opportunity of being alone with Nicky to inform him about the legacy?

I stared at the earl's clear-cut, classical profile and knew instantly that he would never resort to such underhanded tactics. I felt a stab of guilt for even thinking such a thing of him.

His gaze lifted from the fire and returned to me. He said, "I thought you told me that you taught children. This Watson fellow looks to be about my age. He most certainly is not a child."

I was so surprised by the change of subject that I just stared at him.

"Well?" he said a little irritably.

"The bulk of my clients are children, but I occasionally teach adults as well. In fact, Mr. Watson is the second gentleman student I have had this spring."

Savile gave me a look I couldn't quite read.

"And did this other 'gentleman' also drive over by day, or did he stay in the house here?"

I was beginning to see where he was going, and I felt myself beginning to get angry. "He was from London, so he stayed in the house."

"And how old was this 'gentleman'?"

"He was about my age," I said. "Not that this is any of your business."

"Perhaps not, but I think I know more of the world than you do, Gail, and I tell you now that you are asking for trouble if you continue to have strange men staying in your house."

I felt the blood rush into my cheeks. "These 'strange men' are here to learn how to ride a horse, my lord, not for any unsavory reason. I can assure you that nothing happens under this roof that is not entirely proper."

"I am quite certain that *your* intentions are entirely proper," he said grimly. "I am not quite so certain about the intentions of the men you might bring in."

I stared at him incredulously. "Are you implying that one of my clients might attack me, my lord?"

"It has been known to happen," he replied, "and you are virtually unprotected,

Gail. The MacIntoshes live downstairs, and Mr. MacIntosh is totally lame. Nicky is a child." He was looking more and more grim. "It is not a good idea to have strange men staying in this house with you," he repeated.

I hated to admit it, but he was beginning to frighten me. Since Tommy's death I had never had anyone but women and children to stay in the house.

"Nonsense," I said bravely. "Mr. Curtis was a perfect gentleman the whole time he was here."

This was true, but I remembered the way I had caught him looking at me sometimes, and I bit my lip.

"Isn't there an inn in town where your male clients could stay?" he asked.

I shook my head. "Nothing that would be suitable."

"Well, think about what I have said." He looked at me, his eyes very golden. "And consider any male over the age of seventeen dangerous."

I leaned back in my chair, crossed my arms, and regarded him speculatively. "I am just wondering if I ought to send *you* to sleep in the stable," I said.

He smiled, and I felt my breath begin to hurry in a way that was definitely frightening.

"Ah," he said. "Every rule has an exception, and I am yours."

But you are not mine, my lord, I thought. *And you never will be.*

Surely it could not be regret that I was feeling?

I stood up. "I will think about what you have said, Savile. In the meantime, I am going to make my usual evening check on the horses, and then I am going to bed."

He stood up. "I'll come to the stable with you."

"That is not necessary, my lord," I said. "I can assure you I shall be perfectly safe walking down to my stable. I do it every night."

"I could use the air," he said blandly.

Together we went to the front door, where I slipped an old hunting jacket of Tommy's over my short-sleeved dress and picked up a lantern. Outside, the April night was dark and still. I looked up at the brilliant star-filled sky and said softly, "I wonder where your brother-in-law's comet is."

"Oh, it cannot be seen in our own skies," Savile replied in a voice as quiet as mine had been. "It's somewhere way out in space. Gervase found it with a telescope."

Savile carried the lantern, and when the ponies in the paddock saw us coming they

171

nickered and came to the gate. We entered the stable and Savile hung the lantern on a hook on the wall so that we could see. Sampson and Noah were already lying down and the rest of the horses were drowsing and looked at us with heavy eyes.

All of the horses, mine as well as Savile's, were wearing rugs, and I decided that the night was warm enough to leave the windows open. Savile helped me to change the water buckets, substituting the full ones in front of the stalls for the half-full ones inside. Then he collected the lantern and we moved to the door of the stable.

We paused again as we came out into the night, standing close together under the great dome of starlit sky. I felt a shiver pass through me and a flame licked under my skin and part of me knew that I had to defend myself against this man and part of me didn't want to.

I drew in a long, unsteady breath. "We had better get back to the house," I said. "We want to make an early start in the morning."

"Yes," he said, and his voice sounded oddly faraway. He began to walk forward and I followed.

CHAPTER 10

Our trip to Savile's stud farm was accomplished fairly smoothly. Grove and I rode a little behind the earl's curricle, with Grove and his placid Domino acting as a barrier between my mare and the middle of the road. In general, Maria behaved very well. She shied once or twice at what she obviously thought was a horse-eating vehicle, but with the curricle in front of her and Domino beside her she managed to feel sufficiently protected from menace and soon quieted down.

It had rained lightly the night before, so the road was neither muddy nor dusty. The traffic was light, the April sky was brilliantly blue, and the sun was warm on my head and my back. I rode beside John Grove and watched the back of the earl's shapely golden head as he patiently answered what appeared to be an endless stream of questions from my ever-curious son.

At Epsom we turned off the highway and began to travel westward along a smaller country road. Epsom, the home of the Derby, is one of England's most famous racecourses, and race meetings were held there during both the spring and the fall. A number of stud farms were to be found within the vicinity of Epsom, as there were within the vicinity of any of England's larger courses. The closer a farm was to a course, the less distance an owner had to walk his horse to get there.

Unlike Newmarket, which was a preserve of the aristocracy, Epsom attracted racegoers of all classes. During an Epsom race meeting, thousands of spectators would flood the grounds, and dicing, gaming, wrestling, and boxing all vied with the horses for attention. I had never before been to a race meeting at Epsom, but Tommy had gone once with his father and had told me all about it.

The road we had turned onto was far prettier than the highway. I regarded with pleasure the brilliantly colored spring wildflowers that grew along its wide, grassy margins: blue speedwell, yellow cowslips, pale primroses, and in some places I even saw early marsh orchids. Birds sang loudly from the thickets and hedgerows, and fields of wheat stretched away on either side of the road, flowing over the gently rolling landscape.

"Rayleigh is only a few miles farther along this road, ma'am," Grove said. "Close enough to walk the horses to the racecourse the morning they are due to run." He grinned his gap-toothed grin at me. "We like to keep 'em safe at home for as long as we can. Less chance that way of 'em being nobbled."

As I knew that disabling the favorite was an all-too-common practice of English bookmakers, this information did not shock me.

The hedgerows and fields on our left soon gave way to a six-foot-high iron fence. I could not see what was behind the fence due to the tall elm trees that were planted all along its inside perimeter.

"This is it now," Grove said, waving his hand toward the fence. "Rayleigh."

We followed the fence for another mile before we reached a great iron gate. It swung open for the earl, and Grove and I followed the curricle as it moved slowly along a wide, gently descending graveled avenue that was lined and shaded with tall elms. Then the carriage in front of us drove out from under the trees into the full sunshine, and we followed.

My breath caught in my throat, the scene before me was so beautiful. On either side of the path, the thick, rich, shin-high grass waved gently in a sea of ripe spring green. Two pastures, so large that the wooden fences disappeared from view, enclosed small herds of mares and foals. The sun shone brightly on black, gray, bay, and chestnut coats. Some of the mares were folded up in the grass, in that amusing doglike way horses have, and one chestnut mare was actually stretched right out on her side, her legs stuck out in front of her, looking for all the world as if she were dead. Long-legged foals played baby games, romping and squealing and batting their tiny hooves at one another, while their mothers looked on with calm eyes, knowing that as soon as the first hunger pang struck, baby would be back.

The road went across a small stone bridge that forded a crystal-clear stream that ran through the pastures and afforded the horses their water.

I sighed.

Grove grunted, as if he perfectly understood my feelings.

Nicky turned around on the curricle seat and called to me, "His lordship says that the yearlings are in another pasture, Mama. And the stallions have their own paddocks all to themselves."

I nodded and waved to indicate that I had heard him.

The mares' pasture fences that fronted the road ended as the path began to rise, and once we reached the top of the small hill I saw the rest of the farm spread out before me. The stable buildings looked as if they were at least another mile away, and as we descended the hill a new fenced pasture appeared to the left of the road.

"This is where we keep the mares who haven't foaled yet," Grove informed me. I looked at the half dozen or so heavily pregnant mares standing together under a clump of trees, lazily switching their tails. The glossiness of their coats told me that they were groomed regularly.

"They look well cared for," I commented to Grove.

"And so they should be," the groom retorted. "The foals those mares are carrying are worth a small fortune each."

Maria, meanwhile, was becoming very excited by the sight, smell, and sound of all these strange horses. I had to keep patting her neck and talking to her, and if she hadn't been tired from her four-hour journey, she might have given me serious difficulties.

I was glad when we finally arrived at the stable yard and I could dismount.

"She did very well," the earl commented, as he lifted Nicky down from the curricle seat.

Maria snorted a few times and began to prance in place. Her nostrils flared as she sniffed the air.

A small, gray-haired man with amazingly bowed legs had come up to us. Savile said, "Mrs. Saunders, allow me to introduce my trainer, Fred Hall."

"How do you do," I said.

He nodded at me. "Fine-looking mare ye've got there, Mrs. Saunders. Nice deep chest. She looks as if she'd be a stayer."

"Thank you, Mr. Hall," I said.

"As you can see, Hall, she is somewhat excited," Savile said.

"Aye, my lord. She probably smells the stallions." He looked at me. "Their paddocks 're on t'other side of the stables, ma'am, and the breezes is coming our way."

Maria certainly smelled something, because she tried to rear. I gave a sharp tug to the rein I was holding and said, "No!"

"I'll put her out by herself, ma'am," Hall suggested. "That way she can buck and rear to her heart's content. When she gets tired she'll begin to eat grass and quiet down."

This seemed to me an excellent suggestion.

Once Maria was safely behind a paddock fence, with a groom to watch her to make sure she didn't do anything foolish, Savile lifted me up to the curricle seat along with Nicky and we drove toward the house.

It was as different from Savile's main residence as it could possibly have been. Instead of authentic medieval castle walls surrounding a Jacobean jewel, Rayleigh was a simple red brick gentleman's house of the sort that could be seen all over England. It was three stories high with wood trim and a central pediment, and the third story was lit by windows in the roof. The shrubbery that surrounded it was simple as well, in harmony with the rolling grasslands of the stud farm.

I guessed immediately that this was a very masculine house. Its situation on a stud farm and its proximity to the race track would lend themselves to gatherings of men. I imagined late nights of drinking and of reckless wagers being placed on horses. I pictured dark colors and comfortable leather chairs and pictures of horses and dogs all over the walls.

The servant who came to take the curricle from Savile was not wearing livery, and my suspicions about the more casual character of the house deepened.

Savile lifted me down from the high seat of the curricle, and the feel of his hands on my waist seemed to burn right through my riding jacket. I didn't look at him as I walked beside him and Nicky through the front door of Rayleigh House.

It was not at all what I had expected. We

walked through the ivory paneled hall and into a small parlor, where the walls were covered with faded pink damask, the furniture was covered with faded crimson silk, and family portraits adorned the walls. This room did not look dilapidated or decayed, however, as my rooms at Deepcote did. This room was muted and soothing and beautiful.

Even at his stud farm, the Earl of Savile lived in elegance.

He said, "I will have my housekeeper show you and Nicky to your rooms, where I am sure you would like to freshen up. Luncheon will be served in half an hour, and then, if you like, I will take you to see the stallions."

"That sounds very nice, my lord," I said.

Nicky's hand crept into mine.

Savile saw it and gave him a reassuring smile. "Don't worry, your room will be right next to your mother's, Nicky."

"It's a very big house, my lord," Nicky said in a small voice.

"Oh, it's not as big as it looks," Savile said carelessly. "You'll soon find your way around without any trouble at all."

If Nicky thought this house was big, I wondered what he would say if he ever saw Savile Castle.

At that moment a middle-aged woman with gray-blond hair pinned neatly into a bun came into the room.

"Ah," said Savile, "here is Mrs. Abbot now. Mrs. Abbot, I want you to take Mrs. Saunders and her son, Nicholas, to their rooms. And show them where the dining room is, will you, before you take them upstairs."

"Certainly, my lord," said Mrs. Abbot. "Will you follow me, ma'am?"

With Nicky's fingers still clinging to mine, we trailed out of the parlor after the housekeeper.

The dining room was paneled in late seventeenth-century wood, and several extremely large paintings of ships at sea looked down on the long, rectangular mahogany table at which we sat.

"In a house like this I would expect to see pictures of horses, not boats," I commented as I took my place next to Savile.

He grinned at me. "My grandmother had the ship paintings hung. She was brought up on the south coast and said that if she had to endure hours of talk about horses, she demanded to have something to look at that *she* loved."

I reminded myself never again to say anything that might cause him to smile at me.

Nicky said politely, "They are very nice

pictures, my lord."

We had a nice, civilized luncheon of soup and cold meat, then Savile took us to see his stallions. I had told Nicky upon my return from Savile Castle in the winter that I had had an opportunity to look at only one of Savile's stallions, and that he was going to let us take our choice from the three he owned.

The stallions were kept in three separate, strongly fenced paddocks, and I watched as the one nearest to us, a tall, red-gold chestnut with a white blaze on his face, trotted around the railings of a white-painted wooden fence, his mane and tail flying, the muscles under his gleaming coat moving visibly in the bright afternoon sun.

"He's magnificent," I said.

"That's Rajah," Savile said. "He's the youngest of the three and consequently the least proven as a stud. He had a splendid record on the racecourse, though — he won the Guineas at Newmarket two years ago."

"What is the Guineas, sir?" Nicky asked.

I saw a flicker of surprise cross the earl's face at Nicky's betrayal of ignorance on the subject of one of the most prestigious races in the country. As I listened to Savile explaining about the Guineas to my son, I reflected, not for the first time, on the fact that Tommy's death had hurt Nicky in more ways than one.

After watching Rajah for about ten minutes, we walked along the dirt path that led from one paddock to the next, Nicky between us. As we came up to the fence where a dark bay was contentedly eating grass, he raised his head to look at us and then came trotting slowly to the rails. He was as glossy and smooth as polished mahogany, the shape of his head was classic, and his long legs were unblemished. From the slightly stiff way he moved, however, I guessed that he was no longer young.

"Hello, boy," Savile said in a gentle voice. He held out his hand and the stallion took the sugar he was offered.

"This is Monarch," the earl told us. "He's eighteen years old, but I can assure you that he is still very interested in girls."

This provoked a giggle from Nicky.

"He looks wonderful," I said.

"He's a grand old fellow," Savile said affectionately, bestowing another piece of sugar upon the bay.

"Why didn't you give sugar to Rajah, sir?" Nicky asked.

"Stallions are tricky creatures, Nicky," Savile replied. "It is never a good idea to give food out of your hand to a stallion. One day

183

you may find yourself missing a few fingers."

Nicky looked horrified.

"His lordship does not mean that stallions are vicious, sweetheart," I said quickly. "It is just that they tend to be somewhat aggressive."

"Why?" asked my innocent son.

I gave Savile a look that was an unabashed cry for help.

He came to the rescue. "You see, in the wild, a stallion is the head of a herd," he explained to Nicky. "He has to be suspicious and aggressive if he is to protect his mares and their foals from danger. It is a trait that domesticated stallions have inherited from their wild ancestors, and it is especially strong in stallions that are standing at stud."

"But you gave sugar to Monarch," Nicky said.

"Not all stallions are the same, and Monarch has always been a very sweet-tempered horse."

Nicky looked thoughtful.

"Why don't we look at the stallion in the next paddock," I suggested brightly, and Savile gave me an amused look as he began to walk in the suggested direction.

The stallion in the last paddock was also a bay and one of the most enormous horses I had ever seen. He snorted when he saw us

184

and then ostentatiously turned his back and looked off into the distance, his head held imperiously high, his neck an arch of arrogance, the whole of his strongly muscled body exuding insolent disdain.

"Centurion is not famous for his friendly disposition," Savile said. "He is, however, a Derby and a Gold Cup winner and he is much sought after as a sire."

"Why is he so unfriendly, sir?" Nicky asked.

Savile replied thoughtfully, "It often happens that the most competitive horses, the ones with the real fire, the real drive to win, are the ones who remain essentially untamed. It's an important part of their nature, and if a man tries to squelch it he either drives the horse into absolute rebellion or he kills all the fire that makes the animal what he is."

It both surprised and moved me that an aristocrat such as Savile should evince so deep an understanding of the nature of an animal such as this one.

The three of us leaned on the fence, and this time Nicky failed to get between us. In fact, he was on the other side of the earl and evidently perfectly content to remain there.

Savile's arm brushed against mine.

My heartbeat accelerated.

He didn't move and I didn't either, afraid to seem as if I were making too much of what was essentially an extremely casual contact.

The three of us stood there for five minutes watching the supremely beautiful and arrogant Thoroughbred totally ignore us, while I tried to get control of my breathing.

"I like him," Nicky said at last, and it was as if the sound of his voice broke a spell that was holding me captive. I reached up, ostensibly to brush an insect away from my cheek, and then I stepped away from the earl.

"Do you?" Savile said to Nicky. "Why?"

"He's like a prince," Nicky said.

"And he knows it," I added dryly.

"Take a Centurion colt to market and you will realize a very considerable sum of money, Mrs. Saunders," Savile said. "Neither Rajah nor Monarch will command as much."

At that point Nicky finally decided to insert himself between us. "Are you going to choose him to be the father of Maria's baby, Mama?"

I frowned. "I never thought of trying to sell a foal of Maria's to a racehorse owner, Savile. After all, she herself has never raced. She has no record."

He shrugged. "To be honest with you, I

186

don't think that will matter a great deal. It's true that you will not get as much as you would if you had a mare with a winning record, but Centurion foals are in very high demand. There are not that many of them, you see. I am very particular about the mares I allow to be bred to him."

I lifted my eyes to him in surprise.

"And you would accept Maria?"

"Maria is one of the loveliest mares I have ever seen." The eyes holding mine were very golden. Savile's voice had dropped suddenly, become soft, almost caressing. I felt a throb deep within my body. For some reason, Tommy's words came rushing to my mind: *"She reminds me of you, Gail."*

I must be insane, I thought in agitation. Did I really think the earl was trying to make love to me? In broad daylight? In front of my son?

I went back to looking at the stallion. "And what is Centurion's stud fee, my lord?"

"Two hundred fifty pounds."

"Two hundred fifty pounds!" My eyes swung back to him, this time in shock. "Have you taken leave of your senses, my lord? I cannot afford to pay two hundred fifty pounds for a stud fee."

"Ah, but you are not to pay me until you have sold the foal," he reminded me. "The Duke of Harwich bought the last Centurion foal for over a thousand pounds."

By now I was beyond shock. "Dear God," was all I could say.

Nicky grabbed my hand and began to pump it excitedly. "That's a lot of money, Mama!"

"It surely is, sweetheart."

"If your goal is to make money, then I recommend that you choose Centurion," Savile said.

I was trying to think. "What if there is something wrong with the foal? What if I can't sell it?"

"Then there would be no charge. I guarantee healthy foals," Savile said blandly.

I looked once more at the splendid, untamed prince standing so arrogantly in his paddock.

"He wouldn't hurt Maria?" Nicky asked doubtfully.

"Centurion likes mares much more than he likes people," Savile assured him. "He will take very good care of her."

"You'll have to pull her shoes, though, or she might take good care of him!" I shot back.

"Don't worry, we know how to deal with prickly ladies around here, Mrs. Saunders," Savile said gravely, and once more I had the uneasy feeling that he was not talking about my mare.

Then he smiled down at Nicky. "Do you want to see the yearlings?"

"Yes, sir!"

We set off in another direction, and Nicky skipped along beside the earl, talking and asking more questions.

I had never before realized how much he would enjoy being around a man who was the right age to be his father.

Nicky was obviously sleepy at dinner, so I left Savile at the dining-room table with his bottle of port and took my son upstairs to put him to bed.

Nicky fell asleep almost immediately, but I waited in my room for another hour, afraid to go back downstairs.

By now there was no longer any point in trying to conceal from myself that I was strongly attracted to the Earl of Savile. The merest brush of the man's arm against mine did more to my nerves than had any of the romantic tactics that other men had tried during the six years since Tommy's death.

The plain truth was that I did not want to be alone with him. I did not trust myself.

At last I decided that it was late enough for me to seek him out and decently make my excuses about needing to go to sleep. I smoothed down my rose-colored afternoon frock — Savile had thoughtfully told me not to worry about bringing an evening dress — and marched down the stairs to the library, where the butler had told me his lordship could be found.

✓ He was sprawled in a comfortable-looking armchair in front of the wood fire when I came in the door. The bottle of port next to him looked as if it had had some serious inroads made upon it. A huge portrait of a male Melville in tights and Elizabethan ruff gazed arrogantly out at the room from over the fireplace.

I said, "Nicky is asleep, my lord, and I believe I am going to follow him. It has been a long and tiring day."

He turned to look at me and then slowly got to his feet. He ran his fingers through his hair, dislodging a few strands so that they fell across his forehead. He leaned his hands on his desk as if for balance, looked at me somberly, and said, "You should send that boy away to school, Gail. He is being smothered alive at home."

All my thoughts of sexual attraction disappeared as if by magic.

"You know nothing of the matter!" I said furiously. "In fact, you scarcely know Nicky at all. I can assure you that he is perfectly happy at home with me at Deepcote and doing his lessons with Mr. Ludgate."

He leaned farther forward on his hands, his eyes commanding mine. "Mr. Ludgate is an old man, and so is Mr. MacIntosh. The boy is obviously starved for the company of someone whose range of interest is wider than cooking and books."

The red that had been hovering before my eyes since he'd first brought up the subject of Nicky leaving home now deepened to a bright crimson. The fact that I was secretly afraid that he might be right only made me angrier.

"When I want your opinion you can be sure I will ask for it," I snapped. "In the meantime, Nicky is my son and I know what is best for him."

"You're asking him for the kind of companionship you ought to be getting from a husband," Savile said bluntly. "And that isn't doing Nicky any good at all."

At those words, something in me snapped.

"How dare you!" I snarled, and, striding swiftly across the room, I stopped at the desk and raised my hand to strike him.

He caught my wrist in midair. "Oh no you don't," he said softly. Then, still holding my arm, he came around the desk until he was standing beside me. Before I realized what he was going to do, he had pinned my arm to my side and his lips were coming down on mine.

Fire leaped through my veins at the touch of his mouth. I knew I should push him away. I even raised my free hand to his shoulder to do it, but my fingers stilled against the blue wool of his coat and did nothing. A moment later my arm slid around his neck, opening my body so that it pressed full-length against his.

It was not a chaste kiss. My mouth was open, our tongues probed each other, and I tasted the heady sweetness of port on his breath. I was standing on my toes, and when he let go of my captured wrist I slid that arm around his neck as well.

I felt his hands circle my waist. Then one of them came up to cup the back of my head and the other covered my breast. The intense thrill of pleasure that went through me at that caress frightened me back to my senses.

I put both my hands on his shoulders and pushed hard. It took a moment for him to realize what I was doing, but then he let me go.

I jumped back from him as if I had been released from a slingshot.

"Oh God," I said. "Oh God!"

I stared at him in utter terror.

"Gail," he said. He was noticeably out of breath. "Don't look that way, sweetheart. Please don't look that way."

"What way?" I managed to croak.

"Frightened. Believe me, I am not trying to extort payment from you for taking your mare. I never meant this to happen. I just lost control. . . ."

I had never suspected him of such a thing. Such low tactics were beneath him; I knew that. It wasn't Savile I was frightened of; it was myself.

I was scared to death by how much I wanted him.

This had never happened to me before. Making love with Tommy had been sweet, but I had always been content to let him be the one to initiate it.

Much as I had loved Tommy, I had never burned for him the way I burned now for the Earl of Savile.

I said hurriedly, "I think I had better go upstairs, my lord. Right now."

The fire behind him lit his hair to a brighter gold. The eyes that were watching my mouth had an unmistakably hungry look to them.

"Yes," he said. "I think you had better."

"Good night," I said, and rushed out of the room.

193

★ ★ ★

The elegantly hung four-poster was extremely comfortable, but I did not get much sleep that night. Both my body and my mind were aroused, the one aching for something it could not have and the other worrying about what Savile had said about Nicky.

Nicky was perfectly fine at home, I told myself with defiant determination. Savile knew nothing about the matter. My boy was happy and healthy, both in mind and body.

The more I thought about the earl's words, the more my indignation swelled. Easy for Savile to tell me to send Nicky away to school! Would he also care to tell me how I might pay public-school tuition?

Of course, if I could sell Maria's foal for anything near the sum that Savile had quoted to me, I might manage it, I thought.

Then the image of the earl's face as it had appeared as he looked at me right before I left the room flashed before my eyes.

"I just lost control," he had said.

I did not think he was a man who lost control very often.

Of course, I had lost control too.

It doesn't matter, I told myself. *I have nothing to worry about. Tomorrow Nicky and I will go home and I will probably never see him again.*

It was disconcerting, how unutterably depressing I found that thought to be.

I turned on my other side and went back to worrying about Nicky.

So passed the night.

At about five in the morning it started to rain. I heard the drops tapping steadily against my windowpanes, and when the chambermaid came into my room at eight she raised the blinds on a bleak, gray day. Nicky and I went down to breakfast together, and Savile was already there, drinking coffee and reading the *Morning Post*.

He looked up and smiled courteously when we came in. My face in the mirror that morning had borne the unmistakable shadows of sleeplessness, but his looked perfectly normal.

For some reason, I found that I resented that.

"What a vile day," I said as I put a boiled egg and a muffin on my plate and came to sit at the table, making sure to keep a place between us.

"I know," Savile replied. "I am sending you and Nicky home in the chaise. This is not weather for an open carriage."

Nicky carried his own extremely full plate to the table and took the place directly to the earl's left. "Are you coming with us, sir?" he asked, hope shining naked in his crystal-blue eyes.

Savile folded his newspaper and put it aside. "I am afraid not, Nicky," he answered gently. "I have an engagement in London later today."

Nicky made no attempt to hide his disappointment.

"Perhaps you can come to visit when you bring Maria back to us," he suggested.

"Perhaps," Savile said in the same gentle voice, and I knew that he would not come.

He turned to look at me, and when he spoke his voice was all business. "Hall will keep Maria here until he is certain that she is in foal. We can make arrangements then to return her to you."

"Thank you, my lord," I said.

He nodded. He was sitting only one place away from me at the table, but I felt as if he were a million miles away.

One did not need to be a savant to comprehend that he bitterly regretted his lapse of the night before.

Was he afraid that I was now going to pursue him?

If he was, he flattered himself.

I said to my son, "Hurry up and eat, sweetheart. His lordship has things to do, and we need to get back home."

Nicky, who was like a tuning fork when it came to my feelings, immediately put down his fork. "I'm not hungry, Mama," he said. "I'm ready to leave whenever you are."

I looked at his full plate and felt a sharp pang of conscience. I promised myself that I would have Mrs. MacIntosh cook him an immense meal as soon as we reached Deepcote.

I said to Savile, "Nicky and I will wait upon your convenience, my lord."

Savile looked at Nicky's plate and a muscle jumped in the corner of his jaw.

"I will order the chaise, then," he said.

I stood up. "That will be splendid. We shall be waiting in the front hall in fifteen minutes."

Savile stood up. "All right."

I forced myself to hold out my hand. "Thank you, my lord, for your generosity."

He seemed to hesitate, then he took my hand into his much larger grip.

It was as if a streak of lightning leaped from his fingers into mine. We both disconnected the handshake, as if we had been burned.

"Gail . . ." he said, and the businesslike tone was quite gone from his voice.

But I backed away from him. "Goodbye,

my lord," I said firmly. Then I took Nicky's safe little hand into mine, turned, and walked out of that room.

CHAPTER 11

The lilac trees in the garden at Deepcote were in flower when I got the notice from my landlord that would change my life.

My dear Mrs. Saunders,

I have just completed the sale of Deepcote to a Mr. William Northrup. Mr. Northrup and his family wish to take possession of the house as soon as possible, therefore I will not be renewing your lease.

I will appreciate it if you will have vacated the premises by the thirtieth of June.

Your devoted servant,
John Mar

I sat staring at the letter before me in a state of shock. June thirtieth was exactly four weeks away. How on earth was I supposed to relocate myself and my business, which included seven horses, within such a short period of time?

I went immediately to get my copy of the

lease, to make certain that Mr. Mar could in fact do this to me. After fifteen minutes of closely perusing the document, it became brutally clear to me that he could.

In exactly twenty-eight days I would be out of a home.

I stood at the morning-room window, looking out at the lilac trees in all their misty beauty, and tried to think rationally about how I should approach this disaster.

As I saw it, the most immediate problem was the horses. If I wanted to continue my business in a new location, I had to hold on to them. A good school horse is worth his weight in gold, and I had four of them: two ponies and two geldings. Then there was my beloved old Noah; Squirt, Nicky's pony; and Maria.

Maria! At least I could do something about her, I thought. I would write to Savile and ask him to keep her at Rayleigh until I had a place for her. She was still there because she had not been success-fully bred on her first try with Centurion, and Savile was keeping her until she came into season again so that they could try once more. I was certain that he would not mind keeping her until I had found a home to bring her to.

That left me with three horses and three

ponies. Not to mention Nicky, myself, and the MacIntoshes.

It would be nothing short of a miracle if I could find a new establishment within a month's time, I thought. I didn't even know how to go about looking for something. Tommy had been the one who found Deepcote for us all those years ago.

Inevitably, the name Sam Watson popped into my head. I knew that if I asked Sam, he would take in my horses. I knew that he would also take in Nicky and me and the MacIntoshes.

Last week Sam Watson had asked me to marry him. I had put him off, not saying *yes* but not exactly saying *no* either. In fact, I wasn't sure what I wanted to do about Sam Watson.

I liked Sam. Equally as important, Nicky liked Sam. And I had begun to think of late that Nicky would benefit from having a father.

So said part of me.

The other part of me remembered a pair of golden eyes and a kiss that had scalded me to the innermost part of my being.

I shook my head as if to clear it, and the lilac trees blurred before my eyes. When I could once more see them clearly again, I made some decisions:

I would write the letter to Savile asking him to keep Maria.

I would consult my solicitor in Highgate to see if he had any advice for me about securing a new establishment.

Ⲩ Sam was away from Edgerton at the moment, but he had told me he would return sometime next week. If my solicitor told me that he would be unable to find me a new establishment within the allotted period of time, I would tell Sam that I would marry him.

Let fate decide, I thought recklessly, and went off to write the letter to Savile.

Four days after I had received notice that my lease was being terminated, the Earl of Savile drove his phaeton into my stable yard. My traitorous heart leaped when I saw him give the reins to Grove and jump down to greet Nicky, who had come racing from his vegetable garden when he saw who it was.

I watched from my bedroom window as Savile ruffled Nicky's hair and gave him a light punch upon his arm, and I saw my son's face light up like a candle. Then Savile rested a friendly hand upon Nicky's shoulder and the two of them began to walk toward the house, the boy craning his neck to look up into the face of the tall man beside him.

Two minutes later, Mrs. MacIntosh was knocking excitedly at my door.

"Lassie, lassie, ye'll niver guess who is here!"

I opened my door. Her apple-round face was glowing as brightly as Nicky's. " 'Tis none other than his lordship himself!"

Part of me was so eager to see him that I wanted to race down the stairs, and part of me didn't want to leave the safety of my bedroom. "Did he say why he is here, Mrs. MacIntosh?" I asked.

"Not to me. But he wants to see you, lassie. Did you not write to him? Perhaps he knows a place that we can lease!"

"Perhaps he does," I replied slowly.

"Comb your hair, lassie, before you go down," the little Scotswoman ordered. Obediently, I went to my dressing table, picked up my old bone comb, and ran it through my hair. Mrs. MacIntosh followed me and with her fingers she softly brushed the hair away from my ears.

"That's better. Come along with ye now, and don't keep his lordship waiting."

She had put him in the drawing room. She beamed at me as I walked slowly from the stairs toward the door. There was no doubt that she regarded Savile as our savior. I didn't know what to think. All I knew was that I was much too glad that he had come, and that my gladness had nothing at all to do with my lease.

The door was slightly ajar, and with sudden resolution I pushed it all the way open. He was there, standing alone in front of the window, his back to the room. He turned as I came in, and even from across the room I could see the gold of his eyes. I wondered how I could ever have thought they were brown. His slightly disordered hair and his unfashionably tanned skin also glowed warmly golden in the sun that streamed in through the window.

I stepped into the room but remained close to the safety of the door. "Why are you here?" I asked in a voice that was slightly deeper than my normal tone.

"I'm here because you've loss your lease, of course," he replied. He moved away from the window and crossed the tattered carpet in my direction. "I've come to bring you and Nicky back to Savile Castle with me. All the horses can go to Rayleigh until we find you another place to live."

I stared at him in absolute shock. I had not expected this.

He stopped in front of me and looked down.

"I've told my cousin John to start making

inquiries. He'll find you something, Gail. You don't have to worry about that. In the meantime, however, you need a place to live."

"I don't have to be out of Deepcote for almost another month," I said, "and I have clients scheduled during that time."

"Cancel the clients," he commanded. "Tell them that you will reschedule them when you have found a new establishment."

His lordliness was beginning to get my back up. I encouraged the feeling. It was much easier for me to deal with him when I was angry. "And why should I do that?"

"Because it will be much better for you and Nicky to come to Savile. My sister is staying with me for the summer, and her three children — two of whom are boys Nicky's age — are staying with me as well. It will be a wonderful opportunity for Nicky to have some normal companionship, Gail."

I bristled at the "normal." "I'll have you know that Nicky knows several boys his own age, my lord."

"Who?"

I folded my arms across my chest defensively. "The sons of some of our local farmers."

The aristocratic eyebrows rose. "I meant

boys of his own class."

"Nicky and I are not of the nobility, my lord."

"Neither are my nephews. They are the sons of a gentleman, as Nicky is."

I clasped my elbows with my hands and shook my head. "Lady Regina was present at the reading of George's will, and I simply can't take a chance that one of her sons will tell Nicky what was in it."

"Good God, Gail," Savile said. "Ginny has said nothing to her children on the subject of George's will."

"How can you be sure of that?" I demanded.

"First of all, parents do not confide that sort of thing to their underage children, and second of all, I asked her."

I scowled.

"Charlie and Theo will be delighted to have a friend to stay for the summer. They'll take Nicky swimming and fishing, they'll play knights and pirates and ride their ponies all over the estate and play ball and fly kites . . . you know, all the things that boys do during their summer vacation."

I had to admit that it sounded like a heaven-sent opportunity for Nicky, who had never had much chance to do any of those things.

I wasn't so sure about how heaven-sent staying in the same house with Savile was going to be for me, however. He stirred something in me that no other man had ever touched.

"Are you certain that Lady Regina will not object to my presence?" I procrastinated.

"Savile Castle belongs to me, not to my sister," Savile said a trifle grimly.

"Yes, but if she is acting as your hostess . . ."

"Ginny is staying with me for the summer because her husband has gone to a scientific conference in Heidelberg and she is expecting another child and did not feel up to accompanying him. She will be very happy to have you to augment my own boring company, I assure you."

"And you think that Mr. Melville will be able to find me another establishment?"

"I do not promise that he will find something within a month, but by the end of the summer he should certainly have located something for you. You will have to discuss with him what it is that you are willing to pay."

I drew a deep breath. His logic was perfect, I thought. I would be a fool to turn down such an opportunity.

"Well then," I said, "I do not see how I can refuse your offer, my lord." I gave him a slightly unsteady smile. "You must know that I have been worried to death. Your generosity has lifted a burden from my shoulders."

"I am glad to hear that," he said, his face inscrutable.

I thought of Sam, who was to return to Edgerton the following day, and then I looked once more at Savile.

Two more days and I would probably have opted to marry Sam.

I looked once more at the golden-haired earl standing before me.

Fate, I thought, *had decided.*

Savile decided to leave Mr. and Mrs. MacIntosh at Deepcote until the final month of my occupancy was up. If I didn't have a new place by then, Savile said he would send them to his hunting box in Leicestershire, where they could live until our future was resolved.

"If I bring you to Savile Castle and allow you and your superior cooking into my kitchen, my own cook is certain to resign," the earl told Mr. MacIntosh humorously. "And, since I fear that nothing I can offer will ever lure you away from Mrs. Saunders, that will leave me in quite a quandary."

"Ye're right, my lord. Nothing will iver

induce me to leave my lassie and the wee Nicholas. We will be happy to do whativer ye suggest," the flattered Mr. MacIntosh replied.

Several hours after Savile's arrival, Grove pulled into my stable yard with the earl's chaise and a handful of postillions who were going to transport my horses to Rayleigh.

One of the postillions was a small, thin youngster whose task was to ride Squirt to Savile Castle so that Nicky would have his own pony for the summer.

The chaise was for our baggage, and for Nicky and me if the weather should turn ugly.

Savile had thought of everything.

I had to admit, it was pleasant to have all my arrangements made so easily. All Nicky and I had to do was pack.

Before I went to bed that night, I made my usual trip down to the stable to check on the horses. Savile offered to come with me, but I shook my head.

"I've lived here for eight years," I said to him. "I need to be alone to make my goodbyes."

The summer sky was still not completely dark as I left the house. I stopped for a moment in the middle of the stable yard to gaze around me at the familiar scene. I had come here with such happiness, a young wife and mother, and then had come the terrible grief of my husband's death. Deepcote was inextricably linked with my greatest joy and with my deepest sorrow. Deepcote would always mean Tommy to me.

I leaned against the paddock fence, and Fancy and Polly, turned out of their stalls once more by the need to stable Savile's animals, came over to nuzzle my hands, looking for treats.

Tommy's voice sounded in my ears: *"I think I've found the perfect place for us, Gail. It's got a good-size stable and two well-fenced paddocks and the house ain't that bad. Well — at least the roof don't leak!"*

I remembered standing at the door of the drawing room, holding Nicky in my arms. "My God, Tommy," I had said, "this is absolutely dreadful."

We had looked at each other, and then we had begun to laugh. I laughed so hard that tears came to my eyes. What had decrepit furniture and tattered rugs meant to us in those days?

I patted Polly's neck and thought about the young couple who had come to Deepcote eight years before.

Tommy was dead, killed instantly by the kick of a horse as he had bent over to pry a stone out of a rear hoof. The iron horseshoe had caught him squarely in his left temple.

Tonight, as I stood alone in the middle of the place where we had once been so happy, I realized that the girl I had been when I married Tommy was buried here along with him. I was a woman now, a woman who had learned to rely on her own capabilities and strengths because she had a child depending upon her and no one else to turn to.

I placed my hands on top of the fence, rested my cheek on them and listened to the softly breathing night.

"Goodbye, Tommy," I whispered. "Wish me luck."

No answer came whispering out of the dark, but my ears didn't need to hear what my heart already knew. Tommy had always wanted me to be happy.

CHAPTER 12

The red and white hawthorns were out all along the roadside and the scent of the coming summer was in the air on the day that we left Deepcote. Savile and Nicky and I rode on the front seat of the phaeton, a seat that was really meant to accommodate only two. Neither Nicky nor I was very big, however, and the earl assured us that there was plenty of room for him. The chaise, driven by Grove and carrying our meager baggage, followed along behind us.

I started out by asking Savile about his nephews, because I knew that was the subject in which Nicky would be most interested.

"Charlie is the oldest, he's ten," Savile said obligingly. "He's very smart — he's like his father in that — and he's also very imaginative. He makes up his own games and has been known to spend entire days living in make-believe worlds of his own creation."

"What kind of worlds, sir?" Nicky asked.

With his long whip, Savile competently flicked a fly off the back of one of his horses.

The horse's gleaming coppery hide never even twitched. Savile said, "He once spent an entire week being a castaway who befriended a monkey on a jungle island."

Nicky laughed delightedly.

"And Theodore?" he prompted.

We had been driving under the shade of a short avenue of beeches, and as we came back out into the sunlight Savile's eyes crinkled a little at the corners to adjust to the brightness. For the first time I noticed that his lashes were several shades darker than his hair.

He said to Nicky, "Theo has always been horse-mad, but lately he has also grown very fond of fishing. The way he has been going these last weeks, I am beginning to wonder if we are going to have any fish left in the lake."

"Your nephews sound like they are great fun, sir," Nicky said wistfully. "Do you think that they will like me?"

"I am very sure they will," Savile replied, giving my son a reassuring smile.

Savile's being nice was very difficult for me to handle and I tried to get a grip on my fluttering stomach.

"I am surprised you do not have a house-party at Savile for the summer, my lord," I said with an attempt at lightness. "Isn't it customary for the ton to entertain one another at their country homes during the warmer months?"

"Well, actually I do have something of a house party at Savile, Mrs. Saunders," came the surprising, and unwelcome, reply.

I whipped my head around and said accusingly, "You said nothing to me about any house party! You said your sister was the only person staying with you!"

"I said that my sister was staying with me," he corrected. "I did not say she was the only person."

Perhaps he had not, but he had certainly led me to think so. "Who else is there?" I asked suspiciously.

"Well, there is my cousin Roger Melville, whom you met the last time you stayed with me." He paused briefly and shot me a quick look. "Then there is also Lady Devane and her three daughters, and her father, Mr. Cole."

If I had not been sitting in a phaeton I would have leaped to my feet.

"What! Are you mad, Savile? I never would have come with you if I had known those people were staying in your house."

Nicky said nervously, "What is wrong, Mama? Why don't you like the people his lordship has staying with him?"

214

I hid my hands in the folds of my skirt so that Nicky would not see my fists opening and closing. The look I gave Savile was scorching. He had done this on purpose, waiting until Nicky was present before he told me about the rest of the house party.

"I don't have the proper clothing for a house party," I said to Nicky tersely.

He knew it was more than that, but he said, "Oh," and fell silent.

"I shall be happy to advance you some of the money you will make on Maria's foal if you wish to purchase some clothing," Savile said.

I wanted to hit him so much that my hands were trembling. "No, thank you, my lord," I said emphatically.

The faintest trace of a smile pulled at the corners of his mouth. He said, "Don't you want to know why I have invited such an unattractive group of people to stay with me for the summer?" His eyes left the road and shot me another quick look. "And I don't mean you, Gail."

I didn't say anything.

He continued smoothly, "One month after George's death, in what has to be a stroke of supreme irony, Harriet found that she was in the family way."

That got my immediate attention. "No!"

"Yes. And of course, if the child is a boy, he, rather than Roger, will be the new Lord Devane."

"Good heavens," I said, completely diverted.

"Precisely. Mr. Middleman and I discussed this potentially explosive situation, and we both decided that it would be best if neither Roger nor Harriet was officially put in possession of Devane Hall until the succession was quite clear. That is how I earned the joy of housing both Roger and Harriet until Harriet's child is born."

Silence fell as I contemplated this astonishing news. The roadway slipped by beneath the phaeton's wheels and the chestnuts maintained their steady, perfectly matching trot. Finally Nicky said tentatively, "Did you say there would be other children there besides Charlie and Theodore, sir?"

"Yes. There is my niece, of course, the boys' younger sister, Caroline, who is three. And then there are my cousin's children — Maria, Frances, and Jane."

"Oh," said Nicky. I could see that he was finding the prospect of so many strange children a bit frightening.

"I expect the girls will be spending most of their time with their governesses," I said brightly.

"That is so," Savile said.

Nicky, who had had very little experience of small girls, looked relieved.

"You will all sleep and eat together in the nursery, of course, but Mr. Wilson is in charge of the boys, and he's a very good-natured young man. His father is a friend of my brother-in-law's, and when my sister was looking for someone to take the boys in charge for the summer, Gervase thought of George Wilson. He's studying law at the Inns of Court and was looking for employment for the summer." Savile gave Nicky an encouraging smile. "I'm sure you'll like Mr. Wilson, Nicky. He is young enough to remember what boys your age like to do."

At the words "sleep and eat together in the nursery" I felt Nicky press closer to me on the seat. His thin body was very tense. "Oh," he said, attempting to sound casual, "then I won't be staying with Mama?"

I should never have agreed to come, I thought. I wanted to put my arm around my son and hug him to my breast. I wanted to tell Savile to turn the phaeton around immediately and take us home.

I hadn't thought about the fact that Nicky would be expected to conform to the ways of an aristocratic household. I hadn't thought that he wouldn't be sleeping in the room next to mine or taking his meals with me. I hadn't envisioned this kind of separation.

I looked at Savile and bit my lip, trying to think of a way out of the situation I appeared to have gotten Nicky into. At the same moment, the earl turned and looked directly at me over the top of Nicky's head.

His eyes were grave. His face was stern. He shook his head slightly but definitely, then turned back to the road.

"I realize that you might be feeling a little overwhelmed, Nicky," he said cheerfully, "but I can assure you that dinner in the nursery will be far more fun than a long, boring evening with the adults. We dress up for dinner every night, and my cook always serves five separate courses."

"*Five* courses, sir!"

"Always. Dinner goes on for a very long time."

"I could never eat five courses," Nicky said.

"Neither can I," I said. "Perhaps I could join the nursery party, my lord."

"Absolutely not," came the instant reply. He added in a humorous voice, "One of the reasons I invited you to visit was to provide me with relief from the company of my relatives."

Nicky actually chuckled.

I scowled at the earl's profile, but he gave no sign of noticing.

I stared at the passing landscape, chewed my lip, and wondered how I could ensure that no one said anything to Nicky about George's legacy.

Predictably, Nicky was struck with wonder at the magical sight of Savile Castle materializing in the distance. The other time I had been to Savile, it had been encompassed by snow, and today the sight of its high round towers soaring above the clear waters of the surrounding lake made it look more than ever like a fairy castle out of the pages of Thomas Malory.

The horses' hooves crunched on the gravel of the causeway. A long, low stone wall, which had been hidden by the snow on my last visit, separated the causeway from the water of the surrounding lake, which lapped very gently against it. The island that contained the gatehouse was also visible today, and I was able to see how truly small it was. From the island we crossed over the last expanse of water and drove through the immense gate in the medieval walls and into the castle courtyard.

Thick carpets of lawn stretched on either

side of the drive, and carefully trimmed and shaped evergreens softened the stone walls of the house. Beds of flowers, with each bed planted according to color, lined the paths that left the driveway to circle around to the back of the house, where, presumably, the stables were hidden.

The phaeton came to a halt in front of the stone-arched front door of the house, and the butler and two footmen in the earl's blue and gold livery came out the door so quickly that one would have thought they had been standing there all morning, waiting for us.

One of the footmen went to the horses' heads.

Savile jumped down, then turned to help me alight as well.

I didn't want him to touch me, but there was no way I could avoid it. I rested my hands lightly on his shoulders and he lifted me down. I turned away from him immediately to look at the house.

Nicky came to stand beside me.

"It's so big, Mama," he said a little breathlessly. "Why, it's even bigger than Rayleigh."

I put my hand on his shoulder and squeezed it gently.

"Uncle Raoul! Uncle Raoul!"

Two boys came tearing around the side of the house and began to run across the lawn in our direction. They skidded onto the gravel drive, came to a halt in front of the earl, and stood grinning up at him delightedly.

"You're back!" the smaller one said.

"As you see, I am back, Theodore," Savile returned, "and I have brought with me another young man who is going to be staying with us for a while." He reached out, gently removed my hand from Nicky's shoulder, and drew him into the orbit of the two other boys.

"This is Nicky Saunders," he said. "Nicky, these are my disreputable nephews, Charlie and Theo Austen."

Charlie and Theodore took turns grabbing Nicky's hand and pumping it furiously.

"Are we glad to see you!" Theodore said fervently. "This whole place is infested with *girls*."

Nicky's smile was a little tentative, but it was a smile. "I'm glad to be here," he said.

"May we take Nicky up to the nursery and show him where he is going to sleep, Uncle Raoul?" Charlie asked.

Savile turned to me. "Allow me to apologize for my nephews, Mrs. Saunders. I assure you, they have been taught manners. I can only assume that in the excitement of the moment they have forgotten them."

The two little boys looked abashed. "We're sorry, Uncle Raoul," Theodore said.

"Mrs. Saunders," said Savile, "may I present my nephews, Charles and Theodore Austen."

Both boys had smooth, shiny hair cut in a neat fringe over their foreheads. Charlie was dark haired, however, while Theodore was blond, like his mother. Both of them had large, long-lashed brown eyes.

"How do you do, Mrs. Saunders," they chorused.

"Hello, boys," I said with a smile. "I am very glad to meet you."

"Thank you, ma'am," said Theodore.

"Sorry if we were rude, Mrs. Saunders," Charlie said with a beguiling smile. "It is just that we are so happy to have reinforcements against all these girls."

I grinned.

"Someday you will not feel that way, Charlie," Savile said.

Charlie looked unconvinced.

"May we take Nicky with us, Mrs. Saunders?" Theodore asked charmingly.

"Of course," I replied.

There was a spring in Nicky's step as the three boys walked together back across the drive toward the side of the house. I could see Theodore gesturing largely as he talked to Nicky, no doubt explaining to him the horrors of the female invasion.

"Feel better?" Savile asked me softly.

I didn't look at him. "A little," I said.

At that moment, Lady Regina came out of the front door of the house. "Oh good, you've brought Mrs. Saunders, Raoul." She came up to the side of the phaeton where we were standing, kissed her brother on the cheek, and held out her hand to me.

"I am very glad to see you, Mrs. Saunders. Welcome once more to Savile Castle."

Her smile was gracious if not precisely warm.

I said, "Thank you, Lady Regina. It is kind of you to have me."

"Do you think we might go inside?" Savile said.

The smile his sister gave him was much warmer than the one she had given me. "I think we might manage that, Raoul." As the three of us started walking toward the front door she looked around. "I take it that my boys have already kidnapped your son, Mrs. Saunders."

"Yes, Lady Regina. They took him off to the nursery."

She chuckled. "Their noses are out of joint because Harriet's girls are here. I only hope the boys don't plot anything too grisly to make their disapproval felt."

She did not sound overly worried.

"They had better not," the earl said. "The Melville girls seem to be quiet, timid little things. I don't want them to be upset or frightened, Ginny."

I thought of Harriet and her father. "Timid?" I said.

"Harriet's probably knocked all the spirit out of them," Lady Regina said cynically. "She doesn't care about her daughters. All she wants is a son so that she can hang on to Devane Hall."

"Well, there is still the possibility that she may get one," Savile said.

"I know you will be devastated to hear this, Raoul," Lady Regina said, "but Mr. Cole has been called away to London on business."

"Oh, what a shame," the earl said with a mixture of amusement and relief. "We must say a prayer that his business is time-consuming, Ginny. Harriet is much more pleasant when her father is not around to stir up all her grievances."

The relief I felt at this piece of news was enormous. I wouldn't put it past Albert Cole to call Nicky a bastard to his face.

We stood for a moment longer in the middle of the Great Hall while Savile and his sister consulted about bedroom arrangements, and I looked at the immense stone fireplace, which was even more fabulous than I had remembered, and registered my relief about the absence of Mr. Cole.

"I told Mrs. Ferrer to get the blue end bedroom ready for Mrs. Saunders," I heard the earl say to his sister.

She didn't answer, but the words must have produced some kind of a reaction because something about her body posture caught my immediate attention. After a rather long pause she said, "All right, Raoul. I will ask Mrs. Ferrer to show her up now."

He nodded. "Luncheon will be in half an hour, Mrs. Saunders, and then I would like to show you the castle grounds."

"Very well, my lord," I replied slowly, still trying to puzzle out what had caught my attention about Lady Regina.

The earl's sister told a footman to summon the housekeeper, who appeared in less than two minutes. I followed her up the great, almost theatrical-looking Jacobean staircase, with its open well formed by arched Ionic columns and its mythological figures worked in grisaille along the wall. We walked through Raoul the Seventh's gloriously carved Renaissance Great Chamber, then took the route that was familiar to me from my previous visit. This time, however, we did not stop at the middle of the bedroom passageway, but continued on to the very end, where Mrs. Ferrer opened the last door on the left before a narrow set of carpeted stairs at the hall's end.

I noted the stairs with pleasure. Due to the nature of my parents' death, I always looked for an escape route when I stayed in an unfamiliar place.

This room was half again as large as the bedroom I had occupied on my earlier visit, and although the drapes and the bed hangings were several degrees less faded, there was nothing else about the room that suggested to me the reason for Lady Regina's reaction.

For Lady Regina did not approve of my being given this room; of that I was quite certain.

My eyes went slowly around the bedroom, taking in the carved four-poster with its blue tapestry hangings, the mahogany writing table with its handles made to look like brass lion-head masks, the mahogany cheval glass, the pair of gilt beechwood chairs with blue velvet upholstery on either side of the coal-burning fire, and the large, carved wardrobe against the east wall.

At this moment a footman came in carrying my pitiful-looking portmanteau. Behind him came a chambermaid carrying a jug of hot water.

The footman put down my baggage and the chambermaid poured the hot water into the porcelain bowl on my bedside stand.

"There is a rather small dressing room and a water closet through that door, ma'am," the maid said, nodding to the door near the middle of the west wall of the room. "Due to the size of the dressing room, I am afraid that your clothing will have to be hung in the wardrobe in this room. Would you like me to unpack for you now?"

"Yes," I said quietly, "that would be nice."

I let the maid hang up my clothes, and when she volunteered to take a few of my dresses to have them ironed, I agreed. After she left, I looked at the three dresses that were left hanging in the wardrobe.

The sight was depressing in the extreme. My clothing, which was barely adequate for the social amenities of life in a small village, was woefully inadequate for the demands of a country-house visit.

I told myself that I didn't mind, but I did. No woman likes to appear at a disadvantage, and I knew that both Harriet and Lady Regina would regard my unfashionable wardrobe with scorn.

I could tolerate Lady Regina's disdain more easily than I could Harriet's.

"Oh well, there's nothing I can do about it," I said aloud, trying to sound offhand. "As long as Nicky is happy, I must be content."

I didn't bother to change my brown cambric traveling dress, as I had nothing better to wear, but I washed the travel grime from my face and hands and combed my hair in front of the cheval glass. Then I went downstairs to luncheon.

I met John Melville in the Great Hall and he came to shake my hand and welcome me to Savile Castle. His smile looked genuine and his brown eyes held what appeared to be admiration as he looked into my face.

I appreciated the look; it fed my badly faltering self-confidence.

"Rotten luck, losing your lease like that, Mrs. Saunders," he said. "Don't worry though, I shall find you something even better, I promise."

"I should be so grateful if you could, Mr. Melville," I replied. "My late husband found Deepcote for us, and I'm afraid I haven't the smallest idea of how to start looking on my own."

The warmth of his smile increased. "Don't

worry," he repeated. "Are you going in to luncheon, Mrs. Saunders?"

"Yes, I am."

"It is always laid out in the family dining room," he said. "May I escort you?"

"That would be very nice," I said, and the two of us began to walk slowly across the Great Hall.

"Do you have an office in the house, Mr. Melville?" I asked as we passed through the music room, with its black-and-white marble tile floor.

On my previous visit Lady Regina had told me that the music room had originally been used for occasional banquets, plays, and entertainments, and also as a dining hall for servants. Today it took its name from the harpsichord, pianoforte, and two harps that stood in each of its four corners. There was a modern Egyptian-style sofa placed along one of the walls, and four Egyptian-style chairs flanked the opposite wall, presumably for the comfort of listeners.

"I have my office at the top of the Constable's Tower," John Melville answered me.

I turned to him with a smile. He was not a particularly tall man, but I am not particularly tall either, and I had to look up to meet his eyes. "What wonderful views you must have," I enthused.

He grinned. "That's why I chose it. I spent most of my boyhood summers here at the castle, and I love it dearly. I can never get enough of the sight of the walls reflected in the still, clear lake water on a summer's day."

"The castle seems to be some sort of summer refuge for boys," I said with a laugh.

"My aunt and uncle always had a kindness for children," John Melville said. "And Raoul, of course, draws them like a magnet."

"Does he?" I asked curiously.

By now we were passing through the drawing room, which Lady Regina had told me had originally been called the King James dining room, since it was the room where King James (along with other royal visitors) had dined. A life-size bronze statue of the king, placed there when the house was built, still surveyed the room from the auspices of another great Jacobean chimneypiece. On the opposite side of the room was a huge portrait of Savile's grandfather, who in the preceding century had turned the room from a state dining room for royal visits into a drawing room.

"Yes," John Melville said, referring back to my question about Savile. "It is a thousand pities that he has no children of his own."

"I am surprised that he has not married again," I said.

"Considering that during the last six years Ginny has thrown every eligible young lady in the ton into his path, it can be nothing short of a miracle that he has not married again," John Melville returned with a soft laugh.

"He must have loved his wife very much," I said.

"He was exceedingly in love with her," John Melville replied. "So much so that I doubt he will ever remarry."

By now we had passed through the formal dining room and entered the breakfast room.

The first person I saw as I came in the door was Harriet. She was wearing a bronze silk afternoon dress that made her skin look sallow, and, since she was seated, I could not get a good look at her figure. Her normal stoutness probably masked her condition anyway, I thought meanly.

She scowled when she saw me. "Well, well, look who is here," she said in a tone I can only describe as nasty. "It's Mrs. Saunders."

She made *Saunders* sound as if it were a barnyard word.

I stared directly into her eyes, and after a moment she shifted her eyes back and forth and then looked away. With a flash of intuition, I wondered if Harriet thought that I was a witch too.

If she was indeed laboring under the delusion, I thought delightedly, then perhaps I could make use of it.

"Good afternoon, Mrs. Saunders," said a light, faintly amused voice, and I turned to look into the eyes of Roger Melville. Clearly, he had seen the same thing in Harriet's face as I had. "I am so glad you have come," he continued. "This family party stands in crying need of a little enlivening."

Lady Regina said repressively, "Mrs. Saunders is here so that her son can be a companion for Charlie and Theo, Roger."

"Of course, Ginny," Roger said, and the malicious glint in his blue eyes was very pronounced. Of course, I understood that Roger had no reason to love Harriet, but I most certainly did not want him to use me as a pawn to annoy her. I shot him a repressive look.

At that moment, Savile walked into the room. He looked from where his family was seated around the table to where I stood empty-handed next to the sideboard. "Why are you not eating, Mrs. Saunders?" he said. "We had a long ride in the open air this morning. I know that I am starving."

John Melville handed me a plate. "We've only just got here ourselves, Raoul. I was recommending that Mrs. Saunders take some of the cold fowl."

I smiled at him. "That sounds very nice, Mr. Melville."

One of the three footmen standing beside the sideboard cut me a piece of the aforementioned duck, which I took to a seat at the table as far away from Harriet as I could possibly get. Savile piled his plate high and came to take the place next to mine.

"While you were gone I had more complaints about the miller, Raoul," John Melville said as everyone resumed eating. "This time it was Henderson who came to see me. You might want to talk to Jarvis yourself when you get a chance."

All the good humor disappeared from Savile's face. "I will speak to him this afternoon," he said. He looked at me. "Perhaps Mrs. Saunders will come with me, which will give me a chance to show her some of the countryside."

"Very well," John Melville said.

Everyone else was silent.

"Perhaps Nicky would like to come with us, my lord," I said brightly.

"Nicky will do much better with my nephews," Savile said calmly. He cut a piece of roast beef off the slice on his plate, put it in his mouth, and began to chew. He looked thoughtful.

I sneaked a peak at Lady Regina. She looked resigned. When she saw me looking at her, the look of resignation changed into a restrained smile.

"The grounds are well worth looking at, Mrs. Saunders," she assured me.

"I am looking forward to it," I said faintly. I ate another small bite of my cold fowl.

Lady Regina began to tell her brother about a letter she had received from her husband that morning, and we all listened politely to the list of dissertations that had been presented in Heidelberg on the subjects of astronomy and mathematics. It was very impressive, if incomprehensible.

Fifteen minutes later, Savile turned to me and smiled. "The phaeton will be at the front door in ten minutes, Mrs. Saunders," he said. "I'll meet you in the front hall."

I stood up. "Very well, my lord."

I excused myself from the luncheon party with what I hoped was composure and went upstairs to don my bonnet and gloves.

CHAPTER 13

Savile was waiting at the foot of the stair-case, and as he turned to smile up at me I knew beyond the shadow of a doubt that I was lost.

How had this happened? I asked myself in bewilderment as I walked beside him out to the phaeton. How had this one man, whom I had seen but a few times over the course of the last five months, managed to turn my world upside down?

I should never have come here. I had no business being here. I had known that, and yet I had let him persuade me. I, who prided myself on my independence, had allowed myself to be packed up like a child being hustled home from a school where there has been an outbreak of typhus.

I knew why I had done it.

I also knew that I had been wrong, but I doubted that I was going to change my mind.

"Why so pensive?" Savile asked. We had reached the phaeton and were standing to-gether next to the passenger's side. "Are you still worried about Nicky?"

"A little," I said. "It's a difficult habit to break."

He put his hands around my waist. They felt so warm and strong and right. I rested my hands on his shoulders, feeling the superfine cloth of his coat under my fingers, and he swung me up to the seat.

"I have no intention of trying to separate you from your son, Gail," he said as he claimed the seat next to mine and picked up the reins and the whip. "I often take the boys on outings during the summer," he smiled at me, "and you will always be welcome to join us."

His smile was like sunshine.

"That would be nice," I said gravely, my eyes on the dappled gray backs of the pair he was driving this afternoon.

Savile set his team in motion. "You will notice that Savile Castle does not have the sort of park you will see in many of the newer country houses," he said, and I had to repress a smile at the note of faint hauteur in his voice when he said the words *newer country houses.*

"Do you mean those newfangled seventeenth- and eighteenth-century edifices, my lord?" I asked.

He chuckled appreciatively. "Precisely."

We passed through the immense gate in

the medieval walls and came out onto the graveled drive. The thick green grass on either side of the drive sloped down to the clear water of the lake, and I could hear the water slapping gently against the shore. I said, "How large is this island, my lord?"

"It is only a mile square, and the outbuildings, such as the kitchen, take up a great deal of room. The more extensive grounds belonging to the castle are on the other side of the lake."

"Your kitchen is still located in a separate building?" I said in surprise. "Your servants must find that excessively inconvenient."

"There is an underground tunnel connecting the kitchen to the main house, so the food does not have to be carried through the weather," came the serene reply.

It occurred to me that there were some definite advantages to living in a small house.

As we were heading over the causeway, I asked, "Are we going to the mill?"

"Yes," Savile said. "The drive to the mill will take us through some of Savile Park, so you will be able to see it."

I thought for a minute about the ramifications of the earl's going to see the miller. "Does the mill actually *belong* to the castle, my lord?" I asked with what I hoped was concealed disapproval. Mills usually were at the service of a whole village, not merely one household.

"It has for centuries," came the easy reply. When I made no answer he glanced at my face, then continued pleasantly, "It is not quite as extraordinary a thing as you may think, Gail. I employ well over a hundred people on a permanent basis, and when I have a special project under way, like the rebuilding of the stables, there might be double or even treble that number to feed. A working mill to grind wheat into flour for bread is essential to the running of a large estate such as Savile."

I had never lived close enough to a large estate such as Savile to know such things. "I can see that it must be," I said a little ironically.

A cloud covered the sun. Savile lifted his face to scan the sky, and it occurred to me that it was an incongruously countryman type of thing for a great earl to do. He continued, "The mill does not just work for the castle, of course. For a reasonable fee, it grinds wheat for my tenants and the local villagers." A muscle tightened under the smoothly shaved skin at the corner of his jaw. "I have had trouble in the past with my present miller, Jarvis, producing less weight in flour than is brought to him in wheat, and

John has spoken to him about it several times. Evidently John has received complaints again. It's time, I think, for me to talk to Jarvis myself and make it clear that I will not tolerate having the local people cheated."

I looked at Savile's jawline and decided that I would not like to have him angry with me.

When we reached the other side of the causeway, instead of taking the main road westward, which I had done before, we turned onto a local path and followed the lake northward. I looked at the castle across the water and saw for the first time that in fact only three of the walls were close enough to the lake to be reflected in the water; the fourth wall was backed by what was probably a half a mile of gardens and estate buildings.

Several rowboats were bobbing in the water on the edge of the island across the lake from us. Aside from the causeway, the boats appeared to be the only way off the island, as no footbridge was within view.

High evergreen trees appeared to the right of the path, obscuring my view of the lake. Then the phaeton made a turn around them and the view of the lake and the castle reappeared, but now I was also looking at a topiary garden that formed a background to what looked like an extensive collection of Greek statues. There were garden benches placed at strategic intervals so that one could sit and contemplate the beauty of the statuary, and in the center of the garden was a marble fountain that was a statue of a nymph, with water trickling through her hands.

Savile stopped the phaeton so that I could take a closer look at this extraordinary spectacle. "The topiary garden has been here forever," he said, "but my father added the Greek statues."

"They are very nice," I said faintly.

He shot me an amused look. "There's a maze, too." He gestured to the left side of the path and the high, immaculately trimmed boxwood. He added blandly, "I don't know if it's as up to snuff as the maze belonging to your friend Mr. Watson. You'll have to try it one day and see if you get lost."

"How did you know that I got lost in Mr. Watson's maze?" I asked him in surprise.

"Nicky informed me," he said.

"And you remembered?"

A flash of gold from his eyes made me remember vividly a certain intimate moment in the library at Rayleigh. "When it comes to you, Gail, I forget very little."

"Oh," I said nervously. "Ah."

A smile quirked the corner of his mouth. He picked up the reins and drove on.

The shrubbery gave way to an attractive expanse of neatly scythed lawns and wide-spreading oak trees. Then my once-more astonished eyes beheld what looked like a Greek temple set on the shore of the lake, its white columns looking bizarrely out of place in this quintessentially English setting. Savile stopped the phaeton once more.

"It's a bathhouse," he informed me. "My father had it built when Palladianism was popular."

"Goodness," I murmured faintly. I looked from the Greek temple to the medieval English castle walls and tried not to smile.

"My mother used to have picnics here for her guests," Savile said. "They would eat off china plates and sip champagne out of crystal glasses and imagine themselves to be nymphs on the banks of the Aegean, or some such nonsense."

I could not help myself. I laughed. At the sound, he looked at me and grinned.

"My nephews sometimes use it for swimming," he said. "It does actually have a Roman-style pool inside, but mostly the boys prefer to swim in the lake."

His words instantly distracted me from his smile. "They swim in the lake?"

"Yes. All the Savile children swim. The lake is too close to our lives for us to take chances."

"Nicky does not know how to swim," I said tensely.

"Then we shall just have to teach him," came the cheerful reply.

I folded my arms across my chest in speechless disagreement. I had no intention of risking my boy's life in that lake.

"Gail," he said quietly. Sincerely. "I promise you that Nicky will be well looked after while he is here. Can't you take a few weeks to relax? For years you have been carrying burdens that no other woman I know could carry. Relax, sweetheart. Give yourself a holiday."

I tried not to think about what that "sweetheart" did to my nervous system. Problems don't go away because one decides to take a holiday, I thought resolutely. I didn't say that to him, however, I just folded my hands in my lap and gazed straight ahead. We drove on in silence and I was glad to see the next building come into view on the right side of the path. It was a charming half-timbered cottage with a thatched roof, set off from the road by a hawthorn hedge and a painted white fence. It sparkled in the sun, and the flowers in the front garden were vibrant with color and lovingly cared for.

Once more Savile stopped the phaeton.

"What a charming cottage!" I said with overly enthusiastic approval. "Does it belong to one of your tenants?"

"Actually, it is part of the castle park," Savile said quietly. "My grandfather had it built at a time when rustic cottages were all the crack. When I was a boy, John and I used to sleep out here on hot summer nights. It was always much cooler by the lake than in the nursery. Sometimes we would catch a fish for breakfast and cook it ourselves on the lakeshore."

Somehow I had never envisioned the Earl of Savile catching and cooking his own breakfast.

I looked once more at the cottage. I knew whole families who would have been ecstatic at the thought of having that cottage to live in, and Savile had used it for a toy.

Not for the first time, I realized that I was out of my depth.

We started forward once again, the carriage passing under the hanging branch of a beautiful old oak.

I tried to reestablish our earlier rapport. "Your cousin told me that he spent many of the summers of his youth here at Savile," I said pleasantly.

But Savile was looking up and frowning. "That branch has come down too far over the road. I shall have to tell John to send someone out here to cut it down."

He returned his attention to me. "John's father, who was my father's younger brother, was killed in the American war, so John really grew up here at Savile." His eyes were back on the road, which curved to follow the narrowing lake. "As I told you before, John is not an ordinary kind of steward, Gail. He is my cousin, my second-in-command, if you will. Most certainly he is not my servant." He clucked to one of the horses. "As a matter of fact, at the moment he is also my heir."

The wide expanse of the lake narrowed rapidly, and in a few minutes the road was following along the steadily flowing River Haver. The grassy verge on either side of the river was sprinkled with rocks, which increased in size as we drove along.

At one point the phaeton bumped over a rock and I was thrown against the earl's shoulder. I righted myself hastily. The whole side of my body that was next to him was warm with awareness.

"At one time you could get a ship along the river all the way to the Thames," Savile told me, "but it has dried to little more than a stream in places."

"Well, it looks impressive enough," I said.

"Yes, it still runs quite strongly here." He frowned. "There is the mill up ahead of us."

The stone building with its high water-wheel, its rushing waterfall, and its millpond did not look very different from thousands of other mills that dotted the English countryside. *Clack-clack-clack* went the mill wheel as it turned with the push of the water, and the ducks on the millpond looked the same as the ones that floated on the millpond at either Hatfield or Highgate.

Two carts were parked together in the shade of an elm tree and two men stood together at their horses' heads, talking. Their lethargic postures changed dramatically as Savile drove in and they turned to watch him with intense interest.

The stout miller, whose clothes were covered with flour and dust and who looked like every other miller I had ever seen, came out the door of his mill. "My lord!" he cried with great geniality. "How glad we are to have you home once again!"

"Will you hold the horses for me, Gail?" Savile asked me.

"Of course," I said, and held out my hand for the reins, careful that my fingers did not come into contact with his.

The earl swung down from the carriage

and went to meet his employee on the steps in front of the mill.

They spoke for exactly two minutes, and even from where I sat I could see that after one minute the miller had gone pale and was sweating. He tried to say something and Savile cut him off. The earl then turned and beckoned to the two men who were standing in the shade of the elm. Both men jumped, then half walked, half ran to join Savile and the miller on the steps of the mill.

Two more minutes of conversation ensued, at the end of which time the two men were smiling and the miller looked even paler than he had before. Then Savile rejoined me at the phaeton.

"He was cheating?" I asked as I transferred the reins back to him and he started the horses up again.

He didn't reply, just nodded. After we had driven for perhaps a minute he said with feeling, "God, Gail, I really believe that greed is responsible for more evil in this world than almost anything else."

"You are probably right," I replied.

"There is no need for Jarvis to cheat on the weights. I pay him a good salary. He has a house to live in, a wife and only one child to feed. He is much better off than many of the local farmers, who have suffered bitterly from the drop of the price of corn since the war. And these are the men he is cheating. His neighbors, for God's sake."

I sighed. "I have always had a strong belief in the doctrine of original sin, my lord. It seems to me that most of the time there doesn't have to be a reason for people to be mean. Unfortunately, they just are. It's why I have always valued people like Nicky and my late husband so much. They are the pure of heart to whom Christ promised the Kingdom of Heaven."

"You sound as if you loved your husband very much," he said, his eyes looking steadily between the ears of his grays.

Darling Tommy, I thought. *He did have a heart of gold.* "Yes," I said. "I did."

Silence fell as we negotiated the wooden bridge over the rushing water of the Haver.

"There's a grotto upstream from here," Savile said in a brisk, informative kind of voice. "My grandfather was a crony of Horace Walpole's and he put it in during the Gothic rage."

We were driving through what seemed a wide-reaching expanse of woods. "There's a hermit's cave in the wood here, and a tree house," Savile said in the same voice as before.

It seemed to me that, contrary to the earl's words, the park at Savile must be quite as extensive as any other country-home park.

"Other haunts of yours during your boyhood?" I asked lightly.

At that a faint, reminiscent smile touched his lips. "Yes."

I pulled my eyes away from his mouth and said, "For how many years have you held the title, my lord?"

"Eleven," he replied, "I succeeded when I was twenty-one."

I thought that twenty-one was dreadfully young to assume responsibility for such a vast estate.

"You've shown me improvements made by your father and your grandfather," I said. "Have you made any improvements during your own tenure, my lord?"

A breeze had begun to blow off the water and it ruffled the neatly brushed hair above his brow. I stared at it in fascination.

He said, "As I mentioned before, I rebuilt the stables. I am also presently doing extensive repair work on the castle outbuildings." He flashed me an engaging grin. "And the water closets are the most modern engineering obtainable."

I had to admit that my thoughts at the moment were not on water closets, but I said obligingly, "Water closets are definitely preferable to Greek temples."

"My thought precisely."

"Your wife did not go in for Greek temples or Turkish tents, I suppose?" I asked, conscious that I might be treading on tender ground.

"My wife did not care for the country at all," came the level reply. "She preferred to spend most of her time in London."

I was silent while I digested this reply. Probably it didn't mean anything at all, I decided. There were many successful aristocratic marriages where the partners spent a good part of the year separated from each other. It was not the sort of marriage I would have wanted for myself — indeed, it was not the sort of marriage I had had — but it had probably not seemed at all odd to the Saviles.

"I see," I said.

We drove out of the coolness of the woods and onto a wide expanse of grass that was dotted with artfully arranged clusters of trees. Deer and sheep grazed peacefully on either side of the road.

"Now this is quite lovely," I said with satisfaction, looking around.

I felt his eyes on my face. "Yes. It is."

I turned to look at him. The intent look in his golden eyes was unmistakable. My stomach turned over. He turned back to his horses.

"Capability Brown did the original park," Savile said smoothly, "but I didn't like the excessively formal look of the trees, so when I inherited I got Humphrey Repton in to thin out the clumps. It looks more natural now and I like it much better."

"It is very serene-looking," I managed to say, looking at the peaceful scene before me. My insides were not peaceful at all.

He nodded. "I'm thinking of putting up a footbridge from the island to this part of the park to make it more accessible."

We discussed this plan with great assiduity as we drove toward the causeway that would take us back to the castle. When we passed through the medieval gate, Savile promised me meaningfully, "After dinner, I will show you the gardens behind the house."

Two footmen came out the front door as soon as we pulled up, and one of them went to the horses' heads to lead them to the stables. Savile and I walked in the front door and I was happy to see that there was no one else in the Great Hall. I needed to steel myself before I met the other household members again, as at the moment I was definitely feeling too vulnerable.

I turned to Savile and, testing whether what he had said about my access to my son was true, said, "I would like to see Nicky now to make certain that he has settled in comfortably."

"Of course," Savile replied promptly. "In fact, the present is probably a good time, as they will be getting ready to serve dinner in the nursery and all the children should be present. If you come with me, I'll take you up to the third floor myself."

I followed him past the magnificent fireplace and up the Jacobean stairs to the second floor, where we turned right toward the bedroom wing where I was staying. We passed through the succession of small sitting rooms and turned down the long bedroom passageway, which we took all the way to the end to the narrow staircase that was next to my room.

"This stair goes directly up to the nursery floor," the earl told me. "I thought you would be comfortable knowing that you were so close to Nicky."

I was grateful to him for his thoughtfulness and I could not hold back a smile. "Thank you, my lord."

He gave me a long, level look I couldn't quite read, then said, "Come along with me and I'll take you up."

I put a hand on the banister and then turned to him.

"Where does the downstairs come out?" I

asked, my mind once more running to the subject of escape routes.

"It comes out right next to my apartment, actually," Savile said calmly, then began to walk up the stairs ahead of me.

So then of course I knew why Lady Regina had not wanted me to have this room.

CHAPTER 14

The nursery was enormous, taking up, as I later discovered, almost a quarter of the third floor. My mind was so preoccupied with what I had learned from Savile about the staircase, and what it might mean, that it took me a few moments to look around and get my bearings after we had walked in the nursery door. When finally I noticed my surroundings, I discovered that I was in what looked to be an immense playroom. From the doorway I saw two rocking horses of different sizes, a large dollhouse, an extensive collection of dolls, a corner filled with carved wooden blocks, and a large wooden table in the center of the room.

Cries of "Uncle Raoul! Uncle Raoul!" went up almost immediately, and as the Austen children made a dash for Savile, I looked around for Nicky. After a moment I saw him in the corner to my right, standing in front of a display of toy soldiers set out upon a large board. Then he looked up, saw me, and came running.

I reached out my arms for him and he

hugged me around the waist, but then he pulled away from my arms. He looked up at me, his eyes bright. "Theo has put together a whole map of the Battle of Waterloo using toy soldiers, Mama," he said in a rush. "You can see the English and the Prussians and the French and all of their positions!"

He had my hand now and was tugging me in the direction of this military shrine.

A little girl's voice cut through the noise in the room. "Up," it demanded. "Uncle Raoul! Pick me up!"

"I sometimes wonder if you have legs, Caro," Savile said humorously, but when I turned to look he had a golden-haired little girl riding on his shoulder with her hands tucked securely into his.

"She's such a baby, always wanting attention," Charlie said scornfully.

"She is, after all, only three years of age," Savile returned mildly. His voice changed subtly. "I hope you are well, Miss Elleridge?"

"Thank you, very well indeed, my lord," came the gentle feminine voice. "It is always wonderful to see how much the children love you."

I looked at the woman who had to be the girls' governess. She was of indeterminate age, with soft, faintly wrinkled skin and a cap worn over her neat mouse-colored hair. Her eyes looked intelligent, however. And kind.

"And if you look here, Mama, you can see the Belgians under the Prince of Orange," Nicky was saying.

"This is all very interesting, sweetheart," I said.

"Come and make your curtseys to his lordship, girls," the soft-voiced Miss Elleridge said, and three small girls who had been standing in the corner stepped forward.

These had to be George's daughters, I thought, and I stopped even pretending to listen to Nicky as I looked at the products of the union that should never have happened.

Mercifully, the girls looked like their father and not like their mother. Much as I hated George, I had to admit that he had been a good-looking man. The three little girls who stood so shyly in front of Savile were pretty and blond, and, from the hesitation I heard in their voices, they were also as insipid as their father had been.

"Good afternoon, my lord," each one said as she curtseyed.

The youngest, who was probably younger than Caroline, peeped with a mixture of curiosity and envy at Savile's niece, then lowered her eyes.

"Good afternoon, Maria. Good afternoon, Frances. Good afternoon, Jane," Savile returned gravely. He lifted Caroline down from his shoulder in a froth of petticoats. She started to protest, but Miss Elleridge took her hand and said firmly, "Come along, Caroline. I want to fix the ribbon in your hair."

"Mama!" Nicky said. "You're not listening to me."

I gave him a guilty smile. "I must confess that soldiers are not of the greatest interest to me, sweetheart. I'm sure that these are all perfectly splendid, but . . ."

I felt Savile come up to stand behind me. "I have found over the course of my life that ladies are rarely interested in toy soldiers, Nicky," he said.

"I like toy soldiers, Uncle Raoul," Caroline declared, pulling away from the governess as soon as Miss Elleridge had finished with her ribbon. She shot a defiant look at her brothers, who looked disgusted. "I like soldiers much better than dolls."

"And you, Jane?" Savile asked. For the first time I noticed that he was holding the hand of George's youngest. Or rather, she had her little fingers tightly wrapped around his thumb.

She said in a firm little voice, "I like dolls."

The firm voice surprised me and I looked at her again. Her eyes were brown, not blue like the two older girls', and her babyish chin had a determined tilt to it.

Perhaps this one is more like Harriet, I thought.

"Well, there are certainly enough toys in this room to occupy the lot of you," I said pleasantly, looking around. "Actually, it seems to me as if there are enough to occupy every soldier on Theo's board."

Lady Regina's children and Nicky laughed. George's children regarded me solemnly.

"There are more toys in the cupboards, Mama," Nicky informed me, pointing to the old oak cupboards that lined the walls of the room.

"Shall we show her?" Theo asked, exhibiting all the signs of proud ownership.

"I should love to see your toys," I said.

For the next forty minutes I was taken on a tour of the nursery toys. Savile sat on an old settee by the window with Jane on his lap and George's other girls on either side of him and talked to them while Charles and Theo and Nicky and finally Caroline showed me what was in the cupboards.

The first cupboard Charlie opened for me was filled with educational board games and

I believe I looked at every one of them. I looked at backgammon and chess and learned in detail how many times each of these games had been played by the Austen boys and who had beaten whom and how.

We moved on to other cupboards, which held a variety of items such as balls, carved animals, drums, kaleidoscopes, skipping ropes, tops, and toy boats. Some of the toy sailboats were quite magnificent, and when I heard that the boys sailed them on the lake, I heard again a warning note in my brain.

"Nicky does not know how to swim," I said. "If you boys are going to be around the lake, you must be certain he does not go into the water."

Nicky gave me a look that said, *Traitor.*

"You don't know how to swim?" Charlie asked my son.

Nicky gave me that look again. "No," he admitted starkly.

"We'll have to teach you, then," Charlie said. "I'll ask Uncle Raoul to have the pool in the bathhouse filled." He looked at me. "It's where we all learned to swim, Mrs. Saunders. It's not deep, so it's quite safe."

I was quite certain that I didn't want Nicky being taught to swim by boys his own age, but from the look on my son's face I knew that this was not the time to say so. I said instead, "Are there no girls' things in this nursery other than the dollhouse and the dolls?"

The boys immediately lost interest in showing me the toys.

"Of course there are, Mrs. Saunders," said Miss Elleridge, stepping forward. "In fact, the girls and I were just to the village today, where we picked out quite a large collection of paper dolls. And this cupboard over here holds the toy tea sets and some material and silks and designs for making samplers."

"I didn't go to buy paper dolls," Caroline informed me. "I don't like them."

"I did not tell Miss Elleridge to buy them for you, Caro; I told her to buy them for your cousins," Savile said. "Unlike you, Maria and Frances like cutting out paper dolls."

"How do you know what they like, Uncle Raoul?" Caroline demanded.

"I asked them," Savile returned mildly. He looked at Miss Elleridge. "Where is Mr. Wilson? I should like to introduce him to Mrs. Saunders."

"Lady Regina asked to see him for a few minutes, my lord. I expect he shall be back shortly."

Savile lifted Jane from his lap and set her on her feet in front of him, then he stood up. Maria and Frances rose as well, and I noticed how they stood as close to him as they could get without actually touching him.

"Come along, Nicky, and we'll show your mother your bedroom," Savile said. "By then, Mr. Wilson should have returned."

We went through a large schoolroom, where there was a big round table that was so old it looked as if it had grown out of the floor like a mushroom, and down a narrow passageway.

"The playroom and the schoolroom are the focal point of the nursery, and there are four passageways leading away from them, rather the way spokes come out from the center of a wheel," Savile told me. "The passageway we are presently in has all of the boys' bedrooms off of it, as well as the bedroom and sitting room for their tutor. The opposite passage has the same for the girls. Then there is a passageway with rooms off it for the nurserymaids, and the fourth passageway is the infants' nursery."

Savile Castle was well set up for children, I thought. Of course, for a family to still be around after almost eight centuries, the production of children would have to be one of their priorities.

I thought about John Melville's comment to me about the unlikelihood of Savile's marrying again and wondered if perhaps Savile's cousin and heir was indulging himself more in hope than in reality.

I was glad to see that Nicky's bedroom was not very different from his bedroom at home — in fact, it might even have been a trifle smaller. He would have been very uncomfortable if he had been put into an elegant room like mine.

As I listened to my son chattering away, I admitted for the first time that Savile had been right when he said that Nicky would be better off in the nursery with the other children.

Mr. Wilson was in the playroom by the time we returned, and I was relieved to find that he did indeed seem a sensible, trustworthy young man. His hazel eyes met mine directly and his smile was full of natural good humor. I managed to get him aside for a few minutes to inform him that Nicky did not know how to swim, and he assured me that he would be particularly vigilant whenever the boys were in the vicinity of the lake.

Then it was the nursery dinner hour, and Miss Elleridge, in the nicest possible way, made it plain that Savile and I were de trop. Three nurserymaids were clearing the large table in the middle of the room and setting out china and silver plate when the earl and

I went back down the staircase that led to the passageway next to my bedroom.

The earl did not stop to chat. "Our dinner will be served in an hour," he said briefly. "We'll gather in the drawing room as usual."

"Yes, my lord," I said formally, and turned aside to open my bedroom door. When I turned back to close it, he had disappeared, his feet perfectly silent on those conveniently carpeted stairs.

I wore my old yellow muslin evening dress to dinner. There was nothing I could do to improve its looks; it would have to serve as a regular alternative to my blue. I simply had nothing else.

The maid whom Lady Regina had sent to help me dress looked at it with an incredulity she tried without success to disguise.

"I know," I said gloomily. "I actually do have one very nice evening dress, but as I can hardly wear it every night, this one is going to have to be put back into service." I stood in front of the cheval glass and smoothed the muslin over my hips. The plain scoop neck and puffed sleeves looked pitifully out of date.

"You could tie a velvet ribbon around your neck, ma'am," the maid, whose name was Mary, suggested. "That has become very fashionable lately, particularly if you have a pin to attach to the ribbon."

I gave her a pleased look. "I do have a pin," I said. "It's a small cameo brooch that once belonged to my mother."

"Let me go and get some ribbon, ma'am, and we'll see how it looks," Mary suggested.

Mary's arrangement actually looked quite nice, and consequently I went down to the drawing room with a little more confidence than I might otherwise have felt.

All the Melvilles with the exception of Savile were gathered in front of the bronze statue of King James. The first person who saw me when I walked in the door was Roger Melville. He smiled at me, his blue eyes celestial.

"Mrs. Saunders, how wonderful to see your lovely face. We have all grown extremely tired of what is a relentlessly family party and are thrilled to have a non-Devane amongst us." He paused, then added guilelessly, "Oh dear, perhaps I should not have said that."

I felt myself grow rigid at the implication that I might be a family member through my relationship with George.

"Roger," John Melville said warningly. He turned to me. "How did you enjoy your tour of the estate today, Mrs. Saunders?"

I drew a deep, steadying breath. "I was very impressed, Mr. Melville," I said. "His lordship started off by explaining that the Savile park is not as extensive as the parks of other, newer country homes, but that certainly did not seem to be the case to me."

"You have, of course, visited at so many country homes," Harriet said sullenly.

Everyone ignored her.

"Dear Raoul," Lady Regina said with a chuckle. "In his heart he thinks that everything about Savile Castle and its environs is perfect. I have seen him look down his nose at utterly magnificent vistas while he muttered to me under his breath, 'And they call that a lake?' "

I laughed, and at that moment Savile walked into the room. Our eyes met across the gathered company and I wondered that everyone present did not feel the sparks that instantly leaped between us.

Powell appeared in the doorway almost immediately after the earl. "Dinner is served, my lady," he announced correctly to Regina, and we began to line up for the nightly procession into the dining room.

The earl escorted Harriet, whose waistline was noticeably larger when she heaved herself out of her chair; Roger escorted Lady Regina, who appeared much more mobile than Harriet even though her waistline was almost as large; and the ever-pleasant John Melville got me.

"Any news from your father, Harriet?" Lady Regina asked courteously when we were all sitting around the table in the family dining room and the soup course was being served.

"Yes, I received a letter from him today," Harriet said. She peered eagerly into her soup plate to see what it contained, then picked up her soup spoon. "His business is taking longer than he thought and he is going to be delayed a few more days."

"Thanks be to God," John Melville murmured softly, and I could see his sentiment reflected upon every Melville face at the table, Savile's included.

Harriet began purposefully to eat her soup, and Lady Regina turned to make conversation with me. "How is your son getting on with my boys, Mrs. Saunders?"

"Very well, thank you."

From the one sip of soup I had taken I knew it was mulligatawny and too heavily seasoned with curry for my taste. I put down my spoon.

I said to Lady Regina, "I spent almost an hour in the nursery this afternoon and was very surprised to discover that what appears to have impressed Nicky most is Theodore's battle arrangement."

Lady Regina cast her eyes upward. "Theo and his soldiers," she said with resignation. "I don't know where he gets his bloodthirsty tendencies — not from my husband, certainly."

"He gets them from his Melville blood, Ginny. How can you even ask?" Roger had finished his soup and now he put down his spoon. "We've always been a violent lot. How do you think this castle got built in the first place? As an abbey?"

Lady Regina frowned.

"All small boys like to play with soldiers, Ginny," Savile said soothingly. "It doesn't necessarily mean that Theo will be wanting Gervase to buy him a cavalry commission."

"I must tell you that I was deeply surprised to see how interested Nicky was in the soldiers," I confessed to Lady Regina. "I think it was the battle formation that fascinated him. It was really quite detailed."

"Theo insisted that it had to be exact," Savile said. "I had to look up every single regiment so that he could place them exactly where they were on the fateful day. It is that interest in the details of the real world that is so interesting about Theo. And *that* reminds me of Gervase, Ginny. All mathematicians must be interested in exact details."

Lady Regina bit her lip. "Do you think so, Raoul?"

He nodded. "Now, when I play soldiers with Charlie, we make up our own battles. Charlie is interested only in what he can generate from his own imagination."

Lady Regina must have read my feelings on my face because she suddenly smiled at me and said, "You didn't know that my brother still plays with toy soldiers, Mrs. Saunders?"

"No," I said, "I did not."

"It is one of my most closely guarded secrets," Savile said. "I rely on you, ma'am, not to give me away."

I could not look at him. "Never," I said lightly.

The too-spicy soup went out and the fish, a boiled carp, came in. The wineglasses were refilled.

"And do you cut out paper dolls too, Raoul?" Roger asked sweetly as he took an overlong drink of his wine.

"Not as frequently," Savile replied. "Caroline still likes the active toys her brothers use, and until this summer I had no other little girls to play with."

Harriet shot him a suspicious look.

"My girls should not be playing," she said.

"They should be studying their letters and their numbers. They should be learning to draw and to play an instrument."

I said, unwisely, "All children need to play."

Harriet glared at me. "Yes, you're such an expert on children, aren't you? You're an expert on how to get them, at any rate!"

Savile started to say something, but suddenly I had had quite enough of Harriet.

"Lady Devane," I said, "I do not know what unfortunate circumstances in your own marriage have left you so embittered, but I can assure you that I am not connected with them. If you suspect your husband of having had an affair with me, then allow me to assure you that that did not happen. My own marriage was an exceedingly happy one, and my son is well loved by me and was well loved by my husband. I have no idea why Lord Devane left a sum of money to Nicky, but I suspect it had to do with things farther back in the past than relate to either you or me."

I pushed my fish plate out of my way and leaned forward. My voice deepened as I said with crystal clarity, "And if I find that you have disturbed my son's peace of mind by suggesting that he might be connected to Lord Devane — in any way at all — I will see to it that something extremely unpleasant happens to you."

My voice sounded so menacing that I actually frightened myself.

Absolute silence reigned in the room. I happened to glance at one of the footmen standing by the sideboard and saw a surprised little smile on his face. It was quickly gone, however, as his expression returned to one of gravity and disinterest.

"Bravo," John Melville said to me under his breath.

Roger's eyes were large and bright. "What do you have to say to that, Harriet?"

Harriet's slanted brown eyes were burning into mine.

"I hope you understand me, because I mean it," I said.

Her eyes shifted. I could imagine her thinking of all of Aunt Margaret's deadly herbs. "I understand you," she muttered at last.

I leaned back. "Good," I said.

The earl said coolly, "I believe we are ready for the next course, Powell."

CHAPTER 15

After dinner the ladies withdrew to the drawing room and the men remained in the dining room with their port. I did not excuse myself tonight but instead talked to Lady Regina; we shared stories of what it was like to be a mother. Harriet sat in brooding silence, staring into the empty grate of the fireplace.

Somewhat to my surprise, I found myself feeling quite comfortable with Savile's sister. She was truly involved in the upbringing of her children, not the kind of woman who shuffled them off to the convenient care of nursemaids and tutors and then forgot about them. That involvement gave us a common ground.

"It is true that I was brought up here at Savile," she told me, "but the house I presently live in is nothing more than a simple gentleman's residence. My husband is not a poor man, but neither is he vastly wealthy. It is only when they come to Savile that my boys get a taste of what it is like to live this sort of life."

Lady Regina might not be wealthy, I

thought, but I was quite certain that she was rich as Croesus compared to me.

"Devane Hall is not as imposing as Savile Castle either," Harriet said, making her first contribution to the conversation, "but Papa has poured a great deal of money into improving it." She set her jaw in a way that gave her an unfortunate resemblance to a bulldog. "It isn't fair that Roger should get the benefit of all of Papa's money."

I had noticed before that Harriet's speech was much more genteel than her father's and had wondered how that came to be. It was only later that I discovered that she had been sent away to school in Bath when she was a child so that she could learn to be a lady. The first thing they had corrected was her speech. Unfortunately, the one thing they had not been able to correct was her soul.

It did not take the gentlemen very long to rejoin us and it did not take Savile very long after that to propose showing me the rose garden.

"I would like to say good night to Nicky first," I said, glancing toward the doorway as if it were an escape route from deadly danger. Perhaps after I made my good nights in the nursery I could decently retire to my own bedroom, I thought.

"We'll have the children brought down to us, shall we?" Lady Regina asked, effectively scotching my scheme. She wrinkled her nose. "I am not precisely in the condition to favor climbing all those stairs more than twice in one evening."

I felt immediate contrition. "Of course you are not, my lady." I took a deep breath and added heroically, "Nor is Lady Devane."

So the children were fetched, and the Nicky who bade me a buoyant good night did not seem the same boy who had huddled next to me on the seat of Savile's phaeton that morning.

He's beginning to grow up, I thought.

Once the children were out of the room, Savile turned once more to me and again proposed showing me the rose garden. Everyone else in the room began ostentatiously to talk at once as I accepted, trying not to betray by a quiver in my voice the sudden loud beating of my heart.

"Aside from the kitchen garden, the rose garden is the only garden that lies within the castle walls," Savile informed me genially as he escorted me toward the French doors that led off the drawing room onto the wide stone terrace. "There are more extensive gardens, of course, beyond the eastern wall, but we'll save those for another day."

Behind me I heard Lady Regina ask John Melville what he thought of the new brewer's building.

We walked across the terrace to steps that led down to a stone-paved path that followed the perimeter of the entire house. The sides of the path were planted with lady's mantle, lavender, and achillea, which also grew in pockets between the stones of the pathway, giving the whole picture a lovely look of relaxed abundance. We turned the corner of the house in silence, passed under high hedges topped with a rose arch, and entered into the rose garden.

It was quite gloriously beautiful, so artfully managed that it looked utterly natural even though I knew that this could not possibly be the case. Climbing roses grew everywhere, even up the old medieval castle walls. There were white roses with glossy dark foliage, roses of a pale, delicate pink, and brilliantly colored yellow roses, brighter than butter. There were magnificent plantings of beautiful shrub roses, the colors a deep red, pink-red, and white, and sprinkled in among all these displays of the queen of flowers were poppies, geraniums, and lady's mantle.

We stopped to look around and to inhale the heady fragrance.

"It is beautiful, my lord," I said sincerely.

273

"Everything about your home is utterly beautiful."

I could tell from the look on his face that my words had pleased him.

It made me feel very happy to have pleased him.

Things were clearly going from bad to worse with me.

We walked through the garden, ostensibly admiring the flowers, but all the while we both knew that we were here for something else. Then we were standing next to the great medieval wall and looking up at the setting sun, which was glistening off the chimney pots on the roof of the house. Savile put his hands on my shoulders and turned me so that my back was to the wall and I was facing him. The sinking sun shone slantingly onto his face, gilding his skin and his hair. The look on his face as he scanned my countenance was hard and intent, not at all his usual genial expression.

He said, "I have not been able to get you out of my mind. You haunt my nights, and lately you have even been keeping me from my work during the daytime hours as well."

"Oh," I said brilliantly. My heart had begun to hammer in my chest and the pulse to race in my throat. I put my hand up to my neck to hide it from him.

"I want you to know that you're perfectly free," he said. "I didn't invite you here to pressure you into becoming my mistress. You are welcome to remain here for as long as you want. John will find a new establishment for you, just as I promised he would, and I will leave you strictly alone."

I didn't speak. I couldn't speak.

"Do you understand me, Gail?" he said. "My desire for you has nothing to do with how welcome you are in my home."

"Yes," I said, my mouth dry. "I understand, my lord."

A tendril of hair had fallen forward across my forehead and he reached out to brush it back, letting the lock slide through his fingers as if he were feeling the texture of silk. The touch of his fingers sent shivers through my entire body.

"All you have to do," he said, "is say no."

I swallowed and tried to speak, but words just wouldn't come. He waited. Finally I whispered, "I don't know."

He raised his hands and cupped my face as if it were a rose he was admiring. He bent his head to mine and kissed me.

My back was against the hard stone wall and my face was turned up to his. He kept on kissing me and after a moment I opened my lips and kissed him back. His strong body was pressed against me, and of its own volition my body softened and bent into place along the hard lines of his.

I reached up to slide my arms around his neck and the rest of the world seemed to disappear. I no longer smelled the roses or felt the stones of the wall through the thin muslin of my dress. All I felt was the body of this man as it pressed against mine, the demand his mouth was making on mine, and the desire that was rising within me with all the vitality of sap rising in the springtime.

He had me hard up against the wall by now and his hands had come up to caress my breasts. Our mouths explored each other's hungrily, and my hands moved urgently up and down his back, feeling the strength of it even through his expensive black superfine coat.

I was lost, and we both knew it.

A voice broke through the intensity of our mutual desire.

"Raoul, where are you?"

Lady Regina had to repeat herself three times before we managed to break away from each other.

We stood a few feet apart, trying to catch our breaths and straighten our clothes. Savile's hair was hanging over his forehead and wordlessly I smoothed it back for him.

Savile's raw-sounding curse was still rasping in my ear when his sister and his cousin John joined us in the garden. "Harriet and Roger are going at it with a vengeance, so we decided to escape and join you," Regina said pleasantly.

"I can well imagine that there is no love lost between the two of them," I said evenly, proud that my voice was under control. I was extremely grateful for the rapidly failing light, however, as I was very much afraid that my lips were swollen. Fortunately, my hair was too short to become really disordered.

"So how do you like our rose garden, Mrs. Saunders?" John asked.

"It is very beautiful," I replied.

"I was just telling Mrs. Saunders that the rose garden is a new addition to the grounds," Savile said.

His voice sounded perfectly normal as well.

He turned to me and continued, "Originally this section within the walls housed many of the outbuildings. That is why the bedrooms look out on the kitchen garden and not on the rose garden. The original occupants did not wish to look from their bedroom windows and see the bake house and the potting shed."

"One can perfectly understand that, particularly when the kitchen garden is so pretty," I said. I feigned a small yawn. "I beg your pardon, but I must be more fatigued than I had thought."

"Tea will be served in less than half an hour," Lady Regina told me. "Shall we all return to the drawing room?"

We returned to the drawing room, and since no one stared at me I imagined that what I had been doing in the garden was not emblazoned on my face. I drank my tea and ate a slice of buttered bread, then took my candle from among those laid out near the drawing-room door and made my way upstairs to my room.

The bedroom windows were open to the warm summer air and I went to stand in front of them and listen to the sounds of the night. Somewhere a nightingale was pouring out its soul in ecstasy and I felt a lump come into my throat.

Mary came into the room with quiet efficiency and asked if she could help me undress. I accepted her assistance with a smile, and when she offered to have my yellow gown pressed so that it would be ready for the day after tomorrow, I accepted that offer as well. I got into bed and waited until she had left, then I rose and returned to the windows.

The nightingale was still singing and I shut my eyes and listened, breathing in the scents of the night and trying not to think. Then, very slowly, I went to the wardrobe and took down from the top shelf a package of herbs.

I remembered so vividly the day that Aunt Margaret had given me my first packet of this particular herbal mixture. It had been precisely one week before Tommy and I were married, and she had come to my bedroom and handed it to me and said, "Wait to have children, Gail. You are so young. You and Thomas need to establish yourselves. Take a dose of these every day, and wait."

Aunt Margaret had been too late with her herbal mixture, however. Six months after Tommy and I were wed, Nicky was born.

I looked now at the package I had brought with me from Deepcote. After Nicky's birth I had realized that Tommy and I could not afford another child, and I had begun to make the mixture myself. I assumed it was efficacious, as for the duration of my marriage I had never found myself in the family way.

After Tommy's death I had never had occasion to use those herbs, but I had brought them with me to Savile. My decision to become Savile's mistress had been made before that kiss in the garden.

It took him almost an hour and a half to come. I had left the candle burning next to my bed and was sitting up against my pillows, looking at the pages of a book but registering very little, when I heard a soft knock at the bedroom door.

"Come in," I called quietly.

The door opened and he was there, so tall that his head barely cleared the doorway. He was wearing only his white dinner shirt and his dress trousers. He shut the door behind him and said, "I was stuck in the library with Roger. I was beginning to think I was never going to get rid of him."

I closed my book and put it on my bedside table. "I knew you would come," I said.

At that he began to cross the room in his distinctively long, lithe stride.

"Gail," he said. He reached the bed, then sat down on its edge and looked for a lengthy, searching moment into my eyes. What he saw there must have reassured him, because he lifted one of my hands, turned it, kissed the blue veins that were visible at my wrist, and murmured, "Thank God."

Under his lips, my pulse accelerated like that of a racehorse.

"My lord," I breathed.

He looked up. "Raoul," he said. "I want

to hear you call me Raoul."

I wet my lips. I tried to slow my breathing, slow my pulse. I said, "Raoul."

He smiled his wonderful smile. "It seems as if I have been waiting forever to hear you say my name."

He was like sunshine — warm, life-giving sunshine, and imperceptibly my body lifted toward him.

He kissed me, his body bending over mine, his fingers resting on my neck, his thumbs rubbing gently up and down my collarbone. He kept on kissing me, and my arms went up to circle him and hold him close.

I kissed him and kissed him, loving the feel of his strength against me, the feel of his shirt under my hands, the smell of his skin, the texture of his hair.

His mouth finally lifted from mine and moved down to follow the line of my arched throat. "Gail," he muttered. "God, Gail, what you do to me."

"Mmm . . . The feeling is reciprocal," I said shakily.

He pressed me back against the pillows and I felt his hands beginning to move on my all-too-responsive body. I placed my hands between us and began to unbutton his shirt. He lifted himself away from me, balancing on his hands and remaining perfectly still until I had finished. Then I pulled his shirt free of his trousers and slid my hands under the loosely hanging cambric to touch his warm, bare skin. And once again he moved.

How can I describe what happened between us that night? The mechanics of love are the mechanics of love, and I suppose what happens between one set of lovers does not vary so very much from what happens between another. What differs, however, is the feeling. What differs is the fire, the passion, the intensity. The tenderness.

That night Raoul and I became lovers. When I felt him surge inside me, when I held him close and felt him penetrate deeply into my body, making us one, we became lovers. When I felt the hot, drenching pleasure that his thrusting organ gave me, when the piercing beauty of the nightingale entwined itself indistinguishably with the way his golden body moved with mine on the moonlit bed, when at last my insides rocked with explosions of pleasure so intense that my whole body shook with them, then we became lovers. And after it was over, when he lay quietly with his body all along mine and his golden head resting in the hollow between my neck and shoulder, I knew that no other man would ever mean to me what this man did.

That thought should have made me sad, because I knew I could not have him. But the summer was only beginning then, and I had not yet begun to dwell upon the fact that eventually we would have to part.

Raoul left me sometime during the early morning and we met again at breakfast. He was at the table when I walked in, and the smile that he gave me was little more than the deepening of a fold at the corner of his eye.

My heart completely turned over.

I went to get a plate of food from the sideboard and took a place at the table that was not next to him.

Lady Regina was the only other person at the table and she gave me a pleasant greeting.

"John and I are going to inspect the new outbuilding work this morning, Mrs. Saunders," Raoul said, "but the boys have coaxed me to have the bathhouse pool filled so that they can swim this afternoon. Would you care to have lunch on the bathhouse grounds while the children enjoy themselves?"

"Nicky does not swim," I said.

"So you have told me. But he really should be taught, and that is one of the reasons I agreed to fill the pool."

"All of my boys learned to swim in the bathhouse pool," Lady Regina said. "So did Raoul and John and I, for that matter. If Nicky is to spend the summer here at Savile, I think it would be wise for him to learn to swim."

I looked at her in surprise. "Do you swim, Lady Regina?"

She smiled at me. "Yes, I do. And since you are visiting here for the summer, I would like you to call me Ginny, and for you to allow me to call you Gail."

I looked at her in stunned surprise. Considering the way she had received the news of what bedroom I had been given, I would never have expected such congenial treatment.

"Th-that is very kind of you, Lady Regina," I said.

"Ginny," she corrected firmly.

"Ginny," I repeated faintly.

She looked at her brother. "Do you mind if I join your picnic this afternoon, Raoul?"

He had been regarding her with an oddly thoughtful expression, but his response to her question was instantaneous. "Of course not. I shall extend the invitation to the rest of the family as well."

Ginny sighed.

I brought the subject back to the issue that

concerned me most. "Just who is going to teach Nicky? Mr. Wilson?"

"I am quite sure that the boys have managed to extract a promise from my brother to swim with them," Ginny said.

Raoul chuckled. "Don't worry, Mrs. . . . ah, *Gail*." He gave his sister his blandest smile, then turned back to me. "I taught both Charlie and Theo to swim. I am sure I will have no problem with Nicky."

I didn't think he would, either.

"Now, Ginny," Raoul said, "shall I have them send out the china and crystal for you to dine off of, or do you merely want a basket luncheon with a few footmen?"

"The basket luncheon," Ginny said immediately. "We shall have to feed the children as well."

"Excellent," Raoul said. He stood up. "I told John I would meet him in fifteen minutes, so I hope you ladies will excuse me."

We assured him that we would, and I forced my eyes not to follow him as he left the room.

CHAPTER 16

After breakfast Ginny took me for a walk in the gardens that lay beyond the castle walls. We descended the terrace steps and took the path that would lead us by the stables, which were partially screened from our view by several plantings of evergreens. It was amazing to me how the relatively small area within the castle walls had been so completely transformed from what must once have been a teeming medieval household into the elegantly ordered surroundings of a nineteenth-century nobleman.

"Raoul has had the stable block almost completely rebuilt in the last five years," Ginny told me as we strolled along the stone pathway. "The carriage house in particular was quite ancient and it was also much too small to house my brother's collection of vehicles, so he had it torn down and completely rebuilt. He even installed a carriage wash!"

It was a beautiful summer morning, and the Savile flags that topped each of the four castle towers were rippling in the soft southeasterly breeze. The path took us closer to the stables and I looked at the impressive stone buildings that were spread in front of us.

"None of the buildings looks new," I said.

Ginny gave me a pitying look. "Of course they don't. They look exactly as they always did, only bigger. Raoul insisted that the new carriage house must be built of exactly the same stone as the old one. The masons were able to use some of the stone from the original building, of course, but they had to bring in a great deal more from the local quarries."

I thought of all the stone that must have been hauled across the causeway to satisfy Savile's whim.

"It must have cost a fortune," I said before I could stop myself. I felt my face flush. "I beg your pardon, Ginny, I should not have said that. It is none of my affair how the earl chooses to spend his money."

The earl's sister smiled. "It did cost a fortune. And it is costing Raoul another fortune to rebuild the outbuildings as well. He is employing an enormous number of people, however, and God knows that since the war there are far too many people in this country who desperately need work."

I knew that what Ginny had said was true. The great majority of the soldiers and sailors who had defeated Napoleon had returned to an England whose wartime economy had collapsed, leaving them with little or no means of earning bread for themselves and their starving families.

"Yes," I said, "it is a dreadful situation. I am certain the men who are employed here at the castle are very grateful to be working on the earl's rebuilding projects."

"Of course they are," Ginny replied matter-of-factly. "And that is precisely why Raoul has undertaken them. Did he tell you that he has also built a model village to house all of the additional workmen and their families?"

"No," I said quietly, "he did not tell me that."

One reached the gardens by passing through what must once have been a postern gate in the castle walls behind the stable block. Ginny and I emerged from the shadows of the walls, and the first sight I had of the gardens was of a sea of emerald-green grass with sunlight shining off the lake water. I drew in my breath.

"Come and sit down," Ginny said. "I wouldn't mind getting off my feet for a minute or two."

"Of course," I said quickly.

She made a face at me as she led me

toward one of the flower beds. "I'm afraid I am feeling this pregnancy more than I did my other ones. I must be getting old."

I hesitated. Then, since she had been the one to bring up the subject, I asked, "How far along are you?"

"Seven months."

"That is a good enough reason for feeling tired," I said briskly. "You have just walked too far."

She shook her head, pressed her hand briefly to her back, and sighed as she took her seat on a garden bench. She did look tired, I thought.

I sat beside her, looked around me, and exclaimed, "What a pretty garden!"

And indeed it was a very pretty garden. All the flower beds had been separated into individual colors, a pattern that was unusual and quite striking. The white garden in which we were sitting, for example, had a weeping pear, white foxgloves, and silver foliage plants that were particularly beautiful.

A high wall of evergreens separated the garden from what Ginny told me were the castle outbuildings.

"In medieval times the castle had to be completely self-sufficient, of course, and even today we produce most of what is needed for the household right here on the estate," she said. "It is certainly easier and cheaper to brew ale for hundreds of people in one's own backyard than it is to have it hauled from a distant place and then have to store it."

If I had been overwhelmed before by the scale upon which Savile lived, this conversation with his sister served only to intimidate me further.

Ginny got slowly back to her feet. "I will leave Raoul the pleasure of displaying the outbuildings to you."

She turned to go back to the house, saying in a conversational tone, "A man like Raoul should be in the government, of course, but as long as Lord Liverpool and the Tories are in power he will have nothing to do with Westminster."

"Does he cast his vote in Parliament?" I asked cautiously, not wanting to seem too curious.

"Oh, he votes against Liverpool's government all the time, not that it does much good, unfortunately. At the moment they have the majority."

We strolled along in the sunshine, and in my mind I tried to reconcile the fiercely tender lover I had known last night with the great noble I was hearing about today from his sister.

Ginny's words had somehow made him seem very distant from me.

I wondered if perhaps that had been her intention all along.

When we arrived back at the house it was to discover that Harriet had just received a letter from her father saying that he would arrive at Savile later in the day. That gave Harriet a reason to forgo the picnic, which she had not been very interested in in the first place.

Roger was the only one who did not attempt to conceal his glee at Harriet's decision to remove herself from the outing.

"Really, Roger," Ginny scolded him as the three of us waited at the front door for the low-slung curricle and Roger's horse to be brought around, "you must try for at least a modicum of civility when you address Harriet."

"Why?" Roger replied. His pale hair shone like silver in the summer sun and his eyes were as clear and as blue as the sky above us. "I don't like her. I resent her quite bitterly. In fact, I have strong doubts that the expected little bundle is George's at all. I wouldn't put it past Harriet to have gotten herself in the family way just to keep her hold on Devane Hall."

"Roger!" Ginny was truly appalled.

As the same thought had crossed my mind, I was considerably less horrified by Roger's suggestion than Ginny was.

"How can you say such a dreadful thing?" Ginny demanded.

"Easily," Roger assured her.

At that point, the horses arrived from the stables. Roger swung up into the saddle of his bay Thoroughbred, and two footmen assisted Regina into the low front seat of the curricle. I got in on the other side and picked up the reins, and one of the footmen climbed into the seat behind us. We headed toward the causeway.

The sight of a Greek temple nestled under wide-spreading English oaks was still incongruous to me, perhaps even more so today as a picnic had been set out on the perfectly scythed English lawn. Lawn chairs were set in a circle in the shade of one of the oaks, and baskets of food and flagons of drink reposed upon a large trestle table that was covered with a pristine white linen tablecloth.

From within the equally white columns of the bathhouse came the shrieks of boys' voices and the deeper sound of men's laughter. Roger went to stand in the doorway and look in, offering comments, while Ginny and

I went to sit in the lawn chairs under the trees.

"Raoul and John," Ginny said to me over the voices and the sounds of splashing. "I often wish my husband would play with his children the way my brother does, but it is just not his way."

"I believe some men relate to their children better as they grow older," I said.

"Yes, I believe that is true." She shook her head. "Gervase loves his boys, of course, but in fact it is Caroline who can get him to do anything. She manipulates him shamelessly."

"She is a beautiful little girl," I said sincerely.

"She is a handful," Ginny returned. "The tantrum she created when I said she could not come today! But she would have insisted that she be permitted to swim with the boys, and that I simply could not allow."

The two of us talked on about our children. Eventually the splashing from within the temple stopped, and, about half an hour after we had arrived, the gentlemen emerged to join us for lunch.

My eyes went immediately to Raoul. He was wearing a blue jacket and a shirt with no neckcloth, so the strong column of his neck was bare. His neatly brushed wet hair looked light brown, not gold. He said to his sister, "But where is Harriet?"

"She received word from her father that he would arrive this afternoon, so she decided to wait for him at the castle."

"Oh dear," said another voice. "So Cole really is coming back?"

I looked with a little shock and surprise at John Melville. I had been so completely attuned to Raoul that I had not even noticed his cousin's presence.

A younger voice spoke from the region of the bathhouse stairs. "Did you bring the food with you, Mama?"

"Yes I did, Theo," Ginny said. "I expect you're starving after all that activity."

"Famine stricken," Charlie assured her, clattering down the bathhouse steps in a very unclassical manner.

"Well, go and tell Edward that I wish him to open up the baskets," Ginny said.

I looked at my damp-haired son. "Did you like the pool, Nicky?"

He grinned at me. "I put my face in the water, Mama, and I floated! I just lay there in the water and I floated!"

"Good heavens," I said. In fact, it sounded like the sort of thing a dead body did, and I can't say it gave me a great deal of confidence. I looked at Raoul. "How can learning to put his face in the water help to keep him from drowning?" I demanded.

"It's just a start, Gail," he said peacefully. Then, to Nicky: "Why don't you run along with Charlie and Theo and get some food, Nicky."

Nicky ran off happily, and Savile came to take the chair next to mine. "If one is afraid to get one's face wet, then one can't swim, it's as simple as that," he explained. "That is why the first thing to do in teaching a child to swim is to get him accustomed to getting his face wet. Now that he is comfortable doing that, Nicky will be able to learn how to stroke. He'll be swimming by the end of the week."

John had taken the seat opposite mine, and he must have seen my doubtful look because he joined in to second Raoul. "It's true, Mrs. . . . Gail." He gave me a nice smile. "We're all islanders here, and I can assure you that we know about things like that."

The picnic was perfectly lovely, my first real experience of what it meant to live a life of leisure. The food was plentiful and hearty, tending toward the kind of meat pastries a boy would like rather than the more exotic dishes that I was certain Raoul's mother had served to her guests, and we helped ourselves from what the footmen had laid out upon the trestle table. Raoul had two rowboats tied up on the shore in front of the bathhouse grounds, and had promised that after we had eaten he would take the boys out for a boat ride while John Melville took me in the other boat.

Lady Regina had opted to stay behind to rest in her chair, and Roger said he would keep her company. "I cannot understand this relentless desire you have to keep busy all the time," he complained to Raoul, "but I can assure you that I do not share it."

"I can well believe that, Roger," Ginny said dryly. She poked a cushion behind her back to support it and beckoned to one of the footmen to bring her a footrest. "The most exercise you ever get is the flick of the wrist that it takes to deal the cards!"

Roger was not at all put out. "You know me well, my dear Ginny," he said smoothly.

"I have no intention of conversing with you," she warned him. "I am going to take a nap."

"Dearly as I love your conversation, I can assure you that I will survive an hour or so without it," he said. "In fact, I believe I will take a nap as well."

John looked disgusted.

Raoul looked incredulous.

I said to him, "If that boat overturns, you

promise me you will rescue Nicky?"

He turned to me. His hair had dried while we ate lunch and it once more shone golden in the sunshine. "I promise," he said.

I turned to John. "And if our boat overturns, you promise you will rescue me?"

"I promise," he said with a smile.

"Then let's go, Uncle Raoul!" Theo shouted, and we all moved off toward the boats, leaving Ginny and Roger behind us.

I had an extremely interesting boat ride with John, who was quite forthcoming about the difficult situation that presently prevailed in the Savile household.

We had rowed around to the opposite side of the castle, where the shore was wooded, and John rested on his oars and let the boat drift as we chatted. The afternoon was as perfectly sunny as the morning had been, and for the first time I could see glimmers of Melville blond in his mostly brown hair.

"Poor Raoul," John said. "He is so good-natured that he lets himself be taken advantage of by his family. There is no reason for him to feel any obligation to house Harriet and Cole this summer. Cole is as rich as Golden Ball. He can well afford to take care of his daughter until the child is born, and we all know where we stand in regard to Devane Hall."

I trailed my fingers in the water, enjoying the coolness against my warm skin. I said, "From what I understood from Lord Devane's will, Roger should be able to support himself as well. Didn't Lord Devane leave him a rather large sum of money for just that purpose?"

John snorted. "The money was for Roger to pay off his debts, which Raoul made him do. Roger lived for a while on the power of his being the new Lord Devane, but he wasn't even able to collect one quarter's rents before Harriet turned up in the family way. Once that happened, Roger's credit closed down completely. In short, he is in worse financial trouble than he was before George died. If Harriet's child is a boy, I don't know what Roger is going to do."

I sprinkled a little of the lake water onto the nape of my neck. "Learn to live within his means, I expect," I said.

"I doubt that he will ever learn to do that," John said bluntly. "He never has yet. That's why he comes periodically to sponge off Raoul, and Raoul, as head of the family, can never find it in his heart to turn him away."

"Generosity is an admirable trait," I murmured.

John looked down at his hands, which were resting on the oars. "There is no doubt that Raoul is generous — too generous, some may say."

"Well, I can certainly understand your complaining of his generosity when it saddles you with unwelcome tasks like finding a new home for a strange woman and her horse business," I said lightly.

His brown eyes lifted immediately. "Gail! I never meant you!" he said. "Believe me, I am more than happy to assist you. Nor have I ever before objected to any of the small, simple acts of kindness that Raoul has asked me to perform. It is just Roger and Harriet who rather stick in my craw." He gave me his nice smile. "Please don't take my words as any reflection upon yourself."

I smiled and nodded and allowed myself to be assured that I was just a small, simple act of kindness and nothing more.

I wore my blue dress to dinner, and when I arrived in the drawing room the only ones present were Harriet and her father.

"So you're back again, missy," Mr. Cole said as I marched straight-backed into the room.

"I might say the same about you, sir," I returned.

He was wearing the same type of old-fashioned suit he had worn when I had seen him last and yet another brilliantly hued waist-coat. He stretched his lips in a strange grimace and it took me a moment to realize that he was smiling at me.

"I figure that since we must needs be living under the same roof for the next few months, we might as well be civil to each other," he said.

I shut my mouth, which had dropped open in shock. "Yes," I said faintly. "I will certainly agree to that."

"Mind you, I still don't cotton to the idea of my money going to that boy of yours, but since I'll soon have a grandson of my own, there'll be plenty left for him."

I thought of asking him how he could be so certain that this time Harriet's child would be a boy, but then I decided that such a query would not be in the spirit of his proffered peace.

At that point, Ginny came into the room. "Mr. Cole," she said pleasantly, "I hope your journey was a good one?"

"Thank you, my lady, it was fair," the merchant replied.

Wonder of wonders, I thought. I had been certain that Harriet would have told him of my threat against her and had girded myself to face a blast of hostility.

I had no idea what could have mellowed

his attitude toward me, but I was more than happy to go along with it.

Roger sent word that he was dining with friends in the neighborhood, so dinner at the castle was actually quite civilized. The children came down to say good night, and as I hugged Nicky he gave a big, jaw-cracking yawn.

I chuckled. "I know someone who will sleep well."

"I didn't sleep too good last night, Mama, because the room was strange and I missed you," he confessed. "But I think I will sleep good tonight."

I felt a totally selfish twinge of gratitude that he had missed me. Then I thought of what I had been doing last night and I felt a much deeper twinge of guilt.

"What do you have planned for tomorrow, sweetheart?" I asked.

"Mr. Wilson is going to take us back to the pool so I can practice my swimming in the morning, and then in the afternoon we are going to go for a ride to the Home Woods. Charlie and Theo have a tree house there, Mama, and there is a hermit's cave as well!"

"My, that sounds like fun," I said.

He nodded vigorously. "I'm glad we came

to Savile Castle, Mama. I didn't want to, but now I'm glad we did. I'm having fun."

"It's good for you to have boys your own age to play with," I said.

"That doesn't mean I want to go away to school!" he said hastily.

"There is no possibility of your going away to school, Nicky," I said a little sadly. "We cannot afford it."

In his pleasant, well-bred voice, Mr. Wilson said, "I think it's time we were returning upstairs, Nicky."

I hugged my son and watched him return to the troop of children heading back upstairs to the nursery under the supervision of Mr. Wilson and Miss Elleridge.

Raoul had seemed preoccupied all during dinner, and he excused himself right afterward, saying that he had to go somewhere. He left the house even before the port was served, leaving the rest of us to finish the evening without him.

The time after the children went to bed seemed very long, and by the time I went upstairs after the tea tray had been removed I felt utterly miserable.

He would not be coming tonight and I felt abandoned. I told myself that I was being foolish, that I could not expect him to stop the rest of his life just because he had a mistress, but the fact remained that I felt abandoned.

I dismissed Mary, got into my big empty bed, blew out my candle, and snuggled down, grimly determined to go to sleep.

But sleep would not come. My mind was too filled with what I had heard today from Ginny and from John, and my body was too filled with memories of the sensations that Raoul had awakened the preceding night with his lover's touch, to allow me to find any rest.

Two hours after I had blown out my candle, I heard the faint rattle of the door latch being lifted. I bolted up in bed and watched as a tall, shadowy figure stepped silently into my room, his candle shaded with his hand.

"Gail? Are you still awake?" Raoul asked softly.

"Yes," I said.

He took his shading hand away from the candle and came silently across the floor. He put the candle on the table next to the bed and sat beside me.

"Where were you?" I asked before I could wonder if it was within my rights to question him.

"Out looking for Roger."

"Oh." There was a note in his voice that told me I had indeed overstepped my place.

"I'm sorry I deserted you," he said. He reached out to smooth my tumbled hair off my brow. "I was afraid you might have gone to sleep."

"Well then, you would have just had to wake me," I returned.

He grinned at me, his teeth very white in the darkness of the room. He was wearing riding breeches, not dress trousers, and his shirt was open at the neck and hastily stuffed into his waistband. He looked as if he had been in a hurry, and my heart began to sing.

"I didn't think you were coming," I said.

"Are you mad? I've thought of nothing else all day." He pulled his shirt over his head and dropped it on the floor, stripped off his breeches as well, and swung his long legs into the bed next to me. He said my name, then his body crushed mine down into the softness of the mattress, and soon the words of Ginny and John didn't matter because I couldn't think at all.

CHAPTER 17

"Come for a ride with me tomorrow morning," Raoul said before he left me for the night.

"That would be lovely," I murmured in languorous response.

And so several hours later we met decorously in the dining room under the benign eye of Powell, where I had coffee and a muffin and Raoul had coffee and an enormous plate of everything that was on the sideboard. Then we walked down to the stables to collect our horses.

Raoul swung up onto the back of an immense black Thoroughbred gelding. I had never in my life seen a horse so big.

"His name is Satan, but it's a disgraceful misnomer," Raoul informed me. "He's not even remotely mean; in fact, he's actually timid."

"Timid?" I echoed, looking in amazement at the huge black standing quietly under his rider in the misty morning air, while a groom tightened the girth of my saddle.

"He was a complete failure in the hunting

field — afraid of the hounds, afraid of the horns, afraid of the fences. I use him to hack about the estate, which is all he's good for."

"Why do you keep him?" I asked curiously. A fearful horse is not a joy to ride, as the fright-and-flight reflex is particularly strong in this type of animal.

"I couldn't sell him; he is just the sort of horse who would be sure to be abused," Raoul said. "And I can't just pass him off to someone else on the estate to ride. You see, under this intimidating exterior of his, he has an extremely sensitive soul. The grooms all tell me that whenever I go away to London and leave him behind, he goes off his feed for weeks."

The groom had finished with my girth and I shook off his assistance and swung up into my sidesaddle, hooking my knee around the horn. "You don't take him to London with you?" I looked once more at the magnificent black. "I should imagine he would create quite a stir in the park."

Raoul absently patted Satan's arched neck. "He would be terrified of the city noise. Even new things around the estate and the neighborhood worry him, but he has enough confidence in me to cope with them. London would undo him."

My horse was a delightful little gray Arabian mare, scarcely more than a pony in size but full of spirit. I felt her out as we crossed the causeway and turned to take the path that followed the left side of the lake. Stretching away from the shore on this bank was Humphrey Repton's spacious lawn interspersed with clumps of trees and gracefully grazing deer. We cantered side by side along the wide, grassy path and I noticed how easily Raoul was able to regulate Satan's stride to match the shorter stride of my little gray.

Several miles of park lawn rolled by us and then the path left the open and passed into what Raoul told me was the Home Woods, where Nicky and the boys were going to spend the afternoon. Once we were beneath the trees, Raoul slowed Satan to a walk and I did the same with Narsalla, and he pointed out the different walks to me and explained about the tree house and the hermit's cave. We emerged from the woods just at the place where the lake narrowed into the river and the small wooden bridge crossed the swiftly flowing stream. We continued upriver and after a few miles the landscape changed to fields of ripening wheat. Farmhouses stood along the road, and Raoul told me that all of the land within my vision belonged to the Savile estate and was let out to tenant farmers. We stopped before one of the farm-houses and he turned to me and said, "Do you mind if I look in here for a minute?"

"Of course not," I replied.

No one was about, so he dismounted from Satan and opened the gate for both of us. We tied our horses, then Raoul knocked at the neatly painted blue front door.

It was answered by a worn-looking woman in a faded orange dress. Two little girls peeked out at us from behind her skirt.

"My lord!" she said, her pale blue eyes widening in surprise. "I didn't know you'd be coming." Her hand went nervously to smooth down her already-smooth hair. "I have naught prepared . . ."

Raoul smiled and waved his hand in dismissal. "There is no need to prepare to receive me, Essie. You should know that. I heard about Hal from Mr. Melville. How is he doing?"

The worn face looked even more drawn. "You heared that he broke his leg, my lord?"

"Yes."

"It's bad, my lord. Doctor said he can't get out o' his bed fer a month at the least."

"So Mr. Melville said." Then, gently: "May I see him, Essie?"

She blinked and seemed to come out of a trance. "O' course, my lord! O' course!

Come in, come in!" She stepped aside and said in a low voice to her daughters, "Go out back and play for a little, girls."

The children disappeared as Raoul and I came into the house.

"I have brought Mrs. Saunders with me," Raoul said, introducing me to the woman. "She and her son are staying at the castle for the summer."

The woman bobbed me a curtsey. "How do, ma'am."

Raoul looked at me. "Would you mind waiting while I make a brief visit?"

"Of course not," I replied. "Take as long as you like." I smiled at the woman. "I know how tedious it is to keep a man tied to his bed. I'm sure you need all the assistance you can get."

She gave me a tentative smile in return. "That's so, Mrs. Saunders. My Hal has been like a bear in a cage ever since this happened, I kin tell you." She rubbed her hands in a nervous gesture and asked even more tentatively, "Would you like to come to the kitchen and take a cuppa tea?"

"That sounds lovely," I returned promptly.

Essie and I were drinking tea in the kitchen when Raoul sought me out. She jumped to her feet when she saw him in the doorway and regarded him anxiously.

Savile said, "Well, he's still not happy about his leg, but I think he is easier in his mind, Essie. I just told him not to worry about this quarter's rent, and if the wheat crop is lost we can dispense with next quarter's as well. I think I can get some help in here for Hal, though. Enough, at any rate, that you won't lose your crop."

The anxiety lifted from the woman's face like magic. "Oh, my lord! I knew you would be understanding! I kept tellin' Hal that he had naught to worry about. 'His lordship will take care of us,' I said. But he *would* worry!"

"Of course you should have known that I would be understanding. Did Mr. Melville not tell you not to worry?"

"Well, he did that, my lord, but he didn't give us no specifics like."

"Well, now you have them," Raoul said easily. "I will ask Mr. Melville to hire a general workman to be around the house to help you, Essie, and then when the time for the corn harvest comes, we'll hire a crew of migrant workers to help you out."

"You were very generous," I said as we returned along the road by which we had come. "So generous, in fact, that aren't you afraid that all of your tenants might decide to break their legs? It's far easier to lie in bed and let someone else do your work for you, I should think."

Raoul chuckled. "I don't think there is any fear of that. Hal Jenkins is an exceptionally good tenant — hardworking, honest, loyal. His family have had that farm for over a hundred years. Hal is utterly miserable at being forced to lie in bed, and everyone who knows him knows that as well."

The sun had burned through the morning mist by now and it gleamed off Satan's shiny black coat. Under that huge, muscled exterior might lie a timid, sensitive soul, but there could be no doubt that he was a splendid-looking animal. He and Raoul made a magnificent pair.

"Are you wearing those black boots to match your horse?" I demanded.

He laughed down at me. "How did you guess?"

By now we had reached the wooden bridge just above the Home Woods, and Raoul said, "Let's cross over and go home along the other shore. That way we can look in at the bathhouse and see if the boys are still in the pool."

I agreed and we turned toward the bridge. It was too narrow for two horses to go abreast, so Raoul went first on Satan.

A third of the way across, the big black

gelding stopped as suddenly as if he'd run into glass. Narsalla almost ran into his rear, the stop was so sudden. Then Satan began to snort and back up, and for a minute I thought Narsalla and I were going to be crushed against the wooden rail by his enormous rear end.

Raoul forced Satan to take a step forward to free us, and he yelled to me, "Get off the bridge, Gail!"

I managed to back Narsalla off the planks of the bridge, and we stood on the shore and watched as Raoul tried to persuade an increasingly frantic Satan to go across. Finally, when the gelding refused to respond to all of Raoul's leg and voice commands, he resorted to giving the black a good whack behind his girth.

At that the horse rose straight up into the air.

My heart lunged into my throat as I watched the gigantic gelding come down and knock into the fragile wooden rails on the side of the bridge.

"Get off of him, Raoul, before he kills you!" I shouted.

Raoul had already come to that conclusion and was dismounting right there on the bridge. Then, holding Satan's reins in his hands, he turned the animal carefully and led him to join me on the shore.

Satan's coat was covered in sweat, his eyes were rolling, and he was trembling all over. He was obviously terrified.

"But what could have happened to frighten him so?" I asked, looking around me at the peaceful morning.

Raoul said in a quiet voice, "It has just occurred to me to wonder if there is something wrong with the bridge."

I stared at him. "What do you mean?"

"The main bridge across the river lies farther upstream," he replied. "This particular bridge is only for the use of the Savile estate, and as you can see it is neither very large nor very substantial. The wooden supports are supposed to be checked regularly as part of the ongoing castle maintenance, but perhaps someone forgot. At any rate, I will have John send someone out here immediately to look them over. You and I will return home by the road on this side of the lake."

"Since the bridge may indeed be damaged, we should put some kind of sign up immediately to keep people off of it," I said. "The boys are supposed to come this way after their morning swim."

"You're right, Gail." He thought for a moment. "There is always rope at the tree house," he said. "I'll go and get it and rope off the bridge at this end. And as soon as we get home I'll send someone out to the bathhouse to warn Mr. Wilson not to use the bridge until it is checked."

He had been patting Satan's neck the whole time we were talking, and the horse was beginning to calm down a little. I thought that most men finding themselves unable to force their horse to their will in front of a woman would right now be beating the poor animal unmercifully in retaliation. I looked at Raoul's gentling hand, at his long, tapering, aristocratic fingers, and felt myself slide a little deeper into love.

"Would you mind walking back to the house by yourself?" Raoul asked as we left our horses in the stable yard. "I want to find John as quickly as possible so that I can have that bridge checked."

"Of course I don't mind," I assured him.

The first thing I did when I got to the house was to go up to the nursery, but unfortunately the boys had already gone. Miss Elleridge was there with the girls, preparing to take them outdoors to play.

"Mr. Wilson took the boys to swim in the bathhouse pool, Mrs. Saunders," the governess told me kindly.

"*I* want to swim in the bathhouse pool,"

Caroline announced. There was a martial glitter in her brown eyes.

"Me too," said dark-eyed little Jane.

Her two blue-eyed elder sisters looked doubtful. "A pool would be awfully scary," said Maria, the eldest. "One might drown."

Frances, the middle child, said, "Swimming is for boys, not girls, Caroline."

Caroline stuck her stubborn little chin into the air. "My papa says that I am just as clever as my brothers. And girls can too swim! My mama can swim. She is going to teach me next year, after the new baby is born."

"I want to learn to swim too," Jane said loudly.

Caroline gave her a lordly look. "Well, if you're nice to me, Jane, perhaps my mama will teach you."

Poor little Jane, I found myself thinking. She would have to spend the rest of her childhood being dependent upon other children's mothers for attention because she surely didn't get any from her own.

I left the nursery and descended the stairs to my room, where I changed out of my riding clothes and into one of my unfortunately serviceable morning dresses. Then I went along the passageway to the Little Drawing Room, which was the comfortable room on the second floor where the ladies

315

liked to gather in the morning. Ginny was sitting at a writing table engaged in writing a letter. She looked up and smiled when I came in.

"Sit down, Gail," she said. "I'm almost finished, and I'd love to go for a walk around the garden before luncheon. I've been indoors all morning."

I smiled and agreed, looking around the room to choose a place to sit.

The room was done in green damask with gilt beechwood chairs with green velvet upholstery. A large, gilt-framed mirror adorned one of the walls, and an armoire, with brass handles made of lion masks, adorned another wall. There was also the writing table, with brass lion-mask handles, at which Ginny was sitting. The windows were open to the summer day and I went to sit on the beechwood chair that was closest to them. I gazed toward the stables and thought about Satan's behavior earlier that morning.

More and more I was beginning to think that Raoul's feeling that something was wrong with the bridge might be correct. Animals have a sixth sense about danger that humans don't possess, and in a fearful horse like Satan, that sense was probably very highly developed.

"Finished," said Ginny, and I turned to

look at her. She was wearing a green muslin morning dress that ended at her ankles, showing matching green leather boots. The dress was highwaisted and full, affording as much concealment as possible for her swelling stomach. Her dark gold hair was brushed into a seemingly casual topknot that had probably taken her maid half an hour to achieve.

I said, "Do you want to change your shoes before we go out?" It had rained last night and if we left the garden paths to walk down to the lake I thought we might run into a few muddy spots.

She gave me a surprised look. "No. I'm wearing boots."

I too was wearing boots, but mine were brown and well worn and sturdy.

She must have seen my thought, because she gave me a sudden smile. "These boots are not as frivolous as they might appear, Gail. They have been through their share of mud puddles, I assure you."

I started to apologize, but then her smile won me over. "Perhaps it's the color that fooled me," I said. "They are such a perfect match for your dress."

"I was reared to be a countrywoman and when I am in the country I know how to dress," Ginny told me. "I have never been one to spend my time parading around garden paths in silk gowns and soft leather shoes."

Her voice was scornful and I thought she might be speaking of someone in particular, but I did not feel it was my place to ask who that someone might be.

We had a very enjoyable walk, wandering across the lawns of the back garden, sitting under the cedar tree for a while, then walking under the trees of the small grove. I told Ginny about what had happened at the bridge that morning and she agreed worriedly that the structure ought to be checked.

We returned to the house in time for luncheon, which was not a formal meal but was served individually as each person arrived in the dining room. Ginny and I were eating fruit and a slice of cold turkey and Harriet and Mr. Cole were industriously tucking into beef pies when John came in, a frown between his brows.

"Raoul isn't here?" he asked.

"No. We haven't seen him," Ginny replied. "Did you have the bridge checked, John?"

"Yes. That is what I want to talk to him about."

"Was there something wrong with it?" Ginny demanded.

"As a matter of fact there was," John replied. He took his place at the table and said to the attentive footman, "I'll have some cold meat and cheese."

I frowned and leaned forward. "What was wrong, John?"

"One of the main supporting beams was broken. If Raoul and Satan had gone out onto the middle of that bridge, the whole structure would have gone down with them. Considering the weight of Satan, it's a miracle that it didn't come down as it was."

I thought of the swiftly flowing river under the bridge, and my whole body felt the crash of Raoul and Satan going through the shattered wooden planks, of Raoul being trapped under Satan's body or his head being struck by one of Satan's hooves as they fell, and I felt physically sick.

"Thank God for Satan, then," I murmured almost to myself. "He sensed something was wrong."

No one appeared to hear me.

"What I want to know," Mr. Cole said angrily, "is what kind of a havey-cavey operation you run here, Melville. Don't you have this property maintained at all?"

John went rigid. "I have a very organized maintenance schedule, Cole. This should not have happened, and I intend to find out why it did."

"Well, I for one will be mighty interested to find out the answer to that question," the merchant boomed. "Any one of us could have gone across that bridge and found ourselves takin' a bath!"

"I can assure you that my inquiries will be most thorough," John said as stiffly as before.

I said, "You have sealed off the bridge, of course?"

"Of course. There are men working on it right now."

At that moment, Raoul came into the room. He took his usual place at the table and listened with no expression on his face as John told him the news about the bridge. Then, still without commenting on the bridge, he turned to his sister and put a letter in front of her.

"A messenger just brought this from Austerby, Ginny. I think you should read it immediately."

She frowned, put down her knife, and picked up the letter. We all watched her with unabashed curiosity as she read.

"Oh my God." She looked up. "Do you know what this says?" she demanded of her brother.

"The messenger told me something about it."

At that moment, Roger walked into the room. He looked at Ginny's white face and said, "But what has happened?"

"There's been a fire at Austerby," Ginny said. "Hallard — my steward — writes that the whole east wing has been burned."

"Are you sure he said the whole wing?" Raoul said sharply.

"Here." His sister handed him the letter. "You read it."

He spread the paper before him and we all sat in silence as he perused the words. He looked up. "It could have been worse, Ginny. The servants all got out. No one was hurt."

"I can't believe this has happened," Ginny said a little hysterically. "And Gervase is away at one of his stupid scientific conferences!"

"You don't mean that," Raoul said evenly. "You're just upset."

"But I can't leave Hallard to see to this all by himself. And I can't go down to Austerby myself just now, either!" Ginny was starting to sound even more hysterical.

"I will go down and take a look for you," Raoul said. "I'll assess the damages and see what really happened and what needs to be done to put the house into shape again." He patted her hand. "I really think that if the fire was as bad as Hallard is indicating, there would have been some fatalities. Let me take a look."

"Would you do that, Raoul?" Ginny asked. "I would be so grateful."

"Of course I'll do it," he replied. "I can leave this afternoon and be there by dinnertime."

"You can put up at the Pelican if the house smells too bad," Ginny said.

"Don't worry about me," he said. "And don't upset yourself! I'll take a look for you and come back with a report tomorrow."

Ginny smiled. "You are the best of brothers," she said.

Across the table, the golden eyes met mine with regret. Tonight, I thought, I really was going to have to sleep alone.

CHAPTER 18

It rained that night and I lay awake for a long time listening to the drumming of the drops against the windowpanes and thinking about my future.

What had I done to myself by coming here to Savile Castle? I had been attracted to Raoul Melville in a way I had never felt before with any other man, and I had let that attraction influence my behavior. I had told myself that a summer's dalliance wouldn't harm anyone, that at the end of it I would walk away with everything that mattered to me still intact. I would have my independence and I would have my son, and what more did I really want?

As I lay awake in my lonely bed, the answer to that question was painfully clear. I wanted Raoul. Two nights and two days had been enough to tell me that. My body wanted him and my heart wanted him, and already I could see that the longer I remained around him the worse it was going to get for me.

I didn't try to fool myself by pretending that this arrangement of ours had any chance of ending respectably. The Earl of Savile would not — could not — marry a widow whose social origins were so far beneath his own; one, moreover, whose child's origins were shrouded in scandal and doubt. No, for Raoul our affair was nothing more than a summer arrangement that would end when John found me a new establishment and I went off to resume my old life, as Raoul would resume his.

Deep down I had known that I was doing wrong when I had taken Raoul as a lover. It certainly hadn't taken God very long to let me know that I was going to be punished.

The real irony of the whole situation was that I was stuck here at Savile for the summer. First of all, I had nowhere else to go, and second, I couldn't find it in my heart to uproot Nicky from a situation that was obviously so beneficial for him.

Of course, I could always tell Raoul that I had changed my mind about us.

Hah! I thought bitterly. I had as much chance of doing that as a peasant had of turning overnight into a prince. For as long as I was within the vicinity of that heart-wrenching smile of his, I would be like putty in his hands.

I shut my eyes and huddled down in my solitary bed.

Don't think about it, I told myself as the rain beat dismally against the windows. *Take the summer one day at a time, and when the day comes for your heart to break, worry about it then.*

The rain stopped before daybreak, and the sun came out strongly enough to dry the lawns and allow Mr. Wilson to take his charges outdoors to play shuttlecock and bowls. These were games that Nicky had played occasionally at neighborhood gatherings at home, but he had nothing that remotely resembled the proficiency of Charlie and Theo. I had accompanied the boys outdoors because I felt the need to be close to Nicky that morning, and I could see that his ineptness both frustrated and humiliated him. This, of course, made me feel terrible.

We met John at the side door as we all moved into the house for luncheon and he asked Mr. Wilson what his plans were for the boys that afternoon.

"We're all going for a ride," the tutor replied with a smile.

I gave him a grateful smile. Nicky was a very good rider and right now he needed to do something at which he excelled. I thought that Raoul had been right when he told me that Mr. Wilson was a very fine young man.

At lunch Roger asked me if I would care to go for a drive with him into Henley, the closest town of any size to the castle. "Savile village is closer, of course, but Henley is a coaching stop and there are several large inns in the town as well as some rather nice shops," he told me with an inviting smile.

"There is even an ice cream parlor," Ginny informed me. "Be sure you make Roger buy you an ice."

Roger lifted his fair brows. "Really, Ginny," he said. "Ices are for children."

"I should like to drive into Henley with you," I told Roger. "It sounds a very pleasant way to spend an afternoon."

Truth to tell, with Raoul gone, time was hanging a bit heavily on my hands. I simply was not accustomed to the role of a lady of leisure.

After luncheon, I met Roger in front of the house and his own phaeton was brought around from the stables. The carriage was an extremely high-perched affair, its body a shiny black with yellow stripes, and it was pulled by a pair of glossy black geldings that were as showy as the carriage. Roger took my hand to assist me up into the perilously high seat, then he joined me, lifted the reins, and with a flick of his whip put the flashy blacks into motion.

For the first ten minutes after we left Savile I was a nervous wreck, but, somewhat contrary to what I had expected, Roger proved to be an excellent driver and I found myself able to relax. Some clouds had come in while we were at lunch, which alleviated the heat of the day and made the afternoon quite pleasant. Henley was on the Folkestone road, and as we drove along, Roger kept up an entertaining flow of chatter that made it easy for me to respond without effort. Fields of wheat and hops rolled away on either side of us and we passed several small villages with their gray stone church spires ascending gracefully toward the sky.

We reached the inn just outside of Henley, the Black Swan, an hour after we had left the castle. Roger pulled up in the bustling courtyard.

"Would you like to stop here for a glass of lemonade?" he asked me with a charming smile.

I would much have preferred to stop somewhere less busy than the active coaching inn and asked if there wasn't somewhere else in town where we could find refreshments.

His charm melted into faintly concealed annoyance. "I need to make a brief stop here, Gail, and I thought perhaps you might feel more comfortable indoors in the parlor than out here in the stable yard."

"I did not realize that you wished to stop," I replied with dignity. "If that is the case, a glass of lemonade will be very welcome."

I allowed him to lift me down from the heights of the phaeton and to escort me indoors.

Since it was after lunchtime and before dinner, the public parlor was empty, and Roger found me a seat at a wooden table, ordered me a lemonade, then disappeared toward the back of the inn.

To be truthful, I thought he was answering a call of nature and paid very little attention to his behavior.

I was sipping my lemonade and looking idly around the old, dark wooden building when a man stopped at my table and said in a distinctly upper-class voice, "Excuse me, but did I see you come in with Mr. Roger Melville?"

I looked up. The man who was looking back at me was remarkable because of his extraordinarily dark, sunburned skin. Only his accent, his tobacco-colored hair, and the paleness of his eyes gave away the fact that he was English. "Yes," I said cautiously. "You did."

The man gave me an enigmatic smile.

"May I further inquire if you came from Savile Castle?"

I was beginning to feel very wary indeed. Who was this man and what did he want?"

"Yes," I said again, "we came from the castle. And may I ask who you are?"

"My name is Wickham," he said casually. Without being invited, he sat down across the table from me. "I was once a friend of George Devane's, but I've been in India for the last eight years."

Needless to say, this was not a recommendation to me. "Oh?" I said coldly. "Well, I am not acquainted with you, Mr. Wickham, and I have nothing to say to you. Good day, sir."

"I know who you are," he said surprisingly. "You are Mrs. Saunders."

His pale blue eyes regarded me as if I were a very interesting specimen he was about to dissect. I did not like the man at all. I particularly did not like the way he was looking at me, as if he knew something I did not know.

I said, "Mr. Wickham, I don't wish to be rude, but I wish you will go away. I am not interested in your relationship with Lord Devane. In fact, I am not interested in Lord Devane, period. I am simply waiting here for the return of my escort, and once he arrives we shall be leaving." I bestowed upon him a dismissive stare. "Goodbye," I said.

He bared his teeth at me in what I imagined he thought was a smile. "You don't mince words, do you, Mrs. Saunders?"

"No," I said baldly, "I do not."

He stood up. "I'm putting up here at the Black Swan for a while. Perhaps I will have the pleasure of meeting you again."

"I doubt it," I replied. "Good day, Mr. Wickham."

He sketched me a mocking half-bow and moved away toward the door of the parlor. I watched him go and wondered who he could possibly be and why he had accosted me in such a manner.

Could Roger have insisted that we stop here so that this man could approach me? But why?

I was still puzzling over this problem when Roger came back into the room. "Are you ready to leave, Gail?" he asked as he stopped at my table.

"Yes," I replied. As I stood up I said, "The oddest thing happened while you were gone, Roger. I was approached by a man named Wickham. He knew my name and insisted on sitting down and telling me all about his friendship with George."

Roger's fair brows drew together. "Did he

bother you, Gail? I'm sorry. I had no idea anyone would have the nerve to approach you in here."

"You don't know anyone called Wickham?" I asked.

"No."

"That's odd," I said. "He knew you."

Roger gave me a sharp look. "What did he look like?"

"He was very dark. He was just back from India, he told me. His eyes were light blue and looked quite extraordinary in his sunburned face."

No sign of recognition appeared on Roger's face. He shook his head. "I don't know him."

The landlord, a tall, rather elegant-looking man, appeared at our table. "That will be two shillings, Mr. Melville," he said to Roger.

"Oh, just put it on his lordship's account, Murchison," Roger said carelessly.

"I am sorry, Mr. Melville, but his lordship told me himself that I was not to charge any more of your bills to his account, that you were to pay for them yourself." The landlord's voice was apologetic but firm.

Roger went white to his lips. "Good God, Murchison! It's not as if two bloody shillings are going to bankrupt Savile." Roger took the coins out of his pocket and threw them on the table so hard that they bounced and would have rolled off it had the other man not put out his hand to stop them. Then Roger stalked out of the parlor.

I was left behind, looking at the landlord. The tall man gave me an apologetic look. "I am very sorry, ma'am, but I did not feel I could disobey his lordship's orders."

"I perfectly understand," I said. "I am just wondering, Mr. Murchison, by any chance did his lordship give you this instruction two nights ago?"

The innkeeper thought for a moment, then apparently decided that there could be no harm in replying to my question. "Why yes, he did."

I remembered that two nights ago Raoul had left the dinner table to go in search of Roger. Apparently he had found him there at the Black Swan, and I would have wagered anything that Roger had been gambling. I wondered if the mysterious Mr. Wickham had been Roger's gambling partner.

I went along out into the stable yard where Roger and his phaeton were waiting for me. I allowed a groom to help me up to the high seat and we pulled out of the stable yard rather faster than was safe.

"Slow down, please," I said sharply. "You

are too close to town to be going this fast."

He ignored me.

"Roger. I said *slow down*."

Very slightly he raised his hands and the blacks speeded up. The phaeton's seat rocked unsteadily. I reached out, grabbed the reins from his hands, and stopped the horses.

He had not expected me to do that, and he swung around to look at me, his blue eyes murderous.

"If you wish to kill yourself, then go and jump in the lake and drown," I said pitilessly. "Don't take innocent people with you."

"I do not want to kill myself," he said furiously.

"Then slow down this phaeton."

We stared at each other, and the anger that emanated from him was so palpable that he frightened me. "Didn't you know that Raoul had cut off your credit?" I asked him finally.

He stretched out his hands for the reins. I put them into his fingers and he began to drive forward again, this time more slowly. "He told me he was going to do it, but when Murchison would not allow me to charge two shillings! Well, I rather lost my temper."

This, I knew, was the only apology I was likely to get from him.

"I am sure that Raoul did not mean for

you to be embarrassed like that," I said soothingly, although privately I thought that Roger could certainly have plunked down two shillings for my lemonade without trying to make Raoul pay for it.

"It is exactly the sort of thing that he would want," Roger contradicted me bitterly. "He wants me to grovel, to be humiliated, and all because the luck has run against me of late. The luck never runs against Raoul! He doesn't know what it means to scramble for money like the rest of us do. He's had complete control of Savile and all its resources since he was twenty-one years old, for God's sake."

"Does Raoul gamble too?" I asked with some surprise.

"Oh, no more than is expected. He doesn't have to gamble — he already has everything."

It seemed to me that Roger's argument was definitely specious, but I thought this was probably not the wisest time to point that out to him.

"That damn woman," Roger said viciously. "This is all her fault. I had the title, I had the property, I could have kept my head afloat perfectly well. And then she turned out to be increasing."

"There is a good chance that you will still

be Lord Devane, Roger," I said. "After all, Harriet has certainly shown a propensity to produce girls."

"That is true." The tense expression on his good-looking face relaxed slightly. "Once I have access to the rent roll of Devane Hall, my financial pressures will be alleviated." He shot me a very blue-eyed look. "Although any extra cash I can put my hands upon immediately will certainly be appreciated."

I thought I knew what he was talking about. "If you can convince Raoul to relinquish Nicky's money to you, then I will agree to it," I told him. "Frankly, however, I think your chances of getting Raoul to agree are slender."

"Well," he said lightly, "it's worth a try."

I gave him a pleasant smile. "Certainly it is. I wish you luck."

The rest of our trip was uneventful, but as we drove home through the cornfields my mind was filled with questions. Roger was evidently in dire need of money. Had he brought me out with him to see if he could get me to agree to his trying to get Nicky's money out of Raoul? And what, if any, was Roger's relationship with Mr. Wickham?

We returned home to catastrophe. John met me at the door with news that Nicky's pony had gone berserk in the woods, throwing Nicky into a tree.

My hands flew to my mouth. "Oh my God," I said through their white-knuckled pressure. "Is he all right, John?" Then, as John hesitated: *"Is he all right?"*

"He's still unconscious," John said. "The doctor is with him now, Gail."

"Unconscious." I began to run toward the stairs. "I must see him."

"He's not in his room," John called after me. "We didn't want to haul him up three flights of stairs, so we put him at the end of the hall here, in the countess's bedroom. Come, I'll take you."

We turned to the right from the Great Hall and went into the withdrawing room, which was the room that separated the public from the private rooms on that side of the house. I had rarely been in this section of the house before, and at the time I was in no condition to notice anything, but later I would discover that the withdrawing room was followed by Raoul's businesslike office, after which came a pretty morning room, and then, at the corner of the house, the countess's dressing room, then finally the countess's bedroom, which was where they had put Nicky.

I noticed nothing about the massive and ancient room as I rushed in the door. All I saw was the small figure lying in the huge, silk-hung bed. An elderly gray-haired man wearing a brown riding coat and brown boots was standing next to the bed talking to Raoul. Ginny stood next to the bed, watching Nicky.

I ran up to the other side of the bed and stood looking down into Nicky's still face. His eyes were closed and he was very pale. I bent over him to touch his cheek with my lips and he didn't move. Terror washed over me. "What happened?" I said through lips so stiff I could scarcely speak.

It was Raoul who answered me. "According to Mr. Wilson, he and the three boys were riding through the Home Woods when it happened, Gail. The ponies were perfectly calm when all of a sudden, for seemingly no reason at all, Squirt went berserk. He reared and bucked and plunged off the path, knocking Nicky's head on a low-hanging branch. Nicky came off, and when they ran to see how he was, he was unconscious. Mr. Wilson brought him back home immediately and we sent for Dr. Marlowe."

The bed was quite high but I leaned over it so that I could scan my son's face carefully. There was an ugly bruise on his right temple.

"His brain has had a shock, Mrs. Saunders," the doctor told me gravely. "It is essential that you keep him quiet, even after he wakes up."

I spoke my deepest fear. "He is going to wake up, doctor?"

"Let us hope so," the doctor said.

My heart jolted. "*Hope so?* Is there a chance that he might not?"

"In these cases, when the injured person is breathing normally as Nicholas is, the patient almost always wakes up, Mrs. Saunders. From what I can determine, he has no serious injury other than the blow to the brain, and we must just wait until that heals itself."

By now I was so terrified that I could scarcely breathe. I bent my head until my lips were close to my son's ear. "Nicky," I said in a voice that was sadly unsteady. "Can you hear me, Nicky? Mama's here."

There was no response on the small pale face.

"Gail," Raoul said softly. "Sit down before you fall down." I felt his hand on my arm. "Come. I've brought a chair for you. Sit down."

I obeyed the pressure of his hand and sat in the chair that he had placed next to Nicky's bed. I put my hand over my son's, and it seemed to me that his fingers stirred slightly under mine. My breath caught in hope, and I looked up at the doctor. "How long?" I demanded. "How long before I can expect him to wake up?"

"It might be a matter of hours. It has even been known to be a matter of days," the doctor said. "But you must not expect him to remember anything of the accident, Mrs. Saunders. That is a memory he will probably never recover."

"I see."

"I will take Dr. Marlowe out, Raoul," Ginny said, and as she passed me she gave me a gentle pat on my shoulder. "He'll be all right, Gail," she said. "You know how resilient boys are."

After Ginny and the doctor had gone out, I looked up at Raoul and said, "Squirt would never go berserk like that."

Raoul's face was unreadable. "What if a bee stung him?"

"He would have run down the path. Squirt's instinct is always to run. He would not have taken Nicky into the woods. What really happened out there, Raoul?"

"I don't know," he replied. Then: "Gail — Squirt is dead."

"*What?*"

"Apparently he had some kind of a fit. Wilson said he had never seen anything like it; after he threw Nicky, the pony just flung himself down on the ground and threw himself around as if he were having a major colic attack."

"Colic does not happen that suddenly."

"Not usually, no, but perhaps Squirt got into something that made him ill."

I thought for a few minutes. "The only thing I can think of that might cause the kind of reaction you are talking about is deadly nightshade, and I certainly cannot imagine that you allow that particular plant within the vicinity of your stables."

"Of course I don't," Raoul said soberly. "In fact, I can assure you that no horse in my stables has accidental access to any dangerous plants."

It was a few moments before the word *accidental* registered with me.

"Raoul?" I said fearfully. "You don't think anyone deliberately tried to hurt Nicky, do you?"

He came to stand next to me and gently smoothed a tendril of my hair behind my ear. "I love your ears and your neck," he murmured. "They are so finely modeled, so delicate."

I pushed his hand away. "Answer me! You *do* think someone tried to hurt Nicky!"

I jumped up out of my chair to face him. His face and voice were very sober. "I don't know how to answer you, Gail, but I will confess that I don't like the way that pony died. And I don't like the way that bridge was damaged, either. John swears to me that it was checked on schedule only last month and that at the time it was fine."

"Oh my God," I whispered.

Then he asked the question that scared me almost as much as Nicky's accident. "Gail, is there any reason you can think of for someone to wish harm to Nicky?"

I looked up at him, making myself meet his eyes. "No," I whispered. "I can't, Raoul."

He said carefully, "There are no . . . circumstances . . . attached to Nicky's birth that might render him vulnerable to an ill-wisher?"

His golden eyes were perfectly nonjudgmental, perfectly steady.

I turned my eyes away from him, back to Nicky. "No," I said. "There are no such circumstances."

"Very well." His voice was quiet. "I had to ask, Gail."

"Yes." My voice now was merely weary. "I suppose you did."

I spent the night in the bed of the Countess of Savile, with Nicky lying comatose beside me. There was a connecting door between the countess's bedroom and the bedroom next door, which belonged to the earl, but no one had even hinted that Raoul's proximity might be improper. It seemed that the circumstances of Nicky's illness took precedence over propriety.

Of course, what no one knew was that Raoul never went to his room at all but settled down in a chair on the other side of Nicky's bed to watch with me over my son. I didn't even suggest that he seek his own bed; my need for the support of his presence was too great.

"I once took a knock on the head like Nicky's," he reassured me. "My horse stopped dead at a jump and I went over his neck and hit the ground headfirst. It took me five hours to wake up, and I survived the ordeal perfectly fine, Gail. And I promise you, so will Nicky."

I was immensely grateful for his encouragement and clung to it like a lifeline.

It was two hours after midnight when I felt Nicky stir a little beside me. I scrambled to my knees and bent over him.

"Nicky?" I said. "Nicky?"

Raoul was beside me in an instant. We had kept the bedside lamp burning all night, so Nicky's face was illuminated clearly enough for us to see that his eyelashes were fluttering.

"Nicky," I said urgently, *"can you hear me, sweetheart? It's Mama. Can you hear me?"*

His eyes opened. "Of course I can hear you, Mama. Why are you shouting at me?"

"Oh thank God," I sobbed. "Thank God."

I felt Raoul's warm hand on my shoulder.

"My head hurts," Nicky said. "It hurts bad, Mama. What happened?"

"You had a fall from Squirt, Nicky," Raoul said. "You have been unconscious for a few hours, and your mother has been quite worried about you. I'm afraid that your head is going to hurt for a day or two."

Nicky frowned irritably. "I fell off Squirt? I don't remember that."

"It doesn't matter," Raoul said calmly. "Dr. Marlowe said that you probably wouldn't remember. There is nothing for you to worry about."

Nicky blinked a few times, as if trying to get us into focus. "Is Squirt all right?" he asked.

"Squirt is perfectly safe," I replied softly. "Now, can you sit up for a little and have something to drink?"

Raoul and I managed to get Nicky up to use the water closet and to drink some water. By that time Nicky was in tears from the pain in his head and all he wanted to do was lie down again. We put him back to bed and I got in beside him and held his hand.

"Go to bed yourself," I said softly to Raoul. "You must be exhausted."

But he sat back down in his chair. "I'll wait until he's gone off again."

It did not take Nicky long.

"He's asleep," I said to Raoul some minutes later.

"That's good." He unfolded his long body from the chair in which he had been helping me keep watch, stood up, and stretched. He came across to my side of the bed and stood there silently looking down at Nicky's sleeping face.

I looked up at Raoul.

His hair was hanging down over his forehead, there was a faint stubble of gold on his cheeks and chin, and he looked tired. More than that, he looked worried.

"You do think he is going to be all right?" I asked urgently.

His eyes moved from Nicky's face to mine and he smiled. "He will be fine, Gail. He'll have a hell of a headache tomorrow, but he'll be fine."

"Well then . . ." I was lying back on some pillows, looking up at him, and I thought that my heart was probably in my eyes. How could it not have been? I said, "Thank you, Raoul. It was a great support to have you beside me tonight, and I appreciate it more than I can say."

"Little Gail," he said. He bent over the bed for a moment and kissed me on the mouth: quick, hard, hungry. "I'll be next door if you need any help with Nicky," he said, and I watched him open the door to his bedroom and go through.

CHAPTER 19

The following morning Raoul instituted a search in the stables to see if anyone knew what Squirt could possibly have eaten to have precipitated such a violent colic attack. The inquiry produced no results.

I wanted to keep the news of Squirt's demise from Nicky for one more day, but Raoul thought that he should be told. It was a measure of how enthralled I was becoming with the man that I acquiesced and broke the bad news to my son.

Nicky was very upset. I knew he would be, but, as Raoul pointed out, he would be upset whenever I told him and it wasn't fair to allow him to go on thinking that his pony was alive when he wasn't.

Raoul's words made sense to my head, but it broke my heart to see my child's pain.

Nicky spent the day in the countess's bedchamber, receiving short visits from the nursery set but mainly sleeping. That evening, as the adults gathered in the drawing room before dinner, Ginny asked me if I wanted Nicky moved upstairs to the nursery for the night.

"He's slept a great deal today and the doctor said he would probably sleep through the night, but if you're worried, Gail, it would be very easy to have one of the nursery maids sleep in his room to keep an eye on him."

I was just about to say that I would stay with Nicky myself when Raoul spoke. "Oh, leave the boy where he is for another night, Ginny. The other children wake up so early that they will disturb him, and Dr. Marlowe wants him to stay in bed for at least another day."

"Very well, Raoul," Ginny said pleasantly. "It will be as easy to set up a trestle bed for one of the nursery maids in the countess's room as it would be in the nursery."

He smiled at her. "That won't be necessary. I'm sure Gail will want to spend the night with Nicky again."

Silence descended on the drawing room. I looked around bravely and surprised an expression of what looked to be profound worry on John's face. Roger looked dismayed, Harriet looked morose, Mr. Cole looked angry, and Ginny looked thoughtful.

Powell appeared in the doorway and said, "Dinner is served, my lady."

We formed our nightly procession and paraded into the dining room. Ginny and

Raoul discussed what had to be done to repair Austerby before she and her family could return to live there. John occasionally joined in with a suggestion, and the rest of us made an effort to converse among ourselves with at least a minimal degree of politeness.

I thought with some nostalgia of Mr. MacIntosh's uncomplicated meals and my equally uncomplicated days at Deepcote before the Earl of Savile had driven into my stable yard and turned my life upside down.

After the gentlemen joined us in the drawing room, Raoul, Ginny, Roger, and Harriet sat down to play whist. I did not know how to play whist and John very kindly offered to walk with me in the garden.

Mr. Cole had disappeared after dinner and no one was interested enough in his whereabouts to inquire after him.

There was a mist off the lake and the night air was chilly enough for me to wish I had brought a shawl. Before I quite knew what was happening, John had taken his coat off and hung it around my shoulders.

The warmth was welcome but the intimacy of the gesture surprised me. I looked up at him with a question in my eyes.

He gave me a rueful smile. "Don't worry,

I'm not trying to usurp Raoul's place."

The darkness hid the rush of color to my face. It was perfectly clear that the entire Melville family knew that Raoul and I were lovers and the situation was not a very comfortable one for me. Raoul, of course, could not know that. He probably had affairs like this all the time, with women of the world, who took such arrangements with perfect *sangfroid.* As long as appearances were maintained, the world of the ton did not care what went on behind the scenes. And Raoul was very good at maintaining appearances, as witnessed by the way he had just used Nicky's illness to get me into the room next to his for the night.

Unfortunately, I was not a woman of the world.

I replied to John in a revealingly small voice, "His lordship has been very kind to me."

"I wonder if he has." John's voice sounded rather grim. "It's clear as a pike to me that you're not the kind of woman to take an arrangement like this lightly, Gail, and I don't want to see you getting hurt."

Well, I was going to get hurt, but that was quite my own fault.

"Don't worry about me," I said in an attempt at lightness. "All I really need is a new place to set up my business. Nicky and I shall be fine."

John said abruptly, as if he had not heard my words, "He won't marry you, my dear. Apart from the social gap between you, there is the matter of Georgiana and the child. I saw what their deaths did to him, Gail. I really don't think he will ever allow himself to go through that again."

"I have never expected Raoul to marry me," I said, my voice steady even though my heart ached. "All I have expected of him is that he will find a new location for me to set up my business." I laid my hand lightly on his arm. "And that job, I believe, he has delegated to you. Have you seen anything suitable, John?"

He let me change the subject and we spent the rest of the twenty minutes we were in the garden chatting about the two places for lease he had investigated and their unfortunate lack of suitability.

The tea tray came in at eleven, and, after eating some fruit that I did not want, I collected a light from the table where the night candles were put out, wished everyone good night, and retired.

I cannot tell you how strange it seemed to walk through the rooms that had once belonged to Raoul's wife. The morning room was done in pink silk and furnished with a davenport desk of rosewood with inlaid lines and brass handles in the form of lion masks. Twin pink-silk-upholstered Sheraton chairs stood along the wall, and flanking the wide, pink-silk-hung window were rosewood bookcases with front grilles. The paintings on the walls were pictures of great urns of multicolored flowers. When Ginny had taken me through the apartment that morning, she had said that this was the room the countess had used to write out her menus and to keep her housekeeping books.

After the morning room came the countess's dressing room, which was absolutely sumptuous. The furniture was mahogany banded with satinwood and everything was covered with pale green silk: the walls, the windows, the chaise longue, the chairs.

"Georgiana had it done up to match her eyes," Ginny had said, with an elusive trace of emotion I couldn't place, and I remembered the beautiful green eyes in the portrait in the Melville gallery.

There had been nothing Georgiana could do with the bedroom to make it modern and elegant, however. The walls were lined with centuries-old tapestries, the furniture was heavy oak, and the room was solidly magnificent, not delicately elegant. The hangings on the bed where my child now slept were embroidered with silver, gold, and pearls, and Ginny had told me that they were more than two hundred years old.

Once, Raoul had lived with the woman who had inhabited these rooms. Once, he had loved her very much. Indeed, according to John, he loved her still.

Reluctantly my mind again summoned up the portrait in the Melville gallery. I remembered the smooth dark hair, the green eyes, the long, slim neck, the unmistakable look of aristocracy stamped on every feature of her face. It hurt me to think of her. It hurt me to think that Raoul had loved her, might love her still. I wished with all my heart that he could love me.

When I bent over the bed to check Nicky, I saw that he was fast asleep and breathing normally. I had been inspecting his breathing all day and had seen nothing to alarm me. It was true that he was sleeping a lot, but when he had been awake he had been perfectly alert. His only complaint had been of a headache.

There was no Mary tonight to help me undress, so I got out of my blue dress with a little more trouble than I had become accustomed to. My nightdress and toiletries were already laid out on the massive oak chest that functioned as a table, and I pulled my white cotton gown over my head, combed my short hair, got into the bed next to Nicky, and leaned back against the pillows, listening to his soft, even breathing.

It excited me unbearably to think that Raoul would be coming to bed in the room next door. I thought of what it would be like to be his wife and to lie thus every night, waiting for him, listening for him, and then I banished the thought from my mind.

Why torture oneself by dreaming of the impossible?

Nicky was lying on his side, and I reached over to put my hand on his shoulder, as if to reassure myself that I was still Gail Saunders and not some strange woman who was inhabiting my body.

I don't know how much time passed before the connecting door between the rooms opened, as I knew it would, and Raoul came in holding a candle. He walked quietly on stockinged feet to the side of the bed and looked down at Nicky.

"Is he sleeping?"

"Yes. He's been asleep since I got here."

Raoul's eyes moved from Nicky to me. "He'll be all right on his own for a little while, Gail," he said.

I drew a deep, unsteady breath. "I don't know. I've been thinking about what you said last night, Raoul, and I don't think I want to take a chance and leave him alone." I swallowed. "What if someone *does* wish harm to him?"

In answer to that, Raoul went through the connecting door into the countess's dressing room. I could hear him locking the door that led into the passageway. Then he returned to the bedroom and did the same for the door in there. "Now the only way to gain access to this room is through my room," he said. He came back to the bedside and stood looking down at me. "Nicky is safe."

He was convincing. "Well . . . if you are certain." Slowly I pushed the lightweight cover off of me and swung my legs around to slide off the bed. My feet hit the carpeted floor and I looked up. Raoul towered over me. "Gail," he said, and put his hands on my waist to lift me up to him. I reached up my arms to circle his neck and my feet came completely off the carpet. Our mouths met hungrily and we kissed like people who had been parted for years.

"Gail," he said again, only this time it sounded more like a groan. We were still locked together, my feet still dangling free of the ground, when he began to walk toward the connecting door to his room. He stopped for a minute, and I felt his arms come under my knees, and then he was lifting me high and carrying me through the door and into another tapestry-hung room where a single candle was burning. He laid me down on the bed and stood beside me for a moment to rip his shirt out of his waistband and pull it over his head.

"I'm sure that is a very nice nightdress, sweetheart, but you are nicer by far," he said. "Do you think we could have it off?"

"I might manage that," I replied breathlessly. And as I divested myself of my prim nightdress, Raoul pulled off his black dress trousers. Then he joined me on the bed.

His hands were all over me, searching out the places where I most liked to be touched, caressing me with fingers that were surprisingly hard for the fingers of an aristocrat. I ran my hands up and down his back, over his ribs, loving his lean-muscled body, which glowed golden in the candlelight. I ran a line of kisses up and down his collarbone, pressed my face against the hollow of his shoulder, and rubbed my hand across the breadth of his chest, feeling my fingers slide through the crisp golden hair that grew there.

There was nothing about him that was not beautiful.

His lips went to my breast, and I sucked in my breath and arched my back as shocks of sensation went from his mouth all the way down to my loins. I put my hands on either side of his head to hold him where he was, and, involuntarily, my legs began to part in welcome.

We said quite a few things to each other as the tempo of our drive toward consummation increased relentlessly. Finally the need became overwhelming and the force of his hard, powerful possession gave me an explosive pleasure that surpassed even what I had found with him before. Then, afterward, when he held me close in his arms, the cherishing warmth of his embrace was so sweet that it made tears clog the back of my throat. I closed my eyes and snuggled my head into the hollow of his shoulder.

I felt so safe when I was with Raoul.

Safe. The very word brought Nicky to my mind.

"Raoul," I said urgently. "I have to get up. I have to check on Nicky."

He didn't try to argue with me, just got out of bed and handed me my nightgown. Then he put on a dressing gown to cover his nakedness and together we went next door to check on my son.

Nicky had turned on his back and was

sleeping with one arm thrown over his head. His hair was flung back from his brow, and in the light of the candle his long lashes cast shadows on his cheeks. Looking at him, my heart cramped with love.

And with something else.

"Do you really think the bridge was sabotaged?" I asked Raoul.

We moved away from the bed toward the window so that our voices would not disturb Nicky.

"I don't know what to think," Raoul answered. "John is emphatic about the trustworthiness of the two men who checked it last month. I know most of the workmen on the estate, but these two men are new, so I cannot vouch for them myself."

"If they are new, then how can John be so certain of their trusthworthiness?" I asked sharply.

The moonlight coming in the window cast shadows on Raoul's face. "Apparently they were recommended by someone John has a great deal of faith in. All I can surmise is that the men were not thorough enough in their inspection. I have told John to send other men the next time."

I didn't say anything to that.

"Quite probably I overreacted in suspecting foul play," Raoul said. "I am spoiled by

John's efficiency. Things like that do not happen at Savile."

I thought of what would have happened if that bridge had gone down with him and I shuddered. I did not think that Raoul was overreacting.

He said to me, "You're cold. Where is your dressing gown?"

"No, I'm fine," I said. "I'm just worried."

He reached out to smooth away the worry line that I knew was etched between my brows. "I shouldn't have said anything to you." He sounded as if he was annoyed with himself.

I shook my head in disagreement.

In a sudden, complete change of topic, he said, "By the way, Gail, I have been meaning for some time to ask you the date of Nicky's birthday."

My whole body stiffened and I looked at Raoul suspiciously. "Why do you want to know that?"

He gave me his most genial smile. "Oh, we always have a party for the children's birthdays and I don't want to pass over Nicky's."

I knew very well that this was not the reason for his question. "Nicky was not born during the summer, so you don't have to worry about that," I replied shortly.

"Still," he persisted, "I should like to remember the day with a small gift. I have grown quite fond of Nicky."

We stood staring at each other in the moonlight coming in the window while I tried to decide whether it would matter if he knew the date of Nicky's birth. Finally I decided it would not.

"Nicky was born on December twenty-first," I said reluctantly.

He nodded.

I realized suddenly that if he wanted to, he could easily look up the date of my marriage in the parish register at Hatfield and discover that Nicky had been born too early. I raised my chin and told myself that I didn't care about that. After our nights together, it was certain that Raoul wasn't harboring any mistaken ideas about my chastity anyway.

I said, "So you think the lack of repair on the bridge was an accident?"

He ran his fingers through his disordered hair. "It probably was, just as Squirt's sudden colic was probably an accident as well. When you think about it, the bridge accident could not have been directed specifically against Nicky, Gail. Anyone might have used the bridge that morning."

"True, except that that morning everyone knew the boys were supposed to be going from the temple to the Home Woods and in doing so they would naturally have crossed the bridge."

"There is no saying that one of the other boys would not have gone first. The accident might not have harmed Nicky at all."

"The whole bridge could have collapsed when one part of it went down and everyone could have gone in," I argued.

"I suppose that is true, but I go back to my original question." His eyes were golden in the silvery moonlight. "Who would want to hurt Nicky?"

That, of course, was a question I could not answer. Instead, I turned, went back to the bed, and stood silently looking down at my sleeping son. I felt Raoul come up beside me and then his arm came around me, pulling me against his side. I leaned against the long length of him, feeling his strength and his warmth. It felt so good there in the circle of his arm.

He said soberly, "You've been carrying too much weight for too long on these slender shoulders of yours, sweetheart. I wish you would let me help you."

As soon as I heard my own thought spoken out loud, I knew how dangerous was the situation I had gotten myself into. I could not allow myself to begin to lean on Raoul

Melville. *I could not.*

I stiffened against him and said angrily, "How many times do I have to tell you that Nicky is not a burden to me?"

Raoul bent down and kissed my temple, right in the hollow below where my hair began to grow. "I didn't say that. I didn't mean that."

But I stood rigid within his embrace and would not relax.

"I know how much you love him," he said. "I did not mean to imply that you resent him. All I meant was that there are times when you need help."

I didn't reply.

He sighed.

I said stiffly, "I think I had better stay here with Nicky for the rest of the night."

At that, he turned me around, bent his head, and started kissing me. He put one hand on the back of my head to support it and slipped the other inside the opened top of my nightgown. He caressed my breast and slid his tongue into my mouth and all the resistance drained out of me.

It took exactly one minute before Raoul was carrying me back into his bedroom once more.

I had no defenses against the man. I lay back in his bed and opened my body and let him come into me, deeper and deeper, until we were so deeply joined together that it seemed nothing would ever part us. We rocked together, his hardness softening me and softening me until together we shuddered and cried out and the world dissolved into searing sensation and soul-shattering passion and we collapsed in each other's arms, still one body, one fulfillment, but, unfortunately, not one love.

CHAPTER 20

I was back in bed with Nicky before the sun came up, which was a good thing because he woke with the dawn, ready to rise and go upstairs to the nursery to eat. I persuaded him to remain in bed for another hour and then I took him upstairs myself and stayed to have breakfast with the nursery set.

All of the children, girls as well as boys, were going to spend the morning fishing on the river, and this seemed to me a quiet enough activity for a boy who had recently suffered a head injury. Raoul had promised me last night that he would assign one of the younger, larger footmen to keep an eye on Nicky, so I felt easier in my mind about my son's safety. I would have accompanied the children myself but I was feeling guilty about leaving Ginny in the sole company of Harriet.

Poor Ginny. Not only was she feeling the discomforts of pregnancy, but now she had the added worries of a house whose bedroom wing had burned down and needed to be rebuilt. All of this with a husband who was at a scientific conference in Heidelberg!

"Let's go for a drive to Henley," I said when I found her sitting glumly in the Little Drawing Room staring distractedly out the window at the lovely summer morning. "You need a change of scene and we can do some shopping and get some ices at that ice cream parlor you told me about."

Her face brightened like a child's who has been promised a treat. "What a good idea, Gail. I am so despondent about Austerby. Just the thought of having to rebuild the whole east wing makes me sick. Is Raoul free to drive us, do you know?"

Raoul was nowhere to be found, however. Powell told us that he had gone to inspect some work that was being done at one of the tenant's farms and was not expected back until much later. Roger was gone also, along with his phaeton, so he could not drive us. Mr. Cole and his carriage were also missing from the stables, but since neither Ginny nor I would dream of asking Mr. Cole to drive us around the corner, his absence did not make any difference to our plans.

"I'd drive you but I have a whole series of appointments this afternoon," John told us.

Ginny and I looked at each other gloomily.

"Do you know, Ginny, I am perfectly capable of handling Raoul's grays," I said. "Do you think he would object to my borrowing them so we could go to Henley by ourselves?"

Ginny looked uncertain. "I am just wondering if it would be proper."

"We'll take a groom," I said.

Ginny said in a rush, "To be honest with you, Gail, I am feeling so low that the thought of a drive to Henley is like heaven. I am sure it will be perfectly proper for us to go by ourselves if we take a groom." She added recklessly, "And if it isn't — well, who cares!"

I repeated the question that was my real concern: "And what about Raoul letting me use his grays?"

Ginny gave me a look that held a combination of speculation and amusement. "Raoul would probably let you use the sacred Savile sword if you wanted to, Gail. His grays will be as nothing."

I blushed. "It is true that he is a very generous man."

"Yes, he is. But that is not what I am talking about," came the enigmatic reply.

In the end we decided to go to Henley by ourselves. There was no objection in the stables when Ginny asked for Raoul's grays and the low-slung phaeton to be brought around and we drove off in the peace, sunlight, and warmth of a perfect July morning. Ginny wore a big-brimmed straw bonnet trimmed with green satin ribbons to shield her eyes and her complexion from the sun. I didn't own any bonnets like that since I was accustomed to driving and needed my lateral vision, so I perched a little dab of ancient black straw on my short locks for convention's sake and off we went over the causeway.

The grays were lovely to drive, well broken and willing to move right up into their bits. There was very little traffic on the road, and Ginny spent most of the time telling me about how she was gong to redecorate each room at Austerby when the new wing was built. I made noises to indicate that I was listening with breathless attention, and by the time we reached Henley she was feeling very much better.

She did have to use a water closet, however, so I stopped at the Black Swan.

There was a lull in the inn's usually busy stable yard, and the first thing we saw, standing by itself, was Mr. Cole's old-fashioned carriage.

"Good heavens," said Ginny. "I wonder what that odious Cole is doing here."

I answered, "Perhaps he is meeting a business associate. After all, he can hardly bring the sort of fellow he must do business with to Savile, can he?"

Ginny wrinkled her elegant Melville nose. "That is so." She looked around. "I hope we don't meet him, Gail. Imagine having to acknowledge a man like that in a public place." She shuddered delicately.

We went into the parlor and Ginny got a maid to take her upstairs so she could use the water closet. I didn't want anything to drink, so I went to look at the pictures hung along the dark wainscoting of the parlor wall. I was still standing there, with my back to the room, when Albert Cole came in with someone whose voice sounded oddly familiar to me.

Remembering Ginny's wish not to meet Mr. Cole, I kept my back turned and so was an unintentional eavesdropper on a very interesting conversation.

"I've told you that I'll need some proof of what you're telling me," Cole said. "I'm not one to shell out the nonsense without I've got proof that the information you're selling me is true."

"Oh, it's true all right. It's like I told you in London, Cole. I know where it is, I just have to convince the party holding it to give it up to me."

Suddenly I recognized the voice. It belonged to the man who had thrust himself on me when I had come to the inn with Roger. Wickham, I think he had called himself. I had thought that perhaps he was the man with whom Raoul had found Roger gambling.

It now seemed that Wickham had been hanging around waiting to meet Mr. Cole, not Roger.

Mr. Cole said, "Well, I don't deny that I'm mighty interested in that information, Mr. Wickham, mighty interested. But I have to see it before I'll pay you a cent."

"But don't you see, I need money to convince the party holding the information to give it up to me." Wickham sounded very frustrated, as if this was a point he had been making again and again.

"Well, don't it beat the Dutch," said Mr. Cole in amazement. "You want me to pay you money for information you say you know someone else has? How am I to know that this ain't all one big bamboozle and you're not going to take my money and run away with it?"

"Because I won't!"

Mr. Cole's laugh held genuine amusement. "No, no, sonny," he said. "If you want me to pay you for that information, then you bring it to me. Otherwise you get nothing."

The conversation continued in this vein

for a few more minutes, while I studiously gazed at the pictures of hunt scenes that lined the dark walls of the parlor. At last the two men moved out into the inn's entryway and I heard them parting, Mr. Wickham still without the money he had come to collect.

I wondered a little worriedly what kind of information he was trying to sell to Mr. Cole. Wickham didn't seem the sort to have inside information on investments or things like that. Could this interview have anything to do with the dangerous happenings at Savile Castle?

Although I didn't like Mr. Cole, could I seriously think he would be interested in harming Nicky? The money Nicky had inherited from George was nothing to a man like Cole.

Then Ginny came back into the parlor and I banished the odd meeting from my mind as we prepared to continue on to Henley.

Ginny had a wonderful afternoon. She met a number of people whom she knew, and telling her tale of woe about the burning of Austerby perked her up tremendously. Added to that, the phaeton was filled with her purchases by the time we started for home. I spent the afternoon mainly trailing in her extravagant wake, but I did make a single purchase — a set of marbles for Nicky that I thought he would like.

Once or twice Ginny pointed out a dress that she thought would look well on me, but I shook my head. "I know you must be growing very tired of my two evening dresses, Ginny, but I cannot afford a new one," I said firmly after she had tactfully pointed out the second dress. "Money is extremely tight with me at the moment and it will continue to be tight until John finds a place for me to start up my business again."

She started to say something, then stopped abruptly, and I thought the subject of my lack of money was safely dropped. On the way home, however, she raised it again.

"Gail," she began, "I don't mean to pry, but why have you never married again? Surely that is the most obvious way for you to escape your financial difficulties." Before I could answer, she added quickly, "And don't tell me that you have never had any chances, because I won't believe you."

I looked thoughtfully at the matched set of powerful dappled gray haunches moving in an easy trot in front of the phaeton. One of the horses flicked his tail to swish away a fly, and I said to Ginny, "Finding a husband is not as easy as you may think when one is poor and has a child to support."

"Are you saying that since your husband's

death no man has ever asked you to marry him?" she demanded.

"Well . . ." I dragged the word out reluctantly. "No, I am not saying that."

"I didn't think so," she said triumphantly. She turned her head so that she could see me around the edges of her bonnet, folded her arms across the bosom of her green walking dress, and demanded, "So — why?"

I sighed. "I suppose I didn't want to give up my freedom," I said. "Surely you can understand, Ginny, that it is one thing to be married to someone one loves and quite another thing to be married to someone one only tolerates. That is why, as long as I could keep Nicky fed and clothed, I preferred to do it on my own."

There was quite a long silence. A gig was coming down the road in the opposite direction and I drove Raoul's beautifully mannered grays past the single brown gelding pulling the gig with no trouble. The driver, who looked like a farmer, tipped his hat to Ginny and me.

Ginny said, "I do not know many women who would have had the courage to do that, Gail."

We came around a sharpish turn and found that a big lumbering farm cart piled high with hay was in front of us. I slowed the grays to a smooth walk.

"These are the loveliest horses," I said with enthusiasm.

We walked slowly behind the cart for another hundred yards or so and then the hay cart turned to veer across the fields. I increased our speed to an even trot.

I could have driven those horses all day.

I tried to explain my actions to Ginny. "I was brought up to be independent, you see. My parents died when I was quite young, and my sister and I were sent to live with my mother's sister in Hatfield. As Aunt Margaret suffers from an illness that makes her afraid to leave her home, Deborah and I had a great deal of freedom." I turned my head to give Ginny a brief smile. "It was not that Aunt Margaret did not love us. She did. But she was definitely . . . odd."

"This is the woman whom Harriet keeps referring to as a witch?"

"Yes. She is very interested in herbs. I would trust her over any doctor when it comes to illness."

"It does not sound like an ideal childhood," Ginny said in a noncommittal sort of voice. "No mother, no father, and an aunt who spends all her time in her herb garden and is afraid to leave her property."

I shook my head in decisive negation. "It

was not a bad sort of childhood at all. Deborah and I had each other, you see. We made up to each other for whatever else and whoever else we might have lacked."

"And where is Deborah now?" Ginny asked.

With those words, the pain struck, the pain that would never go away when I confronted the loss of Deborah.

"She died," I said woodenly, staring once more at the gray haunches in front of me.

"Oh, Gail," Ginny said with ready sympathy. "I am so sorry. How very dreadful for you."

"Yes," I said. "Thank you."

Silence fell between us.

"Life has not been easy for you, I think," Ginny finally said in a quiet voice. "You have lost a mother, a father, a sister, and a husband, and you are — how old?"

"Twenty-seven," I said. I lifted my chin. "But I have my son. Many women do not have as much."

Ginny straightened her bonnet. "Nicky is a darling child," she said, and I gave her the smile that praise of my son always drew from me.

"I wonder how the fishing expedition went this morning," I said, and once more we fell back upon the safe subject of our children.

The fishing expedition had been a success and the nursery party got to eat the fruits of their labor for dinner that evening. Our family dinner was not half as pleasant as I was certain dinner in the nursery had been.

The trouble began when Roger appeared in the drawing room with eyes too large and too bright, and the first thing Raoul said to him was, "Have you been drinking?"

"I?" Roger demanded with exaggerated surprise. "How can you ask such a question, dear cousin? You of all people must know that I cannot afford to buy myself even a drink of blue ruin at a local tavern."

"That's so," Mr. Cole said bitterly. "You've taken my money, the money Devane set aside for you as his heir, and you've spent it all. Once my grandson is born and you're booted out of Devane forever, the devil knows or cares how you're going to live."

Roger leaned against the wall next to the fireplace near the statue of King James, folded his arms, and regarded Mr. Cole with infuriating superiority. "Harriet hasn't a very good record for producing boys, Cole," he said nastily. "Allow me to tell you that the betting at the clubs is heavily on another girl."

Mr. Cole's face turned a mottled red and he gripped the carved arms of the oak chair he was sitting in. "After three girls, the odds are the nipper will be a boy! And I'll tell you this, Mr. Roger know-it-all Melville, once you don't have the prospect of inheriting Devane behind you, all your creditors are going to come calling. I'd be mighty interested to see how you're planning to pay them off!"

Raoul said, from his place next to me by the window, "That's quite enough, both of you. You're upsetting the ladies."

"Ladies? There's only one lady here as far as I can see," Roger said nastily.

Harriet said furiously, "Papa!"

Raoul said in a voice that would have frozen hell, "Roger, apologize this instant to Gail and to Harriet."

All of the flush from the wine he had drunk drained away from Roger's face. "I didn't mean you, Gail," he said.

"We are waiting," Raoul said implacably.

"I am sorry, Harriet," Roger said. But he was looking at Raoul and not at Harriet, and I did not at all like what I saw in his eyes.

Dinner was not pleasant. Roger drank too much wine and made veiled, insulting remarks to Harriet, which finally caused Raoul to dismiss him from the table during the fish course.

"I am sorry, Harriet," Raoul said after Roger had left in a fury. "I should have done that sooner, but I hate having to treat him as if he were a sixteen-year-old."

"He's deep in under the hatches, my lord," Mr. Cole said somberly. "I've heard the moneylenders have him in their clutches."

Ginny said, "Good God, surely even Roger can't be that stupid?"

"That is my information, Lady Regina."

It occurred to me as I listened to this conversation that Nicky's money would be an absolute necessity to Roger should he indeed inherit George's estate.

Is there any reason someone might wish Nicky ill? Raoul had asked me that. Now, I wondered if there might be a reason right here. Roger had already asked me point-blank if I would agree to release the money bequeathed to Nicky if Raoul would agree to it.

He must know, however, that Raoul would not agree to such a thing, I thought.

I could not help wondering what would happen to that money if Nicky were dead. Would it go directly back into the estate, giving Roger immediate access to it?

I felt my hands grow icy cold and clasped them together in my lap.

Could Roger be trying to harm Nicky?

I didn't make a noise or a move, so I was surprised when Raoul turned to look at me and asked with concern, "Are you all right, Gail?"

"Yes." I forced a smile and picked up my fork. "I am fine."

"Where do you think Roger got the drink this afternoon?" John asked. "I thought you told the local inns not to serve him."

Raoul sighed. "I did, but he obviously has some acquaintances in the neighborhood."

The footmen finished removing the pickled herrings and brought in roast pigeons stuffed with parsley and butter.

"You could just boot him out of Savile, Raoul," John pointed out. "There is no reason why you have to put up with Roger and his ill humor and his wastrel ways."

I hadn't eaten the herrings but the pigeons smelled all right. I accepted some asparagus from Raoul and cut into my fowl.

He answered John, "I know, I know, but Mr. Middleman and I agreed that it would be best if the two possible heirs to Devane remained here at Savile until this whole issue is resolved."

"And afterward?" John persisted. "Suppose Harriet's child *is* a boy. What are you going to do with Roger then? Continue to support him? Continue to allow him to live here?"

"Then we will have to find a way for Roger to support himself," Raoul said serenely.

John snorted rudely.

Ginny said, "Good luck."

Mr. Cole said, "That kind of young man don't never come to anything good, my lord. He ain't like you, you see. He don't care about anything but himself."

I felt a stab of surprise at how well Mr. Cole had expressed what I thought was probably the essence of Roger Melville.

That night I moved back to my old room on the second floor and Raoul came up the stairs to visit me and everything was normal for three more days.

Then one of the tenants' children was killed by a bow and arrow in the woods.

CHAPTER 21

It happened like this. For three days, Charlie, Theo, and Nicky had been playing Robin Hood in the Home Woods. In fact, for the first two days, I had joined in their game for part of the day. I knew I had to surmount this need I felt to keep a constant eye on Nicky, but when the boys agreed to my tentative suggestion that perhaps they could use a Maid Marian to bring them luncheon, I couldn't resist the opportunity. On the third morning, however, Ginny asked me to go into Savile village with her and I had left the boys to play their game without me.

What had happened next was that Johnny Wester had accompanied his father, who was one of Raoul's tenants, to the mill, where Charlie had met him and invited him to spend the day playing Robin Hood. Johnny's father had given permission and Johnny had enthusiastically accompanied Charlie to "Sherwood Forest" to meet the rest of Robin Hood's band of merry men.

Unbeknownst to me, the faithful Mr. Wilson was not in attendance on that particular morning, as Ginny had given him permission to spend the day with his brother, who was passing through Henley. The boys had pressed the footman whom Raoul had assigned to look out for Nicky into service to play Little John to Charlie's Robin.

The boys had also taken advantage of their tutor's (and my) absence to borrow several of the estate's target-shooting bows and arrows, which were stored in one of the outbuildings behind the castle. Albert, the footman, was unaware that the boys did not have permission to use the bows, so he had gone along with the game. In the absence of Maid Marian, the boys had assigned Albert to remain back at camp (the tree house), supposedly preparing dinner for the merry men, and so both as a guard and as a witness he was useless.

All the boys knew the rudiments of shooting, and afterward they told us in shock that they had not been shooting at each other but at the trees, which were supposed to be the Sheriff of Nottingham's men.

Only somehow Johnny got shot in the chest and was killed.

After Albert had brought the child back to the castle, after it was certain that he was dead, and after his parents had been sent for, Raoul stood our three boys in front of him in the Little Drawing Room and tried to discover exactly what had happened. Ginny and I sat tensely on the settee on either side of Raoul and listened.

"None of us could have shot him, Uncle Raoul!" Charlie cried in distress.

"We were all spread out in a line, see, because we were supposed to be attacking the sheriff's men," Theo said.

"Charlie and Theo and I were all shouting and yelling," said Nicky. "Johnny was kind of quiet, but I could hear the noise he was making as the twigs broke under his feet. Then there was a . . . kind of thud, and he cried out."

Nicky swallowed audibly.

"None of us could have shot him," Charlie repeated. "We were all facing in the same direction, Uncle Raoul! How could we have shot Johnny in the chest?"

"You are quite certain that none of you were in front of Johnny?" Raoul asked quietly.

"No!" Charlie and Theo said emphatically, and Nicky shook his head.

"Arrows don't turn around," Charlie said. "They go straight. And we were shooting away from Johnny, Uncle Raoul. I swear it!"

Ginny said tiredly, "Well, someone shot Johnny, Charlie. He didn't shoot himself."

The three boys were very pale and shocked-looking. "I *know* someone shot Johnny, Mama," Charlie said. "I am just telling you that it wasn't us."

Ginny fell back on motherly scolding. "What on earth prompted you boys to take out the bows and arrows? I can't believe that you could be so untrustworthy."

Silence fell in the room. The three boys looked wretchedly at their feet.

"We're sorry," Theo whispered.

"Yes, well, sorry will not bring Johnny back," Ginny said, falling back on trivial words in the face of the tragic.

"Could there have been a poacher in the woods?" I asked. "Someone who did not want to be heard with a gun so he chose to use a bow?"

"A poacher who was poaching small boys?" Ginny asked.

"No, a poacher who mistook Johnny for a deer," I said doggedly.

Raoul replied somberly, "Anyone from the neighborhood would know that the children use those woods. It is hard to believe that anyone would be careless enough to shoot without being very certain indeed what it was he was shooting at."

"We were being quite loud, my lord," Nicky said in a small voice. "We were pretending it was a battle, you see, so we were shouting all kinds of taunts. A poacher would have known for certain that people were in the area."

The whole picture was growing uglier and uglier.

Powell appeared in the drawing-room doorway. "The Westers are here, my lord."

Raoul got slowly to his feet. He looked sick. "Very well, Powell, I will come immediately."

I wanted so much to go with him, to help him through the horrible task of telling the parents that their child was dead. But I did not have that right.

Ginny said, "I'll go with you, Raoul."

He gave her a grateful look. "Thank you, Ginny. I think a woman's presence will be helpful to Mrs. Wester."

The two of them left the room, leaving me alone with the three boys.

Charlie said wretchedly, "If only I had not invited Johnny to play with us!"

My own feelings were very conflicted. I felt dreadful about Johnny, of course, but I had an utterly terrifying feeling that if Johnny had not been added to the game, it would have been Nicky who was lying lifeless in the anteroom.

I said, "You couldn't have known what

would happen, Charlie. Now I'd like you to think. Did you notice any sign at all that there was someone else in the woods with you this afternoon?"

The boys looked at one another, then slowly they all shook their heads.

"We were very busy with our game, you see, Mrs. Saunders," Charlie said. "I'm not saying that no one was there — in fact it's pretty clear that someone must have been, isn't it — but we were too busy to notice anything."

"That's so, Mama," Nicky said.

I looked at the shocked young faces before me. "No one thinks that Johnny's shooting was your fault," I told them gently. "Sometimes things happen, terrible things, that are very hard for us to understand. I think it would be a good idea for you all to spend a little time this week talking to the rector about what happened to Johnny. Mr. Ambling might be able to help make this a little easier for you."

"Yes, Mrs. Saunders," the Austen boys murmured.

Nicky nodded.

"Do you think Uncle Raoul wants us to stay here and wait for him?" Theo asked.

I thought that the familiar surroundings of the nursery would probably be good for them. "No," I said. "Go upstairs. If you are needed your uncle will know where you are."

The three boys turned to leave.

"Nicky," I murmured as they reached the door, and at my words he turned back into the room. "Are you all right, sweetheart?" I asked.

By now the Austen boys had left the room, and Nicky returned to me, threw his arms around my waist, and buried his face in my breasts. "It was so dreadful, Mama," he said in a choked kind of voice. "Johnny was lying on his back and a big arrow was sticking out of his chest." He began to sob.

I held him so tightly that I was afraid I was hurting him, and the image he had described was frighteningly present in my mind.

I had seen Johnny when they brought him in, and the first thing I had noticed was that he was of a similar size and build as Nicky and that his hair was almost the same shade of brown.

A dreadful conviction was growing within me that the target of that fatal bow shot had been my son.

"Listen to me, sweetheart," I said when his sobs had slowed and he had collected himself somewhat. "From now on I want you to be very careful never to leave the company of the other boys and Mr. Wilson. Do you hear me? Never, ever, under any circumstances, go off on your own."

His blue eyes were huge. "Do you think I am in danger, Mama?"

I hated to frighten him, but I thought the situation was too serious for me to ignore. "I don't know, Nicky, but what happened to Johnny was definitely peculiar. So please be careful."

The blue eyes got even bigger. "Yes, Mama."

"Good boy." I forced my lips to assume what I hoped was a reassuring smile. "Good night, then, sweetheart. I will see you in the morning."

"Mama," said my now thoroughly frightened son, "can I stay with you tonight?"

It was a measure of how frightened I was that I said yes.

Raoul and I went for a walk in the rose garden after dinner, and his response to my decision about Nicky was predictable. "You said he could sleep in your room? Are you mad, Gail? The boy is eight years of age — far too old to be sleeping in his mama's room."

Even though I had expected it, Raoul's reply incensed me. "You are just put out because you won't be able to sleep with me yourself. What do you care that Nicky's life is in danger as long as you get what you want?"

He said in a hard voice, "What are you talking about?"

My voice was edged with panic as I answered, "Nicky is in deadly anger, Raoul. I know it. First there was the bridge, then there was the possible poisoning of his pony, and now a boy who looks like Nicky — a boy who was added into the play group at the Home Woods at the last minute — is killed."

He was silent for a minute. Then he said, "You think that arrow was meant for Nicky?"

"Yes," I said. "I do."

"Christ," he said, and I did not mistake his use of the sacred name for blasphemy.

More silence fell between us. The sweet, heavy scent of the roses was all around us, and from the top of the castle walls a nightingale began to sing. I wondered if it was the same nightingale that had been singing the first night Raoul and I had made love.

The thought of that night softened my feelings toward him. "How was your interview with the Westers?" I asked.

"Hellish." His voice was rough and angry-sounding. "What can one possibly say to someone who has lost a child?"

It occurred to me that I was speaking to a man who had been on both sides of that tragic scenario. It was true that he could have used the comfort of my bed that night as much as Nicky could.

I told myself that Raoul's life was not in danger and that Nicky's was.

He stretched his shoulders as if he was very tired. "I know we've been through this before, Gail, but let's go through it again." He thrust his hand impatiently through his hair, pushing it off his forehead. "You think Nicky is in danger but you have no idea as to why this might be so?"

I drew in a deep breath and didn't answer.

The moon, which had been hidden behind a cloud, suddenly came out and illuminated the garden with a pale, eerie glow. The white climbing roses next to me looked almost unearthly in the pale light. Raoul pressed me further: "No inexplicable accidents ever befell him before he came here to Savile Castle?"

"No, they did not."

His face looked bleached as white as a bone in the moonlight, and his eyes were dark and unreadable. He said, "So it seems we must assume that there is something connected to the castle, or to the people within the castle, that poses a danger to Nicky."

I broke off one of the white roses and began to shred its silky petals with nervous fingers. I said, "Raoul, I have been wondering about Roger. I didn't tell you this, but the day he took me out driving he asked me if I would agree to give up Nicky's inheritance if he could persuade you to go along with such a plan. I told him that I would agree, but that I doubted he would be successful in persuading you." I looked up from the mutilated flower in my hands. "Did he ever approach you about this?"

He was looking down into my face with those unreadable eyes. "Yes, he did, and I told him that I would not consider such a thing."

I said a little breathlessly, "I have been wondering — what would happen to that money if Nicky should die?"

Raoul's reply was slow and deliberate. "It would go back into the estate."

I pricked my finger on a thorn, winced, dropped the rose, and stuck my injured finger into my mouth. I said around it, "And be immediately available to the new Lord Devane?"

"Yes."

I took my finger out of my mouth. "Roger

is in desperate need of money, Raoul. Do you think he might be desperate enough to try to do away with Nicky in order to get his hands on Nicky's twenty thousand pounds?"

Raoul reached out to blot a drop of blood from my lip with his finger. His touch gave its usual lightning shock to my nervous system.

He shook his head. "For one thing, Roger has no surety that he *will* be the next Lord Devane, Gail. And even if he is, he will have the money from the rents that I have been holding. Nicky's money would be nice but not crucial to him." A faint look of contempt crossed his face, the look of a strong man for a weak one. "At any rate, I doubt that Roger would have the nerve," he said.

I did not agree, but I thought I had said enough.

Raoul stepped toward me and put his hands on my shoulders. "I know you don't like to talk about this, sweetheart, but I am utterly convinced that these attacks on Nicky — if they are indeed attacks, and I am now inclined to believe that they are — are related to George's will."

I stood stiffly and said nothing.

"Gail," Raoul said, and his long body bent over me, drawing me toward him until I was pressed against his warm, protective strength, "why did George leave Nicky twenty thousand pounds?"

My body was rigid, resisting the familiar magic of his touch. I said, "I don't know."

He said persuasively, "Sweetheart, I can't help you if you won't trust me. You must know that I would never hurt or betray you. But if I am to be of any help to you at all . . ."

I ripped myself out of his arms.

"Will you leave me alone?" I cried wildly. "Nicky's birth is not a mystery and I have no idea why George left him that damned money! I don't want it, I never wanted it, and I am utterly terrified that it is the reason why someone is trying to kill him! In fact, I have been thinking that for safety's sake perhaps I ought to get him away from the castle altogether."

Raoul's face was hard and bleak in the moonlight. All of the tenderness was gone from his voice when he asked, "Might I ask where you would go?"

"To Aunt Margaret's."

His face grew even bleaker. "I think that I will be able to protect Nicky better here than you would be at your aunt's. The first thing I plan to do is hire some Bow Street runners to act as guards for him, and for the other boys as well, until we get to the bottom of this situation. And I *will* get to the bottom of it, Gail, that I promise you — no matter what I might end up uncovering."

His words sounded as if they might be more of a threat than a promise.

"Will you check on how deeply Roger is in debt?" I asked.

"I will check."

"And there is a man lurking around the Black Swan — his name is Wickham. I overheard him talking to Mr. Cole about selling him some information."

"I will check on this Wickham as well."

The scent of the roses was all around us and the nightingale was still singing his heart out from the castle walls and we stood looking at each other with the chasm of my refusal to confide in him between us.

Raoul said, "It's about time for the tea tray, I think."

"Yes," I said in a hollow voice, "I suppose it is."

I knew from the look on his face that he would not be placated if I tried to move back into his arms now. As we walked together toward the house, I wondered in despair if things would ever be the same between us again.

There was a very large footman sitting in the hallway outside my room when I arrived upstairs. Nicky was already in bed when I went into my bedroom, but he was not asleep.

I put my candle on the bedside table and looked into his face. He looked wide awake. "Charlie and Theo said that I was a baby for wanting to spend the night with you, Mama," he said.

"It is not every day that you see someone killed," I returned reasonably. "I don't think it is babyish to need some reassurance, sweetheart. You are, after all, only eight years of age."

"But Charlie and Theo are sleeping in the nursery tonight. They are not sleeping with their mama."

"Charlie and Theo are brothers. They have each other," I said.

"That's true; they are both sleeping in Charlie's room," Nicky agreed. Then, tentatively: "They said I could sleep in there with them."

It began to dawn on me what my son was trying to say.

"Nicky, would you like to go back to the nursery and sleep with Charlie and Theo?"

"It is just that they will call me a baby if I don't, Mama," he said earnestly. A tuft of hair was sticking up at the back of his head and he looked so precious that I wanted to cry. "It is not that I don't want to spend the night with you."

I thought of Raoul's words and took a deep breath. "If you wish to go back upstairs, that is perfectly fine with me."

"You will be all right alone?" Nicky asked anxiously.

I could almost have laughed, the turnabout was so ludicrous.

"I will be fine," I said.

He began to scramble out from beneath the covers. "Well then, I think I will go upstairs."

I had not yet undressed, and I said, "I'll accompany you."

The footman sitting outside my door went with us and on the third floor we encountered yet another footman sitting in the passageway outside the nursery apartment.

"We'll see that Master Nicky gets safely tucked up for the night," both young men assured me.

Since Nicky clearly did not want me to escort him into Charlie's room, I thanked them and went slowly back downstairs to the bedroom that now would contain neither Nicky nor Raoul but just my lonely self.

Nicky was growing up, I realized, and for the first time I let myself wonder what I was going to do when he really was grown up and I was alone. I had never thought that way before. I had never let my eyes look that far ahead.

Raoul had been right about one thing, I thought. I couldn't try to stop my son from growing up just because I was afraid of what my life was going to be like without him.

I got into my solitary bed and blew out my candle.

Once, perhaps I might have been able to marry again, I thought. Once, perhaps I could have settled for life with Sam Watson.

'Twere all one
That I should love a bright particular star
And think to wed it, he is so above me.

Shakespeare's poignant words sounded in my mind.

Raoul, I thought with something that approached anguish. *Oh, Raoul.*

I had rebuffed him tonight, and he had been very angry. It was not that I did not trust him, it was just that I was utterly convinced that the facts surrounding Nicky's birth had absolutely no bearing on the problem we were faced with at Savile.

I thought about being the one to make the first move and going to him that night, but even if I did go down the stairs to his room,

I was not certain that he would be there, and the thought of encountering his valet was unnerving, to say the least.

So I lay awake instead and tried to occupy my mind by thinking about the people who were living at Savile Castle and trying to imagine who might possibly have something against my son.

Raoul and Ginny I did not even consider.

Roger I had already singled out as a likely suspect.

Who else might have a motive? I wondered.

Harriet? Could she hate Nicky, whom she thought was George's bastard son, so much that she wanted to do away with him? I acquitted the pregnant Harriet of being personally responsible for any of the attacks, but there were plenty of villains for hire now in the postwar world and she certainly could have engaged someone to do her dirty work for her.

It was hard to know what was going on in Harriet's mind. She spoke very little, except to her father, and manifested herself to the rest of us mainly as a heavy, brooding, spiteful presence.

I would not put it beyond her to wish Nicky dead.

Then there was Mr. Cole. He had made

no attempt to hide the fact that he resented George's bequeathing twenty thousand pounds of Cole money to what he considered George's bastard, but could that resentment be so severe that he could try to do away with Nicky? Unlike Roger, Cole still had an enormous amount of money, and now he had the prospect of a possible grandson to inherit Devane Hall.

Of course, there was that mysterious Mr. Wickham and the information he was trying to sell to Cole. But Wickham very probably represented Cole's other business interests and had nothing to do with Nicky at all.

The final member of the Savile household was John Melville, and the only reason I considered John at all was that he was Raoul's heir. I remembered him warning me on several occasions that Raoul would never marry again, and, while I was not foolish enough to think that John feared that Raoul would marry me, I remembered how he had told me several times how much Raoul had suffered when his wife and child died.

Could John hope that the death of another child whom Raoul had grown fond of — Nicky — might reinforce his determination never to marry again?

Upon reflection, I had to admit that this was a ridiculously weak argument.

In fact, the only villain who made any real sense to me was Roger. I wondered if perhaps I ought to go against Raoul's advice and get Nicky away from the castle, but I was afraid that if I was on my own, with no protection for Nicky but myself, he would be even more vulnerable. After all, I wouldn't be hard to find for anyone determined upon mischief.

I would remain at the castle, I decided, and I determined that in the morning I would ask Raoul if he could get a Bow Street runner to keep an eye on Roger as well as on the boys.

CHAPTER 22

It was raining when I woke the following morning and I went down to breakfast with a headache. There was no one in the dining room and I sat drearily at the table sipping my coffee and nibbling desultorily on a muffin.

Harriet came in when I was starting on my second cup of coffee and I stared at her in surprise. She never came downstairs in the morning but had been breakfasting in her room ever since I had come to the castle.

"I didn't expect to see you, Harriet," I said with a note of inquiry.

"I didn't sleep well," she replied gruffly. "I thought that if I got out of my room for a while perhaps I might be able to nap later."

Once again I felt an unwanted twinge of sympathy for George's widow. She really looked miserable. Her skin was sallow and there were dark circles under her eyes. I thought that this wait to see whether or not she was bearing a son must be hellish, and a comparison to Anne Boleyn suddenly popped into my mind.

"You need to sleep or you will make yourself ill," I said in a gentler voice than I had ever used to her before.

"I can't sleep, though," she replied fretfully. "I lie there and I try and I try and I try, but I can't!"

I had had my share of nights like that, so I knew what she was talking about.

"Will it be so very dreadful if this child is a girl?" I asked. "You will still have your title, after all."

"It can't be a girl," she replied tensely. "Papa would be unbearably disappointed if it was a girl. He wants a grandson who will be Lord Devane of Devane Hall. I have to do this for him. I have to."

"But he will still have a daughter who is Lady Devane," I pointed out again.

Her caterpillarlike eyebrows almost joined in the middle, so intense was her frown. "That isn't good enough for Papa," she said. "I wouldn't have Devane Hall, you see. Roger would have that."

What kind of pressure was this to put upon a pregnant woman? I thought indignantly. My Anne Boleyn comparison was appearing more and more accurate.

"I could write to my aunt and ask if she has a recipe to help you sleep," I said tentatively. "I am quite certain that she would be able to recommend a few soothing herbs."

Harriet's dark eyes regarded me with a mixture of hope and suspicion. "Why should you want to help me? You hated me for marrying George. I always knew that."

I sighed. I didn't know the answer to her question myself. I only knew that suddenly I felt sorry for Harriet and that it was hard to continue to hate someone you felt sorry for.

"I don't know why I should offer to help you," I said. I pushed away my scarcely touched muffin. "Perhaps I really mean to poison you."

Her heavy gaze held my face. "I don't think so," she said finally. "You don't care about George anymore now that you've got your hooks into Savile."

Got my hooks into Savile!

God, but the woman was vulgar. I decided that she could lie awake from now until the end of the world and I wouldn't lift a finger to help her.

I rose from the table.

"It doesn't matter what your title might be, Harriet," I said, "nothing will ever make you a lady."

Upon which splendid exit line I swept out of the room.

I stood in the passageway, unsure of where

to go next. There had never been a dearth of things to do on a rainy day when I was at home, I thought. I forcibly restrained myself from going upstairs to the nursery, where I was afraid that I would embarrass Nicky by my overprotectiveness, and decided instead to go to the library and find a book to read.

The library at Savile Castle had an upper gallery that ran around three-quarters of the room, and the walls were hung, as were so many of the rooms at Savile, with portraits of the family and of their friends. The lower part of the room was lined with dark wood bookcases that held an extensive collection of books. The rich colors of the leather bindings glowed in the light of the lamps, which were lit against the dreariness of the day. Outside, the rain poured down, but the library seemed an oasis of light and warmth in the midst of the general gloom.

To my surprise, Ginny was there before me, sitting at a long table with a book of furniture drawings opened in front of her.

I said lightly, "I meet Harriet in the dining room and you in the library. It seems that none of the ladies in the house slept very well last night."

She put a marker in her book. "No, I didn't sleep well. In fact I lay awake all night thinking about Johnny Wester." She rubbed her temples. "My God, Gail, what could have happened? How could that boy have been shot in the chest with an arrow in our own woods?"

I sat down on the opposite side of the table and regarded her somberly. "I don't know, Ginny."

"An accident like this has never happened at Savile before." Her brown eyes were hollow-looking in her strained face. "Oh, we have the occasional poacher, I'm not saying that we don't. But to be poaching in broad daylight! In the castle woods where there might be children about! That's unheard of, Gail. Unheard of."

"I don't know what to think either, Ginny, except that I agree with you that it is an extremely frightening thing," I returned.

"One can't help but wonder how safe one's own children are," Ginny said somberly. "In fact, Raoul has gone into London today with the express purpose of hiring a few Bow Street runners to keep an eye on the children." She crossed her arms over the chest of her rose-colored gown and shivered as if she was chilled.

I asked tentatively, "Do you know if it was determined whether or not the arrow that killed Johnny was a Savile arrow?"

Ginny gave me a sharp glance. "No, I

don't know. I didn't think to ask Raoul about that."

I got up, went to the window that faced the front drive, and looked out at the teeming rain. It was one of those rains that looked as if it was not going to let up all day. "Not a very nice day to be driving to London," I commented.

"No, it's not. But Raoul was determined to go, and I must confess I didn't try to dissuade him. The thought of a deranged archer loose in the neighborhood makes me very uneasy."

I turned around, determined to change the topic before the subject of Nicky could come up. "What book is that you are looking at?"

"Oh this." She picked up the marker. "It is Thomas Hope's *Household Furniture*. Since I will have to redo all the bedrooms at Austerby, I thought I might get some ideas of what is fashionable. Hope is all the crack these days, you know."

"And have you seen anything you like?"

She shook her head. "I am afraid I don't at all care for this new Egyptian look he seems to favor. I find that I much prefer Sheraton." She gave me a charmingly mischievous smile. "Like my brother, I am hopelessly traditional."

I refused to be drawn into a discussion of

Raoul. "I have come for a book also, but I am looking for a novel." I shook my head in amazement. "I must confess, I find it the strangest feeling to have nothing to do. At home I always found rainy days to be the perfect time to do my household and business accounts. And here I am now, looking for a novel!"

Ginny folded her hands on top of the open book and regarded me with interest. "You keep your own books, then, Gail?"

I regarded her in some amazement. "Of course I keep my own books. Who else should keep them?"

Ginny regarded me with even more interest and did not reply.

"Don't you keep your own household accounts, Ginny?" I asked curiously. I knew that my mother had always kept our household books at home. From earliest childhood, I had always assumed that keeping the household books was something that women did. I had certainly kept the household books for Tommy and me. In fact, starting from the age of ten, I had kept the household books for Aunt Margaret. I had always had a head for figures.

Perhaps women of the aristocracy did not keep their own books, I thought. After all, their households were so much larger than the ones I had dealt with. Perhaps they hired stewards to do the work for them.

"I not only keep the household accounts, I keep an eye on the estate accounts as well," Ginny replied promptly. "I have an excellent steward, but it is never a good idea to let the reins fall from one's own hands completely. And if I left the accounts to Gervase, we should be bankrupt in no time!"

I smiled and came back to sit across from her at the table.

Ginny smoothed her hand along the page of the book in front of her, and her long narrow fingers were a poignant, female reminder of Raoul's. She asked, "You like country life, don't you, Gail?"

I replied readily, "I like it very much, but then I have never lived anywhere else but the country so my standard of comparison is somewhat limited."

She raised her eyebrows. "You have never been to London?"

"No. And I confess that I should like to go someday. Nicky would adore to see Astley's Amphitheatre and the beasts in the Tower." I grinned and confessed, "Truth to tell, so should I."

She traced the lines of a particularly outrageous Egyptian-style sofa with her finger. "What about parties and driving in the park and Almack's and all that sort of thing?"

I stared at her in amazement. " 'That sort of thing' is about as far above my reach as . . . as Gervase's comet is," I told her firmly. "My father was a country doctor, Ginny. I would never be granted a voucher for Almack's!"

I did not mention the other things that stood between me and social respectability — the six months between my wedding and Nicky's birth, George's suspicious bequest to Nicky, and the fact that I was living at Savile as Raoul's mistress.

These things should have been apparent enough to Ginny, I thought irritably. I couldn't understand why she should bring up such a subject in the first place.

But it seemed that Ginny was not finished. "Your father was a gentleman, was he not?"

I said grimly, "He was a country gentleman of little consequence and no fortune, and the daughters of such men are not admitted to Almack's."

Ginny gave me an enigmatic look and did not reply.

This was a subject I was determined to drop, and I went back to our original topic. "In the absence of a countess, who does the household accounts here at Savile?"

"The same person who did them when

Savile did have a countess," Ginny said dryly. "John."

"Oh," I said in some surprise.

Ginny said, "That is why Raoul personally does so much of the supervising of the outdoor estate, because John has to spend a great deal of his time going over the tradesmen's receipt books, the servants' wages book, the tax books — in short, the accounts that I do for Austerby, although they are on a much smaller scale than the accounts for Savile."

I said in wonder, "Savile is still rather like a medieval manor, is it not?"

"In a way it is," Ginny said. "Raoul loves it with a passion, you know. He dutifully goes to London each year for the parliamentary session and the social season, but he is always happiest here at Savile."

"I can understand that," I said sincerely. "His family's roots are deep in the soil here and he feels that strongly."

Ginny hesitated. Then: "It posed a problem with Georgiana, Raoul's love of Savile," she said slowly. "Georgiana was a creature of the town. She hated Savile and longed for London every time she was forced to spend a few months down here. It caused some . . . strife . . . between them."

"Oh," I said, at a loss as to how to respond

to the confidence. "Well, if two people truly love each other, surely they manage to make accommodations."

Ginny went back to tracing the ugly Egyptian sofa. She did not look at me as she said, "To be honest, I think what love there might have been between the two of them had waned long before Georgiana died. Raoul was brokenhearted that he lost his son, but Georgiana's death left him feeling more guilty than truly sorrowful."

Ginny's words were certainly putting a different picture on Raoul's marriage from the one given to me by John. It occurred to me that an outsider never really knows what goes on within the intimacy of a marriage, although I could not deny that the idea that Raoul might not have loved the elegantly aristocratic Georgiana gave a lift to my heart.

"If they were such opposites, then why did they marry?" I asked, thinking that since Ginny had introduced the subject she might be willing to answer my question.

"You've seen the portrait of Georgiana," Ginny said. She looked up from her book and her brown eyes met mine. "And what woman in her right mind would not want Raoul?"

I felt myself blushing, and she mercifully looked away.

"It was not until after the wedding that they discovered they had nothing in common," she concluded.

I thought of the instant sexual attraction between Raoul and myself and wondered if perhaps we were in the same situation as he and his wife had been, if history might be repeating itself.

Not on my part. That answer came almost instantly. I loved and admired almost everything about him. Even if I could have, I wouldn't have changed a hair on his head.

On the other hand, there were probably quite a few things he would change about me.

"Why are you telling me all this?" I asked Ginny cautiously.

"It must be the gloomy day loosening my tongue," she replied. "That, and being worried about the mad archer." Once more she rubbed her temples. "There's nothing like a good gossip to take one's mind off one's troubles," she said semihumorously.

"Yes . . ." I said slowly. "I suppose that is so."

I chose a book that Ginny recommended, not one of the gothic romances that had always sounded so silly to me but a delightful book about people whom one could actually imagine knowing. It was called *Pride and Prejudice* and it kept me enthralled for all of the morning and most of the afternoon. In fact, I was still curled up in the library in a large leather chair that faced the fireplace and had its back to the door when Mr. Cole came into the room with a man whose voice I immediately recognized as that of the Mr. Wickham I had met at the Black Swan.

The men did not move very far from the door, and my presence was hidden from them by the back of my chair. At first I was so involved in my book that I did not realize that anyone had come in, but when the men began to talk, and I recognized their voices, I listened shamelessly.

Now, in the normal course of things, of course I would have made my presence known. But things were far from normal at Savile Castle these days and I was fully prepared to put aside the niceties of good manners if it would help me to learn anything that might shed light on the mysterious accidents that had beset us of late.

The two men were speaking in low voices, but, fortunately, my hearing was excellent.

Wickham said, "I am pleased to be able to inform you that I have in my possession the paper that you desire."

"Let me see it, then," Cole returned in a

grim-sounding voice.

Wickham laughed with genuine amusement. "Do you think I'm a fool? I'm not handing it over to you just like that. It would be only too easy for you to rip it up before I could get it back, and then I'd be out all my money. It's not the sort of paper that can be replaced."

It occurred to me suddenly that the name of the villain in *Pride and Prejudice* was Wickham. This Wickham did not seem very much better.

"How did you get your mitts on it?" Cole asked.

"I've been rummaging around among my brother's things for weeks and I finally found it. I didn't think he would have destroyed it; he's too weak to have done that. He's just the sort who would hold on to it, and worry about it, and do nothing. Well, now he doesn't have it any longer — I do. And I plan to do something with it."

Stealing from his own brother. This Wickham sounded like a very pleasant fellow indeed, I thought.

"Does your brother know you've got it?" Cole asked.

"No. But it's not the sort of paper you can deny, is it? Everything is in order, just like I told you."

I heard Mr. Cole pacing back and forth. He seemed to be coming closer to me. My heart began to beat harder and I made myself as still as I could in my chair.

"Well, if you've got the goods all right, then I'll buy them from you," Mr. Cole said at last.

"That's what I'm here for. But you've got to come up with the blunt."

Now it seemed that Wickham's voice was moving closer. My heart was hammering in my chest. *Please, please,* I thought, *stay by the door. Don't come any closer to this chair.*

I couldn't bear to lose the chance to find out something that might bear on the strange accidents we had been having at Savile.

They were still moving closer to me.

"Oh, I can come up with the dibs all right, sonny," Mr. Cole said. "That piece of paper, if it really exists, is easily worth a thousand pounds to me."

"A thousand pounds! It's worth bloody more than that, Cole, and you know it."

I fought to keep myself from trying to make myself even smaller in the chair. My best chance not to be discovered was not to move at all.

"What do you want for it, then?"

"I want twenty thousand pounds."

Mr. Cole laughed. It was not an amiable

sound. "I didn't get where I am, sonny, by playing ducks and drakes with my money. You'll get no twenty thousand pounds from Albert Cole."

I heard the urgency in Wickham's voice as he said, "Think what it will mean to you to have that paper, Cole. Think what it will mean for you to be able to destroy it for good and all. I think that is worth twenty thousand pounds, don't you?"

There was a long, tense silence. Then Cole said, "Ten thousand."

"Twenty and not a penny less."

"Ten," Cole repeated firmly. "That paper ain't worth a penny to anyone but myself. Oh, you can take it to Savile if you want, but he ain't going to give you any money for it. You will only be spiting yourself if you do that, Wickham. Ten thousand pounds. That's my offer, take it or leave it."

There was a long pause, during which I could feel Wickham's discontent vibrating through the room. Then he said sulkily, "Oh, all right. Ten thousand pounds."

I heard the exhale of Mr. Cole's breath and felt his relief. "Very good, very good. I'll have to see my bankers before I can make a payment. You are still staying at the Black Swan?"

"Yes." Wickham's sulkiness was even more pronounced.

"Good, good. Once I have the blunt, I will call upon you there." Their voices began to recede, as if they were walking toward the door. "You shouldn't have come here today, Wickham. It wasn't wise."

Wickham replied, "It was raining and I knew you would never venture forth to Henley, and I wanted to tell you that I had the paper."

"So badly under the hatches that you can't wait an extra day, eh?" Mr. Cole asked sardonically.

Once again the sulky note marred Wickham's voice as he said, "My investments have not prospered as well as yours. . . ."

The voices trailed away as the two of them left the room, and I sat in my chair, staring at the fireplace with my book lying unregarded in my lap.

What on earth was this piece of paper that was so important to Albert Cole? I wondered. Could it have anything to do with the dangerous happenings at Savile Castle?

CHAPTER 23

The rain continued to pour down all day long, and when Raoul still had not come back from London by dinnertime I assumed that he had decided to wait until the following day to return with the runners. When I went upstairs to the nursery, however, it was to find two burly-looking, craggy-faced men, one of whom had two broken front teeth, sitting on chairs outside the schoolroom door.

The boys were in awe.

"His lordship sent them to look after us, Mama," Nicky told me.

"They used to be prizefighters, Mrs. Saunders," Charlie told me with great reverence.

"Uncle Raoul told them to protect us with their very lives." Theo's eyes were stretched wide.

Mr. Wilson said briskly, "His lordship told me that he does not know precisely what is going on at Savile, but that he wishes to make certain the children are safe. That is why he has hired the . . . er . . . gentlemen whom you saw sitting in the passageway."

"Well, I think that is very wise of his lordship," I said. "One can never be too careful, and Johnny Wester's death certainly raises some very serious questions."

All the boys nodded solemnly.

"Er . . . have you seen his lordship?" I asked Mr. Wilson.

"No. He did not return with the gentlemen outside," the tutor told me. "Evidently he had other business to attend to in London."

I tried not to allow my face to show my disappointment and my worry. I might not have known Raoul for very long but I knew that it was not like him to disappear at a time like this.

I spent an hour with the children in the nursery playing a board game and then went down to have my dinner, which, lacking Raoul, was as subdued and dreary as the weather.

Harriet maintained her usual silence. Mr. Cole appeared to be in a good humor, but he too said little. John tried to keep up a courteous conversation with me, and Roger looked restless and bored. Ginny made me want to scream by saying every five minutes, "I wonder where Raoul is," until finally Roger said bitingly, "Ginny, if you say that one more time I shall certainly do something drastic."

Ginny looked furious, and I silently applauded Roger.

I didn't stay around for the tea tray but took *Pride and Prejudice* up to my bedroom and finished it in the warmth of the coal fire that had been lit against the dampness of the night.

A fire in July, I thought. Raoul certainly lived in the height of luxury.

Where was he? Why had he not told me that he wouldn't return this evening? I knew it was not the weather that kept him away. A man who was intrepid enough to drive through a blizzard would certainly not let a little rain slow him down.

Was my refusal to confide in him so great a sin that whatever was between us was finished and this was his way of telling me so?

It was not finished for me, of course. No matter where I went or what I did, it would never be finished for me. But, sadly, there were some things that could not be said between us; there were simply some loyalties that I could not betray.

If he could not understand that, then we were indeed at a standstill.

At that thought, I felt as if a knife turned in my heart.

At two in the morning I gave up trying to go to sleep and went down to the library to get the copy of *Sense and Sensibility* I had seen reposing on the shelf next to *Pride and Prejudice*. I was surprised to find Roger there, sitting at the big mahogany library table with a bottle of wine and a glass in front of him.

He was clearly drunk.

"Well, well, well, look who's here," he said, looking up with a strange glitter in his brilliant blue eyes. "If it isn't Savile's own personal little bed warmer. What are you doing down here, sweetheart? Lonely because Raoul ain't home?"

"No," I said stiffly. "I came for a book."

"Can't sleep, eh?" he asked in mock sympathy. "Got an itch that needs to be scratched? I can help you with that, if you like. I've been wanting to do it since first I laid eyes on you, if you want to know the truth."

I said contemptuously, "You are disgusting, Roger."

He shrugged and poured himself more wine.

"I may be disgusting, sweetheart, but if you think Raoul is going to marry you, you are a fool. My dear cousin is far too aware of his own worth to marry some indigent little widow with a bastard brat."

Perhaps because they echoed my fears, his words struck me to the heart. I struggled to keep my face expressionless. I would have died before I let Roger know that he had wounded me.

There had been a vicious sound in Roger's voice, however, when he spoke Raoul's name, and I concentrated on that. "Why do you hate Raoul so much?" I asked. "He has supported you for years, Roger. I should think you would be grateful to him."

With his silver hair and his blue eyes illuminated by the wall sconces, he looked like an angel, but the expression on his face was excessively unpleasant. "I've told you before. He has too much. Everyone respects and admires Raoul. I could have been just as important, just as highly respected, if I'd been the earl, if I'd been the one who had control of the Savile estate and money. Raoul owes it to me to pay my debts. He always has before, but now he's getting sticky about it. He says I must pay my own way."

He slammed his hand down upon the desk. "Well, I'm going to surprise them all," he said. "You'll see." He stood up, leaned forward across the desk, and gave me what I'm sure he thought was a persuasive smile. He dropped his voice to a coaxing note.

"The lion's away, Gail," he said. "Are you sure you don't want to play?"

"Very sure," I said definitely, and turned

swiftly and left the room.

I went back to the bedroom with my copy of *Sense and Sensibility* and spent the rest of the night reading and thinking about Roger. More and more I was coming to believe that he was the one who was responsible for all of the terrible things that were happening at Savile.

He needed money and having Nicky out of his way would make money available to him immediately if he inherited. There was, of course, the question of Harriet's child, but I was also beginning to wonder how safe Harriet's child would be if it was a boy. If Roger was willing to kill an eight-year-old like Nicky, why should he hesitate to commit infanticide?

I didn't sleep for the rest of the night, and in the morning the sight of my wan face and the shadows under my eyes was distinctly unappetizing. My ugly brown morning dress was loose on me as well, testifying to my lack of appetite during the last few days.

Mrs. MacIntosh would have had a fit if she had seen me, I thought, in an attempt at humor. And Mr. MacIntosh would have gone on a mission to fatten me up. I felt a pang of homesickness for the dear old couple whose love for Nicky and me was unequivocal.

The day was sunny and warm, but still Raoul did not return. The children played within sight of the house under the vigilant eyes of the Bow Street runners as well as Ginny and me, and in the evening I retired to my lonely bed and finished reading *Sense and Sensibility* before I managed to fall into a restless sleep.

At luncheon the following afternoon John told me that he thought he might have located an establishment for my horse business. It was in southern Hertfordshire, he said, not very far from London.

"My correspondent writes that there is a house, a carriage house, a stable with eight stalls, and a fenced paddock with good footing you can use for a riding ring," he said.

A month ago I would have been delighted by the news. Now, I felt my heart sink.

"It sounds perfect," I made myself say. "How long a lease do they want and what is the rent?"

"The lease would be for a year and the rent is a thousand pounds," John said.

"That is too high," I replied immediately.

"Yes; well, my friend thinks I can get them down. Evidently the family has inherited a larger house and are anxious to let this one quickly. I think I can get them to come down a few hundred pounds on the lease."

"Hertfordshire," Ginny said. "Is it any-where near the Cecils'?"

"It is not in the immediate neighborhood, no," John said.

"Well, since I am hardly going to be on visiting terms with the Earl of Salisbury, that scarcely matters, Ginny," I said a little tartly. I didn't need any more reminders of how far my station in life was removed from Raoul's. I turned back to John. "I gather you haven't seen it yourself?"

"Not yet. I thought I would ride up there tomorrow and make certain that everything is in good repair. I understand that it is, but I want to make certain for myself before I begin to negotiate for terms."

I smiled at him across the luncheon table. "I cannot thank you enough. I know how busy you are here at Savile, and it is so very kind of you to take the time to do this for me. And you have been so swift!"

His light brown eyes smiled back at me. "It is my pleasure to assist you, Gail. I know how eager you are to resume your own life, so I have tried to be as expedient as possible."

I wasn't at all eager to resume my own life, unfortunately. I could hardly say this to John, however, so I smiled and thanked him again and pushed away my uneaten slice of roast beef.

"You are getting too thin," Ginny said to me. "I noticed this morning how your dresses are beginning to hang on you."

"I just don't have any appetite," I said. "I am too worried about Nicky, I suppose."

Ginny raised an eyebrow but did not answer. Then she turned to ask John again, "I suppose you have not heard from Raoul?"

"No, I have not," John replied with sorely tried courtesy.

Suddenly I felt that if I remained in the dining room for one more moment I was going to scream. I needed desperately to get away from the house and all the people in it, so I excused myself and decided that I would take Narsalla for a ride by myself around the lake.

When I arrived at the stables dressed in my riding habit, it was to find that the head groom was not keen to let me go out by myself. This annoyed me seriously, so I finally lied and told him that Raoul had said I could take out the little gray Arabian mare whenever I wished. Grove begged to be allowed to accompany me but I refused him curtly, and they reluctantly saddled Narsalla and I was on my way.

I crossed the causeway and turned left, taking the lake path along the deer park and through the Home Woods. I followed the road after that for about five miles more, traveling along the river and through the cornfields, past the Jenkinses' farm, where Raoul had been so kind to the injured tenant farmer, then farther and farther into the country.

Everywhere I looked, the land stretching out around me belonged to Raoul. Taking into consideration his stud farm, his hunting box, and his other lesser estates, I now knew that he owned over eight thousand acres. He had hundreds and hundreds of people depending upon him for their welfare: his tenants, his servants, his family — and he failed none of them. For years he had paid Roger's debts and done what he could to redress George's follies. His sister, his sister's children, John, Roger, Harriet, Mr. Cole, me, all of us alike were recipients of his bounty. Even a frightened black horse, whom anyone else would have sent to the knackers, was given a home at Savile and made useful and happy.

How could one not love such a man? I thought. How could his wife have allowed her desire for the gaiety of London to blind her to the gold in her husband's character?

It was not that he had no flaws. He was too high-handed, certainly, too accustomed to getting his own way. But he was not truly arrogant. Raoul was inherently far too just to be called arrogant.

If the property John had found for me was in good condition, and if he could get the lease down to seven hundred pounds, I would have to take it. I would have to pack up Nicky and my meager belongings and leave Savile Castle and I would never be able to return again.

Nicky was still too young to understand what was happening between me and the Earl of Savile. In another year or so, however, he would no longer be too young, and I couldn't chance him tumbling onto the truth. As always, Nicky had to be my prime concern.

'Twere all one
That I should love a bright particular star . . .

The lines from *All's Well that Ends Well* came into my mind once more.

Oh, Raoul, I thought, *come back to me soon. Please give me just a few more memories to hold on to for the rest of my life.*

He met me on the other side of the lake, at the charming half-timbered cottage that his grandfather had built as a plaything for adults. He was riding Satan, and at the sight of his tall figure on the huge black horse my heart leaped into my throat.

We stopped so that we were facing each other on the road.

"You're back," I said foolishly.

"Yes, I just returned. Grove told me that you were out on Narsalla, that you had assured them in the stables that I had said you could take her out alone."

I knew I was in the wrong, which put me on the defensive. "Good heavens, Raoul," I said tartly, "I make my living with horses. I can assure you that I am perfectly capable of going for a ride by myself."

"Of course you are," he replied mildly, effectively taking the wind out of my indignant sails. "I am sorry that I hadn't made it clear myself."

"Oh," I said. I patted Narsalla's arched gray neck. "Well then, that's all right."

"I have not even been back to the house," he said. "I came looking for you immediately because I have to talk to you."

I gave him a wary look. There was a grave expression on his face and the golden eyes that met mine gave away nothing. I said, "If you are going to ask me any more questions about Nicky's birth, there is no point in our talking. I told you before that I have nothing to tell you."

He said, "I have a few things to tell you, however, and since I would like to say them away from where we might be interrupted by one of the family, I suggest that we stop here at the cottage."

My spirits lifted. "Have you discovered who is trying to harm Nicky?"

"Not precisely, but I think I may be close on the trail."

"Thank God," I said fervently, and I turned Narsalla toward the cottage. Together we dismounted in front of the hawthorne bush that set the cottage off from the road and I loosely tied Narsalla's reins to the white picket fence. Raoul did the same with Satan, then we went inside the fence and sat side by side on the iron garden bench that was placed amidst the flower garden in the front yard. The horses began to nibble the greenery around them, and I folded my hands in my lap and looked up into Raoul's face.

"Well?" I prompted. "What did you find out?"

He took his time answering, slowly removing his gloves and flexing his bare fingers as if he needed time to think. Finally he said slowly, "Two days ago, immediately after I hired the Bow Street runners and sent them here, I drove from London down to Devane Hall."

Suddenly I was not sure I wanted to hear what he had to say. "Why did you do that?" I asked tensely.

I watched his hands smooth the soft leather driving gloves on his thigh. The gold signet ring he wore on the fourth finger of his right hand winked in the sun. He replied, "I must tell you that I did not go in my capacity as executor of George's estate, Gail. I went with the sole purpose of seeing your Aunt Margaret."

Suddenly it seemed that the air did not want to come in and out of my lungs. I forced down my rising panic and said breathlessly, "How dare you?"

He didn't answer that. He said only, "She was very loyal to you, Gail. She told me nothing."

Relief flooded through me, and I said contemptuously, "Loyalty is evidently a virtue you know nothing about."

He said, "So then I was forced to go to see Lady Saunders."

At that I leaped to my feet and whirled to face him. "You *didn't* do that! You didn't go to see Tommy's mother!"

He kept his seat and regarded me steadily. "I am afraid that I did, and a miserable old harridan she is."

I could hear my labored breathing. "She

hates me. She always hated me."

His voice was very gentle as he answered, "I could tell that very easily. She had no compunction about informing me that Nicky was born six months after your marriage, that he was not her grandson, and that you had talked her son — who was besotted with you — into accepting Nicky as his own child."

I turned my back on him, folded my arms across my breasts, lifted my chin, and said nothing. What, after all, was there to say? The picture Lady Saunders had painted fitted all too well with the facts as they must have appeared to Raoul.

Consequently I was stunned when Raoul said next, "So then I asked Lady Saunders if she would tell me the name of the village where you and your husband lived when you were first married, and she did so."

Suddenly I was very, very frightened indeed. Slowly I turned to look at him. I said pleadingly, "You did not go there, Raoul?"

"Yes, Gail, I did."

I took a few steps back from him, in a manner that was reminiscent of the way I had backed away from Roger in the library the other night. In truth, I felt just as threatened, although in a completely different way.

"The minister's wife in Highgate remembered you well," Raoul said.

"Oh God," I said. "Oh God." I shut my eyes.

When I opened them again, he was standing only a few feet from me. With a mixture of anger and bewilderment, he asked, "Why the hell have you been hiding this, Gail? It's not a disgrace, for God's sake! Your sister died in childbirth and you adopted her child as your own. What is so terrible about that?"

My hands were balled into fists at my sides. "I promised Deborah that I would never tell Nicky that he was baseborn," I said. "I promised her that he would always think that he was mine, that I would never tell anyone else the truth about his birth. And he *is* mine! From the moment that Deborah put him into my arms, he was mine! Deborah is dead, and the only thing I can do for her is to give her child the greatest security and love that I am capable of." The look I gave him was scorching. "Even Lady Saunders doesn't know that Nicky isn't mine. Tommy told her that he was. No one knows that Deborah came to Tommy and me four months before Nicky was born and asked us to help her. At least no one except a few people in Highgate — whom *you* had to seek out!"

"I would not have had to seek them out if

you had been able to trust me with the truth," Raoul said quietly.

There was a disquietingly bleak look on his face that somewhat quenched my rage. "I made a solemn promise to my sister," I repeated in a more level tone of voice. "I did not feel I could break it."

After a moment, Raoul said, "In fact, the people in Highgate were remarkably secretive. The minister's wife said nothing to me about Nicky not being yours."

I said, "Then how did you find out?"

"I went to the cemetery. There was a grave for a Deborah Longworth. She died on December twenty-second, 1810 — the day after you told me Nicky was born."

I rubbed my temples, trying to think what I might say to him.

"I gather that George was Nicky's father?" he asked next.

"Yes. Deborah and he were in love and he had promised to marry her. Deborah would never have gone to George otherwise! But then George's father discovered Harriet and began to pressure him to marry the Cole fortune. Deborah had too much pride to remain in Hatfield and watch George courting someone else, so she came to Tommy and me. A month after she left, George finally succumbed to his father's pressure and married Harriet."

My rage was gone, leaving me feeling drained and tired. I thought about what Raoul had just told me and a curious fact stuck out.

"What made you go to the cemetery?" I asked.

"I went to look for Deborah's grave," came the startling reply.

I looked up to search his face. "But . . . if the minister's wife in Highgate had said nothing to you about Deborah, why would you do that?"

"Because I suspected the truth," he said.

I leaned my back against the fence and felt the heat of the wood through my dress. Narsalla nibbled at a piece of my hair, thinking it was part of the shrubbery. "You suspected?" I echoed in amazement.

"Nicky had to be George's son — there was no other explanation for that legacy," he said flatly. "And in my mind I had narrowed the possibilities down to two scenarios. The first scenario was that George had raped you."

The look he gave me was extremely grim. "Aside from the fact that the thought of this made me want to murder a man who is already dead, I didn't think that you would have allowed such a thing to happen."

"Are you mad?" I said incredulously. "George, rape me?"

The faintest trace of humor, the first I had seen since we had begun the conversation, quirked the corners of his mouth. "Precisely. The other explanation, then, was that Nicky was George's son but not yours. Once I began to look around for an alternate mother, the picture became clear."

Narsalla's warm nose nuzzled my neck. I thrust my hands through my hair and stared at Raoul. I felt limp.

I said, "But, Raoul, why didn't you just think that I had had an affair with George?"

"I did think that at first, but I haven't thought it for a long, long time," Raoul said.

My eyes stretched wide in astonishment. "But here I was, having an affair with you. Why should you stop thinking me capable of having had an affair with George?"

He gave me the smile that turned my knees to water. "Because, sweetheart, I gave you credit for good taste."

He began to walk across the small space that separated us and I felt my breath begin to hurry and my heart begin to pound. I tried to summon up the fury I had felt toward him just minutes earlier, but it had died.

I said pleadingly, "You will not tell any of this to Nicky, Raoul?"

A flicker of anger crossed his face. "Of course I won't tell Nicky. But you are going to have a difficult time explaining that legacy to him, Gail."

"I wouldn't if you would just let me refuse it."

He murmured, "It seems to me that this is where we started," and he bent his head and kissed me.

The two horses regarded us with interest as we moved from the fence to the garden seat. I was wearing a riding habit and Raoul was wearing riding clothes and it was a little difficult for us to get our hands where we wanted them to be.

We settled for kissing.

I loved him so much, I thought. I kissed his ear, his nose, his jaw. I ran my fingers through his hair.

"We could move into the cottage," he murmured after a while.

"That is an excellent idea," I replied, and he stood up first and pulled me up by my hand to stand beside him. Then he leaned over me again and I bent like a reed before his superior height, his strength, his need.

From down the road came the sound of children laughing. Raoul and I leaped apart like guilty things surprised.

"Mama!" Nicky shouted.

"Uncle Raoul!" cried the Austen boys.

"We're going fishing! Do you want to come?" everyone called.

Raoul gave me an extremely frustrated look.

"Tonight," I said, and smiled.

CHAPTER 24

I didn't get much sleep that night either, but I awoke feeling invigorated, not depressed. Before Raoul returned to his room, he had told me only that he was "making serious inquiries" about the situation regarding Nicky. I had not pressed him further because I felt that the inquiries must be about Roger and I knew that it had to be difficult for Raoul to consider such dreadful things about his cousin.

After breakfast John left to look at the property he had found for me in Hertfordshire. Raoul saw him off with a cheerful, encouraging word, and I must confess that I found it more than a little dejecting that Raoul seemed not to be overly concerned that I might soon have somewhere else to live.

What did you expect? I scolded myself. *You always knew that your sojourn at Savile was going to be a brief one.*

But it hurt bitterly to think that he regarded our being together so lightly.

I won't think about it, I told myself, and I

went down to the stables to take Narsalla for a too-reckless ride through the countryside. As I was passing the Jenkinses' farm I stopped on impulse, and Mrs. Jenkins and I had a pleasant cup of tea together in her kitchen.

When I returned to the house, Ginny informed me that a mysterious young man had arrived from London and had been closeted with Raoul in his office for well over an hour.

"Something is going on," Ginny informed me. "Between Bow Street runners all over the house, and now someone who looks like a law clerk taking up Raoul's entire morning! Well, something is certainly happening."

The two men emerged from Raoul's office at about one o'clock and went into the family dining room for luncheon. Apparently everyone had been on the watch, for the entire household, with the exception of John, magically appeared at the same time in order to share luncheon with Raoul and his guest.

Raoul introduced his companion as Mr. Robert Slater. Mr. Slater was pleasant and quiet and seemed to be a gentleman.

"Are you a solicitor, Mr. Slater?" Ginny asked as she helped herself to some grapes from Raoul's greenhouse.

"No, my lady, I am an investigator," the young man replied calmly.

This caused a minor sensation at the luncheon table.

"An investigator!" Roger said. "Do you mean someone who ferrets about in other people's private business and then reports upon it for money?"

Mr. Slater's thin, intelligent face was expressionless. "I wouldn't describe my profession in quite those terms, Mr. Melville."

I remembered Raoul's "inquiries" and said nothing.

Ginny gave Roger a repressive look and said, "Don't mind my cousin, Mr. Slater. I can assure you that the rest of us don't."

Mr. Cole wiped the whole bottom part of his face with his napkin. "Well, if someone hired you, sonny, then I'd sure like to know who it was and why."

Raoul leaned back a little in his chair. "*I* hired Mr. Slater, Cole," he said. "As I'm sure you all know, I have been extremely concerned about these so-called accidents that have been occurring here at Savile recently, so I asked Mr. Slater to investigate the matter for me."

Roger asked in a silky voice, "And what did Mr. Slater discover?"

Raoul looked around the table. "If everyone is finished with luncheon I think it would be a good idea if we adjourned to the library, where we may be private."

We all got up from the table with alacrity and followed him. I saw as we came into the library that five chairs had been set in a semicircle around the front of the big table. On the opposite side of the table sat a thin, pale, nervous-looking man whose hands were clasped tensely in his lap.

Raoul gestured us to the five chairs. "Please be seated."

We all took our seats. I sat between Ginny and Roger, with Harriet on Ginny's other side and Mr. Cole on the end.

Raoul and Mr. Slater went behind the library table and took the two other chairs that had been set there, Raoul sitting in the middle, next to the nervous-looking man. He lightly clasped his long-fingered hands on the table in front of him, regarded them with a faint frown between his straight brows, and began to speak.

"Over the past weeks it has become increasingly clear to me that the dangerous things that have been occurring at Savile Castle recently have been directed against Nicholas Saunders."

I felt Ginny turn to look at me, but I kept my eyes focused on Raoul.

He went on, "I saw no immediate significance in the matter with the bridge, which could simply have been the result of neglect. But then Nicky's pony was poisoned."

Roger spoke up. "There is no proof that that pony was poisoned. It could simply have colicked."

Raoul's brows rose in disbelief. "Possibly. But the suddenness and violence of the attack spoke more of poison than it did of colic." Once more he looked down at his loosely clasped hands, then he looked up and said quietly, "Then there was the death of Johnny Wester."

Mr. Cole shifted noisily on his chair. "Well, it don't make sense to me how you can think that the death of the Wester nipper had anything to do with young Nicholas."

Raoul's face was set hard. "I believe that Johnny Wester was killed on the mistaken assumption that he was Nicky," he answered. "Remember, no one but the boys knew that they had added Johnny to their game. And Johnny is very similar in height and coloring to Nicky. I believe that whoever shot that arrow thought that he was shooting at Nicky."

My hands were clasped tightly in my lap. For a brief moment, Ginny's hand closed over them and squeezed comfortingly.

From behind the library table, Raoul went on, "Naturally I began to ask myself what possible threat Nicky might pose to anyone that it should become so essential to get him out of the way."

The room was deathly quiet.

Raoul said, "At first my thoughts turned to Roger."

Roger yelped in protest but Raoul ignored him. His somber golden eyes moved slowly from Mr. Cole, to Harriet, to Ginny, to me, and then, at last, to Roger. He said, "I knew you needed money, Roger, and if Nicky were dead, the money set aside for him in George's will would be available to you. But the more I thought about this possibility, the less I liked it."

"Thank you, Savile," Roger said ironically.

Raoul continued to hold his cousin's restless blue gaze captive. "For one thing, there was no guarantee that you were going to inherit the Devane estate at all, and if you did you would probably be able to stave off your creditors, at least initially, without the extra twenty thousand set aside for Nicky."

I frowned and shifted in my seat so that I could look at Roger. I was not as sure of him as Raoul appeared to be.

Raoul's eyes left Roger's face at last and went back to the contemplation of his clasped hands. "No matter how I tried, I could not put aside my belief that the danger to Nicky originated with that legacy. However, it was not until I traveled to Sussex a few days ago that I began to understand what it was that must be at the root of these attacks."

I froze in my chair. He couldn't do that, I thought in horror. He had promised me that he would never tell!

Raoul did not look at me as he continued, "I don't think any of us ever had any doubt that Nicky was George's son. A man like George does not leave twenty thousand pounds to a boy whom he has met in passing on the street."

Ginny did not look at me either. Roger and Harriet and Mr. Cole did. I felt their eyes burning my skin.

Raoul said, "We all assumed that George was Nicky's father and that Gail was Nicky's mother, and that is where we were wrong."

I will never forgive him for this, I thought. *I will never forgive him.*

It was then that Raoul dropped his bombshell. He lifted his gaze and for the first time since we had come into the library he met my eyes. He said, "Nicky's mother was Gail's sister, Deborah, and she and George were married."

I stared back at Raoul incredulously. "What?"

He nodded gravely. "The paper you heard that fellow Wickham trying to sell to Cole? It was the record of the marriage. This gentleman here," he nodded to the man sitting next to him, "is the parish priest of Hawton, a village where George had a small property. George and your sister Deborah were married there by license in February of 1809."

"That ain't so!" said Mr. Cole.

"That can't be true!" Harriet cried in a strangled voice. "George and I were married in July of 1809!"

There was absolute silence in the room as we all registered what this might mean.

Deborah's marriage was legal and Harriet's was not.

"My God," I finally said in a shaky voice. "Does this mean that Nicky is George's legitimate son, Raoul?"

"His legitimate son, Gail, and his heir."

"My God," I said again. I could not take it in.

Roger said sharply, "And just where is Gail's sister, Savile?"

"She is dead," Raoul said gently. "Gail has reared Nicky from the time he was born."

"Fine words indeed, my lord, but where's your proof?" Mr. Cole said scornfully. "If there is no official marriage record, then there is no marriage."

"That is true, Raoul," Ginny said. "If the marriage between George and Deborah did indeed take place, there should be a record of it in the parish register at Hawton."

"Slater?" Raoul said. "Will you tell us what you found at Hawton?"

"Yes, my lord," the young man said. His level eyes regarded the five of us seated before him. "The whole page from the book that listed the marriages for the months of January, February, and March of 1809 was ripped out. When I asked Mr. Wickham here," Slater nodded to the man sitting on the other side of Raoul, "what had come of the page, he said it had fallen out of the binding and been lost." Slater curled his lip. "There was nothing wrong with the binding of that book, my lord. That page had been ripped out, pure and simple."

Wickham. The name rang familiarly in my mind and I looked at the clergyman and frowned. This was not the Mr. Wickham I had met.

"Papa!" Harriet said shrilly. "What are they saying?"

"Now, there ain't nothing here to concern you, Harriet," Mr. Cole replied. "There ain't a scrap of proof to back up any of this. It's all Savile's speculation."

"Cole is right," Roger said, agreeing with

445

the merchant for probably the first time in his life. "A missing page in a parish register is no proof of anything."

For the first time, the thin pale man sitting next to Raoul spoke. "His lordship is telling the truth. Nine years ago, Mr. George Melville came to me and asked me to marry him to a young lady in a manner that would avoid the attention of his father. As both parties were over the age of twenty-one, and Mr. Melville's family held property in the parish and he could be considered a resident parishioner, I did not see how I could fail to withhold my consent."

"I'll bet he sweetened your pocket to do it for him, too," Roger said sarcastically.

A dark flush came across the pale, meager features of the clergyman.

Raoul said, "The witnesses to the union between George and Deborah were Mr. Wickham's wife and his brother, Vincent, who was on a visit before he left for India."

I thought of the dark, sunburned face of the man who had been trying to sell a paper to Mr. Cole, and saw how the pieces of the puzzle were beginning to come together.

"I can only surmise what must have happened after the marriage," Raoul said. "George and Deborah obviously went home and told no one what they had done, but one can only assume that Deborah thought it was only going to be a matter of time before George would reveal the truth to his family. Then George's father brought the Coles to Devane Hall and began to pressure George to marry Harriet."

A sound came from Harriet and once again I felt that uncomfortable stab of pity.

Raoul went on, "The financial situation at Devane was desperate. If Uncle Jack could not pay off some of his debts, he would lose Devane Hall completely. This was the kind of pressure that was brought to bear on George." Raoul shrugged. "One must assume that George shared this information with Deborah."

"Of course he must have, the spineless worm," I said scornfully.

Ginny said, "Why didn't the girl simply insist that George tell his father the truth? Or if he was afraid to do it, why didn't she go to Uncle Jack herself?"

I answered that question. "Deborah would have had too much pride. And when she found herself with child, instead of telling George she came to me." I put my hand up to shade my eyes. "She didn't tell me about the marriage for the same reason, I imagine."

"That is what must have happened," Raoul agreed. "She ran away to you, and a month later George married Harriet."

Harriet moaned and stood up so abruptly that her chair fell over. I had not thought her heavy body capable of moving so quickly. "Oh God, oh God, oh God," she said.

"I am sorry, Harriet," Raoul said gently. "This must be dreadful for you. Would you like to go and lie down?"

"Yes, yes, yes." Her voice grew higher with every *yes*, and I became afraid that perhaps we were going to have to deal with hysterics.

Ginny went to her and put an arm around her shoulders. "Let me summon your maid for you, Harriet, and you can go to your room. Come along now . . ."

Ginny's soft murmuring could be heard as the two of them left the library.

I sat in the sudden silence that their exit had produced and thought about what Raoul had just revealed. I remembered how Deborah had been during the last months of her pregnancy. Something terrible and destroying had happened to her when George had caved in and married Harriet.

Roger said, in his light, brittle voice, "Mr. Wickham, one can't help but wonder why the minister who performed this secret marriage was so reticent on the subject. Surely you knew that my cousin's subsequent marriage to Harriet Cole was bigamous."

"I did, of course," Mr. Wickham said wretchedly. "But Lord Devane came to see me shortly before the second marriage took place, you see, and he told me that he would be forced to remove me from my living if the first marriage should become known. I . . . I do not have many connections, Mr. Melville, and at the time I had a young family to support. I did not think I could afford to reveal what I knew."

"It surprises me to learn that George had the backbone to make such a threat," I said contemptuously.

"Oh, it wasn't Mr. George Melville who came to me, Mrs. Saunders," the minister said in surprise. "It was Lord Devane. His father."

A brief silence fell, during which time Ginny came back into the room.

"George did tell Uncle Jack, then," Raoul said.

"Oh yes," said the minister. "Lord Devane was quite furious. He wanted me to give him the page from the register upon which the marriage was recorded. I would not do that, however. There were other marriages recorded on that page, you see. So I told him that I would tear the page from the book and hide it and that no one would see it unless I should have to produce it to verify one of the other marriages, which was unlikely as everyone was still living in the parish."

For some reason it made me feel slightly better that George had told his father about his marriage to Deborah.

"Yes, well, this is all fine talking, my lord, but you ain't got the proof," Mr. Cole said. "And I'll tell you this, there ain't no way I'm going to allow you to brand my girl a whore and my grandchildren bastards! I'll take you to court and we'll tie that bloody estate up for so long that it will molder into the ground before I let that happen!"

"There is proof, of course," Raoul said softly. "Even if you have the register page in your possession, there is still the sworn testimony of Mr. Wickham here, and of his wife and his brother. There is Mr. Vincent Wickham's testimony that he offered to sell you the page from the marriage register and that you agreed to buy it."

"I never did that," Mr. Cole said immediately.

I said, "Oh yes you did, Mr. Cole. I heard you. You were talking to Mr. Wickham here in the library. I was sitting in the chair in front of the fire and you didn't see me. You agreed to buy the paper for ten thousand pounds. Mr. Wickham wanted twenty thousand but you wouldn't give him that much."

Mr. Cole surged to his feet. "You're lying, you jezebel!"

I leaped to my own feet. "Murderer! You tried to kill my son! I'm going to see to it that you hang, Cole! I'm going to stand there and watch as you choke to death! I'm going to . . ."

Cole had turned purple, as if he were indeed choking, and was advancing upon me. Suddenly, Raoul's arm was around me and he was holding me against him. Restraining me, actually.

"That's enough," he said to Cole in a voice that stopped the older man dead in his tracks. "You must accept the fact that while I may not have the register paper in my possession — I assume you have destroyed that — I have enough evidence to establish that Nicholas Saunders is in fact Lord Devane's legitimate son."

"Well, we'll just see about that, my lord," Mr. Cole replied. He was breathing heavily. "Harriet and I will be packing our bags and leaving Savile, and the next you'll be hearing from me will be from my solicitors!"

"It will be a futile enterprise, Cole, but if you desire to pursue the matter, then by all means do so," Raoul said coldly.

As the merchant stomped from the room, I looked up at Raoul incredulously. "Are you just letting him go like that? He tried to murder Nicky!"

"We don't have any proof of that, Gail," Raoul returned.

"We don't need proof! It's perfectly obvious that he's guilty."

"We need proof if I am to ask Sir Robert Warren, our local magistrate, to arrest him," Raoul said.

I glared up at him in furious frustration. "Well then, are you going to try to find some proof?"

"I can promise you, Gail, that I will do my damnedest."

"He deserves to be hanged," I said again. "He may not have succeeded in killing Nicky, but he killed poor little Johnny Wester!"

"Yes," Raoul said quietly. "I know that, Gail."

I felt like screaming, I was so angry.

Ginny said, "Speaking of proof, is there anything beyond your word to verify that Nicky is Deborah's son, Gail?"

I gave her my reluctant attention. "I'm quite certain there will still be people living in Highgate who will remember that Deborah was the one who was with child, not I."

"What about the midwife?" Ginny asked.

"I suppose she could be traced if she has moved," I said. "She was not that old a woman."

Roger said acidly, "Congratulations, Gail. It seems that you have just found a new home for your horse business — Devane Hall."

I shut my eyes as the full ramifications of what had just happened began to sink in.

"Oh God," I said. "I am going to have to tell Nicky who he is."

"Yes," Raoul returned in a very gentle voice, "you are."

CHAPTER 25

"Take him for a ride," Raoul suggested. "You can stop at one of the buildings along the lake to talk, but get him away from the house. You both need to be alone together when you tell him."

It was half an hour after the meeting in the library. Everyone else had left the room, and for a few minutes at least Raoul and I were alone. He was standing next to the window, which had been closed against the cool and cloudy afternoon. I was standing facing him, with my hands on the back of a carved oak chair.

I said acidly, "True. It is excessively unpleasant to have tremendous personal surprises sprung on one in the midst of a large group of people."

He said, "I'm sorry I did that, Gail, but I didn't know about the marriage for certain until Slater arrived this morning with Wickham." He leaned his shoulders against the pale green wall next to the tall window, regarded me with a mixture of bewilderment and anger, and said, "Why in God's name didn't your sister ever tell you that she was married? Didn't she know that she was depriving her child of his birthright?"

I repeated what I had said earlier: "Deborah would have had too much pride to push herself in where she was not wanted."

He shook his head in sharp disagreement. "This was not a personal matter, Gail. This was a matter of law." His mouth hardened. "And a matter of justice as well. Nicky should have been acknowledged as the heir to Devane Hall."

"Well, from what you have told me, my lord, Devane Hall would have to have been sold if Nicky inherited," I flashed back, furious that he was criticizing Deborah. "I am quite certain that Deborah knew that Nicky would be much better off with me and Tommy than he would have been with a profligate for a grandfather and a spineless . . . creature . . . for a father!"

His mouth retained its hard line for a few more moments, then it softened very slightly. "Perhaps that is so," he conceded. "She could not have foreseen that your husband would be killed and you would be left to support the boy on your own."

I said evenly, "I believe I have told you before that I have never found Nicky to be a burden."

His reply was just as even. "I know you have not, Gail. That is not what I meant."

I wasn't sure what he had meant, but I decided not to pursue the subject. It didn't take a genius to see that the subject of Deborah was not one on which we were ever likely to agree.

I said instead, "Are you certain it is safe to take Nicky for a ride? You don't think Mr. Cole will keep trying to harm him?"

"Cole is not a fool," Raoul replied. "Even if something should happen to Nicky now, Harriet's marriage is still invalid. Once the information about Deborah's prior marriage was made public, Nicky was perfectly safe from Albert Cole."

I looked at him suspiciously. "You sound as if you don't intend to pursue the matter of Mr. Cole any further."

"I have assured you that I will not let the matter of Johnny Wester's murder drop, Gail," he replied a little irritably.

I let my thoughts turn to the man who had been my other suspect. "What about Roger? If something happens to Nicky, then Roger will inherit Devane. Do you think I can trust him not to harm Nicky?"

Raoul replied in a supernaturally patient voice, "I know you don't like Roger, Gail, but I do not believe that he is a murderer."

I felt myself flush. "I suppose you think that I am being hysterical."

His smile was warm and reassuring. "Not at all. You have had good cause to be concerned about Nicky's welfare. But I can honestly tell you that I think it is safe for you to take him for a ride around the lake."

So I fetched Nicky from the nursery party that was playing bowls on the lawn and induced him to come riding with me by promising that he could ride Narsalla. I rode one of Raoul's extra hacks, and Nicky and I set off over the causeway under an overcast, midafternoon sky.

We did not speak much until we had reached the lakeside cottage. Nicky was doing fairly well with Narsalla but there was no doubt that she was a bit of a challenge for him. There was color in his cheeks and his eyes were sparkling, however. Clearly he was enjoying himself enormously. Like me, Nicky always preferred to ride a high-spirited horse, and he had been missing Squirt badly.

He was not pleased when I suggested that we stop at the cottage.

"Why, Mama? I am just beginning to get the feel of her. I don't want to stop now."

"I must talk to you, sweetheart. It's important."

"You can talk to me anytime, Mama,"

said my bewildered son.

"I know, but this is a very important, very private kind of talk. Let's just let the horses nibble the grass for a bit and we can have our discussion, shall we? It won't take long, I promise."

"All right." He gave in with the sweet unselfishness that had always been his mother's, and slid down from Narsalla's back. After he had tied her he turned and asked suspiciously, "You're not going to talk about sending me away to school, are you?"

"No, sweetheart, it's nothing like that."

He gave an exaggerated whistle of relief.

"Come and sit on the bench," I said, but when I had him there beside me I didn't know how to begin.

How do you tell a child that something you have led him to believe all his life is untrue?

I inhaled deeply and began slowly, feeling my way. "I want to tell you a story, Nicky. It is about my sister, but it is about you too, so will you please be patient and listen?"

Nicky gave me an alert look. Like all youngsters, he was interested in anything that pertained to himself. "All right, Mama," he said.

I stripped off my riding gloves and ran them nervously through my fingers as I talked.

"When Deborah and I were quite young," I began, "our parents were killed in a hotel fire and we were sent to the village of Hatfield to live with my father's sister, my Aunt Margaret. Deborah was a few years older than I and the kindest, most gentle person whom I have ever known. We were very close — much closer than sisters usually are."

"That was because you had no parents, I expect," Nicky said wisely.

I smiled at him. "Quite probably." I drew in a deep breath, consulted the heavy gray sky, and continued. "Now, Hatfield village lies close to Devane Hall, which was the home of an uncle of the Earl of Savile. At the time that Deborah and I were living in Hatfield, this Lord Devane had one son, whose name was George, and he was a very handsome and personable young man."

I looked into Nicky's clear blue eyes. "Are you following me so far?"

"I think so, Mama. Lord Devane was the earl's uncle."

"And Lord Devane had a son named George, who was just a year older than my sister, Deborah," I clarified further.

There was a faint line of puzzlement between Nicky's finely drawn brows, but he nodded that he understood.

I looked down at the gloves I was mangling

between my fingers. "Well, what happened next, Nicky, was that Deborah and George fell in love. But Deborah and I had no money, and because of this George knew that his father would never allow him to marry Deborah."

Nicky nodded again. Even at eight, he knew what it was like when one had no money.

I went on, "But George and Deborah loved each other very much, and so they decided that they would get married secretly."

I could see that this romantic tale of people whom he had never known and did not care about was not holding Nicky's attention. I said sharply, "Pay attention, Nicky. This is important."

His eyes left the horses and came back to me. "Yes, Mama," he said with an effort.

"This is what happened," I said firmly. "George and Deborah got married in secret and didn't tell anyone. Then George's father tried to make him marry Harriet Cole because the Coles were rich and George's father had gambled away all of the family's money."

Now I had truly caught Nicky's attention. "Do you mean Maria, Frances, and Jane's mama?"

"Yes, that is who I mean. And, as you can imagine, it upset Deborah very much to see George paying attention to Harriet, especially since George was already married to herself."

I could see Nicky struggling to follow this.

"What happened was this, Nicky," I said simply. "Deborah found out that she was going to have George's baby, and because she was very upset at the way George was behaving, she ran away from Hatfield. I had been married to Tommy Saunders for a few months, and of course Deborah came to stay with me."

Suddenly an apprehensive look came across Nicky's childish face, a look that said he did not think he was going to like what was coming next. He didn't say anything.

I put my arm around his shoulders and held him against me. "My beloved sister died right after she gave birth to her baby, and with her last breath she gave me her child for my own. And for eight years now you have been my own, Nicky, the child of my heart even if you are not the child of my body."

Silence. His body was stiff, resisting my embrace.

"I'm not your son?" he said at last.

The note in his voice was anguishing.

I said softly, "You are the son of my sister, Deborah, and of George, Lord Devane, Nicky. In fact, in case you are interested, you yourself are the new Lord Devane. Not Roger. Not Harriet's child if it is a boy. *You.*"

I waited for him to ask me about this, but he said nothing.

Finally, "You lied to me," he said. I looked down into his white face, into his huge and stricken eyes.

I felt as if a knife twisted in my heart. "I love you more than anything in the world," I said. "That love is not a lie. It never has been."

I felt a shudder go all through him and he jerked himself away from me and jumped to his feet. "How could you love me and lie to me like this? Why didn't you tell me? I could have understood it. You should have told me!"

I held out a pleading hand. "Sweetheart, Deborah never told me that she and George had been married! I thought that you were baseborn, and neither your fa— neither Tommy nor I wanted you to suffer that stigma. Can't you understand that?"

He didn't understand what I was saying. He was, after all, only eight years of age, and his world had just been turned upside down. His mother was not his mother. That was

462

all he could comprehend at the moment, all that he could understand.

He was devastated. I had known that he would be.

Suddenly he whirled away from me and ran toward the horses. In a flash he had untied Narsalla's reins and was swinging up into the saddle. The little mare reared a bit as he swung her recklessly away from the cottage and toward the lake path. Then they were away at full gallop. I could hear the sound of hooves pounding even after they were out of my sight.

My chest was tight with fear, but I let him go. For the moment, I understood, Nicky needed to get away from me.

The gray clouds were low and thick by the time I got back to the castle. The flags flying from the four towers were scarcely visible in the late afternoon gloom.

The first person I asked for when I came in the door was Roger. I wanted to make certain that he was in the house and not loose somewhere on the grounds, free to make mischief with Nicky.

Powell told me that Roger had gone to his room right after the meeting in the library and was still there.

Next I asked for Raoul.

"I believe his lordship is in his office," Powell replied, and that is where I went.

One of the understewards was with Raoul when I looked in, but he said, "Come in, Gail. Barrett and I have just finished."

I came in as the young steward went out, greeting me with grave courtesy as he went by. Raoul gestured me to the chair that faced his desk.

"How did it go?" he asked gently.

"It went the way I thought it would," I replied. "He was extremely upset. In fact, he ran away from me, Raoul. I did not chase after him because I thought that would do more harm than good, but I am worried. He is riding Narsalla, and you know how high-spirited she is and Nicky is upset and . . ."

I could hear the rising panic in my voice and I forced myself to stop talking.

Raoul got up from behind his desk and went out into the hallway to tell the footman who was stationed there that he wanted a message sent to the stables that a search was to be instituted immediately for Master Nicky.

"And when he is found, he is to be told that I wish to see him."

"Yes, my lord," I heard the footman reply.

Raoul came back into the room, resumed his chair, frowned at me, and said abruptly,

"You look as if you have lost ten pounds, Gail, and there was never very much of you to begin with."

"Yes, well, living in constant fear is not a very effective appetite stimulant," I retorted.

"It is almost all over now, sweetheart," he said soothingly. "You can start eating again."

I sighed and rubbed my temples. "You really think that Nicky is safe?"

"I'm sure of it. As a matter of fact, I am sending both of you to Devane Hall tomorrow. That is what I was talking to Barrett about when you came in. He is leaving immediately so he can get there first and make certain that things go smoothly for you when you get there."

I dropped my hands and stared at him in shock. "You want me to go to Devane Hall tomorrow?"

The eyes that met mine were a clear, pure amber. "Yes. I think it is important to establish Nicky as the rightful Lord Devane immediately. You don't need to go about in the neighborhood if you don't wish to, Gail, but you should be in possession of the premises." He smiled. "I will even have Mr. and Mrs. MacIntosh driven down from Deepcote to join you. Perhaps Mr. MacIntosh's cooking will start you eating again."

"Oh," I said. Then, tonelessly: "That will be nice."

"Devane Hall has turned into a tidy little property," Raoul said. "You will have no more occasion to worry about Nicky, Gail; his future is fixed. And you don't have to worry about your legal relationship to him either. I have contacted my solicitor and we have begun the paperwork to have you declared his guardian. I will be the executor of his property until he reaches his majority, but under the law you will remain his mother, sweetheart."

I couldn't stop myself from saying, "Is it really necessary for us to leave tomorrow? It will be so upsetting for Nicky to leave in such a rush."

He answered my real concern, "I can't come with you tomorrow, Gail, but I will join you as soon as I see to a few things that need my attention here. I'm not deserting you, sweetheart, I promise you."

Powell came into the room. "My lord, I just thought you might like to know that Master Nicky has been found and he is all right. He will be coming to see you within the next ten minutes."

I shut my eyes as relief flooded my heart.

"Thank you, Powell," Raoul said.

I opened my eyes, and as soon as Powell had gone I said sharply, "I don't want you to talk to Nicky about . . . about what I just discussed with him, Raoul."

"I have no intention of interfering in your relationship with your son, Gail."

"Then what do you want to talk to him about?" I demanded.

"I wish to talk to him about his responsibilities as the new Lord Devane. Specifically, I wish to talk to him about his responsibilities toward his sisters."

It took me a moment to realize that Raoul was referring to Harriet's children.

"Mr. Cole will take care of them," I said. "He has a ton of money."

Raoul replied, "It is not just a matter of money, Gail. It is a matter of branding these little girls as bastards."

I sat staring at him.

"Is there something that can be done?" I asked at last.

"I will discuss that with Nicky."

"Raoul, Nicky is eight years old!"

"He is also Lord Devane, and during his lifetime he will be responsible for the welfare of a great many people. One is never too young to learn that one's responsibilities are a part of one's privileges."

I couldn't quarrel with him. I didn't want

to quarrel with him. All I wanted was for him to hold me and tell me that he loved me so much that he couldn't live without me, and that regardless of my unimpressive origins, he wanted to marry me.

But there was small chance of that, I thought as I got wearily to my feet. He was sending me off tomorrow and he seemed remarkably cheerful about the idea. Of course, he wasn't planning to break off our affair. He would come to visit me at Devane Hall as he had promised, I had no doubt of that, and he would expect to continue where we had left off at Savile.

What he didn't know, of course, was that once I left Savile I would never lie with him again.

A knock came at the door and a small voice said, "Did you wish to see me, sir?"

"Yes, come in, Nicky," Raoul replied.

Nicky looked surprised when he saw me. "Hello, Ma . . ." His voice trailed off. His face was white and pinched-looking and his hair and the shoulders of his coat were wet. I glanced out the window and saw that it had begun to rain.

"Well, I'll leave you two together, then," I said quietly.

Both males looked at me and nodded and neither of them replied.

I did not go down to dinner that night. I did go upstairs to the nursery to say my usual good night to Nicky, and I found a very subdued scene. Harriet's girls were gone, of course, and the Melville boys, who hadn't yet been told what had happened that afternoon, were very unhappy that Nicky would be leaving the following day.

I said as little as I could, just kissed Nicky good night as I always did. The fact that he called me Mama and clung to me for an infinitesimally brief second made me feel considerably better.

Then I went back to my room, finished packing my paltry belongings, and went to stand at the window to look out at the rain.

Raoul came at midnight, when the rain was pouring down, sending the heavy wet scent of the garden wafting through my open window.

"Aren't you chilled, standing there?" he asked as he came in and shut the door behind him.

"No. I have always liked the smell of summer rain," I replied.

"You're all right about going down to Devane tomorrow, aren't you?" he asked. "You can stay one night on the road and Barrett will be there when you arrive. You shouldn't have any trouble moving in, Gail."

A rush of cool air had come in through the window when the door opened and I absently rubbed my hands up and down my arms for warmth. "I must confess that I don't quite understand the need for such a rush, Raoul."

"I feel it is important for Nicky to be in possession of the premises."

"You don't really believe that Cole is going to take this to law, do you?" I asked. "As you yourself pointed out this afternoon in the library, even without the parish register there is too much evidence against Harriet's claim."

Raoul shrugged and turned to lock the door. "Who knows what a man like Cole will do when he is enraged?"

I shivered. "That is true. Perhaps you ought to send one of those Bow Street runners along with us to keep a watch on Nicky, just to be certain that he is safe."

"As a matter of fact, I am planning to do just that," Raoul surprised me by replying.

I said sharply, "Then you *don't* think that Nicky is safe!"

"I do, but it never hurts to make certain."

I crossed my arms tightly across my chest. I was not happy.

"Gail . . ." Raoul was approaching me.

"Please don't think that I'm deserting you, sweetheart. I'll come to Devane myself sometime next week, I promise. I just cannot get away at the present time."

"Yes, Raoul," I said tightly. "I understand."

He put his hands on my waist, bent his head, and nuzzled the place where my neck and shoulder joined. I felt the faint roughness of his beard scratching my tender skin. I linked my arms around his waist and leaned my body all along his, letting my head fall back so he could have access to my throat.

His fingers moved along my ribs. "You're too thin," he said again. "We'll have to get Mr. MacIntosh to fatten you up."

"You make me sound like a Christmas goose," I murmured.

He chuckled, a deep, baritone sound that sent shivers all through me.

Our lovemaking that night was slow and deeply intense. Every move we made, every word we said, was indelibly engraved upon my heart. The unhurried thrusts of his body rippled through mine, letting me hold on to the feeling of him, the smell of him, the taste of him, giving me time to memorize saying goodbye to the whole heart-shattering experience that was loving Raoul.

It was not the same for him. Raoul was an

aristocrat with an aristocrat's view of sexual matters. He saw nothing wrong with shunting me off to Devane Hall and then maintaining our arrangement under the cover of his visits as executor of George's will. He would expect to arrive at Devane Hall the following week and find me willing to pick up with him where we had left off.

But I could not — would not — do that to Nicky. There would be enough scandal about the way Nicky had come to inherit Devane Hall as it was. I would not add to the talk by letting the neighborhood know that I was having an affair with the Earl of Savile.

Nor could I explain my feelings to Raoul right now and risk losing my treasured last moments with him. Instead, I ran my fingers over his face, the way a blind person might do to learn it, and agreed to all that he was telling me about how I should go about taking charge at Devane Hall.

I lay there awake long after Raoul had gone back to his room, listening to the rain and fighting off the feeling of desolation that threatened to overwhelm me.

The bitter truth was, all that I wanted out of life was to be Raoul's wife. I couldn't imagine anything more wonderful than to live with him always, to help him take care of his beloved house, to have his children, to wake up every morning with his tousled golden-haired head on the pillow beside mine.

But I had to accept the fact that this would never happen. My name had been somewhat cleared by the revelation that I had not had an affair with George, but the daughter of a country doctor, a woman who had earned her own living by giving riding lessons to Cits, such a woman was not the kind of person who married a great nobleman like the Earl of Savile. I understood that. It was just that the knowledge of it was breaking my heart.

CHAPTER 26

There was at least one good thing about the trip to Devane. Nicky and I were enclosed together in a chaise for hours on end and we had a chance to settle some things between us that badly needed settling.

"I'm sorry I ran away from you yesterday, Mama," he started by saying in a polite, brittle little voice after we had left the causeway behind us and started on the road that would eventually take us to Hatfield village and Devane Hall.

We were seated beside each other on the dark blue velvet squabs of the chaise, but the stiffness in Nicky's shoulders made it clear to me that he preferred me to keep as far to my side of the coach as I could, while he would keep to his.

I said quietly, "You were upset, darling, and you had a perfect right to be upset. I understood that. I still understand that. But you know, what has happened is not as dire as it may appear to be. Deep down inside, you are still the boy you always were. Nothing can change Nicky from being Nicky, you know."

"His lordship said the same thing to me yesterday," Nicky said in the same brittle little voice as before.

I was silent, trying to decipher what it was that I heard in that voice.

"Are you still angry with me for not telling you before?" I asked.

"No. I can understand that you could not break your word to your sister, Mama. I'm not angry."

It was true that he didn't sound angry. He had been angry yesterday, but not today.

I was frustrated as well as baffled. I wanted to put my arms around him and hold him against me and tell him that I loved him, but I sensed very clearly that he had put up a wall that he did not want me to breach.

We rode for perhaps an hour in intermittent silence, with either one or the other of us pointing out a particularly interesting sight on either side of the road. Finally, out of desperation to talk to him about a personal topic, I asked, "Did his lordship discuss your . . . er . . . sisters with you yesterday?"

I was going to have a very difficult time thinking of Harriet's children as Nicky's sisters.

Nicky's skin looked almost translucent in the light from the window. The shuttered blue eyes, which had always been as clear as glass to me, had shadows under them.

"Yes," Nicky answered. "He explained to me that I had an obligation to Maria, Frances, and Jane. And to the new baby as well. His lordship and I are going to discuss it more fully in the future, but he thinks I should give them the property at Merion. He says we should not turn our backs upon them and leave them dependent upon Mr. Cole."

I frowned. "Why should you do that when their grandfather is perfectly capable of supporting them?"

Nicky replied carefully, "His lordship said it has something to do with recognizing them and making them respectable. After all, it was not Lady Devane's fault that my father married her when he should not have."

I didn't have any reply, and we drove for perhaps another half an hour in silence.

Finally I could stand it no longer and I turned to my son. "Nicky, what is the matter?" I cried. "You are treating me as if I were some distant aunt whom you see but once a year and whom you do not very much like! I don't care who gave birth to you, I'm still your mother! I don't love you one little bit less than I did last week, when you knew nothing of this at all! And I don't see why you should love me any less either!"

He turned to look at me. "Have you really loved me, Mama, or have I just been your responsibility — the way his lordship says Maria, Frances, and Jane are going to be my responsibility?"

I looked at him in stunned astonishment. His face was white as paper and the skin around his eyes looked bruised. But at last I understood what he was thinking.

I said matter-of-factly, "I am going to kill Raoul. Positively, I am going to kill him."

Nicky's eyes widened. "W-what do you mean, Mama?"

"I mean that he has pumped you full of all these noble sentiments about your duty to those who need your protection, and now you think that this is the way I have always regarded you." I gave him a piercing look. "Am I right?"

His eyes dropped away from mine and he plucked nervously at the knee of his breeches.

"I suppose so, Mama."

I said in a moderated tone, "Well, let me tell you something that might surprise you, Nicky. I am not a nobleman and my feelings in no way, shape, or form resemble those described to you so movingly by the Earl of Savile."

"You don't have to yell, Mama," Nicky said. "I am sitting right next to you."

"I have taken care of you for all these years because I love you," I shouted. "You have been the greatest joy in my whole life. I would die for you. How can you possibly think that I could have found you a burden?"

Nicky's haggard face lit with a slow smile that was at the same time radiant and a little shy. "I love you too, Mama," he said.

"Oh, sweetheart . . ." I enveloped him in my arms and hugged him so tightly that I was probably in danger of cutting off his air supply. But his return embrace was equally tight.

"It doesn't matter that you didn't tell me, Mama," he said breathlessly from somewhere in the region of my shoulder. "His lordship explained to me how terrible it is to be baseborn, so I understand why you did not want that to happen to me."

"Oh, Nicky," I said. Tears were running down my face and I pressed my cheek against the silky hair on the top of his head. I sniffled.

"Mama," Nicky said warningly, "you're not crying, are you?"

"No. I never cry."

"You're crying into my hair!"

I laughed unsteadily and let him pull away from me. I fumbled in my reticule for a handkerchief.

Once I had blown my nose, we were able

to settle down for a question-and-answer session that helped to clear the air between us even more. He wanted to know about Deborah, of course, and I talked a great deal about our childhood together and about her deep, abiding goodness.

Finally we came to the question that Raoul had posed to me the day before. "But, Mama, if she had married Lord Devane, then why didn't she *tell* you? Why did she let Lord Devane marry Maria's mother if she knew it was wrong?"

I reached over and picked up his hand. I said soberly, "When Deborah ran away to me, and your father didn't come after her, I think he broke her heart. I don't think she wanted you to go to him, Nicky. I think she wanted you to be with me because she knew that I would love you better." I sighed. "Perhaps she would have changed her mind once you were born and she realized that she would be depriving you of your rightful place in the world, but she died two days after you were born, Nicky. There wasn't time."

There was a long silence as we listened to the sound of the wheels as they rolled along the road.

Finally Nicky said in a tight little voice, "My father doesn't sound like he was a very nice person."

"He wasn't bad, sweetheart," I said quickly. "He was just weak."

"He did bad things," Nicky said.

"He was afraid of his own father, you see. That was at the root of much of his bad behavior. He was afraid of his father." I was still holding Nicky's hand. "He tried to make reparation to you, you know."

Nicky looked up at me. "What is reparation, Mama?"

"Reparation means to make amends, to give a person compensation for a wrong one has done them," I clarified.

A faint frown indented Nicky's brow. "What kind of reparation did he make?"

"He left you twenty thousand pounds in his will, Nicky," I said. "Somehow he found out about you, and he left you money. In fact, that is why his lordship first came to Deepcote — he came to bring me to the reading of your father's will. So you see, he did not forget about you completely."

Nicky said, "I'm glad my mother didn't send me to live with him, Mama. I'm glad she gave me to you."

I put my arms around him and held him against me once more. "I'm glad too, sweetheart."

"Don't start crying again," he warned.

"I won't."

A huge yawn bisected his face. The emotional upheaval of the last few days must have been exhausting for him. "Why don't you take a little nap," I suggested. "We won't be stopping for another hour."

"All right," he said, and snuggled his head against my shoulder in exactly the same way as he had done since he was an infant. I almost did start crying again.

In precisely one and a half minutes he was asleep. I sat and held him and told myself that I should be perfectly happy, that at least I still had Nicky to live for.

Just driving through the village of Hatfield brought back memories that were a bittersweet mixture of pain and joy. On one hand, Deborah and I had never been made to feel welcome there, and that had been painful. On the other hand, I had met Tommy there and had known all the sweetness and glory that went with first love.

One of these days I would visit our old haunts, I promised myself. They would bring Tommy back to me, and a visit by Tommy would always be welcome in my heart.

Nicky, of course, had a million questions, and I had to point out to him all the local shops and the houses of all the village bigwigs.

"Where does Aunt Margaret live?" he wanted to know.

"Her house is not on the main street. I will take you to visit her in a day or so, and you will be able to meet her," I promised.

I had not had a chance to write to Aunt Margaret before leaving Savile Castle, and I wanted an opportunity to write from Devane Hall to explain what had happened before I landed on her doorstep with Nicky in tow.

Our arrival at Devane Hall went quite smoothly. From the expression that I had seen on the face of the young steward Raoul had sent ahead of us, I had suspected that it would. He had looked determined enough to prepare a medieval castle for the arrival of the king and all of his immense entourage.

The MacIntoshes had arrived earlier in the day and Mr. MacIntosh had already taken over in the kitchen. Mrs. MacIntosh came to greet us, at the last minute holding back from coming into the marble-floored front hall and looking a little shy.

Nicky spotted her, however. "Mrs. MacIntosh!" he shouted, and raced across the green marble floor to land in her open arms.

"Master Nicky! It's that grand to see you, laddie," she said, beaming all over her highly colored face. She held him away from her so that she could look at him. "Ach, but no, I must call ye 'my lord' now, mustn't I?"

"Don't you dare," Nicky said. He looked around. "Where is Mr. MacIntosh? In the kitchen? Where is it? I want to see him."

"Here I am, laddie," came a deep Scottish voice from the doorway leading to the back of the house. Mr. MacIntosh came in, leaning heavily on his cane, and was greeted by Nicky in the same fashion as his wife had been.

I had followed Nicky over to Mrs. MacIntosh and now she turned her attention to me. "How are ye, lassie?" Her shrewd eyes looked me up and down. "Ye're too thin," she pronounced. "Didn't they feed you in that castle place?"

"The food was awful," I confided. "Everything was drowned in sauce."

"Well, MacIntosh is doing a roast chicken for dinner tonight," she said, "with an oyster soup to start." She turned and called out to her husband, "Come and look at this lass, MacIntosh. She's naught but skin and bones."

After the MacIntoshes had finished with their analysis of my physical condition, and after the rest of the servants had been greeted and introduced to Nicky and me, we went upstairs to the bedrooms, which the housekeeper, a woman named Mrs.

Miller, had assigned to us.

Mrs. Miller had given me the apartment that should have belonged to the baron and his wife, an apartment that consisted of one large bedroom and two adjoining dressing rooms. I thought of objecting, but then I thought that Nicky certainly did not want to occupy such a large apartment and that it was silly to leave it empty until he was old enough to use it. I decided I might as well keep it for a while.

Nicky did not want to occupy the nursery by himself and I agreed. I was still a little uneasy about his safety and I asked if he wanted to sleep in one of the dressing rooms that adjoined my bedroom.

I saw him struggle with his decision. He wanted to sleep in the dressing room, of course, but he knew from his time at Savile that boys were not expected to be so dependent on their mothers.

"What do you think I should do, Mama?" he asked cautiously.

"You must do whatever you feel comfortable with, sweetheart. If you don't want to sleep in the dressing room, we'll put you in the room next to Mr. Barrett. And his lordship has sent along one of the Bow Street runners. We can have him sit outside your door."

In the end, that is what Nicky decided to do.

I slept fitfully in the big bed, the bed that I knew Raoul would expect to share with me when he came.

What would he do when I rejected him? For reject him I must. For Nicky's sake, I had no other choice. Nor for my own sake, either, if the truth be told. I could not go on trusting to Aunt Margaret's herbs forever. Nor could I continue to go against what I knew in my heart was morally correct.

I lay awake for hours, wishing uselessly, hopelessly, passionately, that a miracle would happen, that Raoul would smile at me, as only he could smile, and say, "Well then, marry me, Gail," and everything would be wondrously all right.

But the reality was that Raoul was as high above me as Gervase's comet, and I was planted firmly on the earth and could never hope to reach him.

I finally fell asleep near dawn and didn't wake until after ten.

A wonderful impression this would make on my new household, I thought with dismay, and quickly got dressed with the help of a stiff and silent young housemaid. I went along to the dining room, where I helped

485

myself to a muffin and the coffee set out on the sideboard. Then I went in search of the kitchen, where I had a long chat with the MacIntoshes, who told me everything that was happening at Highgate village.

It was close to noon when I decided that I needed some air and that I would go in search of Nicky, whom Mrs. MacIntosh told me had been taken on a tour of the stables by Mr. Barrett.

I thought about Nicky as I strolled along the graveled path that led to the Devane stables, wondering what I was going to do to keep him entertained for the rest of the summer. Devane Hall was not the kind of small, understaffed, homelike place where Nicky had grown up. This was a much larger establishment, where all the work was done by servants, and I could see that a young boy — even if he was the owner — could be very lonely there.

The sleeping arrangements of the preceding night were just the first in a series of problems we were going to have to face now that Nicky's rank had been so unexpectedly elevated.

He was probably going to have to go away to school.

My mind shied from the thought.

I can't cope with the idea of sending Nicky

away now, I thought a little desperately. *Not now, when I am facing the loss of Raoul. . . .*

It hurt just to think his name.

I heard the sound of wheels on the gravel behind me and turned to see a phaeton approaching the stables from the direction of the front gate. I stared at the driver in stunned amazement. It was John Melville.

He stopped the phaeton and looked down into my face. "Good heavens, John," I said. "I didn't expect to see you."

He gave me his pleasant smile. "I came to make certain that everything at Devane Hall was the way it should be. I told Raoul that he should have waited for me to return before sending you on."

"Well, he sent that nice Mr. Barrett, you see," I explained. "And truly, everything in the house seems to be in order."

"Well, I am here to make certain that it is." He glanced ahead, in the direction of the stables. "Are you going to the stables, Gail? May I give you a ride?"

I hesitated. I would have preferred to walk, actually, but John had put his brake on and was looking at me so expectantly that I smiled and put my booted foot on the stair and stepped up into the phaeton with him.

CHAPTER 27

After we had rounded the curve in the path, John surprised me by veering off the drive to the stables and heading his phaeton toward the Devane Home Woods.

"Where are you going?" I asked sharply. "I thought we were going to the stables, John."

"I need to talk to you, Gail," he said. "I was so distraught when I learned that Raoul had sent you away from Savile that I came after you immediately. Please, you must give me a chance to talk to you."

The urgency in his voice was unmistakable.

I was utterly confused. "Of course you may talk to me, but why can we not speak at the hall? Why is it necessary to carry me off into the woods?"

"You will see in a moment," he said. "There is something I must show you. It has to do with your sister and George."

I couldn't imagine what on earth John could have to show me, but I had to admit that my curiosity was piqued.

"What can it be?" I asked.

"Have patience, Gail. We will be there in a moment."

A few minutes later John pulled up in a small clearing beside a small wooden footbridge that went across the little stream that ran through the woods. Unless there was an unusually large amount of rain, the stream was never deep. At this time of year it was only knee deep and in the spring it was perhaps as high as one's waist.

"We get down here," he said to me.

There was something about his manner that was beginning to make me feel slightly uneasy.

I said, "What is the reason for this, John? After all these years, what can be left in this place of Deborah and George? And what is the point of my seeing it anyway? Surely we know all we need to know about that sad relationship."

John didn't answer. He just wrapped his horses' reins and climbed to the ground. He came around to my side of the phaeton and lifted his arms to me. "Come along, I'll help you down."

I shook off his assistance and slowly, warily, alighted from the phaeton.

What is the matter with me? I thought. *Surely I can't be afraid of John!*

But there was an expression in his brown eyes as he looked at me that I had never seen there before, and I found myself taking a step away from him, back in the direction of the pathway that led out of the woods. My heart began to beat swiftly.

He came after me with the speed of a cat, and before I quite knew what had happened, his hands were on my shoulders.

I pulled back sharply but he didn't let go.

"Release me this instant!" I said indignantly.

He shook his head slowly. "I'm sorry, Gail. Believe me, I'm really sorry. But I simply can't let you live. You're too much of a threat to me, you see." The look he gave me was bizarrely regretful. "I'm very much afraid that I'm going to have to kill you."

My mouth dropped open. His fingers were biting into my shoulders.

"What are you talking about, John? What kind of threat can I possibly be to you? Are you insane?"

"No, I'm not insane. I saw right from the start that Raoul's feelings for you were different from anything I had ever seen him show before. Ginny saw it too." He gave a resigned shake of his head. "Don't you see? I simply can't take the chance that he will marry you. I can't lose my position as his heir. I love Savile too much to lose it." The brown eyes that held mine did not show the slightest trace of remorse. "And if I have to kill to keep it, I will," he said.

"Raoul isn't going to marry me!" I said in astonishment. "I am the daughter of an undistinguished country doctor, John! You are insane to think that the Earl of Savile would dream of marrying a woman whose social status is so far beneath his."

Once more came that slow shake of the head. "Who can be sure what Raoul will do? He is certainly besotted with you, Gail, and I simply can't take the chance of you producing any new heirs to stand between me and my rightful inheritance. I've slaved for Savile since I was eighteen years old. I deserve to inherit after Raoul, and I'm going to make very certain that I do."

My initial stunned amazement was turning into panic. I tried to pull away from him again, but his fingers tightened cruelly on my shoulders.

I would fight him if I had to, but I knew that my chances of outmuscling him were slender. I had to try to talk some sense into him.

I said reasonably, "Raoul is not very much older than you are yourself, John. There is nothing to say that he won't continue as

Savile's master for the next forty years."

John smiled and said softly, "Do you know, somehow I rather doubt that he will."

My blood turned to ice.

Think, Gail, I told myself desperately. *Think.*

I said, "If you shoot me, someone is certain to suspect you, John. Someone has to have seen your phaeton drive in the front gate."

"But I'm not going to shoot you, sweetheart," he returned.

I wondered how I could ever have found his smile pleasant.

"I have a much more clever plan than that," he said.

Delayed realization burst upon me. "Nicky was never the target of those attacks at Savile, was he? It was me all along! Raoul thought it was Mr. Cole trying to kill Nicky because he was George's true heir, but it wasn't!"

John looked genuinely amused. "That's right. The broken bridge was aimed at you and Raoul both, and if it hadn't been for that stupid horse of Raoul's, it would have succeeded. Then the groom I bribed gave the nightshade to Nicky's pony by mistake instead of your mare. Another piece of bad luck on my part."

"What about the death of Johnny Wester?" I asked grimly.

"For two days you had been the extra person in the woods playing that game with the boys, Gail. When I heard the voices of Charlie, Theo, and Nicky, but not the voice of the fourth person, I assumed it was you. I had no idea that your place had been taken by the Wester boy." He shrugged. "My bad luck again."

"It was Johnny Wester's bad luck, too," I said bitterly.

"I suppose," John said indifferently.

It was his indifference that frightened me most. He was still holding my shoulders and his body was very close to mine. I shivered with a mixture of fear and repulsion and asked, "If you're not going to shoot me, what are you going to do instead?" I raised my chin and tried to inject a note of scorn into my voice. "It had better be more effective than your previous attempts, or you will be in trouble."

"Actually, I'm rather pleased with what I have come up with," he said with quite a charming smile. "I'm going to drown you."

My whole body jerked away from him. His fingers tightened again. *"What?"* I said.

"Yes. I plan to hit you over the head and then hold you facedown in the stream until you drown. When you're found, people will think that you were climbing down to the stream to pick some flowers — I will thoughtfully supply the flowers, Gail — and that you tripped, hit your head on a rock, fell into the stream, and drowned."

I stared at him in horror.

"What do you think of that, eh?" he asked, as if he genuinely wanted my opinion.

"You're insane," I said.

"Not insane, just ruthless," came the reply. "Now, my love, if you will come along with me, let us move closer to that delightful little stream."

The time to fight him was at hand and I began to struggle in earnest, trying to pull away and to bite him and kick him at the same time. I screamed as we struggled. He moved me toward the stream and I screamed and screamed again.

He laughed as he evaded my kicking feet. Finally he grabbed my arm and twisted it up behind my back. Excruciating pain shot all through my upper body. I was breathing in deep, racking gasps of air.

Nicky, I thought in despair. *Thank God I can count on Raoul to take care of Nicky.*

And then, unbelievably, Raoul's voice came from the other side of the clearing. "Let her go, John, before I am forced to shoot you."

We stopped struggling and stared across the clearing to the man who was standing next to the parked phaeton. We had not heard him come because of my screaming.

John pulled my arm higher and the pain ratcheted through me.

Raoul raised his pistol, which glinted in the sunlight. "There is one sure way to make you let her go and I can assure you that I shall have no hesitation about taking it. The top of your head is well above Gail's; it's not a target I am likely to miss."

I heard John's breath hiss as he inhaled sharply and then let it out. Slowly, reluctantly, he let go his grip on my arm. Then he dropped it completely and I ran across the clearing to stand in Raoul's protective shadow.

He spared me a quick, worried look. "Are you all right, Gail?"

I was rubbing my sore shoulder. Panting, I said, "Yes, now that you are here."

Raoul's eyes went back to his cousin.

"*How* are you here?" John asked. He was very white. "You could not have discovered I was gone until Tuesday evening."

"I didn't, but as soon as I did, I had my own horses put to," Raoul replied.

It was now Wednesday noon.

I said breathlessly, "Good heavens, did

you drive through the night?"

"Yes," came the brief reply.

I stared up at him. The line of his mouth was harder than I had ever seen it.

"Raoul, did you *suspect* that John was involved in this?"

Raoul's eyes were trained on his cousin, and the hand that held the gun on him was rock steady. "I wasn't sure, Gail. I began to wonder after I learned about Cole trying to buy that page from the marriage register. If he had managed to get his hands on that, then there was really no need for him to kill Nicky. And also there was the question of how a stranger like Cole would go about having the bridge tampered with and the pony poisoned. Those kinds of things seemed to indicate someone who was more familiar with the estate and the estate's personnel than Albert Cole could ever be."

I was having a hard time digesting this completely unexpected information.

"But you told me you thought the attacks were directed at Nicky," I said.

"I did, at first. But then, when the truth about Deborah's marriage emerged, I began to change my mind. Even if Nicky were dead, Cole's grandchildren would not have inherited Devane Hall, Gail. It would have gone to Roger. So what was the motivation for Cole to want Nicky dead?"

"You thought John might be trying to kill me?" I asked faintly.

"Suffice it to say, I was concerned enough to want to get you away from Savile before John returned," Raoul said.

So *that* was the reason for Raoul's hustling me to Devane Hall so quickly, I thought in wonder.

Raoul shot me a quick look. "I don't think anything in my life had frightened me more than learning that John had left Savile yesterday morning. I drove like a demon out of hell all night, praying that I would get here in time."

"However did you know that we were here in the woods?" I asked.

"One of the gardeners saw the phaeton come this way, and then I heard you screaming. You have a good pair of lungs, sweetheart."

"Thank God," I said fervently.

"Yes." He turned back to John. "I might have suspected you sooner if it hadn't taken me so long to figure out a motive for you."

A shaft of sunlight was touching John's brown hair, bringing out the hidden Melville gold. He looked slender and forlorn and no threat to anyone. It amazed me.

"But you figured it out at last?" he asked.

"Yes. I finally did."

Oh God, I thought. *Oh God, oh God, oh God. I don't want to be here. I don't want to hear Raoul tell John that he was insane to think that he might ever dream of marrying me.*

Raoul said, "You saw how I felt about Gail, didn't you, and you were afraid that I would marry her and you would lose your place as my heir?"

The expression on John's face was stark, but not as stark as I'm sure the expression was on mine.

"Yes," John said. "That's what I feared."

Raoul nodded. His gun never wavered. "Well," he said pleasantly, "what are we going to do with you, John?"

I finally realized that I wasn't breathing. I took one deep, conscious breath, and then another.

I tried to focus my mind on what was happening between the two men.

"You're not going to turn me in to the local magistrate?" John was asking hopefully.

That got my attention.

"Are you insane?" I demanded of Raoul. "This man is a murderer. The Wester boy's parents deserve to know that the man who killed their child is going to be punished."

"I was thinking of the scandal, Gail," Raoul replied. He gave me a quick, golden-eyed look. "This is the sort of thing that one likes to keep within the family."

I was suddenly and completely furious. "Well, you are not going to keep this dirty little secret in the family because I won't let you! This . . . scum . . ." I gave John a look of utter loathing, "killed a little boy. And let me tell you, my lord, that I don't care if that child is only a tenant's brat. His life is as precious to his parents as Nicky's life is to me. So if you don't go to the magistrate about John, then I will." I put my hands on my hips. "The rest of us don't live in the Middle Ages anymore, my lord, even if you do!"

I glared at him.

"I don't either, sweetheart," he replied. "But we don't live in a perfect world, either. There is no proof that John killed Johnny Wester, and if the case ever went to trial there is a reasonable chance that he would be acquitted."

"He confessed to *me* that he killed Johnny," I said.

Raoul was shaking his head. "I don't want a trial, Gail," he said implacably. "I don't want a public exposure of Harriet's illegal marriage; I don't want scandalous speculation about the fate of her 'poor bastard children'; I don't want you to be forced to testify in front of the press; and I don't want to face heart-wrenching stories about Nicky as the 'lost heir' every morning when I read my newspaper over the breakfast table."

He shot me another quick look. "I know you want vengeance, sweetheart, but to my mind the disadvantages of forcing John to stand trial outweigh the advantages."

John said, "Raoul is right. That is precisely what will happen, Gail. And in the end, I'll probably be acquitted anyway."

"I did not say that you would probably be acquitted, John. I said there was a reasonable chance that you would be acquitted," Raoul said.

"John has to pay for Johnny Wester," I said stubbornly.

"I agree," Raoul said. "And that is what we are going to do."

Both John and I gazed at him with fascination.

Raoul put away his gun, reached into his pocket, and took out a packet. "This is a ticket on the boat from Dover to Calais, along with enough money to enable you to live without starving for a six-month period. After that, John, you will be on your own."

John scowled. "What do you mean? Are you saying that you are banishing me from England?"

"That is exactly what I am saying, John. I don't want you in England. I don't want you near my family. In fact, I never wish to see you again."

I thought that the bleak note in Raoul's voice as he said that last sentence was one of the most painful sounds I had ever heard. I thought of his telling me how he and John had played together as boys, how they had slept out in the cottage and fished for their breakfast in the morning.

What must it be doing to him, to know that this cousin, whom he had loved, had wanted to kill him?

I thought of an objection. "How are you going to know if he comes back, Raoul? You can't keep people posted at all the ports, for heaven's sake."

"I hear things," Raoul said. "Don't I, John?"

"Yes," John said with difficulty.

"Perhaps," Raoul said, "in fifteen or so years, when Gail and I have a handful of children to stand between you and Savile, perhaps then you may come back. But not until then, John. Not until then."

At first Raoul's words sailed right over my head. I was standing beside him, looking at John and fretting about the solution that Raoul had come up with, and the full ramifications of what he had said didn't strike me right away.

Then his words repeated themselves in my brain:

"In fifteen or so years, when Gail and I have a handful of children to stand between you and Savile, perhaps then you may come back."

I felt my back go rigid. Had I heard correctly? Could that possibly mean what it sounded like?

Did Raoul intend to marry me?

I turned to stare up at him, but his attention was all for John.

"I have left a letter with Ginny," he told his cousin. "It says that if anything happens either to Gail or to me, you are the one who is responsible."

John's hands hung loosely at his sides. All the fight had long since gone out of him.

Raoul began to walk across the clearing with the packet in his hand. I watched his back, his neatly cut dark gold hair, his wide shoulders under his brown driving coat, his long, booted legs. He gave John the packet and said shortly, "The boat leaves on Friday."

"May I return to Savile to pack my things?" John said.

"I'll have them sent on to the King's Arms in Dover," Raoul said implacably.

502

"Yes," said John, and slowly, with bowed shoulders, he walked to his phaeton, climbed into the seat, backed his horses, turned them, and drove away.

Raoul and I were alone together in the clearing.

"I'm sorry, Gail," he said, "but I truly think that this is the best way."

I swallowed. I nodded. I said, "Yes, all right. It's true what you said about the unfairness of exposing Harriet's children to the scrutiny of the press."

We were standing a few feet apart and I could see that there was a strained look on his face and that his eyes were their darkest gold.

"Raoul, I'm so sorry about John," I said softly. "I know how painful his betrayal must be for you."

He made a gesture as if he were brushing a cobweb away from in front of his face, then he came closer to me. He said, "I should have told you my suspicions before I sent you away. If anything had happened to you, Gail, I don't know how I would have lived with myself."

I said, "Why didn't you tell me, Raoul?"

"Because they were just suspicions. It was . . . very difficult for me to believe that John could be guilty of the terrible things I suspected him of, you see."

"Oh, Raoul." I took two steps forward and put my arms around his waist and my head on his shoulder. "I am so sorry," I repeated. "I know how much your family means to you. The truth about John must have broken your heart."

His arms circled me and held me close.

"Nothing would have been as bad as losing you," he said.

I shut my eyes. *I'm not going to ask him anything,* I thought. *It has to come from him.*

"I would have asked you to marry me sooner if I hadn't had this dreadful doubt," he said. "You see, if what I suspected was true, a marriage announcement would only have put you in greater danger."

I pressed my face into his shoulder. I was afraid to move, afraid that I might wake up and find out that I was dreaming.

"Gail?" he said. "Did you hear me?"

I nodded. I lifted my face from his shoulder. "Yes," I said huskily. "I heard you. But are you sure, Raoul? What will Ginny think? After all, this summer you and I . . . well, you know."

"Ginny will be delighted," he said firmly. "As a matter of fact, she informed me after you left for Devane that if I didn't marry you I was a fool."

I felt my eyes get bigger. "She did?"

"She did." He smoothed his thumbs along the lines of my cheekbones. "I think I fell in love with you the moment you put me to work painting your bedroom," he said with a grin.

I smiled up at him.

He ran his thumbs along my cheekbones once more. His face was grave. "Under the circumstances, I'm sure you're wondering why I didn't court you in the usual way, why I lured you to Savile and made you my mistress."

"No, Raoul," I said honestly. "I understand that, truly I do. George's legacy certainly didn't make me look as if I were an honest woman, did it?"

He surprised me by shaking his head. "It wasn't that."

I stared at him in surprise. "It wasn't?"

"No." He gave me a crooked smile. "It was worse than that."

"But what was it?" I asked in profound amazement.

He looked embarrassed. I had never before seen Raoul look embarrassed. He said, "Every time we made love, I lived in dread that you were going to call me Tommy."

We looked at each other.

"Are you serious?" I asked after a minute.

"I'm afraid that I am." The look he gave me was definitely sheepish. "I'm not proud of it, Gail, but there it is. I'm not proud that I was jealous of a dead man, but I was." He gave me the crooked smile again. "In a way, I still am."

Could this be Raoul? I wondered. There was a strained look over his cheekbones and the eyes that looked at me were troubled.

I said very carefully, "I was a girl when I married Tommy, Raoul. He was a wonderful boy, and we were happy together, but I loved him the way a girl loves a boy. I'm a woman now, though, with a woman's heart and a woman's strength. My feelings are deeper and more profound than they were ten years ago. I love you the way a woman loves a man." I shook my head in astonishment. "I can't believe that you didn't see that."

"It was too important to me to believe it," he said. "I loved you too much."

"Oh, Raoul," I said. "Oh, darling. There is nothing I want more in this life than to marry you."

I raised my face for his kiss. We leaned in to each other, his tall frame hard against mine, my arms around his waist holding him tight.

"We'll do it in a month," he said against my mouth. "I'll have the banns called at

Savile and then we'll do it."

"All right," I said.

We kissed some more.

"Raoul," I said, "is this going to present a problem for you socially? I'm a nobody, after all. Will people look down on you for marrying me?"

"Don't be an idiot," he returned. He kissed my hair, my forehead, my cheeks, my nose. "I'm the Earl of Savile. I can marry whomever I choose to marry."

For some reason, this arrogant statement did not outrage me at all.

We kissed some more.

Finally I said, "We have to get back to the house, Raoul. Nicky will be looking for me."

With great reluctance he let me go.

"All right."

We began to walk slowly toward his phaeton.

"What will we do with Nicky?" I asked. "He cannot live here at Devane by himself, Raoul."

"Of course he can't. He will live with us at Savile until he comes of age. I shall appoint a steward to look after Devane, and we shall come on periodic visits to make certain that all is well here and that the people in the village know who Nicky is." He lifted me into the phaeton and I could feel the heat of his hands penetrate right through the fabric of my dress.

He got in next to me and said mildly, "I really feel that it is in Nicky's best interest to go to school."

I sighed. "I know, Raoul, but he doesn't want to go."

"We'll give him time," Raoul said. "We'll have Ginny's boys come to Savile for the holidays, and I have a feeling that a year from now, Nicky will have changed his mind and will want to go back to school with Charlie and Theo."

I rather thought that Raoul was right.

I thought that it was going to be very comforting to have a man to advise me as Nicky grew up.

I thought that it would be wonderful to have a baby.

I thought that I had never been happier in my entire life.

I smiled up at him and I felt the radiance glowing in my face. "I love you so much," I said.

"If you look at me like that, Gail, I cannot answer for the consequences," came the stern reply. Then: "Do you think we have to wait four more weeks?"

"I don't see why," I replied, "as long as you are discreet."

He grinned. "Discretion is my middle name, sweetheart," he said. "Discretion is my middle name."

The employees of Thorndike Press hope you have enjoyed this Large Print book. All our Large Print titles are designed for easy reading, and all our books are made to last. Other Thorndike Press Large Print books are available at your library, through selected bookstores, or directly from us.

For information about titles, please call:

(800) 257-5157

To share your comments, please write:

Publisher
Thorndike Press
P.O. Box 159
Thorndike, Maine 04986